JACK THE BODILESS

JACK
THE BODILESS

< A NOVEL BY >

JULIAN MAY

VOLUME I
OF THE GALACTIC MILIEU TRILOGY

ALFRED A. KNOPF

New York

1992

Aux les bons copains—enfin!

I will praise you, for I am fearfully and wonderfully made!
My soul knows how marvelous are your works.
You were aware when my very bones were formed,
Growing secretly inside my mother's body
As a plant's root grows beneath the earth.
You knew me before I was born.
The days of my life were all written in your book
Before they had ever begun.

PSALM 139

Whereas in the familiar closed systems of physics the final state is determined by the initial conditions, in open systems, as far as they attain a steady state, this state can be reached from different initial conditions and in different ways.

LUDWIG VON BERTALANFFY, *A Systems View of Man*

God writes straight with crooked lines.   SPANISH PROVERB

JACK THE BODILESS

[PROLOGUE]

SNOW GROTTO PLANETARY PARK, KANNERNARKTOK TERRITORY

SECTOR 14: STAR 14-661-329 [SIKRINERK] PLANET 6 [DENALI]

GALACTIC YEAR: LA PRIME 1-400-644 [17 MAY 2113]

It was a dark and stormy night, as so many nights were on Denali, where topography and climate conspired to produce some of the Galaxy's worst weather. Worst from a human point of view, of course, unless that human was addicted to Nordic skiing . . .

The mind of the supervising Lylmik entity named Atoning Unifex smiled as Its material essence hovered above the blizzard-lashed park. Denali was a rugged planet, wintery throughout most of its year, the veritable haunt of the Great White Cold celebrated in a certain Earth song that was very familiar to the First Supervisor. On most of Denali's continents, glaciers and permanent snowfields spread wide amidst a fantastic landscape of dazzling peaks, black precipices, and crags that thrust up like the broken tusks of primordial monsters. Denali had no sapient indigenous lifeform. No rational creatures had as yet evolved on it when it was assigned to the Human Polity by the world evaluators of the Galactic Milieu. Its most famous honorary native son, Saint Jack the Bodiless, was conceived before the first Earth settlers arrived.

The hardy people who originally colonized Denali in the mid-2000s had hailed from Alaska and other parts of the United States having severe winters. They were quickly joined by Canadians, Siberians, Samoyeds, Lapps, and a host of others who craved a life of challenge that could be lived in a setting of wild natural beauty. The World-Mind those human colonists engendered might have been expected to be as dark and moody as Denali's weather; but for some reason the very opposite mental climate prevailed, and Denali was an invigorating place with an aether that fairly glowed with friendliness and verve. The original rationale for establishing the colony had been the planet's deposits of valuable gallium ore, and this was still a major economic resource. But Denali had also become a popular vacation resort, first appealing mainly to Human Polity winter-sports fans (including the famous Remillard clan of New Hampshire) and later attracting hordes of like-minded Poltroyans as well.

Atoning Unifex let memories crowd to the fore of Its consciousness, recollections that had been repressed for aeons. This small planet had been loved by both of them . . .

She, of course, had been born here, living and working in the colony's capital city of Iditarod until a fateful tragedy had taken her to Earth, where the two of them had so improbably met. On the very brink of their great adventure she had spoken casually of her own experiences as a native of Denali, and they had laughed together over the unexpected mutual reminiscences. The shared laughter had come to an end long ago, but the memories remained in a deep level of the Lylmik's ancient mind, guarded and cherished and eventually becoming almost too precious to contemplate. The pain that had once darkened these memories had long since faded, and their scrutiny at this particular time was now actually appropriate.

And so Atoning Unifex lingered there in the middle of the storm, Its mind in a state that a human being would have recognized as part reverie and part prayer, thinking of a person who had once been a woman, who had twice loved deeply, and who had mothered Unity in countless nonhuman minds in a distant Galaxy.

Finally the Lylmik uttered the mental equivalent of a deep sigh. The epilogue of the comedy was nearly complete, but One waited upon the inimitable Uncle Rogi, who kicked at the goad as usual, dawdling while cosmic destiny hung suspended.

Unifex focused Its mind narrowly on the subsurface snow cavern that sheltered Rogatien Remillard from the raging snowstorm. It saw a hunched, lanky man sitting beside a tiny tent, taking off his ski boots. Like other members of his famous family, Uncle Rogi possessed the genes for self-rejuvenation. His face was that of a raddled fifty-year-old, belying his actual age of 167 Earth years. His gaunt cheeks were frost-reddened, and his nose and eyes watered a little when he forgot to mop them with the red bandanna handkerchief he carried up the cuff of his old L. L. Bean Penobscot parka. He had tossed aside his knitted toque, and sweaty silver curls straggled over his forehead and ears. He was whistling as he peeled off the archaic twentieth-century ski garb and stripped faded red long johns from a pale and sinewy body. Then he lowered himself with exquisite care into a geothermal pool in the center of the small snow cave. The telepathic emanations from his ever obstinate and uncoadunate mind were happy ones.

Uncle Rogi said to himself: If the storm lasts, I'll forget about the final leg of my trek and call the park's shuttlebug and go wallow for a week in the lodge's après-ski entertainments casino cabaret string quartets Lucullan food good company perhaps a new science fiction novel savored in the Wintergarden while the bar waitrons keep the drinks coming and I check out the snowbunny crop!

The old man settled deeper into the steaming water, smiling.

Poor Uncle Rogi! Unifex had other plans for him. But Rogi had had a good enough holiday, ski-touring more than 200 kilometers throughout the beautiful park during an unusual three-week spell of calm bright days. Now the weather pattern had changed, and whether Rogi was willing to admit it or not, he was adequately refreshed and recreated after his first stint of journalistic labors. It was time for both of them to get back to work.

Unifex descended toward the planetary surface. The negligible physical substance of the Lylmik mind-receptacle deflected only the tiniest of the hard-driven snowflakes and easily penetrated the three-meter-thick crust of ice and snow above the grotto where Rogi had elected to camp. The place was typical of the subnivean hollows that gave the Denali planetary park its name: an irregular cave as big as a good-sized room, melted from the permanent icefield by the heat of a small geothermal spring. The walls and ceiling were ice, but the rocky floor was cushioned with a dense lichenoid carpet of tough gray and lavender saprophytes. Close to the shallow burbling pool grew larger and more fragile exotic lifeforms, sessile animals that resembled scarlet onions with peculiar flowers that gave off a pungent sulfurous scent if they were bruised. As the mildly carnivorous blossoms of the onion creatures bent toward Rogi's exposed shoulders, he flicked hot water at them by way of discouragement.

The walls of the grotto were cupped and dripping near the ground and glittering with crystals of hoarfrost in the cold upper reaches. There thin tendrils of vapor coiled golden in the light of Rogi's antiquated electric lantern before disappearing into a natural flue. Touring skis were propped against one wall, and a backpack lay near the little tent. On the far side of the chamber was the closed entry door, fashioned of harmonious translucent plass, that led to the enclosed surface-access tunnel and modern latrine. (Park visitors were strictly forbidden to dig down into the snow grottoes directly, or to camp in undesignated "virgin" caves except in emergency situations.)

Here and there on the nacreous walls were circular openings, not quite large enough to admit a human hand. From several of these, and from a larger hole at ground level where runoff water from the spring exited, came a glitter of tiny eyes and an occasional peevish hiss. The natural inhabitants of the grotto, hotblooded eight-centimeter "ice crabs" temporarily displaced by the human who had come to spend the night, were keeping a close watch on developments. The crabs considered these alien invaders to be a great nuisance, in spite of the fact that they usually brought along something worth stealing.

A determined onion flower began to nibble experimentally on Rogi's wet shoulder blade. He reached for his backpack, unzipped a compartment, and brought out a battered leatherbound flask. A stiff tot of Armagnac and a guided puff of alcoholic breath caused the lifeform to shrink back from the poisonous exhalation, blanch to a muddy mauve color, and broadcast its disgust on a primitive telepathic mode. The entire plantation of scarlet carnivores desisted from snack attacks forthwith.

Rogi nodded in satisfaction, took another snort, and sank more deeply into the hot spring. Up on the planetary surface the hurricane wind roared in the darkness, and there was a distant rumble as an avalanche let loose somewhere. The grotto trembled slightly. Ice spicules sifted down toward the bather, glittering until they melted just above his head. Rogi began to sing softly:

> "For the wolf wind is wailing at the doorways,
> And the snow drifts deep along the road,
> And the ice gnomes are marching from their Norways—"

Unifex joined in:

"And the Great White Cold walks abroad!"

The old man in the pool leapt like a speared sturgeon. "Bordel de merde!"

It's only me, Uncle Rogi.

"Dammit! One of these days you're going to give me cardiac arrest doing that!"

[Laughter.] I apologize. It was the old college song. I had been thinking of it myself just as I arrived. It brought back all kinds of memories.

"Now look what you made me do." Rogi was accusing. His eruption had splashed hot water over the onion animals and they were flailing in wild distress, the tiny teeth of the flowers chattering like elfin castanets. "You know the park rules about disturbing the native life-forms! These little chompers are sensitive. If any of 'em decide to croak, I could be blamed and end up paying a helluva fine—"

Calm yourself. Look. I've restored them.

"Damn good thing," Rogi muttered, climbing out onto the not-quite-lichens. The clumps of red onions were swaying luxuriously now, and a delicate humming sound filled the grotto. "Don't often hear *that.* It's their full-tummy serenade."

It was the least I could do.

Rogi chuckled. Naked and steaming, he retrieved the brandy flask, which fortunately hadn't spilled, and tucked it into a safe place. "I'm feeling pretty hungry myself. Want to share some chili cagado with me, mon fantôme?"

Thank you. But no.

"Too substantial for your Lylmik guts, eh? You used to love it."

Unifex's thought was wistful: I don't suppose you brought along any Habitant pea soup . . . ?

"Ate the last of it two days ago."

The Lylmik's mind sighed.

Rogi squatted and set up a small microwave campstove. He dipped a pot of water from the spring, peered into it, and extracted a black gelatinous blob and a glass-shrimp that were swimming languidly about the container's bottom. The invertebrates were returned to the pool and the pot set inside the stove to boil. Rogi had tossed in two Aqua Pura tablets for seasoning, since Denali bred tough microorganisms as well as tough colonials.

"So you couldn't resist coming after me." The old man dried himself with a diminutive towel and put his long johns and socks back on.

Unifex said: It was a species of sentimental journey. I had felt compelled to avoid Denali during her first-cycle sojourn here.

Rogi hesitated. "You want to tell me about the two of you? All I know is the little bit Cloudie and Hagen told me—and they didn't know all that much."

Not now. Perhaps later.

"M'mm." Rogi took the seething pot out of the stove and filled two bowls and a large cup, adding a different-colored cube to each container of water. After four seconds of effervescence, the highly compressed food reconstituted and the pungent aroma of chili rose from the first bowl, and the smell of cinnamon-apple cobbler from the second. The cup was full of black coffee. Rogi added five lumps of sugar and a shot of Armagnac to the latter, and sprinkled almost 200 grams of grated natural-state Tillamook cheddar onto the chili.

A sibilant, yearning chorus came from the crab holes, and there was a frantic blinking of eyes. Rogi chuckled wickedly. "Cheeky little bastards. Remember how they used to eat Adidas if you left 'em outside the tent in these snow caves?"

Unifex laughed. It said: I note that you wear inedible Salomon ski boots now. Very comfortable-looking. I like the new Rossi boards, too. But isn't it rather imprudent of you not to wear an environmental suit?

"For sissies! I been skiing my brains out for a hundred fifty years in this outfit and I haven't froze my bizoune off yet. You'll notice that my wrist-com's modern enough. Keeps me alerted to weather changes. And if I get snowed in or come a cropper or even run outa coffee or munchies, the Ski Patrol or a robot monitor'll home in on its transponder-locator and take care of me. I knew this storm was on the way. I figure to spend the night here, then call for a shuttlebug to fly me back to the park lodge tomorrow if she don't blow out as per forecast. Wouldn't mind at all spending the last week of my vacation lolling around in style—"

I'm sorry, Uncle Rogi. I've come to collect you.

"I'm booked for seven more days, dammit!"

You are well rested and quite able to begin work on your Memoirs again—as am I. Take your time finishing your meal, but tonight you'll sleep in your own bed back home in New Hampshire.

"Back to Earth *tonight*—? That'll mean hopping the hype at maximum displacement factor. I'll be a nervous wreck!"

I'll take you myself . . . more gently.

Rogi's eyes narrowed and he squinted at the portion of air from which his invisible companion's thoughts appeared to emanate. "So! You Lylmik *do* have a mitigator for the pain of hyperspatial translation—just like Ti-Jean always said you did."

Yes. Jack was perceptive as always. But the device is not yet appropriate for general use among our client races in the Galactic Milieu. You will make no mention of it.

Rogi spooned down chili and drank coffee. "I wouldn't dream of violating the glorious Lylmik master scheme . . . But what's the damn rush to get me humping again on the Memoirs?"

One has one's reasons.

Rogi rolled his eyes hopelessly. Then for some time he ate in silence, his mind idly recapitulating the things he had already written and shuffling through what would come next, in the period following the Great Intervention. "Gonna take another book, big as the last one, to cover the thirty-eight years of the Simbiari Proctorship. Be a pain in the ass for me to get all those family shenanigans sorted out, too."

Unifex said: I want you to skip over most of that and begin immediately on Jack's early life and disincarnation, and the growing threat of human opposition to Galactic citizenship. Then you will describe Dorothea's part in the earlier drama, and finish up with your view of the Metapsychic Rebellion, making a Milieu Trilogy. The events of the painful Proctorship years, the time before the Human Polity was admitted to the Galactic Concilium, have been covered well enough by Philip and Lucille in their own autobiographies. But they never knew Jack's full story, or Diamond's—

"Or yours, mon cher fantôme."

Or mine.

"I'll have to backtrack some to make it hang together, you know. Start out with a kind of retrospective digression. And I'll still need a lot of fill-in help from you to give a proper overall picture."

I realize that.

"Is that why—" Rogi paused. He swallowed hard, banishing a certain thought before it could be formulated, even subvocally. "Eh bien, mon fils. I reckon you know what you're doing by now."

Beyond a doubt. To paraphrase one of your favorite fantasy writers, even the most modest intellect can hardly help learning a thing or two after six million years.

The old man grinned with forced cheerfulness at the vaporous air. "Six million . . . Ah, those self-rejuvenating Remillard genes! A real drag, immortality, eh? Not that I'm ready to knock it myself yet, you understand. Um . . . do you know . . . can you foresee when I'm . . ."

Not really. Moi, je ne suis pas le bon dieu, j't'assure! But I do intend to see to it that you survive at least long enough to finish the family chronicle.

"Well, thanks all to hell for small favors."

Rogi licked the last of the apple cobbler from his spoon and drank the dregs of the coffee. Then he switched the stove to the dishwashing mode and thrust the tableware inside. A moment later, he began to pack everything away, singing the chorus of Dartmouth College's "Winter Song" under his breath.

At length the Remillard Family Ghost said: Are you ready, Uncle Rogi? The trip home will take only a moment. There will be none of the usual discomfort of hyperspatial translation experienced in a starship.

"Not in my underwear, dammit!"

The old man began to throw his clothes back on. He managed his pants and shirt before he disappeared abruptly from the snow grotto, and all his gear with him.

The lichenoid cast a faint phosphorescent glow about the newly darkened chamber. There was a rustling sound, then a medley of plops as the crablike exotic animals came rushing from their burrows to scavenge leftover bits of Earth cheese. Outside the snow grotto, the Denali blizzard wind howled.

FROM THE MEMOIRS
OF ROGATIEN REMILLARD

I still have the nightmare sometimes. I had it on the night that I was unceremoniously translated from the planet Denali to Earth at the truncated end of my skiing holiday and commanded to resume writing these Memoirs.

As always, the dream played itself out in a weird, accelerating time-lapse mode. There is nothing terrifying about the scene at first. A beautiful mother holds an infant, completely wrapped in a blanket, and she looks up from the baby as a fourteen-year-old boy approaches. This older child of hers has a strangely ominous aura about him. He has come hurriedly home from his classes at Dartmouth College on a blustery day, and he wears black turbocycle leathers and carries a much-modified visored helmet tucked under his arm. His eyes are gray and his mind opaque, and his smile is tentative and quirkily one-sided as he accepts his mother's invitation to open the blanket and see his new little brother for the first time . . . in the flesh.

The black-gloved hands are trembling slightly with an emotion that the older boy despises and tries vainly to check. And then the baby lies revealed, unclothed, perfect. And the minds of Marc and Teresa mingle in joy:

Mama he's all right!
    Yesyes YES!!
Papa was wrong the genetic assay was wrong—
    Yes dear wrong wrong wrong little Jack's body is normal
    and his mind *his mind . . . !*
Mind?
    Oh Marc dear his mind just speak to him it's wonderful
    don't be afraid to wake him . . .

The baby's delicate eyelids open.
And in my dream, there are no eyes.

I hear laughter, and I recognize the voice of Victor. But it can't be Victor because he died twelve years before Jack was born; and for nearly twenty-seven years before that he was helpless, disembodied as Jack would be but unlike Jack deprived of all metafunction, all physical and mental contact with the world outside himself. In my dream, the devilish laughter fades in a smell of pine and a cataract of pain. Tears pour down Marc's face for the first time in his austere young life. The eyeless infant smiles at us—

And suddenly the *real* nightmare takes charge.

No eyes. Only a void, a starless darkness that is somehow alive with fearsome knowledge. My dream races on, and Teresa and young Marc are gone. There is only a pathetic little child shackled to complex life-supportive equipment, and while I watch in horror, his human form begins to disintegrate.

I try to tear my gaze away from the awful sight, but I cannot. Faster and faster, the self-destructive process programmed by his own body proceeds.

The child's despairing mother blames her own hubris for his suffering. His father, Paul, countering his own pain with clinical detachment, finds the disincarnation bleakly fascinating. Marc sees his first glimpse of Mental Man. Denis Remillard and Colette Roy and the other scientists of the Human Polity call the child a prochronistic mutant, an anomaly born out of proper time, too early in the scheme of biological evolution, a throw-forward in the pattern of orderly human development. Four of the exotic races of the Galactic Milieu, pitying, call the little boy pathetic and doomed. The enigmatic Lylmik refuse to discuss his case at all, except for flatly prohibiting his euthanasia.

In the dream, my mind is shrieking: No no Ti-Jean no God no how can you let his body die while his brain lives the brain the wonderful potent superbrain God why why—

Then I see the brain naked.

I plead: Let it die too let the poor thing die stop the machines the genetic engineering attempts the futile meddling let him go in peace let him go!

A monster that does not know its self sees the brain as the Great Enemy, and in a cataract of flame the machines are stopped.

I hear the laughter of the dead fiend again as Victor savors the hideous irony of the situation. For the brain that is Jack the Bodiless does *not* die, but lives. Impossibly, it lives, impervious, sustaining itself in some arcane psychoredactive fashion, nourished by the atmosphere and by photons, enduring and adapting and learning and growing in wisdom and grace and dieu de dieu I am so afraid of it paralyzed with dread even as it tries to reassure me and in my dream I call its name:

Ti-Jean! Jack!

This horrifying mutant, this *thing*, is still my dear little great-grand-nephew Jon Remillard, a brilliant and vibrant little human person only three years old, trapped in 1.7 kilograms of unsupported humanoid encephalic protoplasm.

None of Jack's eventual triumph penetrates my nightmare. I know only my own fear and revulsion and a demonic whisper: *Who will be the next to disincarnate? Perhaps you, Rogi?* . . .

Then Marc is at my side again, much older. This time his dark armor is the glistening wet body-monitoring coverall of a cerebroenergetic enhancer, the perilous mind-boosting device outlawed by the Galactic Milieu. Marc studies the bodiless thing that is his mutant brother with open admiration. And a paradoxical envy.

I see a warning reflected from eyeless depths, and Marc sees it, too.

Jack's mind tells us: No. Human is better. For you, Marc. For all of you.

Marc smiles and shakes his head, denying. Mental Man is the inevitable, the culmination of all rational being—and there is no need to wait upon evolution's laggard pace for His coming. He can be summoned—

Suddenly I see three persons suspended in interstellar space: a faceless woman clad in a suit of diamonds, a blazing plasma that enfolds the first Mental Man, and a black armored shape leading an interstellar armada in opposition to the other two. The Metapsychic Rebellion of humanity against the Galactic Milieu has begun.

At my dream's climax, a blue-and-white planet explodes, haloed by a mass death-shout. And in that terrible moment the Galactic Milieu, the benevolent confederation that saved the human race from its own folly and gave us the stars as a playground, itself begins to die . . .

The dream always ends at this point, before the final resolution, and I return to consciousness freezing and paralyzed, with a half-strangled scream caught in my throat.

Peace! T'en fais pas, Rogi! Calm yourself and relax. It all happened long ago, and now at last in the writing of this personal chronicle you have a way of exorcising the nightmare once and for all.

Perhaps you already know me from the introductory volume of these Memoirs. If you do not, let me introduce myself briefly. My name is Rogatien Remillard, and I am sometimes called Roger but more often simply Uncle Rogi (pronounced, appropriately enough, as "rogue he") by those who find my Christian name impossibly ethnic. It is of French origin, and the Remillards are a sizable family who originally were colonists in Québec and later migrated to the northeastern United States, where there was a large but unobtrusive Franco-American population.

I have for most of my life been a bookseller in the college town of Hanover, New Hampshire. I have a small antiquarian bookshop, The Eloquent Page, where rare old twentieth-century fantasy and science fiction books printed on carefully conserved paper are offered to connoisseurs at atrocious prices. Although I belong to a family of acknowledged mental giants, my own intellectual and metapsychic functions are meager. This has not prevented me from being caught up in the chequered careers of my more illustrious relatives. On the contrary, I have played at times a rather significant role in the family's machinations—something that Milieu historians have seen fit to ignore—and I have witnessed from my worm's-eye view the rise and fall of many a Galactic worthy and villain, including two saints and one notorious individual whose misdeeds were so appalling that he was known as the Angel of the Abyss.

I have never married, but I have loved unwisely several times. I have faced imminent death on quite a few occasions and survived through improbable happenstance. I have killed three persons in cold blood, even though I am the most easygoing and peaceable of men, and one of them was a person I loved deeply.

My fraternal twin brother, Donatien, and I were born in the year 1945, in the New England mill town of Berlin, New Hampshire. Our young father had already been killed during World War II, and our mother died giving birth to us, so we orphans were raised by our kindly aunt and uncle, who had six children of their own.

But no members of the Remillard clan except my brother and I had the "immortality" genes, whose existence was not confirmed until after the Intervention, nor did they possess the genes for higher mindpowers. (It was many years before my twin brother and I discovered that we were not unique in our metaphysic operancy.) How we two responded to our more frightening metafunctions is a story that I have already related at some length. In brief, I learned to live with such powers as telepathy, psychokinesis, and metacoercion, while Don was ultimately destroyed by them, tragically killed when he was only forty-four.

I was rendered sterile by a childhood illness. Don had ten offspring, and all of them inherited the genes for high metafunction and self-rejuvenation; but only the two oldest children were able to utilize their extraordinary mindpowers. Circumstances made Don's oldest child, Denis, become a foster son to me; and it was he who founded with his operant wife Lucille Cartier the so-called Remillard Dynasty, which eventually included many of the most powerful minds the human race has ever known. Don's second son, Victor, was not as intellectually brilliant as his older brother; but his metapsychic mindpowers were probably even more formidable, and he used them ruthlessly for his own self-aggrandizement until he was finally struck down, immediately prior to the Great Intervention, either by me or by the mysterious being I had learned to call the Family Ghost.

From time to time, especially when I am drunk and morose and seized with that melancholy feeling of inescapable doom that francophones call malheur, I have been tempted to believe that the Family Ghost is nothing more than a construct of my own imagination. But if that is true, then by default *I* am responsible not only for the Great Intervention but for the Metapsychic Rebellion as well, and ultimately for the even more momentous events that came afterward, bringing the long story full cycle.

But that would be too farfetched a practical joke, even for le bon dieu, who is so full of them.

So let me begin this Galactic Milieu Trilogy without further maunderings, first with a retrospective.

[2]

A RETROSPECTIVE DIGRESSION
BERLIN, NEW HAMPSHIRE, EARTH
30 MARCH 2040

Rogi drove into the town of his birth late on a dreary spring afternoon, bringing Teresa and little Marc with him from Hanover, as he had been instructed to. Wrathful and profane protests to the contrary had got Rogi nowhere: Paul had been adamant. This time Rogi, too, would come to Berlin and participate in the annual ritual because Denis had insisted upon it. And that was that.

It always seemed to rain on Good Friday, but at least this year the rain was warm, and it was making short work of the remnant patches of street ice and the old gray mounds of snow that still lay about in the sun-starved nooks of town. By Easter, Rogi told himself subvocally, Berlin would be nearly washed clean. The pussy willows in the gardens along the Androscoggin River, where the smoke-belching paper mills once stood, would have snowdrops and blue Siberian squill and pink hellebore blooming beneath them, and the first robins would sing in the budding sugar maples, and the townsfolk in their Easter finery would stroll the riverside paths.

And with luck, before *next* Easter, Vic would be dead.

"Why will that be good?" Marc piped up. "Who is Vic, Uncle Rogi? And why will it be a good thing for him to die?"

"Oh, merde et puis merde," Rogi muttered.

Teresa said: Rogi for heaven's sake!

Secure in his little car seat in the back of the big Lincoln groundcar, the child turned from his interested scrutiny of the town to attack his great-granduncle with a precocious mental probe that made Rogi yelp with sudden pain. Marc's chubby face reflected in the rearview mirror revealed nothing but solemn curiosity, and his own mind was guarded with its usual indomitable screen. He was two years old.

Marc stop that! Teresa said.

"Yes, Mama," said the boy. The probe withdrew almost as quickly as it had penetrated, leaving only a lingering ache behind Rogi's eyes. But the cute little tyke had nearly mindsucked him like a plass pouch of orange juice.

"Shame on you for invading Uncle Rogi. I want you to apologize!" Teresa's uneasiness, which she had carefully concealed during the hour-long drive from Hanover, now tinged the exasperation that she projected to the old man on his intimate mode:

For the love of God Rogi can't you control yourself for my sake and Marc's if not for common decency?

The two-year-old said, "I'm sorry, Uncle Rogi."

"You're forgiven," the old man said. And then to Teresa: Once we get to Vic's house the kid will read the whole family like billboards no matter how they try to screen Denis is an integral *idiot* asking you to bring Marc along to this damned charade does he actually intend to use this *baby* in a metaconcert forchrissake and whatthehell good is a lowwatt mind like mine the whole goddamn thing is a farce a sop to Denis's guilt the lot of you should have put an end to it years ago and Paul should have more sense than to upset you in your condition—

Marc asked, "Does Uncle Rogi think making this Vic dead will hurt you and Maddy, Mama?"

"No, dear. Not at all. I'm fine, and so is Maddy, safe inside me." Rogi TRY to stay more securely on the intimate mode! Better yet think of something else like watching where you're going if you insist on driving manually. Look isn't this High Street where we turn? "Marc, dear, you've misunderstood Uncle Rogi's thought. The Vic he was thinking about is Victor Remillard, who is Grandpère's brother. We're going to see him and pray for him. Victor is very, very sick. He's been sick for nearly twenty-seven years, ever since the Great Intervention."

The small boy was prodding and thrusting now at his mother's mental shield, as a frustrated kitten scratches at a closed door. But there was no easy way through the maternal barricade; nature, compassionate of metaphysically operant parents, had rendered most of them proof against the onslaughts of their loving offspring.

"But why should Vic be made dead? Open to me, Mama, so I can understand better! I *want* to understand. Being dead is bad, isn't it? How can it be good for Vic?"

"Dear, stop poking at me. How many times must I tell you to respect the integrity of other minds? And you must call him Granduncle Victor, not Vic. Politesse, dear, always! . . . When a person is very sick and unable to get well, it's usually better for him to die and go to heaven rather than live on and suffer."

Rogi uttered a short, explosive laugh. "Heaven! That's rich."

Teresa said calmly to the child, "Uncle Rogi is being ironic, Marc. Do you remember what irony is?"

"Yes, Mama. But I'd rather discuss death with you now, please."

"There isn't much time, but I'll do my best, dear."

Rogi had slowed the car as they drove through the central district of Berlin. The town had undergone great change since the last time he had been here, and now seemed gussied up and gentrified almost beyond recognition. The older buildings that were worth rehabilitating had been expertly restored and framed in plantings, and the new structures looked as though they had stood there from time immemorial, mellowing gracefully. There were small parks at every other block, quaint wrought-iron streetlamps already glowing against the early dusk, even though it was still two hours until sunset, and not a trace of shabbiness was anywhere to be seen. Even in the pouring rain the old cottages and frame apartments of the core residential area seemed to glow in their coats of fresh paint, many done in classic New England white with dark shutters, while others sported the cheerful ice cream colors traditional to southern Québec.

Teresa continued in her attempt to explain mortality to the child. The tiny head with its thick mass of black ringlets had lowered as she spoke, apparently in obedient concentration. But all at once Rogi felt Marc renewing his quest for more interesting data, drilling into his own all-too-vulnerable cortex. Rogi exerted all of his adult coercion to fend off the infantile probing, addressing the boy with considerable precision on the intimate mode so that Teresa would have no hint of what he said:

Stop that digging you snoopy little foutriquet! Dammitall I'll tell you if you stop pestering me! Vic is a bad man or at least he was bad before he got sick the baddest man that *I* ever knew and the sooner he's dead the better off for all of us now is THAT plain enough for you?

Yes Uncle Rogi.

You'll find out pretty soon what this Good Friday thing the family does with Vic every year is all about just keep QUIET and watch and listen and it'll sort itself out. Afterward if you still have questions ask Grandpère Denis.

I—I don't want to. I don't like Grandpère. I'll ask you. On the way back home. Will that be all right?

I suppose so. Now let me alone while I try to find this place. I haven't been here in twenty-four years. Damn everything looks different up here! I guess I'll have to turn on the computer.

"—and so the elements of our bodies that were formed ages and ages ago in the hearts of giant exploding stars, elements that we only borrowed for a little while, must be returned to the Galaxy for reuse," Teresa was saying. "But even if our bodies die, our minds will live on in the Mind of the universe and be happy with God and all our friends and loved ones in eternal light. That's what heaven is."

"Will I die?" Marc asked her.

She grasped his tiny hands and kissed the top of his curly head. "Not for a long, long time. You have—you have a very special body to go along with your special mind."

"Will *you* die? And Uncle Rogi?"

"Your Uncle Rogi has the same kind of special body that you have. He won't die for a long time, either, and neither will Papa. I don't have the same kind of body you all have, but if I get old or sick I'll have myself regenerated so that I can stay with you. Do you remember what regeneration means?"

"Like Grandmère. In the regen-tank."

"Exactly. When I get old I'll go to a place that fixes me, just like Grandmère Lucille did, and I'll be made young and strong again. She'll be coming back to us very soon now. You'll hardly recognize her. She'll look as young as Aunt Cat."

The car's guidance system, having digested the code designation for the Victor Remillard estate on Upper Hillside Drive that Rogi called up, now switched on the vehicle's autopilot. Rogi sighed and sat back in his seat while the car drove itself, using satellite reference points. In his reactionary heart of hearts, Rogi considered such refinements obscene, even worse than the now obsolete computerized highway speed-strips. They took all the fun out of driving. A man might as well take the bus! Or one of those bloody flying eggs that wafted around on preset flight paths set up by Air Traffic Control. Up until now, Rogi had refused even to consider learning to fly. But he was weakening. One had to move with the times—even these days, when the damned times seemed almost to zip along at the square of the speed of light.

The dashboard chimed and a robot voice spoke. "You will arrive at your destination in approximately three minutes. Prepare to resume manual control of the vehicle." Rogi mumbled under his breath.

Marc asked his mother: Will we meet Papa and Uncle Philip and the others at Granduncle Victor's house?

Yes. They're all flying in.

The car had turned off Hillside Drive, following a narrow lane shaded by massive white pines and hemlocks. This manicured imitation of the primeval forest of New England opened at length into an expanse of lawn, sere with winter, and a magnificent vista of the Androscoggin River beyond. Parked near the house were five egg-shaped rhocraft—three Wulf-Mercedeses, a Mitsubishi, and a sporty green De Havilland Kestrel belonging to Severin Remillard. Paul's scarlet Maserati was nowhere in evidence.

The house from which Victor had directed his commercial empire prior to the Great Intervention was fully as ugly as Rogi had remembered it: a looming pseudobaronial pile of brick, stucco, and false timbering, built in the 1930s for some satrap of the extinct paper mills. It had leaded glass windows, pointed gables, and a slate roof that gleamed oily in the rain. Rambling decayed extensions with fanciful cupolas mounted upon them had once been stables, garages, and servants' quarters. Inside the main building were ten huge bedrooms, an oak-paneled library, a pretentious drawing room with an attached conservatory (the latter devoid of vegetation), a vast echoing ballroom, drafty hallways paved in marble, a modern kitchen and formal dining room that would have done credit to a small hotel, an empty indoor swimming pool, and a superlative state-of-the-art security system.

Victor Remillard had lived in this house since 2009, from the time of Remco Industries' first great prosperity. With him were his younger twin brothers Louis and Leon, and his widowed sister Yvonne Fortier, all of whom he had rendered nonoperant in early childhood, turning them into his creatures. In 2013, when Victor's criminal schemes were thwarted and he was reduced to a sense-deprived, helpless vegetable, the house became his place of exile. Louis, Leon, and Yvonne were promised immunity from prosecution by Denis and his politically influential friends provided they lived quietly in the old place, caring for Victor, supervising the small staff of domestics and nursing attendants, and staying out of the public eye.

Beginning in 2016, when his youngest son Paul was two years old, Denis Remillard and his wife Lucille Cartier and their seven powerfully operant children had come once each year, on Good Friday, to visit Victor. Denis explained to Yvonne, Louis, and Leon that he and his family were praying for Victor's spiritual recovery.

Yvonne, Louis, and Leon never really understood what Denis meant by that; but they were grateful that they had escaped federal prison after aiding and abetting Victor in his crimes, and they willingly performed their assigned duties according to Denis's instructions. Since they were virtual "normals," they did not take part in the annual metaconcerted prayer ritual except to see to the needs of the operant visitors, who eventually came to include the spouses of Denis and Lucille's adult children. Without Denis's knowledge, Yvonne, Louis, and Leon themselves prayed every day of their lives that Victor Remillard would never awaken from his mysterious coma to reassume his domination over them. In point of fact, the trio prayed that Victor Remillard would die.

And finally, this year, it looked as though their petition might be granted.

Aurelie Dalembert stood at the casement windows of the library, looking out at the rain and sipping sherry. In spite of the roaring fire in the big fireplace, the room was chilly. Cecilia, Maeve, and Cheri sat in uncomfortable damask chairs as close to the hearth as they could get, fortifying themselves with hot tea.

"Any sign of the Prima Donna yet?" Maeve O'Neill asked sharply.

"No," Aurelie replied. "Rogi's bringing her and Marc. In a car."

Cheri Losier-Drake, the youngest of the Remillard spouses at twenty-three, suppressed a tendency to shiver and reached for the silver teapot. "Every year this damned prayer vigil gets weirder. My nerves are a wreck. If only I could have a drink! Cele, you're a doctor. Surely a single brandy couldn't hurt."

Cecilia Ashe gently laid a hand on her sister-in-law's arm. A surge of calming redaction flowed from her brain to that of the other woman. "You know we mustn't . . . Did that zap help a little?"

Cheri sighed. "Must have. Parni gave a happy kick."

"It'll all be over soon." Aurelie's voice was soothing.

"Can't be soon enough," snapped Maeve. She downed the last of her tea in a gulp, plunked the fine china cup and saucer down on the table with a rattling crash, and went to get another birch log from the cradle.

"I find the notion of an annual prayer ritual fascinating," Cecilia said. "It's touching—this concern for the family black sheep."

"It's easy to tell that it's your first go-around," Maeve said, tossing the log onto the blaze. A shower of sparks fled up the chimney. "I don't know how much Maury told you about it, but we don't actually pray, you know. Denis links all of our minds in a coercive metaconcert, and *he* does the praying. Or whatever. It's Sevvy's opinion that the whole thing is nothing more than a colossal guilt compensation on the part of Denis. Because he's refused to pull the plug on Vic for all these years."

Cecilia, who had married the widowed Maurice Remillard seven months earlier, assumed a professionally bland expression. "That might be one explanation. But there are others."

"I think we're coercing Vic to die," Cheri said tersely. "And a consummation devoutly to be wished!"

"Amen," said Maeve. She had thrown still another piece of wood on the conflagration and now dusted her hands and plopped back into her chair. "And if Paul's right, and the infamous invalid is finally sinking, this might be the last year we'll have to put up with Denis's obsession."

From the window, Aurelie said, "I see car lights. It's Rogi and Teresa. And I've farspoken Paul. He and Denis will be here soon. The express Vee-route from Baltimore to Boston was OS and they lost time in a holding pattern. It's a scandal, the way the traffic jams keep getting worse and worse." She came to the fire and poured herself a cup of tea before sitting down with the others.

Cecilia said, "As a neurosurgeon, I find the whole matter of Victor Remillard's mysterious coma fascinating. Is it true that his body has remained in perfect condition up until just recently?"

"He's got the immortality gene complex like all the rest of these lucky sods," Maeve said, with a bitter laugh. "Thank God the regen-tank therapy is perfected at last. Can you imagine how poor old Lucille must have felt? Turning into a decrepit old crone of seventy-two in spite of the best that cosmetic surgery could do, while her husband, who's only a year older, still looks like a graduate student!"

"This will be the first Good Friday that Lucille has missed," Cheri said.

"Probably planned it," Maeve decided. "Nine months in the tank, then—tah-dah!—reborn, young and gorgeous." She patted her thick-ening midsection. "It's a crock that we still have to do babies the old-fashioned way. Look at us! Aside from Aurelie and Anne the virgin-martyr, we're a bloody maternity ward. That's all these dynastic Remillards seem to want out of us women: babies. Sometimes Sevvy seems positively irrational on the subject! I wonder if that's why Jenny and Galya divorced him—"

"Teresa's nearly due, isn't she?" Aurelie remarked, changing the subject abruptly. "And Cat has only another month to go."

"No, seriously," Maeve persisted to Cecilia. "They're planning to use artificial gestation to help populate some of the ethnic planets. Why *not* make it a general thing? I don't mind being pregnant twice, but I'll be damned if I'll go through it again and again just to help fill the Human Polity with superior Remillard minds. But if we could pop the fertilized eggs into incubators—"

"We've had the technical capability for a long time," Cecilia admit-ted, "and it is useful under certain circumstances. But it's far better for the baby to grow inside its mother naturally. There are both physical and psychological factors involved. That's why the Reproductive Stat-utes restrict artificial gestation so drastically."

"What do the Simbiari Proctors know about it?" Maeve flared. "Damned egg-laying salamandroids! They don't risk their lives having babies." She sprang to her feet and strode over to the window. The car had pulled up to the porte cochère at the entrance to the mansion, and the obsequious Louis and Leon were hurrying to greet the arrivals.

"This pregnancy of yours is going much better than the last, Maeve, dear." Aurelie tried to be consoling. "If you can just restrain your contraredactive tendencies—"

"—and avoid stress," Maeve finished in an arch tone. "You can talk.

Six kids already, and ready to keep it up till your ovaries pack it in. You drop babies as easily as an Indian squaw."

Cheri said, wearily, "Try to calm down, Maeve. Give the rest of us a break."

The Irishwoman said, "Oh, I'll simmer down soon enough. Just as soon as we finish with this ghoulish wake for the living dead!" She stared out at the rain-swept sky. "If my feeble farsight's not mistaken, that's Paul's egg coming now. Shall we go find our husbands and get this damned thing over with?"

Paul used his creativity to shield them from the rain as he and his father hurried from the egg to the house. Once Denis stumbled, and would have gone to his knees if Paul hadn't seized his arm. "Papa, you're still too weak to be out of the hospital. This was a mistake."

Denis shook his head stubbornly. If anything, he looked even younger than his twenty-six-year-old son, who was nearly 30 cents taller than his father and sported a debonair mustache to enhance his image as a rising planetary statesman. Both men were dressed in sober suits and topcoats, and water from the sodden lawn threatened their highly polished shoes. Lucille had always insisted that the family dress in a semiformal fashion for the Good Friday ritual; and even in her absence they had automatically complied.

"I'm quite all right," Denis insisted. "You know very well I was scheduled to leave Johns Hopkins next week. There's nothing whatsoever wrong with me physically. Tucker Barnes was probably right when he diagnosed me as suffering from exhaustion and acute depression aggravated by Lucille's absence."

"All the more reason for us to postpone Good Friday."

"No. That's unthinkable, especially under the circumstances."

They reached the porte cochère, and Paul canceled the metapsychic umbrella. The entry hall was brightly lit, and Louis and Leon hastened to open the front door and relieve Paul and Denis of their coats. The twins were sixty-two years old, stocky and balding and hollow-eyed, for all that they possessed the precious self-rejuvenating heritage. Unfortunately, it tended to express itself differently in different individuals, and the complex interaction of the thousands of genes involved was still poorly understood. Aunt Yvonne, who was a year older than the twins, was still pallidly youthful; but these two poor devils would always look middle-aged, like Uncle Rogi. Paul masked his disesteem as he greeted his uncles with cool formality. Would *he* retain his vitality and good looks as the years passed? Denis had, but he was a slightly built blond man, while Paul was robust and dark, as Rogi had been in his youth.

And Victor.

"How is he?" Denis asked.

"The nurse had to adjust the machine again," Louis said.

"The rate of hemoglobin synthesis continues to decrease," Leon added. "Heartbeat and respiration are normal, he assimilates nourishment and excretes, skin and muscular tone are nearly normal, and the EEG is as usual."

"Nevertheless," Louis finished, his voice completely neutral, "unless therapy is started soon to relieve the anemia, he'll eventually die."

Denis was already heading for the red-carpeted central staircase. "Paul, get the others together and bring them up at once."

"Papa! Wait . . ."

Denis halted and turned around, one hand on the banister.

Paul took a breath, sealed off his inner thoughts with as much strength as he could muster, and readied his coercion. "Papa, I've thought the matter over all throughout our flight from Baltimore. I won't let little Marc participate in the metaconcert. We don't know enough about the way mind-linkage affects the participants."

Denis's face wore a gentle smile. He did not meet his son's eyes. "Victor is failing, Paul. We may not have another chance, and we're lacking your mother's input this year. I assure you that the program I use is entirely benign. And Marc's mind is more powerful than that of many adults. Far stronger than those of the wives and Brett."

"Papa—*no*. Marc's my son. A baby. The rest of us are consenting adults. I've always had reservations about this Good Friday thing, and yet I've gone along with it because it was so important to you. But I can't put a tiny child at risk. Uncle Rogi's agreed to participate. He should help a little."

Denis turned away. "Very well." He continued up the stairs, letting his mind rove on ahead of him to the sickroom. The nonoperant day nurse looked up from her plaque-book as he entered Victor's room.

"Good afternoon, Mrs. Gilbert. We're nearly ready."

"Oh, Professor Remillard! I've been wanting to talk to you, but Mr. Philip and Dr. Severin said you were too ill—"

"I'm feeling better." He calmed her redactively. "Draw the drapes, will you, please? I'll just check the machine."

He stood at his younger brother's side for a few moments, looking at the pale, tranquil face of the man he was certain had damned himself. Then he went to the console of monitoring and life-support equipment set up at the foot of the big canopied bed.

The nurse persisted. "Doctor Cournoyer was here yesterday. He'd like to discuss Mr. Victor's deteriorating condition with you. The urgent need for therapy if the anemia is to be arrested."

Denis did not reply. He finished his inspection of the equipment, drew a chair up to the bedside, and sat down. His extraordinary bright blue eyes now lifted and caught those of Mrs. Gilbert, holding her hypnotized as she stood with the drapery cord in one hand.

"When my brother's coma was pronounced irreversible many years ago and the authorities allowed me to take responsibility for his care, they assumed I would do the usual thing—order the cessation of intravenous hydration and gastrostogavage so that he would soon die. For reasons that seemed valid to me, I did not follow this course of action. Instead, Victor has been given food and water and ordinary nursing care for more than twenty-six years. Up until two months ago, his body maintained itself in perfectly normal condition through self-redaction. And his mind, although incapable of any external manifestation, apparently continued to function as well. Victor is blind, deaf, and mute, unable to respond to any sensory stimulus, incapable of voluntary movement, incapable of telepathic communication, coercion, or any other external metapsychic manifestation . . . But he still thinks. A mentality such as his would not have continued to live unless he *wanted* to. Do you understand, Mrs. Gilbert?"

"I—I think so."

Denis inclined his head, so that the terrible eyes were shuttered and he suddenly seemed to be only a very weary, very frail young man. "If Victor is declining now, it's also because he wants to, and we will undertake no special measures to arrest the deterioration. Only carry on as usual. Is that clear?"

"I—yes." The nurse slowly closed the draperies, then touched a switch that lit two shaded brass sconces on either side of the bed. The only other illumination in the room came from the machine readouts, the small lamp at the nursing station, and a single candle in a ruby-glass cup, mounted beneath a wall crucifix opposite the bed.

"Please ask my family to come in now."

"Yes, Professor." She went out, closing the door softly behind her.

Denis lifted the coverlet and took out Victor's arms, folding them across his breast. The comatose man was dressed in gold silk pajamas, and none of the life-supportive equipment was visible. His handsome face had lost its usual ruddiness to the anemia but seemed otherwise normal, with the hint of a smile lingering about the bluish, motionless lips. Victor's crisply curled black hair had no more strands of silver in it now than it had had twenty-six years before, when he was struck down by . . . something on top of Mount Washington at the start of the Great Intervention.

Victor Remillard had killed nearly a hundred people without compunction, including his father and several of his own siblings. He had stolen billions of dollars and violated a bookful of criminal, financial, and commercial regulatory laws. He had conspired with the maniacal Kieran O'Connor to seize control of Earth's satellite laser-defense system. And he had very nearly managed to murder the cream of operant humanity, the three thousand delegates of the Last Meta psychic Congress, on the very day of Intervention.

Victor had also had the opportunity to ruminate over his sins ever since, thanks to his brother Denis.

"Vic," Denis whispered. "Vic, have you found the truth? Have you finally discovered where you went wrong?"

Mind wide open and completely receptive, Denis listened.

Rogi was at the tail end of the procession as they trooped up to Vic's bedroom, the seven metapsychic stalwarts of the Remillard Dynasty, their brave spouses, and him—scared shitless. At least baby Marc had been spared. The nurse had taken charge of him when Teresa declined to put him into the care of poor fey Yvonne, who now stood downstairs in the hall with Louis and Leon, the three of them watching with haunted expressions as the others climbed the stairs.

The bedroom furnishings, of dark and massive oak, were exactly as Rogi remembered them from twenty-four years earlier. The life-support gadgetry was more compact and sophisticated now, and there were new rugs and draperies and hangings about the bed. But the blackened old crucifix with its red vigil light was the one poor lost Sunny, Don's wife, had nailed up as a newlywed in the cottage on School Street; and the face of the man lying in the bed still struck Rogi with a terror so profound that he found himself reeling and had to clutch at the back of a chair to keep from fleeing the room.

The participants in the ritual were ranging themselves about the bed in couples. On the left side, nearest Victor's head, stood Philip Remillard, portly and comfortably homely, oldest of the seven siblings and the shrewd CEO of Remco Industries. With each passing year he reminded Rogi more and more of good old Onc' Louie, the hardworking mill foreman who had raised him. Philip's elegant wife, Aurelie Dalembert, stood calmly at his side, fingering a crystal rosary. She and her late sister Jeanne, who had married the second son of Denis and Lucille, had made careers of being wives to men destined for greatness and mothers of their children. Maurice Remillard, as fair and mild-looking as Denis but more sturdily built, had recently taken an extended leave of absence from the Department of Sociology at Columbia University to join his three younger siblings, Anne, Adrien, and Paul, as an administrator in the Human Polity of the Galactic Milieu. His second wife, Dr. Cecilia Ashe, wearing country tweeds in contrast to the dark suits and dresses of the other women, was looking down at the comatose man with clinical interest. Next to her stood Severin Remillard, who had been Cecilia's colleague in the Department of Neurology at Dartmouth Medical School and her unsuccessful wooer. He was a tall blond man with a dashing air and an iconoclastic view of the Galactic Milieu, which Rogi tended to sympathize with. Severin's third wife, Maeve O'Neill, formerly a successful Irish horse-breeder, was a ravishing redhead, now pale as milk and with her large eyes alight with apprehension, flinching away from her husband's proffered arm.

On the right side of the bed's foot, standing hand in hand with their minds entwined in mutual redactive commiseration, were Catherine Remillard and her husband Brett Doyle McAllister, colleagues in a Child Latency Project at the Polity capital, where both were also Intendancy bureaucrats. Next to them were Adrien Remillard and the wealthy pop sculptor Cheri Losier-Drake. Like Maeve, Cheri looked unhappy and anxious. Her husband, for all his metapsychic talents, was often considered by family detractors to be a rough-hewn, slightly unfinished prototype of the youngest and most famous member of the dynasty, Paul. Paul Remillard was not only tall, built like an athlete, and endowed with princely good looks, but he also possessed what was perhaps the most powerful set of metafaculties in the entire human race. He had married the acclaimed coloratura soprano Teresa Kendall. Besides Marc, their eldest, they had an infant daughter named Marie. The unborn child Teresa carried, also a girl, was to be called Madeleine.

The only unmarried sibling, Intendant Associate Anne Remillard, came up to Rogi with a sardonic twinkle in her ice-blue eyes and coerced him to stand at her side near Catherine and Brett, on the side of the room nearest the door. Denis himself stood next to them, at the very foot of the bed.

As always, the Remillards faced the crucifix and recited La Oraison Dominicale in the French language of their ancestors. Aurelie, Cecilia, and Teresa, who were also Catholics, joined in the prayer. Rogi was too petrified to utter a sound.

Then Denis spoke softly. "Thank you all for coming. Especially you, Cecilia, because I realize this family custom must seem bizarre to you this first time . . . and you, Uncle Rogi, for reasons that I know you would rather I didn't discuss."

Someone coughed, and there was a general shuffling of feet.

"For Cecilia's sake," Denis continued, "let me explain what we are about to do. I intend to link all of our minds in a metaconcert and pray in a very special way for my brother Victor. For over twenty-six years he has lain in this room, in a deep coma. We know from the monitoring machine that he thinks. Orderly thought patterns that are almost certainly rational are generated by his brain. But he is totally cut off from the world of sensation, receiving no input at all as far as we have been able to ascertain. Victor is alone with his thoughts, alone with his memories, alone with recollections of the terrible crimes he committed. It has always been my personal prayer—my hope—that Victor would ultimately repent of what he had done, and when this was accomplished he would either recover or pass peacefully into death."

Denis paused and turned his gaze upon Rogi, who was caught by those coercive blue eyes like a jacklighted deer, too frozen even to feel fear. And then Denis looked away.

"Recently, Victor's body has suffered a severe decline in hemato-poiesis, the manufacture of blood cells. In a person with the self-rejuvenating gene complex, this signifies a very grave prognosis. My brother is dying, and this is probably our last chance to come together on his behalf. Now let us prepare our minds for the meta-concert . . . Cecilia, the process is a very simple one for the partici-pants in the configuration I've designed. Just open your mind wide, with all barriers as low as possible, and *trust me*. I'll do the linkage very slowly, one of you at a time. When the concert is complete, I'll direct it. You need do nothing except relax. Ready?"

Rogi closed his eyes. Immediately, a deluge of memories seemed to engulf him. He seemed to see again his twin brother Donnie, whose juvenile assaults on his mind—nonmalicious in the beginning—had prompted in Rogi the spontaneous development of strong mental shielding. Only once had the two of them conjoined in a self-defensive, triumphant metaconcert. But after that, seeking to renew the experience, Donnie had instead attempted to violate Rogi's self, make the two of them into an inseparable whole. When Rogi refused, Donnie hated him—and hated himself for the hating—until the day that he died.

In the mnemonic flood, Rogi also saw Don's son, baby Denis, at the baptismal font, felt the new young mind bond to him. Denis had made Rogi his adoptive father, taking the love Rogi vouchsafed to him freely after his own father had denied him—in favor of Victor. As young Denis's mind matured and the shy child turned into one of the great minds of the world, Rogi had learned to fear him—even though the love was still there as well—and especially to fear joining mentally with him in metaconcert. Denis would never knowingly harm his beloved foster father; but he was so powerful, so *different*, that Rogi could not help being afraid.

He was very much afraid now.

Rogi's mental screens were still up; he had defied Denis, refused conjunction at the last moment, so that the others had been forced to complete the mind-edifice without him. Rogi was dimly aware of the metaconcert hovering apart from him, engrossed in whatever esoteric activity Denis was conjuring. Elsewhere, deep within the ineffable, immense dynamic field of mental lattices that was called the aether, something without tangible form was looking at Rogi.

Not Denis. Not Victor. Not any of the other persons who had gathered around the bed, nor anyone that Rogi knew.

Something else watched him from deep within a great mental chasm, a thing horrible that encompassed an evil beyond anything he had ever experienced before. Rogi had known Kieran O'Connor and Victor Remillard, the two most iniquitous minds that the human race had ever spawned; but this thing was worse. And it was beckoning to him.

Who are you? Rogi asked.

And it said: *I am Fury.*

Where did you come from? Rogi asked.

I am newborn. Inevitably.

What—what do you want?

And it said: *All of you.*

Rogi's mind screamed its fear and loathing. He seemed to hear laughter—and this time, the voice was recognizably Victor's. Rogi cried out again, pleading, begging for Denis—for anyone!—to come to his rescue. But Denis seemed to be gone, and the minds he had woven so skillfully about him were gone as well.

I require assistance, Fury said, reaching out. *And I'll take you to start with. Silly, flawed old Rogi! But you'll be useful.*

You can't! You can't! . . . See? I told you so!

Now Rogi was laughing hysterically, and the horror that was Fury roared, and the negation of the mental chasm was lit by a crimson radiance that grew brighter and brighter, becoming a red sphere suspended in utter darkness.

He is mine, another voice said. A familiar voice. *You may not have Rogi. Do what you must do, but not with him.*

The red sphere hovered, seeming to become more solid, a glowing thing that Rogi thought he recognized. He took hold of it somehow, and it pulled him away, away, out of the depths, away from the mind-monster named Fury, and back into ordinary reality—

—the bedroom. Severin and Cecilia Ashe bending over the supine figure, she seeking a wrist pulse, he lifting an eyelid to reveal a dilated, fathomless pupil. Denis on his knees, head bowed, hands touching the covered feet of the body, weeping. Paul and Adrien at the machine, where the once-green telltales now blinked red. Anne standing apart, her face frozen. Catherine, Teresa, and the other women together in an agitated group, murmuring. Philip, Maurice, and Brett staring at each other helplessly.

Suddenly, through the closed door, Rogi heard a baby scream.

His paralysis evaporated and he raced to the door, yanked it open. Then he halted, stunned, at the scene in the hall.

Three bodies lay on their backs on the Oriental runner rug. Yvonne, Louis, and Leon, their faces contorted and their eyes wide open, were stone dead.

From the doorway of the bedroom across the hall, Mrs. Gilbert, the nurse, stared down at the bodies in astonishment, while the two-year-old boy in her arms shrieked and struggled like a wild thing.

Rogi's hand went involuntarily to his pants pocket, to the key ring that he always carried with him, the one with a fob like a red glass marble. His strong fingers tightened about the little caged sphere.

It's all right, Rogi said to Marc on the intimate mode. He's gone.

Abruptly, the boy's cries ceased. Flushed and tousled, breathing in noisy gulps, Marc held out his arms to the old man. Rogi took him from the nurse, cradled the small head against his chest, and hurried off downstairs.

[3]

OKANAGON/EARTH
24 AUGUST 2051

He had been summoned.

Coerced. He—the uncoercible!

It was nothing so concrete as a call on the telepathic intimate mode. It was a compulsion, an aching cryptesthetic urge having nothing at all to do with the usual workings of his powerful and orderly young mind. It was a *feeling* (and that, of course, made it totally suspect) that his mother, more than 540 light-years away on Earth, was in danger from some purposeful agency that would cause her irreparable harm. And only he, Marc Remillard, could save her.

But that was counter to all logic; and he had arranged his life so as to subdue in himself the messier, nonintellectual aspects of the human psyche. When irruptions of the feeling function occasionally got the better of him, he counted it a personal defeat, and analyzed the phenomenon rigorously, and strove to bring it under control so as to lessen his susceptibility on the next go-around. But somehow, where his mother was concerned, emotional skewing tended to persist. It was odd that he should continue to love her with such unreasoning ardor in spite of her benign indifference; no amount of metacreative sorting and rechanneling on his part had been successful in transmuting the filial bond with Teresa Kendall into something safer . . .

He had dealt with his father more satisfactorily. Paul could no longer hurt him or even shake his composure. Why, then, he asked himself, should a son's relationship with the maternal parent be so much less amenable to rationalization? It was annoying—and in the present situation, intuition hinted that it might even be dangerous.

But intuition was often illogical, too.

When Marc attempted to farspeak his mother, he discovered that she had her impregnable mental barrier up. And so he was forced to place a call to her from Okanagon via subspace communicator, just as though he were a nonoperant or a metapsychic infant.

When he reached her, Teresa cheerfully denied that anything at all was wrong. She said she missed him, as she said she missed the other three children, off on their various summer jaunts. But they would all be together soon enough, and she was feeling quite well these days, and it was *so* unlike him to be hyperimaginative—and was he quite sure that he wasn't coming down with some exotic bug?

He told her that he would get a scan, and apologized stiffly for his irrational behavior and for disturbing her.

She laughed kindly and said it was probably only puberty, which was bound to be unsettling even to a grandmasterclass young operant like himself. She told him that she loved him, and reassured him once again that everything at home on Earth was fine, and then terminated the communication.

Marc had no way of telling whether or not his mother was lying to him again. The notion that puberty was the cause of his malaise he rejected out of hand; his hormonal secretions were normal for a boy of thirteen, and he was confident that they, like the rest of his bodily functions, were at the moment subordinate to his self-redactive metafaculty. But the maddening compulsion was not imaginary; it was undeniably coercive and focused with considerable precision upon him, and it increased in strength every hour that he attempted futile analysis of its source.

He farspoke his sensible twelve-year-old sister Marie, who was trying to write her first novel at their grandparents' old summer place on the Atlantic shore. Marie told him she had seen their mother last weekend, and things were as normal back at home as they ever were. Teresa was clearly grateful for her time alone. She displayed no overt symptoms of mental dysfunction. She was doing some gardening and was working with every evidence of enthusiasm to transpose an obscure folk song cycle from the archaic Poltroyan into modern human notation.

In Marie's opinion, Marc's premonitions and uneasiness were nothing more than mental indigestion. His giant brain was doubtless suffering overload from all the weird cerebroenergetic experiments he had inflicted upon himself, and he should slow down and smell the flowers before his synapses snapped.

Marc told Marie thanks for nothing.

Next he tried to bespeak his Great-granduncle Rogi, who lived above his bookstore only a block and a half away from the family home. Rogi's puny mentality did not respond to Marc's farspoken hails, and that probably meant that the old man was in one of his downslide phases and stinko again. However, there was only a small chance that Uncle Rogi would know the truth about Teresa anyway. He had always been leery of Marc's parents and the other Galactic celebrities of the Remillard clan, even as he was surprisingly congenial toward Paul and Teresa's aloof eldest son, Marc . . .

In the end, the boy decided that there was no way to resolve the dilemma but to go home and check things out personally, and at all possible speed.

It took three days for the CSS Funakoshi Maru to travel from Okanagon to Earth at the highest displacement factor endurable by masterclass humans. Marc Remillard scarcely felt the pain of the three deep-catenary hyperspatial translations at all. Enmeshed in his premonition, he had also neglected to note that the cost of his ticket on the premium-class superluminal transport had eaten up nearly all of his remaining personal credit-card allowance. When the starship docked at Ka Lei, Marc discovered that he couldn't afford to travel the rest of the way home from Hawaii via express eggliner and taxi. For emergencies, he carried the family corporation credit card, with its unlimited rating; but since he was legally a minor for three more years, no matter how extraordinary his metapsychic quotient, using the card would require parental authorization and thereby alert his father. And the damned premonition seemed to urge that he not let anyone—most particularly not Paul—know that he had returned.

So Marc took the cheapie local shuttle, which took twice as long as the express to fly from Ka Lei to the North American spaceport on Anticosti Island. It was from there that he had embarked for the planet Okanagon the previous June, leaving his BMW T99RT turbocycle in the long-term parking facility. He considered but rejected the idea of sneaking his wheels out without paying. The garage exit was fully automated against that very contingency, and its computer notably sneetchproof, even to the likes of him, and if he blew it and got nailed, he might as well have stayed on Okanagon. There was nothing to do but play it straight. Unhocking the turbocycle reduced the credit on his personal plass to just about zero; but fortunately the BMW was fully j-fueled and ready to roll, and the tolls would be automatically debited to the family account.

Marc removed the cycle leathers from the machine's boot and put them on. He checked the charge and ran an internal test of the circuitry in the cerebroenergetic guidance helmet, then clapped it on, effectively plugging his brain into the bike the moment the hard-hat electrodes came alive at his imperative thought and pricked his scalp. The BMW's instrumentation became part of his own senses, and its operating controls belonged to his voluntary nervous system, answering to his mental commands. There was nothing unique about the cerebroenergetic system except the fact that it was designed to operate a mere turbocycle instead of a starship or another highly sophisticated piece of apparatus. And instead of being manufactured by IBM or Datasys or Toshiba, it had been built by Marc himself.

Ordinarily, he drove his overpowered BMW in a scrupulously law-abiding manner except when he was on a racecourse; but now, in the emergency, he'd crank the bike flat out in the maxcel lanes of the autoroutes and screw the scofflaw monitors with his meta-creativity. If a living police officer spotted him, he'd just have to risk brainwiping the cop.

The mind-controlled two-wheeler with the boy aboard rolled out of the spaceport parking garage, adhering to the speed limit all through the Jacques Cartier Tunnel leading to the Labrador Autoroute on the north shore of the Saint-Laurent. Once it reached the maxcel lanes of the major groundway, the boy hung out the spoilers and commanded maximum throttle. Luckily, no human traffic police eyeballed him en route, and no busybody civilian drivers happened to be alert enough to note his tag number as he scorched past. He reached Hanover, New Hampshire, shortly after noon, having achieved an average velocity of 282.2 kilometers per hour.

The beautiful old college town was swathed in a summer heat wave and seemed nearly deserted. Marc drove the bike in quietly and decided that it would be a good idea to scan things out at close range before going to the house.

He went to the empty parking area of the Catholic Church on Sanborn Road, just around the corner from his home. It was so hot that the birds had quit singing and the tarmac that paved the lot was semiliquid between the bits of gravel. When he unzipped the environmentally controlled leather suit from left shoulder to right ankle and stepped out of it, he felt as if he had stepped into a sauna.

He was able to mentally adjust his body thermostat easily enough; but the feeling of impending disaster had now become almost overwhelming. During the shuttle trip and the drive from Anticosti, he had deliberately refrained from any attempt to farsense Teresa or try to make mental contact with her. The premonition had seemed to warn him that this would be dangerous, that she would inadvertently give away his presence on Earth and somehow preclude his helping her. But now, standing in the dusty shade of a gigantic mutant elm with the cooling engine of the Beemer ticking gently beside him, the boy reached out with the most heavily shielded farsensory probe he could manage and entered the old white colonial-style house at 15 East South Street.

Neither Herta Schmidt, the operant nanny, nor Jacqui Delarue, the nonoperant housekeeper, was anywhere in the place. His mother, Teresa Kaulana Kendall, was in her music studio on the second floor, sitting at a keyboard in front of an open window, playing a soft guitarlike improvisation. As Marc's ultrasense lingered on her face, which was lightly sheened with perspiration, she brushed a damp lock of dark hair from her eyes with a sharp gesture at odds with her tranquil aspect.

Her mind was enveloped in a grandmasterclass screen that no Remillard—not even her husband or her eldest son—had ever been able to breach.

Across the room, sitting stiffly on a ladder-back chair between the computer desk and a bookcase stuffed with old-fashioned printed musical scores, was Lucille Cartier—Marc's redoubtable grandmother and Teresa's mother-in-law. Lucille's rejuvenated beauty was unsullied by sweat, and her dark brown hair, cut in bangs and a classic Chanel bob, was perfectly groomed.

Lucille said, "Now that we're certain that the prognosis for success-ful prenatal genetic engineering is negative, you must agree that only one course of action is possible."

Teresa said nothing. The music she played was technically brilliant but completely lacking in depth or nuance.

Lucille was reining in her famous temper admirably, projecting regret, sympathy, and feminine solidarity at the same time that her coercion was working overtime. "Teresa, dear, there is no other way the family can protect you from the legal consequences of your irre-sponsible behavior. And the child is—"

"Doomed anyhow," Teresa finished, smiling abstractedly.

"Severin himself performed the genetic assay, confirming the pres-ence of at least three intractable lethal traits in the fetal DNA. And I needn't remind you"—Lucille's voice hardened—"that doing those tests makes Sevvy just as much of an accessory to your crime as I am. But he was willing to put himself in jeopardy just to prove to you that the situation is irremediable."

"And I thank you both for trying. And for not reporting me."

"We never considered reporting you to the Magistratum!"

The smallest movement uplifted Teresa's lips. "Of course not. The Remillard family honor—and the honor of the first human Magnate-Designate—would never recover from the scandal."

"You don't know what you're saying." Lucille's words were still objective, composed. But her mental substratum, clearly perceptible to Marc's spying ultrasense, smoldered with outrage. "Any more than you really knew what you were doing when you deliberately flouted the Reproductive Statutes."

"Oh, I knew . . . but I never intended to harm Paul or the rest of the family. I—I only knew that this time the risk was worth taking."

"How you ever expected to get away with it—"

"I had a plan. Once my condition became obvious, I'd slip away to my family's old beach house on Kauai, where only native Hawaiian people and a handful of haoles live now. It would have been easy to make some excuse to Paul." Teresa uttered a small laugh. "He certainly would never miss me, what with the hullabaloo over the upcoming ending of the Simbiari Proctorship and the formal induction cere-monies for the new Earth Magnates at Concilium Orb. I thought that afterward, when the Human Polity finally took its place in the though the secret, once discovered, was no longer worth agonizing over. "Paul never would have known. It took another woman to find out the truth. Well, it will all be over tomorrow . . . Lucille, you mustn't worry about me anymore. You're quite right and I *am* a fool, and that's an end to it. I think you'd better go now and arrange things. I'd like to be alone for a while . . . to do my vocal exercises. You know how I am about letting anyone hear how awful I've become."

"That's nonsense!" said Lucille stoutly. "Your voice is as fine as ever. How many times must we tell you that your singing difficulties are entirely psychosomatic? And this other—this obsession of yours would also respond to therapy if you'd only—"

"Please." Pain flashed briefly from Teresa's eyes. "Just let us be alone together for these last few hours."

"It's *not* sapient! Not at five months!" Lucille's voice was shrill, and her eyes blazed. "It's only your sick imagination hearing it!"

"Yes, of course."

Teresa turned her back on Lucille, took her seat again at the keyboard, and toggled a fortepiano patch. She began to play Chopin's Berceuse. "I'll be ready tomorrow. Just call me. Tell me where and when."

Lucille's mouth tightened as she recognized the lullaby. But she only nodded and left the room, hurrying down the staircase and out of the house to her waiting groundcar. Marc waited until his grandmother drove off and turned away on Main Street before starting to walk his bike toward the house, bespeaking his mother on the way.

MARC: Mama. I've come.

TERESA: *Marc?* It's you? But . . . why, dear? What about the little holiday you were supposed to take with your friends after finishing the undergrad seminar on Okanagon? The trip to the Singing Jungle! I know you were looking forward to a break before beginning at Dartmouth this fall—

MARC: I've come to help you.

TERESA: I told you there was nothing wrong. Nothing that need concern you. [Detachment.]

MARC: I know better. I felt your need. Your danger. There was an irresistible compulsion. You coerced me and I came.

TERESA: Oh no Marc. You know my mind you of all people. I'm weak

Milieu and the Dynasty was settled in as magnates, I'd eventually be exonerated."

"That is by no means a certainty."

"I'm not the only person who thinks the Reproductive Statutes are unjust! Nor am I the only operant who's attempted to circumvent them. For normals, the penalty is only a fine and sterilization and the loss of a few entitlements. Why the Simbiari decided to deal with *us* in such a draconian manner—"

"We operants have more privileges," said Lucille gently, "and we also have more responsibilities."

"To hell with them both." Teresa's voice was level. Her musical improvisation became Bachian, faster and almost frenzied in its intricacy. "To hell with the whole ungodly Proctorship scheme. To hell with the exotics and their Milieu. What fools we all were to think it would be so wonderful to become part of a Galactic civilization."

"There are some normals who would agree with you, and a few operants. But most of humanity believes that the Intervention saved our planet from catastrophe."

"The price—in human freedom and dignity—has been too high."

Lucille Cartier's mental veneer of sympathy thinned momentarily to reveal the thought: *Poor neurotic fool!* And if any love or pity for Teresa tinged this stark judgment, it was imperceptible to Marc.

Teresa seemed to notice nothing and continued equably. "But all this is quite beside the point. My little scheme failed to reckon with your own maternal astuteness, Lucille. You found me out."

Her playing slowed, and the music passed into a minor mode. Almost as an afterthought, she said, "If you and Severin are prepared to perform the procedure, we'd best do it early tomorrow, before Paul comes back from Concord."

"Thank God you've finally come to your senses!" Lucille sprang up from the chair and came swiftly to her daughter-in-law, taking Teresa's hands from the keyboard and drawing her to her feet. "Darling, I know how terrible this is for you. And I'm so sorry it has to be this way. We should have realized what emotional turmoil you were suffering. *Paul* should have known . . ."

Teresa freed her hands. "Not Paul," she said very quietly. There were tears in her eyes now, but the mental façade that she displayed to her mother-in-law was suddenly casual, uncaring—almost as

in the coercive faculty unable to project a compulsion into the next
room, much less five hundred lightyears to Okanagon.

MARC: Unconsciously, you could do it . . . under the circumstances. It
had to be you. It certainly wasn't him.

TERESA: Oh Jesus you can't mean . . . *Marc do you know?*

MARC: Not all of it but enough. I can read your subliminal thoughts
now, Mama. Your barrier is down, and you're thinking so loudly
that I can hardly avoid it! Does—does he really speak to you?

TERESA: Lucille insists it's impossible. He's only five months alive and
his brain hasn't developed far enough even an eight-month fetus is
barely able to conceptualize much less achieve the bilateral cerebra-
tion necessary for even the most primitive form of self-awareness
or communication it's not anything I can understand. I only *know*
it know HE IS THE ONE not you not the others my poor wonderful babies forgive me forgive me I had to do it he must live mutant
or not HE IS THE ONE Marc can you help us how can you *possibly*
help you're only thirteen Lucille and Severin will kill him to save me
but I won't let it happen I'll run away I'll do away with both of us
before—

MARC: **Teresa be still!**

TERESA: . . . Yes.

MARC: I'm here. In the house. Coming upstairs. I know what to do how
to save both of you your unconscious mind was right to call me.
Trust me.

TERESA: Yes.

Teresa did not look up as Marc entered. She stared at her hands, silent
on the electronic keyboard. "You're only a boy. A boy with an amazing
mind, but hardly powerful enough to counter the law enforcement
authorities of the Galactic Milieu. What I've done is a serious crime,
and if you help me you'll be an accessory and liable to the same penalty
as mine."

"As Grandma and Uncle Sevvy will be, too, if they do the abortion."

"The danger of their being found out is infinitesimal, whereas you
would almost certainly be caught if you tried to help me escape."

"I won't be caught. I've already worked it out. Look!" [Image.]

"I see," Teresa whispered. "I see."

She reached out to him mentally, to this oldest child, who had distanced himself from his parents in the earliest years of life, keeping himself to himself, apparently rejecting love as a needless distraction as he cultivated the awesome metafaculties that might someday make him the leading human operant of the new Galactic Age. Teresa seemed genuinely astonished that it should be Marc who would try to save her . . . save both of them. He had shown no particular affection for his other siblings and seemed to have only an Olympian regard for his mother and father. Even now he instinctively froze at her attempted mental caress, as though he knew that love's interface would breach his precious self-sufficiency and render him vulnerable.

As it had.

"Marc, are you sure?" she asked, taking his hand. It was warm, unlike the ramparts guarding his soul's core.

"Yes," he said.

Teresa kissed the young hand, then smiled as she guided it to her belly, which had hardly begun to swell. Marc's muscles tensed, and she feared he would pull away; but then—

"There," she said reassuringly, and the boy relaxed. "You must listen very carefully. His—his thought-mode is like nothing I've ever experienced before, human or exotic. It's rather frightening until you get used to it. At least it was for me! Probe deep. Be open for something quite different. And be gentle, because he feels he must hide, sometimes, like a little frightened animal . . ."

Marc knelt beside Teresa, placed both hands on his mother's abdomen, and closed his eyes. Transfixed, he hardly seemed to breathe for many minutes. Finally he gave a low, inarticulate cry. He opened his eyes and regarded his mother with mingled elation and fear.

"It's all right," Teresa said, smiling. "He's really very happy to meet you. And—yes. It seems that he was expecting you after all."

[4]

HANOVER, NEW HAMPSHIRE, EARTH
24 AUGUST 2051

The antique bell on the front door of The Eloquent Page tinkled, and the teenaged boy came inside. Even before she looked up from her computer inventory check, Perdita Manion was aware that a meta-psychic operant of exceptional stature had come into the bookshop. The mind-signature was not only unreadable; it was encrypted to the point of nonexistence. It could belong to only one person.

She smiled a greeting both with her lips and with her mind. "Well, hello, Marc! So you're back home in time to enjoy the last days of this beautiful New Hampshire summer, are you? I thought you were going to be off-world until the start of the Dartmouth fall term."

"The undergraduate seminar on psychocreative ambivalence at the Okanagon Institute ended earlier than I expected. The Simbiari prof came down with some kind of exotic allergy and couldn't stop dripping green."

"Good heavens!"

"And then there was the big news about the selection of the first human Magnates of the Concilium. Anybody named Remillard was fair game for the local media. So I caught the next ship for Earth."

"But it was your first star trip all alone. Didn't you want to stay on and explore for a bit? Okanagon is such a gorgeous world. All those flowering trees and the singing fire-moths in the jungle gardens . . . Lindsay and I seriously considered settling there in 2020, when the first colonial planets were opened."

Marc's response was edgy and formal. "The planet is certainly very attractive physically, but I found it mentally unsettling. It has such a large cosmopolitan population of nonoperants. Their excessively mer-cantile mind-set has generated a very anharmonic planetary aura."

"Oh."

"I suppose I'm oversensitive. But . . . there's no place like home."

"Well, of course." Perdita Manion offered him maternal sympathy well flavored with humor. Masterclass adolescents had such a difficult time coping, poor things! The brighter they were, the harder it was for them to adapt when they were first cut loose from the hothouse of operant training they had known since early childhood and were forced to swim in the perverse mainstream of "normal" humanity. Her own brilliant son, Alexis, who like Marc had recently graduated from Brebeuf Academy, was a sore trial himself these days—an idealistic champion of the Altruism Ethic one moment and a power-tripping little fascist the next, in spite of the best efforts of the school's operant Jesuit preceptors. It was high time that both boys were off to college, where their psychosocial adjustment to nonoperant people and to members of the five exotic races would be even more closely monitored than their academic progress.

Perdita said, "Alexis will be very glad to see you, Marc. He and Boom-Boom Laroche and Pete Dalembert are planning a fishing trip to Maine next week. I know they'll want you to go along. That might help calm your nerves."

"I'll catch Alex later, Miz Manion—but I'm afraid I may be too tied up with other business to go on the trip."

Marc spoke casually; but for the briefest instant, Perdita caught a hint of anxiety, flashing involuntarily from the expertly shielded young mind. "There's nothing wrong, is there?" she asked.

"Nothing you want to worry about. Just . . . personal stuff."

"And here I am keeping you, when you want to talk things over with your Uncle Rogi. Well, go right on back to his lair. You'll probably find him up to his neck in buyer want-lists. He'll be happy to have a visitor."

She returned to her own work, her subliminal thoughts radiating unqualified love for her own recalcitrant offspring and tolerant goodwill toward Alexis's outré best friend. Perdita Manion did not know that most of her mind was as transparent as glass to Marc's scrutiny. She thought: Thank God Alexis is only an ordinary genius. Since Lindsay's death he's been a handful . . . but what if I'd had to raise a child like Marc? The poor boy!

Marc mind-smiled a salute to her kind heart, ignoring the implication of her other thoughts. Like so many other low-level operants, Perdita had no notion at all of the way higher minds like his functioned; she persisted in judging the personality integration of master-class persons according to her own, nearly "normal," standards. No wonder she failed to understand Alex—much less *him*.

Marc made his way through the close-standing shelves of old-fashioned paged books—fantasy titles, science fiction, and horror novels—that were the stock-in-trade of his great-granduncle. The business catered exclusively to collectors, selling mostly by mail order. The only modern liquid-crystal plaque-books in The Eloquent Page were reference volumes or scholarly studies of the good old stuff.

The bookshop took up the corner premises in the venerable Gates House building on Main Street and had been a landmark in Hanover since before the Great Intervention. Its proprietor, who was called Uncle Rogi by most of the town as well as by the numerous members of the Remillard clan, lived in an apartment on the third floor. Suites of professional offices took up the second floor, and the building also housed a coffee shop, and an insurance office in the annex out back, where there was a garage that Rogi used for his personal groundcar. Marc and his two younger sisters Marie and Madeleine and kid brother Luc had practically grown up in the bookshop, as had their father Paul and their six paternal uncles and aunts before them. The shop was a refuge from the overstimulating ambiance of the Remillard family home just around the corner and down the block, where the elite of Earth's metapsychic operant community, as well as members of the nonhuman races of the Galactic Milieu, were apt to drop in without ceremony and stay for days on end.

A shaggy gray animal strolled out from among the bookshelves and eyed Marc with benignant tolerance.

"Miaow." *Greeting FriendofMaster.*

Hey. Hello yourself cat!

Food?

Don't you ever think of anything else fatso?

The boy bent to scratch behind the ears of Rogi's big Maine Coon cat, Marcel LaPlume. The animal stretched his ten-kilo body and yawned, then gathered his muscles to spring as Marc reached for the doorknob of the back room where Rogi usually worked. The door opened and Marcel streaked inside, muttering telepathic feline complaints against masters who shut out their beloved pets. The back room was sultry with summer heat in spite of the laboring of the antique air conditioner in the window. The unmistakable scent of fine bourbon whiskey mingled with the musty smell of preserved pulp paper. Uncle Rogi, dressed in his usual summertime costume of faded Levi's and a Bean seersucker shirt, was asleep in his ratty old leather-covered recliner-rocker. A half-empty bottle of Wild Turkey and a ham-and-cheese sandwich with two bites out of it sat in front of him in the midst of a pile of videograms and tattered printouts.

The cat Marcel seemed to levitate onto the desk, landing his great bulk without disturbing a single item. He grabbed the sandwich, and his gray-green eyes regarded Marc with sly mockery before he took to the air again. A three-meter leap gained him the sanctuary of a high storage shelf, where he settled down to enjoy his purloined lunch among the piles of century-old pulp magazines shrouded in transparent plass.

Marc came in and shut the door behind him.

"Uncle Rogi, wake up!"

As the boy spoke, his powerful redactive faculty performed a drastic therapeutic maneuver, canceling the alcoholic torpor. The sleeping bookseller's brainwaves jumped into abrupt and highly unwelcome wakefulness. Rogatien Remillard snorted and hauled himself up, muttering curses in the Canuckois French of upper New England that was his natal tongue. His eyes snapped fully open when Marc sent a terse telepathic message arrowing into his mind.

"*My* help? Batège! What kind of trouble have you gotten yourself into this time? And what are you doing back home so early? Don't tell me you've been thrown out of another school workshop for gross insubordination—"

The old man broke off, coerced firmly into silence. Marc said on the intimate mode: It's not that at all Uncle Rogi. This is serious business. A family emergency. You've got to come home with me right away and for God's sake put a lid on it while we're in range of Perdita Manion! . . . Do you still have your old canoe and camping gear stashed in your garage?

Yes. But—

Good. We'll be needing them and your groundcar too. Do you have any cash available?

You know damn well I do and I always will until the foutu credit cards conquer the universe. [Suspicion.] How much cash?

Three or four kay.

Grand dieu! What kind of trouble have you—

Get it and let's go.

Without any further mental exchange, the bookseller rose and put the bottle of whiskey away in a file cabinet. He took a filthy old book-shipping Jiffy bag from the shelves of packing materials, extracted a wad of durofilm bills from it, and stuffed the money into his pants pocket. Then, with the boy following, he went into the front of the store.

"Marc and I will be going out for a while, Perdita. If Professor Dalembert comes for his copy of Murray's *Mamelons and Ungava*, be sure to point out the cracked hinges. But it's still a steal at three hundred."

"You two run along, and I'll hold the fort," Perdita said comfortably. "Nothing's happening at all on a lazy summer afternoon like this."

Marc's laugh was strained. "That's nice to know. Uncle Rogi and I just may take the rest of the day off and go canoeing. Good to see you again, Miz Manion."

The old man and the boy exited into brazen sunshine. High in the buttermilk sky a single egg-shaped rhocraft soared westward over the Connecticut River Valley, seeming to waft as slowly as a toy balloon even though it must have been traveling at several hundred kilometers per hour. There was no other aerial traffic. A sporty black groundcar drove slowly past the post office, where on twin poles the flags of the United States of America and the Human Polity of the Galactic Milieu hung limp. Across Main Street, at the BP energy station, Wally Van Zandt was squirting the petunias in the bed next to the egg-charging pad with D-water, following the common folkloric belief that it would make the flowers more spectacular. Marc noticed that the cost of j-fuel had risen five pence since he'd gone off-world. The damned energy companies seemed to do that every summer. It was high time the manufacturers converted turbocycles and private groundcars to fusion, just like commercial vehicles and eggs. More expensive in the short run for the power plant, but cheaper in the long for the fuel.

Rogi and Marc went around the corner onto East South Street, to Rogi's garage. It was nearly three months since the bookseller had last seen his great-grandnephew, and even in that short period of time

Marc seemed to have grown. The top of his black curls was above Rogi's shoulder level now. The young jaw with its deeply cleft chin was more angular, and the profile was fast losing its childish contour and taking on the distinctive Remillard aquilinity that made Marc's father's face so striking. But the boy's eyes weren't blue like Paul's; they were gray, with a startling luminosity, set deeply in shadowed sockets and topped by oddly shaped brows that were thickest at the temple ends, giving them a resemblance to dark wings. On the rare occasions when Marc neglected to maintain his "social" mental screening, those eyes could flash with a power that was almost heart-stopping.

Rogi, whose own operant mindpowers were unexceptional, was the oldest surviving member of the family. He had experienced the metapsychic usage and abusage of every one of the Remillard stalwarts, and he had no doubt that Marc was the most highly endowed of the lot. He also suspected that the boy might be the most marginally human. For that very reason, Rogi had taken special pains to reach out to him—not always with success. From infancy, Marc had contrived to hide behind a barrier of nearly perfect control and self-containment. More unfortunately, there was something about the boy's mind-set that reminded the old man of his late nemesis, Victor Remillard, the brother of Marc's grandfather Denis. Like Victor, Marc was emotionally cold and prideful, determined to do things his own way while letting the rest of the world go hang. On the other hand, the boy's arrogance seemed not to be malicious, as Victor's had been, but rather the almost inevitable consequent of having a skull crammed with more metafaculties than the human soul could safely support.

Marc had badly needed an adult friend. His father Paul, a fiery politician busy about many things, was undeniably proud of his son's brilliance and his preeminent metapsychic powers; but Paul Remillard seemed to have given up years before trying to establish an intimate rapport with his remote eldest child. Marc's mother Teresa, distracted in his early childhood by her operatic career and her artistic temperament and later traumatized by personal tragedy, loved Marc with the same vague affection she bestowed upon her other three children. But she, like her husband, had failed in her halfhearted attempts to penetrate the boy's personal shell. Rogi had never quite managed to break through that wall of mental armor plate, either; but he wasn't about to stop trying . . .

They went into the garage, and Marc put Rogi to work gathering equipment while the boy himself installed the ancient canoe rack atop the old Volvo groundcar. There was no verbal conversation, and Rogi was patient as he tossed tent, cooking gear, tarpaulins, and nearly all the rest of the camping equipment he owned into the car's trunk and backseat. Marc finished with the rack and revealed how agitated he really was by using his PK to loft the canoe into place, psychokinesis being considered a déclassé metafunction among most operants of stature.

Finally, while the two of them clamped the canoe down, Marc came out with an edited version of the emergency in formally cadenced mental speech:

My seminar on Okanagon ended early. I thought I'd surprise Mama and didn't teleview or farspeak her—just grabbed the first flight to Earth and shuttled from Ka Lei to Anticosti, then drove my bike home. When I got into Hanover I didn't see a soul I knew. I think the whole town is on vacation break. I figured nobody would be at our place except Mama, since Papa's not due back from Concord until the weekend, and the three pipsqueaks are still at the beach at Grandpère's place. I sent my mind on ahead to the house and up to Mama's music studio. I discovered that Grandmère Lucille was there. I listened to what they said—

!! You're too damned good at eavesdropping my lad it'll get you in a peck of trouble one day.

[Impatience!] Never mind that! . . . How much do you know about the genetic heritage of the Remillard family?

[Confusion.] You mean the immortality thing?

Not the multifactorial self-rejuvenation trait. The lethal equivalents!

. . . Aside from knowing the hell our weird family genes have put Teresa and Paul through I have only an incompetent layman's knowledge of the matter.

All four of us children inherit from the Remillard side of the family a dominant polygenic mutant complex: we're smart, we have extremely high metafunctions, and our bodies age up to a certain point and then persistently rejuvenate. The traits have a reduced penetrance and exhibit variable expressivity. You know what that means?

Quelle chierie don't be so damned patronizing. It means some Remillards get a little some get a lot and I'm on the short end of the stick while *you're* up to your young stuckup pif in the good stuff just like your siblings&cousins&father&uncles&aunts&Grandpère Denis—

Exactly. Now, because of Mama's consanguineous relationship through Annarita Latimer, her offspring have an enhanced chance of manifesting one or another of the good traits. Unfortunately, Mama has also contributed a deleterious gene complex to some of us kids. She herself doesn't display any harmful traits, and neither do Marie and I, so it's been assumed that Mama was subjected to a mutagenic factor at some point in her life after Marie's birth in 2039. The deleterious mutagenes appear to be sex linked, and they have lethal expression in male offspring most of the time. Because Maddy's female, she escaped. But she's a carrier. Luc inherited the harmful mutation, but at least he could be pasted back together into a semblance of normality. Mama's stillborn babies and the aborted ones inherited intractable lethal traits that defied all attempts at genetic engineering—

Hence the revocation of your parents' repro license.

But should it have been revoked?

Marc what the hell are you driving at? It's the law.

But is the law just?

The Galactic Milieu thinks so. The Reproductive Statutes are intended to purge the human gene pool of—

The Milieu is a nonhuman organization. How can it know what's best for our race—what genes are good and bad in the long run? Study after study has shown that the human brain is not susceptible to genetic tinkering. The hereditary factors are too complex and interlinked for any eugenic manipulation. What gives those exotics the right to tamper with *physical* aspects of our human genetic heritage that may harm our mental evolution as an unintended side effect?

That's a question without an answer Marc. And it's been knocking around ever since the Intervention and there's no use at all you stewing over it. The Milieu took over the right to control reproduction as a condition of admitting humanity to the Galactic civilization and we accepted it and that's that . . . How come you've all of a sudden got your ass in an uproar about this? Damn you boy let me see what's really on your mind instead of beating around the bush like this!

The Remillard family includes the most powerful metapsychic practitioners on Earth. Who's to say in a crazy mixed-up genetic complex like ours what is an *unacceptable* heritage and what isn't? The genetic assay of Mama's five dead babies showed nothing about their mental potential.

So what? Physically the poor little things were losers. The genetic engineering attempts on them failed. The stillborn ones never saw the light of day and the aborted ones would have been horribly deformed and dysfunctional and destined to die before reproducing.

But the minds of the aborted babies might have contributed something invaluable to the Earth Mind before their disabilities killed them.

Marc I don't understand what you're driving at. Do you mean to say that the brain genes of the babies should have been evaluated along with those for the rest of their bodies? Even I know that it can't be done! Human genetic science has come a long way under Milieu guidance but it can't assay the mind from examining brain tissues any more than it can engineer the mind by tinkering with the brain's DNA. Ordinary evolution is doing just fine transforming our race into metapsychic operants and the Earth Mind is coming along well enough toward coadunation under the Milieu's Reproductive Statutes and I can't see that it matters a hoot whether or not a few poor little crippled babies get to make their contribution—

What does matter is that Mama is pregnant again.

??Impossible!!

I heard her tell Grandmère.

JesusGod. Teresa can't be pregnant now . . .

She is.

Practically on eve Earth inauguration Concilium? And with Paul heading list of newly announced human magnates? Quelle catastrophe your father rest of family put in impossible position! Howcould-shehowcouldshe—

Mama extracted the contraceptive implant herself. It was no trick at all for a person with her creative talents. She feels that she has a solemn obligation—an obligation to the entire human race!—to have this child even if it means violating the statutes of the Simbiari Proctorship.

Sacrénomdedieu! We all knew that she was tottering on the brink after the loss of her last baby. But she seemed to have snapped out of it. Now this! Your poor mama. All that talent! All that beauty! And it's plain what the source of her madness is: she and your father have always had that idiotic dynastic obsession about surpassing Denis and Lucille—

This fetus is five months old. Mama says it speaks to her telepathically in a postinfantile mode.

"Merde de merde!" Rogi exclaimed out loud. "Cette pauvre petite! She's gone over the edge completely."

The canoe was now fixed firmly on top of the old Volvo, and all the equipment was stowed. As the two of them got into the car, the boy seemed gripped by an inappropriate excitement.

"Grandmère Lucille scanned the fetal mind with her redactive deep-sense. She heard nothing but the usual chaotic psychoembryonic cycling one would expect from such a young fetus. She had a discussion with Mama and then . . . went away. Of course, she didn't detect my presence. I went in and spoke to Mama, clarifying the situation, and after that I came immediately to the bookshop to get you."

"But I still don't understand—"

"Grandmère has gone to get Uncle Severin. They'll do an abortion before Papa—or anyone else—finds out. Maybe tomorrow."

"Et alors? It's the only sensible course!" Rogi tapped the garage door opener, backed the car out, then closed the overhead door. Slowly they drove up the street.

"No it's not."

"You have moral scruples? It's understandable. You're young and fresh from the Jebbies at Brebeuf, and they've filled your mind with idealistic notions of human dignity and worth. But this is the real world, Marc! Not even the Church opposes the Reproductive Statutes. If a fetus shows intractable lethal genes, it may be aborted. Your poor Mama is deluded, sick. She needs treatment! Marc, you're thirteen, but you're a mature person. You know what this illegal pregnancy could mean—not only to the family but also to the whole Human Polity. Your parents aren't just private citizens. Paul will surely be nominated First Magnate when humanity is admitted to the Concilium in January. *If* it's admitted! Good God, boy, don't you understand how serious an offense this is? Not even your mother's mental lapse can excuse—"

"Mama is quite sane, Uncle Rogi. I heard the fetus, too."

"You . . . *what?*"

"It's a boy. What I heard . . . I can't describe it, and I certainly can't transmit an image of it to a mentality as limited as yours. You'll have to take my word for it that this baby is something extraordinary. I've listened to unborn babies before, but this one is unlike anything I've ever experienced. God only knows what his metabilities will be."

"And what about his body?" Rogi was bleak. "If he's carrying lethals, odds are strong that he'll be a physical basket case."

"But not certain. Luc's disabilities were modifiable. Regen-tank therapy and genetic engineering for humans become more sophisticated every day. My unborn little brother deserves his chance! I'm not the only one who would say so, either. There are hundreds of millions of humans who believe that the Repro Statutes are unjust and should be changed."

Rogi could think of nothing to say. His deepest, most secret mind-level was saying it all: The law still stood, accepted by Earth as part of the price of the new Golden Age; and in conceiving this child, who might or might not be mentally exceptional, Teresa had committed a Class One felony . . .

They had driven the short block and a half from the bookshop and now stood in front of the Remillard house at 15 East South Street, just beyond the public database, which everybody still called the library. Rogi turned into the driveway, and the two of them got out.

Marc's home was a classic New England white clapboard building, with dark shutters, a small porch, and dormers on the third storey. One of the windows of Teresa's studio was open, and operatic music poured into the humid green shade surrounding the big old place. A soprano accompanied by a full orchestra was singing, in some language other than Standard English, a plaintive song of such thrilling intensity and richness that the old man and the boy were forced to stop at the base of the porch steps and listen, enthralled.

The voice of Teresa Kaulana Kendall always had that effect, even on family members who had heard her recordings countless times. Rogi found that his eyes were filling with tears. That marvelous coloratura, entombed on laser-read record flecks, was preserved forever while the singer herself was silenced, sacrificed along with so many other things for the alleged greater good of the Human Polity of the Galactic Milieu.

And now this new disaster, perhaps presaging a final descent into madness and degradation—if not summary punishment by the Magistratum—had come about because Teresa, like Paul and so many other ambitious human operants, had believed the Lylmik mentors when they said that human beings would someday possess the most powerful mentalities of any race in the universe . . .

"What can we possibly do to help her?" Rogi whispered.

"Help the baby." Marc's correction was chilling. "A mind like that, of such unbelievable potential, must live."

The aria soared to a crescendo, then ended with a soft question that melted, unanswered, into silence.

Rogi said, "Perhaps—if we could prove to the Simbiari Proctors and the Magistratum—"

"Mama hears the baby, and so do I," Marc said. "No one else will. Not yet. And no mechanical scanner has the sensitivity to confirm his mental superiority. His mind is completely anomalous."

"Then there isn't a chance. The forensic redactors will say Teresa's crazy, and your testimony will be discounted as unverifiable because of your relationship to her and your damned superscreening ability that balks mind-reaming. The thing's hopeless."

Marc said quietly, "Not if we get Mama away from here. Hide her until the baby is born naturally. He'll be safe then. A legal entity with full rights to life-sustaining care, no matter *what* his disabilities. The law is clear on that point. Mama will still be culpable, but she can . . . stay out of sight until after the human magnates take control of Polity affairs. Then there's bound to be some way to exonerate her."

"But it's impossible! There's no place on Earth where someone like Teresa, with a registered operant metapsychic identity, can hide from the Magistratum enforcers—from the Simbiari and Krondaku."

"I think there is. A hiding place where no one will think to look for an operant. And even if they do a quick scan of the place, they won't think to zero in and identify Mama."

Marc projected a mental image that made the old man gasp. "You've been there, Uncle Rogi, with the connivance of that book-buying friend of yours. You told me all about it. And that's one reason why I need your help now."

The boy opened the front screen door of his home and looked over his shoulder. "You are going to help. Aren't you?"

Sweat had broken out on Rogi's brow. His emotional tone was one of sheer panic, even though the boy was making no attempt to coerce him. "You know what happens if we're caught?" Rogi asked. "To us and to her? Maybe to the whole damn Human Polity if your father doesn't denounce his own wife for violating the statutes?"

"The risk is worth it! Papa can do what he has to do to save his precious reputation if the fact of her illegal pregnancy comes out. Distance himself from Mama's action. Even cooperate fully if there's a search. But no one will even know she's *alive* if this plan of mine works! And they won't be able to prove we're accessories, either. I can put a block in your mind, and they'll never be able to probe deep enough into mine to get the truth. Later, Mama's bound to be vindicated in the court of public opinion for carrying an exceptional metapsychic to term. The Repro Statutes will be modified."

"You can't be sure of that!"

"On January sixth the Human Polity will be admitted to the Galactic Concilium, to full voting membership in the Milieu. The Simbiari Proctorship will finally be over, and the Green Leaky Freakies won't rule us like children anymore. We humans will finally be able to control our own destiny—our own reproduction as well as everything else. And when we do, we'll show these exotics what real mindpower is!"

Rogi regarded the thirteen-year-old with consternation. "If this unborn little brother turns out to be anything like you, the exotic races may wish they had never Intervened."

Marc uttered a short laugh. Then he said softly, "Somehow, Mama's unconscious mind reached out all the way to Okanagon, to me, the only one who would be able to save her. In the normal course of things, she lacks anything like the mental power needed to span such a distance. But this time . . . I think she was helped. By a metaconcert with that unborn baby! A mind like that must not be lost to humanity. I'll do anything to save him. Anything!"

Rogi felt his heart contract. "And what about your mother, for God's sake?"

"Both of them," Marc said, smiling. "Of course, both of them." The smile vanished like a brief ripple in deep water. "There's not much time. I told Mama to pack some things. We've got to get her out of here right away. I ordered a Hertz egg for us. It'll be here in half an hour. Now I want you to come upstairs and help me reassure Mama."

Marc opened the screen door and went into the house, leaving Rogi standing on the porch.

The bookseller said to himself: This is lunacy! Marc doesn't understand the implications. With Paul's wife a fugitive from justice the Simbiari Proctors might decide to delay the Concilium inauguration. They'd love an excuse! Would Paul even be able to prove he didn't conspire with Teresa? His mind is almost as reamproof as Marc's and they'd suspect he was hiding the truth!

. . . Jésus Christ what a mess! Operant fetuses! Des bêtises! And all we need is another damned superminded Remillard! Aren't there enough of them throwing their weight around and making things tough for us poor lamebrains?

. . . Both Marc and Teresa could even be *imagining* the baby's telepathy. It could be some neurotic thing some weird psychic guilt transference between mother and son and me caught in the middle of it!

. . . Marc can't really force me to go along with his plot. He can't coerce me from a distance and he certainly can't coerce me close up indefinitely and even if he tries it the *fact* of his coercion could be dug out of me by any one of the family Grand Masters as easy as cracking peanuts! The kid'll realize that too.

. . . All I have to do is point this out to him calmly and tell him that his loyalty to his mother is commendable but the scheme to hide her is impossible. I could sneak back to the bookshop right now and call Severin—

No.

Marcdammitlistentoreason—

Rogi listen to *me*. Marc and Teresa are telling the truth.

. . . You're not the kid!

No. You know who I am.

Oh no . . . Oh *shit!*

Rogi mon cher fils tu me fais mal aux noix!

Goddammit I don't feel so chirky myself—

You must help Teresa and her unborn. It is necessary.

Ghost . . . We're talking *Class One felony* pourl'amourdedieu!

[Exasperation.] No more vacillating! There is no time to waste. Do exactly as young Marc tells you. The hazards increase for every moment that you delay.

"You Lylmik bastard!" Rogi hissed, shaking his fist at the sultry air. "The Reproductive Statutes are part of your own Galactic Milieu! Why don't you simply tell your Simbiari minions to make the exception? Why do we have to play these games?"

The screen door opened by itself. Rogi felt a none-too-gentle nudge.

"Merde et contremerde! I'm going! I'm going!" The old man hurried into the house and up the inside staircase to the second floor, continuing to mutter Franco obscenities.

Two flies that had managed to sneak into the house along with Rogi fell out of the air, and their little bodies lay kicking on the rag rug in the entry hall. Then the screen door opened again, the flies were propelled outside, and the door swung slowly shut. The insects crawled groggily about the porch floor for a moment, then spread their wings and flew away.

[5]

FROM THE MEMOIRS OF ROGATIEN REMILLARD, A DIGRESSION

The metapsychic pioneers Denis Remillard and Lucille Cartier had lived in the old house on South Street for more than thirty years while raising their seven amazing children. Paul, the youngest and most mentally formidable of the brood, was born in 2014, the year after the Intervention. He was the only one of his siblings to be educated in utero by means of the new Milieu preceptorial techniques; and by the time he grew to adolescence he was acknowledged as the first human Grand Master metapsychic, with powers that were so overwhelming that he was virtually guaranteed a Concilium seat at such time as humanity's long probationary period ended.

In 2036, when Paul was twenty-two and already media-conspicuous for political maneuvering (read: circumventing the Simbiari Proctorship's more inconvenient restrictive ordinances), as well as being the most brilliant scion of Earth's "First Family of Metapsychology," he met Teresa Kaulana Kendall, a young woman of Hawaiian extraction, who was a celebrity in her own right. She was a musical prodigy who had made her debut at the Metropolitan Opera in New York the previous season singing the fiendishly difficult roles of the Queen of the Night and Lucia di Lammermoor. She was barely nineteen, and the storm of critical and popular acclaim greeting her had been colossal. *The New York Times* had called hers "the Voice of the Century . . . a rare, exquisitely high sopra acutissima that is perfectly controlled and full of ravishing color." Teresa Kendall was also beautiful, and a natural actress, and her stage presence even at that early age had the magical quality that differentiates a talent from a superstar.

The rather inhibited young Paul Remillard found her singing to be an unfailing aphrodisiac.

Even people who ordinarily did not care for operatic music idolized the glamorous young performer. She was also metapsychically oper-

ant, although her higher mental faculties were by no means as spectacular as her vocal abilities. The modern-day disparagers of her legend
like to hint that the voice's effect was a mere psychocreative illusion,
a mesmerizing of the audience by the mindpower of the singer—but
this is patently ridiculous. While it is true that Teresa's popularity owed
something to her coercivity and charm (as is true even of nonoperant
divas), the voice stood on its own merits, unique and phenomenal, as
her recordings prove.

Less than five months after Teresa and Paul's first meeting, they
were married on the Met stage at the close of the 2036–37 season. The
set was from the last act of a Russian fantasy opera that had been
revived especially for her, which she had sung to tumultuous acclaim.
The bride was attended by the production's principals, all still in
gorgeous Slavic costume. (The groom wore conventional black tie.)
The Archbishop of Manchester-in-New-Hampshire, a noted opera
buff and a close friend of the groom's distinguished parents, performed the ceremony. It was witnessed by a mob of singers, stage-
hands, supers, technicians, musicians, and most of the rest of the opera
company; and as the bride and groom kissed, the Met Chorus made
the chandeliers shiver with a recessional version of the hymn to love
from *Turandot*. Sundry Remillards were in attendance—including a
certain elderly bookseller. So were Teresa's mother, the noted actress
Annarita Latimer; her father, the distinguished astrophysicist Bernard
Kané Kendall; and her lovely and spectacularly rejuvenated grandmother, Elaine Donovan.

(The collateral consanguinity of the couple, even had it been acknowledged, would have been no real obstacle to this marriage under
Milieu law. It would be another matter altogether when Marc and
Cyndia Muldowney determined to marry many years later and their
true relationship came to light.)

The production that Teresa had starred in on her wedding night
was, portentously enough, *The Snow Maiden* by Rimsky-Korsakov, a
dark fairy tale with a disturbing ending; but no one thought about
omens at the time. Teresa was captivated by the dashing Paul, eager
to have his children—who would certainly be metapsychic giants—
and confident that she could continue her singing career with a few
minor adjustments to her schedule.

Lucille and Denis turned their big old home on South Street over to the newlyweds and moved to an elegantly refurbished farmhouse on Trescott Road east of Hanover. By then Denis was Emeritus Professor of Metapsychology at Dartmouth College's Metapsychic Institute, and the rejuvenated Lucille was the doyenne of faculty society.

At first, Paul and Teresa seemed to share a union written in the stars. Three mental prodigies were born to them in quick succession— Marc, Marie, and Madeleine. The family was saddened when Marc's twin, Matthieu (actually the firstborn), died at birth; but the small tragedy was quickly forgotten and its import quite unappreciated at the time. Like most opera singers, Teresa had the physique of an athlete, and she had her first three babies easily, retiring from the stage only during the final month of each pregnancy. The precocious infants were nursed backstage, in rehearsal halls, in dressing rooms, and even in the cabin of the luxurious Remco rhocraft that the family corporation provided to shuttle the Prima Donna between her home base in New Hampshire and opera houses in New York, London, Milan, Tokyo, Moscow, and a dozen other Earth metro regions. She also sang on the populous colonial worlds of Assawompsett, Atarashii-Sekai, Cerno-zem, Londinium, Etruscia, and Elysium, on the exotic planet Spon-su-Brevon, the Poltroyan artistic center, and on Zugmipl, where adoring Gi packed the house to the rafters for her week-long engagement in *La Traviata.* In an ultimate tribute, sixteen particularly keen Gi opera aficionados expired in aesthetic ecstasy at the climax of her final performance.

Paul was tolerant of his wife's professional absences. At that time he was deeply involved in the burgeoning new bureaucracy of the Human Polity of the Galactic Milieu. This organization had operated in the beginning as an "apprentice metapsychic government" under the stern guidance of the Simbiari Proctorship and independent of nonmeta Earth governing bodies; but by the time Paul came onto the political scene, twenty years after the Intervention, the pupils were clamoring ever more vociferously to take over the whole school.

Pre-Intervention modes of Earth government had by that time been almost completely metamorphosed into the peculiar republican setup that the Lylmik overlords had deemed most suitable for the Human Polity. This combined the intimate citizen involvement of New Hampshire town meetings on the lowest civic levels with a kind of operant oligarchy in the highest judicial and executive branches. The whole was a tidy representational tree structure, providing a voice in government for each citizen via precinct or township, for each corporation or cooperative enterprise involving more than a thousand persons, for each metro region or city, for each zone—a region often encompassing a former small nation or state—and for each quasi-continental area, called an Intendancy. The highest level of public office, that of Intendant Associate, included both operant and "normal" humans. Nonmetas tended to greatly outnumber persons with higher mindpowers in the lower levels of government, but in the judicial system the opposite situation prevailed.

By and large, the Human Polity shaped up pretty well. Most vestiges of old-fashioned human bloody-mindedness, stubborn nationalism, and fanatical religious opposition to Milieu precepts had melted away on Earth by the fourth decade of the twenty-first century. (The infamous Sons of Earth, in their antiexotic transmogrification, were one of the few dangerous exceptions to this general rule.) Mind-reading exotic overseers and ombudsmen made most forms of political dishonesty obsolete. There was still a certain amount of traditional crime and chicanery and prejudice and injustice, but it was no longer flagrant. Law enforcement was administered by both operant and "normal" human officers, supervised by the Magistratum of the Simbiari Proctorship. The meting out of condign punishment for legal transgressions was swift, and recidivist criminals were dealt with very severely. Members of the metapsychic elite who were convicted of high felonies usually faced the death penalty.

The great majority of "normal" humanity was afire with enthusiasm for the brave new world under the aegis of the Galactic Milieu. It was, of course, somewhat humiliating for the prouder Earthlings to be governed by the humorless Simbiari race, who had been assigned to accelerate our psychosocial maturation. The exotic Proctors, after all, were green; their physiology made them the inevitable butt of cruel human humor, and their severity and jaundiced view of human weakness sometimes provoked hatred and even outright rebellion. On the other hand, poverty and other kinds of deprivation were now obsolete on Earth, the educational system ensured that most people fulfilled their potential, virtue and hard work were rewarded, there was ample leisure, and if one felt hemmed in, there were challenging new worlds to conquer on the colonial planets set aside by the Milieu for humanity's surplus population.

The "normal" overt conscientious objectors to Milieu policies, although never coerced or directly punished for resisting the Galactic social revolution, were denied positions of power, deprived of media publicity, and eventually consigned to the ZPG reproductive class. After 2040, they were also forbidden access to the coveted rejuvenation technology and sequestered from participation in the Milieu's garden of advanced socioeconomic and technical delights. Some of these recalcitrants managed to escape the Milieu via Madame Guderian's notorious time-gate to the Pliocene Epoch. But for the most part, nonoperant misfits such as the religious fundamentalists and other square-peg individuals lived and died embittered and ostracized. Almost inevitably their children became estranged, even those who were educated outside the Milieu-controlled public school system; and when the children reached their majority they almost always rejected the reactionary values of their elders and opted instead for the mental testing and intensive higher education that would prepare them for life in the Human Polity.

The *operant* conscientious objectors to Milieu policy were altogether another kettle of fish, whose adventures will take up a large part of these Memoirs of mine . . .

Three of Paul's older operant siblings—Anne, Catherine, and Adrien—had chosen careers in Human Polity administration, training under the exotic Proctors for the day when Earth's growing operant population would form the highest level of Human Polity government in the Galactic Concilium under an elected First Magnate. After Paul joined his sisters and brother as a member of the North American Intendancy, he rose quickly by dint of statecraft and grandmasterly mental gamesmanship to the highest rank permitted members of a client race—Intendant Associate. From his eminence, Paul coached his lower-echelon sibs, and within two years they were also Grand Master Metapsychics and Intendant Associates. Thus the first hint of the Remillard Dynasty raised its nose above the horizon of the unsuspecting Milieu.

With a minimal bit of coercion, Paul prevailed upon his remaining three brothers to jump on the metapolitical bandwagon as well. Severin abandoned neurosurgery, Maurice gave up sociological research, and Philip, the oldest of Denis and Lucille's children, reluctantly quit as CEO of Remco Industries, the continuing fountainhead of the family fortune. Nepotism being perfectly acceptable to the ethical statutes of the Milieu (although some spoilsport humans cried foul), the seven Remillard siblings linked minds, destinies, and mental constituencies . . . and soared.

Denis and Lucille preferred the academic world, resisting Paul's attempts to draw them into politics. The parents regarded their ambitious offspring with wary bemusement, but the family nonetheless remained very close. In time, all seven siblings achieved grandmasterly status and were elected Intendant Associates.

While Teresa's musical career continued to flourish, Paul devoted himself to the lobbying effort that would culminate in the selection of Concord, New Hampshire, as the capital of Earth and the Human Polity in 2040. This feat earned him the media sobriquet of The Man Who Sold New Hampshire. Paul acquired a smartly trimmed beard to enhance his image as a senior legislator, published several books extolling his vision of Galactic Humanity, and became a fixture on the Tri-D talking heads circuit. His wit, physical attractiveness, and reassuring (to normal humanity) image as a spokesman for the "conservative" metapsychic viewpoint made him appealing to a wide spectrum of human factions—as well as to the urbane Poltroyan auxiliaries within the Proctorship, who dearly loved watching an Earthling outwit the earnest, efficient, scientifically advanced, but undeniably cloddish and dour Simbiari overlords.

Paul and Teresa's fourth child, Luc, was born epileptic, blind, and with severe bodily deformities. The baby's metapsychic armamentarium was enormous but nearly latent. By 2041, the year of his birth, genetic engineering techniques were able to restore Luc's twisted little innards and useless eyes to the human norm. Complete restoration of his body would have to await the advent of puberty, when it would be possible to use regeneration-tank therapy. Redactors had less success alleviating Luc's epilepsy, which was of a puzzling etiology; however, a device implanted in the child's brain eventually prevented the worst of his seizures.

Luc's travails were a source of anxiety and severe nervous strain for Teresa. It became more and more necessary for her to pamper her voice, and she cut back drastically on the number of her operatic and concert engagements. Nevertheless, her repertoire of personal triumphs expanded to include roles such as Manon, the long-neglected Lakmé, Juliette, and the Queen of Shemakha in Rimsky-Korsakov's *Le Coq d'Or*—which had not been mounted by a major opera company since the heyday of Beverly Sills. Teresa's signature role, however, remained the title character of Snegurochka in *The Snow Maiden*, another of Rimsky's gorgeous but psychologically murky fantasies that was scarcely ever performed outside the Soviet Union until Teresa's electrifying portrayal popularized it overnight.

Teresa's personal and professional decline began when her next baby was stillborn, in 2043. A comprehensive genetic assay of the tangled Remillard-Kendall heritage was still many years in the future; but a number of lethal genes were identified in Teresa's germ plasm, and both she and Paul were found to carry the so-called immortality gene of the Remillards, actually a unique polygenic inheritance that augmented the self-rejuvenation capacity present in every human being.

In spite of the genetic problems, both Teresa and Paul were determined to have many more children, just as brilliant as the first four. Their efforts resulted in two additional stillbirths, followed by two lethal-trait bearers confirmed by prenatal testing. The most advanced techniques of genetic engineering having failed to ameliorate the stigmata of the defective fetuses, they were aborted according to the guidelines established by the Reproductive Statutes of the Simbiari Proctorship. Teresa was tormented by depression during this period, suffered two brief mental breakdowns, and little by little began to lose her glorious voice. The final blow came when, in spite of all Paul's efforts, the couple had their reproductive license revoked.

Teresa was pinpointed as the founder of the mutagene complex and received a contraceptive implant. She retired to the house in Hanover, where she clung to sanity by doing vocal exercises in futile hopes of a comeback and dreamed of outwitting the exotic puppetmasters who had imposed their benevolent despotism on virtually all facets of human life—even motherhood.

Paul was bereaved by the tragedy but more philosophical. Of course, his own seed was untainted, and he might have divorced his wife and married again. However, he was still devoted to Teresa even though the intense passion of the early years had cooled, and he was immensely proud of the surviving children. Divorce was a distasteful option, given the climate of the times and the old-fashioned brand of Roman Catholicism espoused by most of the Remillards. Paul might have followed the example of his close friend and rival European Intendant Associate, Davy MacGregor, who like many persons of superior genetic heritage had contributed sperm to the gene pool that would help populate the colonial planets with nonborns conceived in vitro. But the strict anonymity of the banked-sperm setup clashed with Paul's sense of procreative pride. He wanted to know his children . . . and where there was a will, there was also a way.

He had never lacked for feminine admirers; and now that Teresa, although still beautiful, had lost her unique libidinous appeal, Paul put aside his religious scruples and set about to maximize his own genetic potential with discreet and dedicated fervor—and a good deal of willing cooperation from ladies of preeminent chromosomal content. He and Teresa still shared a bed; but as metasensitive spouses do, she knew that her husband was unfaithful.

She never stopped loving him and never reproached him. Nevertheless, it was undoubtedly Paul's continuing betrayal of their marriage that gave a dark impetus to Teresa's determination to have one last, supremely endowed child.

[6]

FROM THE MEMOIRS
OF ROGATIEN REMILLARD

Teresa had obeyed her eldest son and packed.

When I came into her music room, she was showing the contents of her soft-sided carryall to Marc. It contained a portable Tri-D, a plaque-reader, an audio player, a rolled-up Yamaha Scrollo keyboard, two Bose Dinky-Boom amps, a fleck library boîte, a power supply for the above gadgetry, a little toilet kit, a dozen cotton baby nappies, plass overpants, two terry-cloth infant suits, a swansdown bunting that had been a shower gift for her firstborn before the twins were diagnosed, a rain poncho, a ball of twine, a permamatch, a split of Dom Pérignon, and a Swiss Army Champ knife with every kind of thingummy on it but micro-manipulators.

Marc was looking over this collection with frozen incredulity. She, sweetly reasonable, was explaining to her son that the twine was for tying the baby's umbilical cord and hanging up laundry, while the champagne would celebrate Jack's birth.

"Jack?" Marc said faintly.

"His name will be Jon—J-O-N. That's the spelling I prefer. I've explained to him already about nicknames." She acknowledged my entrance with a blithe nod. "Your Uncle Rogi may call him Ti-Jean, of course, in the Franco-American tradition."

"Mama—all this musical stuff!" Marc protested. "I told you to pack only the essentials for survival!"

"These *are* the essentials, darling. I couldn't possibly endure four long months in some dreary rustic backwater without my music."

"But you've no clothes!"

She waved this off with an airy gesture. "I can buy those at the local shopping mall when I get there. Wherever *there* is! Meanwhile, this ensemble should be smart as well as serviceable en route. Don't you think so, Rogi?"

Teresa was not a tall woman, but she gave that impression—larger than life. She wore a stylish polished-cotton jogging suit of her favorite Kendall green and had tied back her shining black hair with a matching green silk scarf. Flung over her shoulders was a hooded sweater of fauve cashmere. She wore medium-weight Raichle hiking boots on her feet. It was a fine outfit for a jaunt up Mount Moosilauke with the Dartmouth Outing Club; but for wintering in the depths of the B.C. mountains . . .

My gaze slid away from hers, and I kept my thoughts hidden. "Uh—Teresa, didn't Marc explain that this place you're going to is a howling wilderness? No malls. No stores at all. Not even a trading post within a hundred kloms."

She shrugged. "Then I shall simply have to throw myself upon the charity of the local inhabitants." She flashed that brilliant smile of hers. "Perhaps I can give little concerts or music lessons in exchange for warm clothes and such."

Marc almost shouted, "Mama, the only local inhabitants in the Megapod Reserve are *them.*"

"Oh," said Teresa. Her exquisite brow knit in a frown of resolute determination. "Well, I'll get along somehow. I was a Girl Scout, you know." She held up a boîte the size of a deck of playing cards. "My fleck library has some excellent references. Along with my opera videos and music recordings and vocal scores, I've duplicated all the books and movies in our family collection downstairs and called up some more from the public library that I thought might be useful. *Camping and Woodcraft* by Horace Kephart sounded wonderfully pioneering from the catalog synopsis. And I couldn't resist some survival books by Bill Riviere and Bradford Angier that I remember reading when I was little and went to stay at Gran Elaine's summer cottage in Maine. Such wonderful Franco-American names those authors have! And for literary atmosphere, I have *Walden* and *The Call of the Wild* and *The Complete Poems of Robert Service.*"

"Mon cul," I muttered.

Teresa didn't even hear me. She sailed serenely on. "The matter of the birth should be easy enough to manage with my training in Lamaze and the obstetrics book I processed into the flecks. Jack says he'll be born easily. He's going to be a small baby. He doesn't quite understand my explanation about the diaper thing yet, but I'm sure it'll sort itself out once he's actually free of the amniotic fluid and experiencing the *concept* of dryness. And he won't really need many clothes inside the house if I keep the heater turned up high, will he?"

"What heater?" I barked. I had been listening to her idiotic prattle with openmouthed horror. "What house? The place is nothing but a broken-down log cabin with a rusty old iron stove, for God's sake, and it's been disused for nigh onto forty years! You'll have to cut wood——"

Teresa flourished her Swiss Army knife. "Fortunately, it has a very sharp saw blade! Of course, I've never had to use it yet, but I expect I'll learn how very quickly. And there would be lots of dry branches just lying about, wouldn't there?"

"Plenty," I said gently. "Only thing is, by the time winter comes, which will happen around the beginning of November at that latitude, the wood will be under three or four meters of snow."

Marc was even more mentally opaque than usual. Maybe the enormity of what he contemplated had finally penetrated that supremely self-confident young ego. He turned to me, a sudden awful decision making his mind blaze.

"I thought you'd just help me take Mama there, Uncle Rogi. She assured me that she'd be able to cope if I fixed her up with plenty of supplies. But I realize now that we'll have to work things out another way. You're going to have to stay in the cabin with her. You know all about wilderness survival and that stuff."

I simply stood there, stunned, with my mind bleeding dismay and pullulating blue funk, while the two of them exchanged nods of agreement.

Marc said to me, "We can pack a few more clothes for her, at least. As for you—I'd planned a provisioning and equipment-buying stop. We're using your camping gear as a basis, and you can make a list of the other stuff you'll need."

Teresa said, "If I'm allowed to take more of my own things, I want my nightgown and a robe and slippers. And if it's really going to be cold, the big down comforter. You'll love that, Rogi, for long nights sitting in front of the fire! We can squish it into a tiny bundle and it won't take up any room at all in the luggage."

I finally managed to overcome my vocal paralysis and blurted, "Now, just a damn minute! We're talking *four months in the wilds?* What's going to happen to my bookshop——"

"Miz Manion will take care of the shop," Marc said, "just as she always does when you're out of town."

With my initial shock slowly receding, I realized that the bookstore should be the least of my worries. I whimpered, "We'll be tracked down and arrested before we ever get out of New England—"

"Not if I toss a few blivets into the system," Marc said. "Uncle Rogi, don't worry. I'll see that you get to the Reserve safe and undetected. I've got everything worked out."

"Well, that's just friggin' dandy!" I said. "And I suppose when Teresa and me are all settled in and comfy in the cabin, with the critters gathering outside licking their chops, *you'll* just fly back home and pretend nothing's happened—and no one will suspect a thing. Not your father. Not Denis or Lucille or your gung ho Intendant uncles or aunts. Not Enforcer Chief Malatarsiss and her squad of Magistratum mindfuckers—when the family's forced to drag you down to Concord and get your young brain peeled like a hard-boiled egg!"

"Nobody," said Marc calmly, "messes with my mind. And I told you I have a plan all worked out."

Teresa smiled, stood on tiptoe, and kissed my cheek. "I'm so glad you're going to stand by me, Rogi. You know, I *was* just the least bit apprehensive about having to cut the wood." Her charm melted me like a popsicle on a griddle. She whirled away into her adjacent bedroom to secure the additional items, and I flung up my arms in surrender.

"Oh, hell. The three of you have got me backed into a corner, and you know it."

Marc had the grace to grin. "Ace coercers—me and Mama and Jack."

The young devil was so confident he had me buffaloed that he didn't even probe my mind. And a damn good thing, too, because I wasn't thinking of the baby at all as Coercer Number Three . . .

I turned away from Marc and stared out the streetside window of the studio, letting my wits freewheel in total discombobulation. Suddenly I spotted a small white ovoid and a larger scarlet one drifting past the tower of the Catholic church.

"Here comes the Hertz service egg towing that rent-a-rho you ordered," I observed. "I suppose I'd better go down and sign it out."

"I'll come with you," Marc said, "to help with the details."

I might have known he had some fairly unusual details in mind.

The Hertz agent waiting for us outside was a pretty young thing in her twenties, normal-minded as they come, and the name tag on her uniform blazer said Siri Olafsdottir. Marc's coercion turned Siri's smile to stone and her lushly fringed eyes into green glass. She stood in the driveway between the two parked eggs and my old Volvo with the canoe on the roof, a credit-card machine in one outstretched hand and a dangling set of plass rhocraft keys in the other, as motionless as a stop-frame hologram image in a Tri-D commercial. Marc had not only paralyzed her but also erased her memory of coming to Hanover, and he later extended the amnesia to include subsequent events involving lawbreaking Remillards. Little pearls of sweat formed on Siri's downy upper lip while she waited in the summer heat, oblivious to any skulduggery.

My terrible young relative sat himself down in the driver's seat of the woman's service egg, getting ready to bamboozle the Hertz firm's computer.

"We tell it she never came here. We tell it that the red 2051 Nissan Peregrine GXX with New Hampshire tag BWS 229 is in the shop for regular maintenance and will stay there for twenty-four hours." He began to mutter into the command mike.

Resigned to my fate, I detached the keys gently from poor Siri's fingers and opened the red egg. It was a luxury model with an over-sized boot. We were going to travel in style. I wondered how Marc planned to fudge North American Air Traffic Control and the ever-vigilant skytroopers, to say nothing of the rho-field neutralizers, the warm-body detectors, and the other alarm systems that guarded the perimeter of the Reserve itself.

"Patience," the juvenile delinquent said. "First we send this good woman on her way." He climbed out of the service craft and said to the Hertz agent: *Into your egg.*

She obeyed like a lovely robot.

Now start up and fly back to Burlington International. You have been out for coffee. You never came here. You never saw us.

The vehicle's door rolled shut. We stepped back as Siri lit the thing up. The faintly glowing purplish net of the safety-jacketed rho-field clothed the egg's outer surface. The machine retracted its pads and hovered half a meter above the ground for a moment. The woman inside now acted perfectly normal—and paid no attention whatsoever to us. She jockeyed neatly out of the driveway, floated to the middle of the street, signaled properly, and swooshed straight up out of sight. A few dry yellow elm leaves swirled in the vortex, then settled back onto the pavement.

Marc checked his wrist chronograph. "Nearly fourteen-thirty. You go get Mama, Uncle Rogi, while I do a few little modifications on our egg's electronic ident system."

"Now, you listen here," I protested. "Even though I do have a license, I'm not all that much of a hot-dogger flying these things—especially cross-country and vector-free. Usually, when I rent one, I just plug into a canned routing and put the thing on auto and take a nap or read until I get to my destination. But there *are* no Vee-routes up in the B.C. boonies where we're heading. The last time I went to this place, I got picked up at the Bella Coola skyport by my friend Bill. I haven't the least idea how to find the Reserve."

Marc had the egg's tool kit out and was removing the panel of the navigation unit. "Don't sweat it. I'll be doing the flying."

"I might have known! Oh, well. What's one more crime added to the stack?"

"Get Mama," Marc repeated. "You'll be driving her in your car to the fairgrounds down on River Road. Stop at a convenience store along the way for a few picnic supplies. Make certain somebody in the store remembers seeing you. Park in the fairgrounds lot, down in the grove of trees near the riverbank. I'll meet the two of you there with the egg, and we'll transfer the equipment and be off."

"But how do you intend to—"

That's enough Uncle Rogi!

His coercion rocked me back on my heels, but an instant later he was radiating soothing vibes and I was climbing the steps.

"No one will see the egg here in our driveway," he assured me. "No one will see it at the fairgrounds." *Trust me!* "Now get upstairs and tell Mama she has three minutes to get down here. We've got a long way to go in a very short time."

The first thing Marc had done in his scheme to foil the bloodhounds was to change the transponder identification code of the Hertz egg (a mere Class Four felony), so that its license tag now became Vermont WRT 661 as far as the sensors of Area 603 Air Traffic Control Syscom were concerned. He flew the thing on manual to our rendezvous beside the Connecticut River and was there long before Teresa and I arrived in the groundcar, which gave him time to program a few more illegalities into assorted computer systems scattered across North America. His creativity blurred the rhocraft so that it blended into the scenery and remained unnoticeable to nonoperant observers, a virtuoso upgrade of an old trick long cherished by operant children.

After the camping gear was loaded in the egg and the canoe hidden in some brush down by the river, we left my car parked in plain sight. The rhocraft, still screened from casual detection, took off at barely subsonic speed from the deserted lot, rose to the local programmed-airway entry altitude, 1,120 meters, and hovered.

Marc let out a great exhalation of relief as he ceased the metacreative camouflaging of the vehicle, which was a bit of a mental strain for him at that age. Then he filed a perfectly ordinary flight plan that allegedly originated in our small local airfield a couple of kloms west of the fairgrounds. We filed for Boston Metro, just as though we were taking an ordinary jaunt to the big city. The display of the navigation unit came up with a menu of optional routes, based upon the heaviness of the traffic patterns at the moment, and invited the driver to make a selection.

Marc chose one of them, saying "Express" into the mike.

The unit said, "Traffic Control regrets that express service to Boston on Vee-2A36 is unavailable at this time due to a minor system malfunction. We apologize for the inconvenience. Service is due to be restored within approximately two hours."

"Fastest alternate," Marc said, unperturbed.

"Thank you. We are programming. Your preset average velocity on the route displayed will be one thousand kilometers per hour. Your estimated travel time to Boston Metro periphery is ten minutes, twelve pip two seconds. Please confirm Vee-route and destination."

"Confirm," said Marc. "Go."

The unit said, "Entering controlled airspace," and the autopilot took over. The red egg went full inertialess and ascended to a cruising altitude of 12,300 meters before we could blink. The halfdome polarized, dimming the high-altitude sunlight, and the landscape of New

Hampshire began to roll beneath us as we zoomed southeastward.

Within a few moments we were part of a stream of ever-increasing numbers of rhocraft that shared our airway. Marc and Teresa were blasé in the face of this spectacle—the boy was now studying a display of aeronautical charts, and Teresa, sprawled elegantly on the rear banquette, told us she was going to take a nap—but I was still unsophisticated enough about egg travel to stare at the swarm of different-sized aircraft flowing along in orderly lines on all sides, the position of each monitored and controlled by faraway computers. We were spaced ten meters apart: private vehicles of every sort, many decorated with spots, stripes, swirls, or other idiosyncratic ornamentation; taxis and other commercial transports; and large and small haulers and service craft with company logos emblazoned on their skins. The odd Simbiari saucer or Poltroyan cigar-shaped orbiter stood out in the mass of multicolored ovoids like an exotic toy in the midst of a flight of gaudy Easter eggs. Up here in the bright stratosphere where the sky was always clear, the faint reticulation of the vehicular rho-fields was invisible. In inertialess flight there was no sound of wind or mechanism, not even a sensation of movement unless one looked down or watched individual eggs glide toward the outer edge of the procession as the traffic computers shunted them to some new vector. Gradually, I began to relax, and even managed to drink a Pepsi from the sack of picnic food.

When we were within a few minutes of Boston, our vicinity display showed a blue police-cruiser blip hard-charging up from behind us in free flight. I was aware of Marc tensing, his mind poised to exert coercion; but no official notification came up on our display or blared from the speaker, and no sigma tractor-beam laid hold of us. The cruiser, beacons scintillating, shot past us on the left like a cobalt meteor and disappeared.

The navigator said, "ETA Boston Metro three minutes. Please indicate new Vee-route or give alternative command. Failure to exercise navigation decision will result in your vehicle being inserted into a holding pattern."

Marc said, "Destination Logan International Airport Departures."

"Departure for which carrier?" the unit inquired.

"United," said Marc.

"Your estimated travel time to Logan International Airport United

Departures via controlled airspace is four minutes seven pip two seconds. Please confirm destination."

"Confirm. Go."

Along with hundreds of other aircraft, we began to descend through a lumpy overcast and decelerate. In an orderly aerial promenade, the streams of eggs separated and went their individual ways, moving neatly through other columns of vehicles, traveling in other directions at other preset altitudes and velocities. It was raining in Boston; but Traffic Control routed the rhocraft around potentially dangerous cumulonimbus cells, and of course no other aspect of the stormy weather had any effect on the vehicles. There were plenty of private eggs heading for the airport, and several dozen accompanied us on our intricate course to the United underwater embarkation area.

Teresa woke up as we landed on the shower-lashed entry pad and were diverted onto the conveyor that would carry us beneath Boston Harbor. She looked around at the familiar skyline in puzzlement. "But what are we doing *here?*"

"Relax, Mama," Marc said. "We're only going to stay long enough for the sensors of the airport to log the fake identification of this egg in short-term memory. When we stop at the departure platform, I'll change the egg's transponder code again. After we exit, we'll fly Vee-free away from the airport into Boston itself, then reenter controlled airspace from the MIT interchange in Cambridge, across the river."

"But why?" Teresa asked.

"My plan should preclude anybody's realizing that we left home by air. They're all going to think that the three of us stayed in New Hampshire and went canoeing. But in case anyone *should* see through my scheme and try to trace our route out of state, I'm covering our tracks. You see, the authorities have a short-term record of every vehicle using the Vee-routes. Three days from now the record will be purged. If somebody thinks to sift Traffic's memory before that, there's a remote chance that they may spot the fact that the Vermont registration of this rhocraft is fake, thus fingering it as our getaway vehicle to Logan Airport. Once we arrive here, however, the bogus egg effectively disappears when I change its transponder code. And so do its passengers. You can fly almost anywhere on Earth from Logan, and if the gate attendant is suitably coerced, you can even do it without a ticket."

"I never would have thought of that," she said.

But Paul would have.

We were now gliding down a cerametal gullet in the wake of a little yellow Saab that had elaborate rosemaling motifs ringing its fulldome canopy. The young couple inside it were locked in a passionate public embrace, having neglected to turn on the privacy screening. Marc was scowling at them.

"But then what do we do?" Teresa asked him. "How will we get to British Columbia?"

"From Cambridge we set a new controlled express course to Montréal, filing our flight plan under the new license code. It's very unlikely that we'll be traced to Montréal, but just to be safe, we pull the same registration switch at Dorval Airport, where huge numbers of rhocraft move in and out every day. Then we hopscotch to Chicago and pull the stunt again at O'Hare. We Vee to Denver and switch, then on up to Vancouver and switch, and finally go to Williams Lake, British Columbia, where we change registration for the last time. Then it's ex-Vee to the hideout and dump you two off, and I return via a completely different routing. If everything works as I've planned, I'll be home in the wee hours tomorrow, and the plan will be working before anyone can sort out exactly what happened."

"Good heavens," Teresa murmured. "How very complicated it all sounds." She had never learned to fly. She thought navigation was a bore—and there were so many tedious rules you had to follow if you wanted to travel at usefully high speeds on the Vee-routes.

Marc continued: "All of those traffic control zones except Williams Lake are very large metros, with hundreds of thousands of eggs flying on the computerized airways every day. I think the chances of the Magistratum seeing through my scheme and tracing us to the Williams Lake end of the sequence before the three days are up are nil. But even if they do, from there we're going to free-fly the final distance—so theoretically, you and Uncle Rogi could be hiding anywhere from the Arctic shore to the Queen Charlotte Islands. Not even the Krondaku would try to comb an area that size with a rough body-scan. And I've got a way to foil the operant-signature farscanners that I'll explain later."

"How long will the entire trip take?"

"If we luck out and express all the jumps from Boston, it would take about three hours to get to Williams Lake. Another half hour or so at ex-Vee max will get us to Uncle Rogi's friend's place out in the bush at Nimpo Lake. We'll probably kill another couple of hours en route getting the food and equipment, but we also gain three hours due to the time-zone differential. That far north, there should still be plenty of daylight left to fly in to the Reserve, and the weather up there is good. I just checked."

Teresa was mystified: "But, darling, what difference does it make whether we land in the Reserve in daytime or at night? And why worry about the weather?"

I knew the answer to that, and so did Marc. He told her soothingly, "Don't be concerned about it, Mama. Just relax."

We were coming into the brightly lit airport departure gate, where there was the usual jam-up of private eggs and taxis and limos discharging travelers onto the platform. People were lined up at standby counters, looking depressed the way they always do. Piles of tagged luggage awaited the attention of overworked porter robots. Babies cried, business travelers slouched, outbound vacationers bounced about excitedly, and the airport police strolled around, keeping an eye on things and muttering into their wrist-coms.

The two people in the yellow egg ahead of us were mushing it up again. Like other private-vehicle arrivals, they would have five minutes of authorized parking before the Port Authority took note of their tag number and required a very good explanation for the prolonged stay. Cautionary signs were everywhere, reminding drivers to tell their guidance systems to exit when the warning flashed on the dashboard.

"Oh, dear," Teresa said, as we came to a stop. "I really think I ought to visit the loo."

Marc had the privacy screening up and was already tinkering feverishly with the transponder. "If you must," he said evenly. "But if you take longer than the allotted five minutes, our ident gets logged in long-term memory, and a human cop comes over to scope us out. The cop could decide to cite us, and then he'd notice that the external license number of our egg and its transponder code don't match—and we could all be dead."

She blinked. "I believe I can wait."

Marc finished his fiddling and slammed the panel back into place.

The warning light had not even come on when he told the command mike: "Exit!"

Smoothly, the conveyor took hold of our egg and sent it back toward the surface. A few minutes later we had reentered controlled airspace at Cambridge under the cloak of our new registration and were hurtling toward Montréal at 2000 kph.

[7]

FROM THE MEMOIRS
OF ROGATIEN REMILLARD

We could all be dead . . .

There were a fairish number of Class One death-penalty felonies on the books of the Simbiari Magistratum, and an operant's deliberate contravention of the Reproductive Statutes was one of them. So was aiding and abetting. Marc might escape capital punishment because of his youth, Teresa on grounds of insanity; but for me—and for Jack— there'd be no tomorrow if we were caught.

But somehow I had a feeling we wouldn't be. The mysterious exotic presence that I called the Family Ghost had ordered me to undertake the trip, and it wouldn't send me to my death. Not unless it no longer needed a human cat's-paw to further its inscrutable designs, a contingency I very much doubted.

The last time the Ghost had actively meddled with my life was a rather innocuous incident in 2029, when I had been commanded to attend a fantasy convention in London. There the Ghost told me to summon Ilya and Katy Gawrys's daughter Mary up from their home in Oxford. The girl was simply to be introduced to a science fiction writer acquaintance of mine named Kyle Macdonald. I would not comprehend the logic behind *that* little transaction for another forty-eight years . . .

I did my best to put aside all worry, settled back in my comfortable banquette, ate potato chips, and tried to relax as our red egg raced through the ionosphere. Following Marc's orders, I compiled a list— or rather, three lists: clothing, equipment, and provisions—of the things we were going to need for the four months or so of our stay in the Canadian wilderness. I hardly noticed when we touched down briefly at Montréal and Chicago. But when we reached Denver, Marc decided it would be safe enough to do some shopping. We traveled ex-vector to the big REI outdoor store at Alameda Square, and Teresa and I engaged in a tornadic shopping spree. We didn't get everything on my lists, but we made a respectable dent in all except the food. An hour later, we were on our way again, with most of the backseat jammed with plunder. Teresa and I began organizing things and packing them into duffel sacks, while Marc engaged in some heavy farsensing, staying in a trance throughout most of the flight to Vancouver Metro. When he finally snapped out of it, he told us that Lucille had discovered Teresa's disappearance and drawn the worst possible conclusions. She had informed Paul of her suspicions, and he was so shocked by the double whammy of learning that his wife was both illegally pregnant and possibly scarpered that he was still in his Concord office, vacillating about what to do.

"He'll figure something out soon enough," I opined grimly. "Call a family council of war, most like. I wonder how long it'll take 'em to think of *me?*"

"Perdita Manion will tell them that you and I went off canoeing together," Marc said, "and they know I could screen us from farsensing if I wanted to. They can't automatically assume we're with Mama— or even that Mama has run away. They certainly won't do anything to precipitate an official hue and cry. And when I return tomorrow and tell them my story—"

"What story is that, dear?" Teresa asked. She was examining a compact Matsushita woodzapper and its instruction manual with fascination. The ionospheric stars shone above our egg's dome, and the vicinity display showed no other aircraft closer than ten kloms.

"It was such a hot afternoon," the boy said, a dreamy expression coming over his face. "Uncle Rogi and I decided to go canoeing on the Connecticut River below Wilder Dam, and we took you along, Mama. Somehow, we capsized in the Hartland rapids. I got a knock on the head. I clung to the overturned canoe, all woozy and witless, while Uncle Rogi tried to save you. He was very brave. I think I remember both of you saying telepathic prayers at the end."

"Oh, how sad!" Teresa exclaimed. "And how clever of you, darling."

My jaw dropped. Good God, was this Marc's foolproof scheme?

"Somebody'll find me and the canoe washed up on the shore down around Ascutney early tomorrow morning," Marc went on. "Too bad they won't find you two—except for one of Uncle Rogi's shoes and Mama's green scarf . . ."

"Do you really think Paul and Denis are going to fall for this fish story?" I inquired, oozing skepticism. "You won't be able to coerce *them* like you did that poor girl from Hertz!"

"No," Marc conceded. "But neither Papa nor Grandpère will be able to prove I'm lying, and my tale will serve as a plausible diplomatic fiction for the family to use, one that will be impossible for any officials of the Magistratum to refute—*unless* they trace this flight. The fact of Mama's illicit pregnancy will probably come out. If only Grandmère hadn't told Papa about it! But she did, and he'll have to satisfy his precious sense of duty . . . Still, I'm virtually certain that Mama's supposed death will get Papa and the family off the hook until after the inauguration of the Magnate-Designates in January."

"But everything really depends on you, doesn't it," I pointed out to Marc. "Whether or not you'll be able to resist the mind-probing of the most powerful human and exotic redactors trying to get at the truth."

He looked sidelong at me with that strange smile of his. "I'll resist," he said. "Count on it."

We made very good time flying in Canada, with nary a sighting of the Air Patrol. Additional farsensing by Marc of the Remillards back home revealed a good deal of backing and filling going on among Paul and his powerful siblings and the latters' spouses. There was no firm consensus on whether Teresa had decamped or simply gone off innocently for the day. None of the items Teresa had taken with her were likely to be counted missing by Lucille, so the formidable family matriarch really had only her suspicions to guide her. Denis, with characteristic intelligence, had undertaken a methodical seekersense dowsing of Hanover and vicinity, searching for the missing woman. I thought this was rather bad news with respect to the canoe-disaster scenario Marc planned to use, since his grandfather was probably the premier aura-scanner of the Human Polity; but the boy only shrugged off my apprehensions.

"If I'm presumably lying unconscious on the banks of the Connecticut while Mama and you have drowned," he said, "my aura would be diminished to the point of undetectability, and yours would be extinct. It doesn't matter if Grandpère fails to scan any of us."

The Vancouver–Williams Lake Vee-route took us almost due north along the valley of the great Fraser River, through a landscape that was, during those years, still fairly well settled by farmers and ranchers. The profligate lumbering operations that had stripped away so much of the Canadian forest earlier in the century were now at an end, and nature was fast reclaiming the remoter parts of the Cariboo and Chilcotin country. As in other marginal parts of the world, many of the people who had struggled here for generations to earn a hardscrabble living had gone away, electing to migrate to the new colonial planets of the Galactic Milieu.

Williams Lake, the terminus of our vectored flight, was then a bush metropolis of ten thousand souls. Here we went first to a hardware store and, using my diminished pocketful of cash, bought items such as wire, nails, spikes, heavy plass sheeting, a couple of lamps that would run off Teresa's little sealed fusion power supply, lots of heavy-duty rope and cord, duct tape, a portable block-and-tackle thingy called a come-along (the cabin was going to need repairs, your average log weighs upward of 150 kilos, and my PK is weak in the extreme), a Swedish saw as backup to the woodzapper and my two axes (I had neglected to sharpen my own camping saw, as usual, so we had left it behind), three metal buckets, a basin, a chisel, and some wedges. Then we went to a drugstore and got vitamins and Chap Stick and lotion and first-aid supplies and pads for Teresa's postpartum needs. At the Bay (Hudson's Bay Company, that is), which Marc was surprised to find looked just like a regular department store, we got ten meters of thick wool duffel cloth, a bolt of white cotton flannelette for baby things and miscellany, some needles and thread, a big pot, a Dutch oven, and a teakettle. At the liquor store we got six bottles of Lamb's Navy Rum, 151 proof, for the comfort of the poor bastard (c'est moi!) who would have to do the hewing of wood and drawing of water. That pretty well wound up the equipment list.

We had obtained some freeze-squeeze camping rations at the Denver REI, most notably hamburger, tomato flakes, carrots, green beans, and ten kilos of dried eggs; but the rest of our food was to be purchased at the Williams Lake hypermarket. Our red rhocraft was now pretty well jammed with stuff, and my money was running low, so we were obliged to halve the quantities of staples on my list. I managed to talk Teresa out of "necessities" such as extra-virgin olive oil, canned liver pâté, smoked char, red wine, and chocolate-covered liqueur cranberries. We did get flour, margarine, lard, dried milk, dried peas and beans, white and brown sugar, pasta, oatmeal, dried fruits and mushrooms, instant potatoes, coffee, tea, instant orange juice, and soup mix. We got salt and baking powder and yeast and dried garlic and onions, as well as peppercorns, bay leaves, chili powder, oregano, and a few other herbs and spices. To Teresa's horror, for she fancied herself a gourmet cook, we got ten kilos of nonperishable Velveeta cheese ragougnasse and a half-case of Spam. We got five kilos of bacon. We got canned Norwegian sardines. We got twelve big Hershey chocolate bars. We got Adolph's meat tenderizer (for which I would later thank the saints). We got broiler foil and giant degradable plass garbags and soap and toilet paper and four liters of chlorine bleach.

Marc said he would bring more food and supplies to us once the excitement died down—positively before the middle of November, when winter would really begin to set in at our refuge. I told him he damn well better not forget, since the food we had would only feed Teresa and me for about three months.

I had insisted upon one last piece of equipment, and left Marc and Teresa to wait for me in the egg while I went into a sporting goods store to get me a gun. Mind you, I wasn't really afraid of the mild-mannered denizens of the Reserve; but I was damn near petrified of grizzly bears, the only kind of wildlife in North America that seems constitutionally unwilling to share the landscape with humanity. I'd read plenty of horror stories about these gigantic brutes, who were mercifully not very common in the lower United States, and I knew that the Canadian Coast Range was crawling with them.

I didn't want any modern photon weapon, either. No, sir! The best of zappers available to the Earthling general public at that time were apt to be unreliable in foul weather, going plasmatic even in drizzle or ground mist. So I picked out a Winchester Model 70 .30-06 bolt-action rifle with a hooded front bead and adjustable rear sights, and a couple of boxes of ammo, paying for them with almost the last of my Human Polity dollars. In a place like Williams Lake, in those days, nobody thought it was unusual for a person to use cash instead of a credit card for such a purchase, nor was there any kind of a rigamarole about registration or a waiting period. A rifle was just another workaday tool in the Canadian boondocks.

The only firearm I had ever used was Cousin Gerard's old .22 Mossberg, which my brother Donnie and I had plinked beer cans with when we were eleven. Don had gone on to become an enthusiastic hunter, but I had never killed an animal in my life. (We will draw a veil over my three homicides.) All the same, just hefting that good old classic piece and sighting down the Winchester's dark steel barrel made me feel all macho and self-confident about surviving winter with a pregnant woman in the midst of a subarctic mountain wilderness.

What a flaming idiot I was.

When we left the town for Nimpo Lake, a tiny resort settlement located just outside the Reserve, it was around 1800 PDT, more than an hour and a half before sunset. The area we flew over now was a high plateau sliced by canyons and dry seasonal watercourses. As we flew west, the rangeland turned into scrubby evergreen forest, and this thickened to clothe low mountains dotted with countless lakes and bogs. On our left hand, rising ever higher toward the south, was the rugged spine of the Coast Range, where many of the peaks topped 3000 meters, and one, Mount Waddington, exceeded 4000.

Some of the wildest and most spectacular scenery in North America was to be found in the part of British Columbia we were heading into. The Megapod Reserve itself had an area of nearly 2,000,000 hectares and extended from the rain-forested Pacific fjords to the eastern slopes of the Coast Range. There were no towns within its boundaries, no tourist facilities or campsites, no roads or trails. Rhocraft were prohibited from overflying it below an altitude of 20,000 meters. The entire Reserve was ringed with rho-field neutralizing generators that would first give warning, then cause trespassing eggs to be shunted into the arms of the law at Bella Coola. Assorted alarm systems around the Megapod Reserve perimeter were designed to betray unauthorized persons afoot or using ground transport who might disturb the rare creatures for whom the Reserve had been dedicated.

Gigantopithecus megapodes.

Called Toki-Mussi, Soquiam, Sosskwatl, and Sasquatch by Native Americans; known to the Tibetans as Mi-Gö and to other peoples of the Himalaya as Yeti; named Jen-Hsüen in China, Almas in Mongolia, Ban Manas in northern India, Abanauayu in the Abkhazian Caucasus, and Gul'biyavan in the Pamir Range, the animals had long been considered to be legendary. The scientists of the Soviet Union, who captured the first living specimen in the high Tien Shan, called it Snezhniy Chelovik, the Snowman. The Canadian biologists who discovered a relict North American breeding band of the huge pongids in a remote valley west of Mount Jacobsen in British Columbia referred to them by the traditional name of Bigfoot and established the first refuge.

After the Intervention, the entire surviving world population of Gigantopithecus, thirty-eight males and twenty-six females, was tracked down by metapsychic means and resettled in the expanded B.C. Megapod Reserve. By 2043, the year of my own clandestine visit, the number of Bigfeet had increased to nearly two hundred, and they were designated as a Galactic Treasure. The giant apes throve in the remote wilderness of the Reserve with the barest minimum of human contact. According to law, only scientists and the trained foresters who tended to the propagation of the native flora and the regulation of other animals indigenous to the Reserve were permitted access. Casual entry by the vulgar citizenry was strictly prohibited.

But there were ways.

I had become interested in the Bigfoot a decade or so before, as a result of acquiring an estate collection of books on the subject. In the course of my advertising the collection for sale, I corresponded with a man named Bill Parmentier, a devoted Bigfoot buff who operated a little fishing and hunting resort on Nimpo Lake. The countryside thereabouts had been reputed to be the stamping grounds of the fabulous Sasquatch since before the arrival of the white man. Bill Parmentier's forebears had claimed many times to have sighted the elusive giant apes—only to be derided as superstitious stump-jumpers by more sophisticated British Columbians. But eventually vindication came. In his videograms to me, Bill displayed interesting family relics: underexposed old photos of strange footprints; people posed beside trees, indicating just how tall a Bigfoot they were sure they'd seen; and even a picture of a tuft of reddish hair, allegedly from a Sasquatch, that had been handed down from a relative who had had the shit scared out of him one day in 1936 while logging in the Bella Coola River Valley.

Parmentier also hinted that he'd seen the creatures himself. Fairly often. Fairly recently. It wasn't tough to manage if you were a local, he said, and knew the ropes.

I let him have the collection of books at a bargain price. And one dull rainy September Sunday after I'd indulged in a few too many highballs, I called him (old-fashioned phone system up there—no teleview) and talked to him in *French*. (Hey! Us Canucks have to stick together, hein?) I begged him to let me see the wonderful living-fossil monsters, too.

He said, "Hell, why not? Work season for the wardens is over the last of August. Been thinking of going in myself to fish."

A week later, I was up there, peeking out the broken window of the abandoned forester's cabin on Ape Lake that he'd stashed me in, trying not to wet my pants as a Bigfoot family eyeballed me from less than five meters away. The father and mother looked like King and Queen Kong dressed in odoriferous auburn fur. Junior was about my height, 185 cents. They ate the fresh peaches I'd set out for bait according to Parmentier's instructions, and then when I indicated mentally that the fruit was all gone, they threw the pits at me and took off.

I tell you, it was an experience!

Then one day years later, I told a certain weird kid about my adventure. I also mentioned that the mental aura of the telepathic Gigantopithecus was spookily similar to that of operant humankind. Marc figured out by himself that the steep mountains surrounding little Ape Lake would tend to foil all but a close-up farscan scrutiny, even when the object of the search had a registered mental signature.

There were a few fishermen having supper at the Nimpo Lake resort when we arrived. In the manner of their kind, they paid absolutely no attention to us when we came into the lobby cum dining room of the quaintly rustic main building, looking for Parmentier. The proprietor remembered me well, whacking me on the back and greeting me in effusive Canuckois. He offered sotto-voce congratulations on my having acquired a lovely new young wife and a strapping stepson.

Briefed by Marc, I had the story all ready. First, we would all have a quick meal. Rare steaks would be just dandy. Then we wanted good old Bill to take us to one of the fishing camps he managed on isolated Kidney Lake in Tweedsmuir Park, just east of the Reserve boundary. We realized it was a little late in the day and kind of short notice . . .

Pas de problème! All I had to do was fly that fancy egg of mine over to the dock pad and dump out the gear. Bill would get the Beav loaded, cranked up, and ready to go while we ate.

Later, when the steaks and delicious garden salad and baked potatoes with sour cream and chives and the blueberry pie with vanilla ice cream were only a memory, the three of us strolled down to the dock. Teresa took one look at our upcoming mode of transport and gave a terrified squeal.

"We're not going in . . . that?"

"Of course we are," said I, heartily.

"But does it really *fly?*" Teresa asked.

Parmentier was just a tad miffed. "Madame, she's flown for sixty years and may well go another sixty. The De Havilland Beaver is the workhorse of the North! She's reliable and cheap and goddam indestructible, and I wouldn't have one of them finicky rhocraft eggs in trade if you paid me."

The twentieth-century aeroplane rode on the glassy water atop two floats. It was vaguely dented and patched, and the windscreen plass was age-yellowed and etched with a patina of fine scratches. But the Beaver's saucy orange-and-white paint job was fresh, and the single propeller was a truly beautiful artifact of varnished laminated wood, without a nick or chip. The aircraft looked elderly but businesslike, and so did its pilot.

Our bags and boxes of supplies and equipment filled the entire open tail compartment and most of the area behind the pilot and copilot seats, leaving a minimal amount of space on the bare metal floor.

"Rogi, you and your boy just crawl in there and squat," Bill directed. "Your lady can ride first-class up beside me."

"No seat belts for us?" Marc was aghast. "But this aircraft has an inertial propulsion system!"

Parmentier guffawed merrily. "Don't hardly need seat belts when you got no seats! Just hang on to that side strap if you feel scared, sonny."

We all climbed aboard, our pilot began throwing switches, and a minute or so later the big radial engine burst noisily into life. Bill warmed her up. Then he advanced the throttle, and the Beaver roared across the lake toward the setting sun, climbing rapidly and making a deafening noise. Teresa was terrified and gripped the edge of her tattered seat. I was aware of Marc flooding her mind with calming redactive impulses, and I could have used a few myself. The aeroplane circled steeply to give us a nice view of the idyllic resort scene below, tumbling Marc on top of me, then came around to a southwesterly heading.

"Next stop, Kidney Lake!" Parmentier shouted.

But it wouldn't be. At an appropriate moment, Marc would seize the pilot's mind with his coercion and compel a course change to another destination, 30 kilometers deeper into the precipitous, glacier-draped mountains. After Teresa and I were dropped off, Marc and Parmentier would fly back to Nimpo Lake. A posthypnotic suggestion would convince Bill that the Remillard family had decided not to fish at Kidney Lake after all. Marc would fly away in the red egg, privacy screens up, and return to New Hampshire by another circuitous route. He would return the Hertz egg to Burlington International Airport in Vermont and take a bus home, fuzzing his identity psychocreatively.

And then the charade would begin.

Marc said to me on the intimate mode: You're certain that this aircraft can fly through the rho-trap barrier?

Sure as hell did before. That's an internal combustion engine. Runs on j-fuel. No dynamic-field technology at all. As I understand it all of the Reserve personnel use antiques like these or old-time helicopters when they fly in to their work sites. But they only go to work during June July and August. Rest of the year the place is officially closed. Deep snow.

And the alarm systems?

Parmentier's got a black box stashed in the Beaver's instrumentation that cancels the alarms. A lot of the locals do. Some of them work in the Reserve part time or ferry in supplies. They also fly into the Reserve during the off-season when they get a hankering for some really spectacular fishing. The wardens wink at it so long as it doesn't happen very often. You saw that rainbow trout lunker mounted above the fireplace back at the lodge? Bill caught that years ago in one of the Reserve lakes.

Gosh! LUST.

But fishermen never go to Ape Lake. It's all milky with glacial silt. No fish. Bill told me there are critters though. Grizzlies and wolves and cats and lots of mountain sheep and goats. A few moose down in the lower end of Ape Creek Valley. And of course the Bigfeet themselves. It's really a gorgeous spot. Very dramatic that remote basin with Mount Jacobsen hanging right over the cabin site and the glaciers calving into the far end of the little lake . . . Of course I wasn't there in winter.

Marc said: You'll manage Uncle Rogi.

I mind-nattered on: Teresa and I will have to lie low for another week until September and then we won't have to worry about having our chimney smoke spotted by anything human. Say! Remind me to steal Bill's map of the area so I have a better idea of the lay of the land. I didn't bother to get a compass because Jacobsen is such a blatant landmark. Only an imbecile could get lost . . . Christ de Tabernacle! I forgot snowshoes! Well I suppose I can make some. I wonder what *else* I forgot . . . Why don't we set up a head-sked and if I think up anything important you can bring it.

Marc said: I won't try to farspeak you from home. It would be too dangerous even on intimate mode when the investigation is on and I'm under suspicion. I'm bound to be under surveillance for a while. But I'll be back sometime between the first and the fifteenth of November with plenty of food and I'll try to think of other stuff you might also need to last you until the baby is born.

I said: We'll be watching for you. *Very* eagerly.

He said: Thank you . . . for everything Uncle Rogi.

Then his coercion reached out and took control of Bill Parmentier's mind, and the last leg of our strange journey really began.

[8]

RYE, NEW HAMPSHIRE, EARTH
24-25 AUGUST 2051

The Hydra hung high in the sky and looked into flames.

They flashed yellow from the sea salt on the burning driftwood and blue around the crackling chewed-over sparerib bones that Adrienne had made them toss in. Silly Adrienne, prancing busily around among the kids and adults, checking to make sure everybody threw napkins and paper plates and potato skins and other barbecue leftovers into the fire. Bossy Adrienne. She was even worse than her mother, Cheri! Always hassling the family with Mickey-Mousery when all a person wanted to do was relax on the beach and go switch-off.

The Hydra considered the tyrannical eldest daughter of Cheri Losier-Drake and Adrien Remillard through the flames' leaping and decided that one day it would certainly take care of her.

< Hello Hydra! Thinking the best kind of thoughts I see. >

. . . God! It's *Fury!* Christalmighty Fury I'm SOglad it's been SO-longSOlong I began tothink you WitchoftheWestmelted! Lately allthis MilieumindLOVEshit crowding out goodstuff.

< Just biding my time Hydra. All things have proper season turn-turnturn waiting for OUR turn. >

[Chuckle.] And here you are at last. Does it mean—

< Yes. Tonight's the NIGHT. >

[Yearningeagernes*sex*citement . . . fear.]

< You don't have to be afraid Hydra never afraid I'll guide you show you how trust me it's going to be *cosmic.* >

Better than the nervebomb?

< Light-years. Taking lifeforce this way is the Ultimate Hightrip. >

Cunning old Fury . . . WHO?

< Look out there on the water. You see? Him. >

!!! . . . ?

<Hydra don't tell me you *are* afraid—>

Goddamfuckshit NO! Just show me how! (He really does deserve it you know. What a prick! So does she the silly superior bitch but I understand why he's the one and it's going to be allright it really is I'LL DO IT.)

<It's just after midnight now. You'll have to wait a bit.>

Right. [Thrill!]

<Act natural. Go to bed like everyone else after the last swim. But NO SLEEPING. If you fall asleep you'll screw me up. I'll tell you when it's time to start and everything else you have to know sweetHydra darlingHydra . . .>

Nervebomb! NERVEBOMB! Please GodGodGod nervebomb nervebomb give it to me give it—*aaaaaah!* . . . Oh Fury how I love you.

The little white trawler rocked, making concentric vermilion rings on the black bonfire-painted Atlantic. Then after a time the boat floated level and quiet again, and the water smoothed. They lay flat on their backs on the deck, hands joined, coming back, watching motionless stars and speeding satellites and listening to the faint laughing and shrieking from the rest of the family on the beach. His wrist-com, which was all he wore, tapped twice on his carpal tendons.

"Midnight, my lovely Cat. Happy birthday."

She uttered a mock moan. "Brett, you beast. Did you really have to remind me? Forty-two!"

"Immortal hypocrite. You know very well that you look like a twenty-year-old." You're glorious and irresistible and I'm mad for you and tonight I need you once again my comfort my love my joy my wife we need each other come banish the last doubts this time rise to me reassure us both . . .

He levitated slightly, turned over, and drifted open-armed above her. She raised her own arms to him and whispered, "I wouldn't abandon you and our work for the world, Brett. Not for the whole Milieu. No one can make me. No one."

Her long blonde hair lay in shining coils on the deck matting and all over her nude body, veiling it from throat to knees. She framed his face with her hands while he kissed her mouth and eyelids and pressed his lips to her warm palms before guiding them to his already awakened sex.

His mind said: They're going to insist. Tempt you with the power. Appeal to your family pride. [Jocosity.] Urge you not to break up the Set!

[Laughter.] You and the children are my family. My pride is in our work, and it will continue as our love continues.

Cat mydearestdarlingsteadfast Cat.

He parted the thick tresses above her breasts and tongued the nipples, increasing the feedback of psychocreative energy that had begun once again to flow between them. She caressed him, deepening the erotic current, intensifying its neural rhythm through the magic that only operant minds possessed. Their bodies closed slowly. Tendrils of her hair rippled and wafted into the air, undulating and questing, stroking his shoulders and flanks, twining with soft strength about his arms and between his legs, drawing her up to him, enfolding both of them in a silken fluid medium that shimmered in the starlight.

They floated, coupled but now motionless, and let the metapsychic tension build, then held themselves on the brink until neither could resist letting their minds ignite the discharge. The wave crested, broke, subsided slowly into a tide of warmth and peace. Its ebb carried away the last vestiges of irrational anger and guilt from his heart and the lingering temptation from hers.

"Together," he whispered. "We'll live and work together. Always."

. . . Even though the Galactic Milieu had demanded otherwise.

The exotic legislators in the Orb World, acting within the mystery they called Coadunate Unity, had weighed the merits of every adult human operant. By means of unfathomable criteria, they had selected only one hundred—out of hundreds of thousands—to be inaugurated as the first human Magnates of the Concilium. No one was surprised that all seven members of the so-called Remillard Dynasty were included on the roster. But Catherine Remillard, alone of the family, had not sought the honor, had made her disinterest emphatic. As a member of the Milieu's governing body, she would be required to give up the Child Latency Project, the work in the Polity Education Ministry that she and her husband, Brett Doyle McAllister, had devoted the past seventeen years of their lives to. The program had borne prodigious fruit—more than fifty thousand latent children between the ages of five and nine raised to operancy by means of the subtle creative-redactive regimen that Cat and Brett had developed together, working in painstaking metaconcert. But their work was not finished. The program was still too primary-oriented to help the majority of latent youngsters, those over the age of nine; but lately there had been hints of a potential breakthrough.

The exotics in Concilium Orb were apparently willing to sacrifice the McAllister-Remillard research partnership for some nebulous greater good, but Cat was not. Late yesterday afternoon, she had notified both the Intendant Assembly in Concord and the Concilium that she was turning down the magnateship. Her decision had caused a sensation.

There was going to be a high old family row, of course. To postpone it and to shore up resolution (and ostensibly to celebrate her birthday), Cat and Brett had fled their research establishment in the capital of Earth and egged to the beachfront mansion in Rye that was the summer home of Cat's younger brother Adrien and his wife, the sculptor Cheri Losier-Drake.

This grandiose old place, which was only half a klom down the beach from the more modest summer home of Denis Remillard and Lucille Cartier, had been in the Drake family for generations, its twenty rooms rendering it a conspicuous white elephant. But all that had changed when Cheri married one of the distinguished offspring of Denis and Lucille. She and Adrien had six children, and Cheri would eventually acquire a horde of operant nieces and nephews that numbered more than thirty. Fortunately, she was a warmhearted child-nurturer and an enthusiastic hostess who championed tribal conviviality, with the result that from late May until September, the enormous carpenter-Gothic house on the beach was almost always full of youthful guests, and Cheri got very little sculpting done. Professional parents would show up when their work permitted, and other relatives were encouraged to join the mob scene for parties, particularly the annual Fourth of July beach picnic and the Labor Day crab-and-lobster feast that traditionally closed the summer season.

Cat and Brett, whose four children were close in age to those of Adrien and Cheri, kept a modified Dutch trawler named Doolittle at the Rye Harbor Yacht Club, less than a kilometer south of the big beach house. Other family boaters—especially Paul, with his splendid Nicholson ketch, and Anne, who had spent the day racing in her

Swan—sneered at the modest McAllister stinkpot. But Brett and Cat had no love for the hard physical labor of sailboating. Putting about in Doolittle was soothing. The fact that the trawler had lately become too small to accommodate their four growing children also suited Brett and Cat just fine . . .

When they were gravity-bound on the deck again, he gently untangled himself from her hair. "There's sure to be a certain amount of family hell to pay over your decision, Cat. But eventually they'll come around. Even Paul. Every operant educator in the Polity appreciates the importance of our work. And no one but you is even remotely competent to evaluate the configurations of our pilot secondary-level project."

She nuzzled his ear. "There's no one else who can make sense of your redactive programming gestalts, you mean. My genius lies in converting *yours* to practical application."

"We're still more than a year away from getting the ultimate refinements really nailed down. But when it's finally ready, millions of kids with latent metapsychic talents will be unblocked and freed to use their higher mindpowers. Kids who would otherwise have been condemned to a lifetime of normalcy—"

Abruptly, she sat up. "Brett, you know we mustn't speak of it like that." Mustn't even *think* about it that way even though we Truepeople know we are the chosen the elite the future the heirs and successors to poor normal humanity God maybe that's why I feel our project is so urgent even more urgent than finally admitting humanity to the Galactic Concilium the division the gulf between Operant and Non *must* be bridged and as soon as possible for our sakes as well as theirs—

"It will be," he soothed her, speaking aloud.

I didn't tell you because there were so many other things on my mind but that wretched Gordo *still* has the metabigot complex encysted I didn't excise it after all the miserable boy simply pulled the wool over the mind of his own shrinkmother!

Brett laughed. He got up and began pulling on his dungarees. A chill breeze had sprung up, and he handed Cat a velour robe. "Gordo's eleven. Perhaps it's time for old Dad to take over his civilizing. With sterner therapy measures."

"Well, we might do well to consider it. Lately, I just can't seem to get through to the child."

Brett said: Don't fret. Not about the world's kids. Not about ours. For now just think of the loving.

She began braiding the extraordinary hair into a single thick plait. Her voice was low, her thought flavor bittersweet. "I do think of it. Of you and me together. Always." And I want it to go on forever and to hell with our responsibilities to operant humanity to hell with the aspiring normals and the arrogant exotics and everything and everyone except you and me and the sea. And stars that are nothing but little lights in the sky—

"Shush. You know you don't mean that."

He swept her into his arms and kissed her one last time, and then they went into the pilothouse and started the engine of the white trawler and headed back to the harbor.

The Hydra skulked among the mooring slips of the yacht club, hiding behind a big garbage dumpster until Doolittle was finally docked among the gaggle of Remillard sailboats, a sturdy snow goose awkward in the company of sleek terns and frigate birds.

Waiting.

Waiting.

Then it was time! Nobody awake on any of the other boats, and the watchman safe in his cubicle watching a porno video and beating off.

< Be very quiet. Use your coercion at max on both of them. >
Yes Fury. [Stumble.] *Shit!* [Terrorexasperation—]
< Damn you QUIET. If they farscan you it's over. Forever! >
Nopleaseno look nobody noticed it's allright—
< Very well. Carry on . . . easy . . . NOW! Hit her first you'll need all your power just to sink her in REMsleep. Yes! That's fine . . . Now get on board quickly! Drag her back to the cabin. Good! Now him! Ready Hydra? Ready at last my sweet Hydra? Really ready? Yes? . . . *Begin at the top of the head* . . . >

Catherine Remillard awoke at dawn, cold and aching and faintly nauseated, hearing the gentle slap of wavelets against the trawler's hull and the voices of three fishermen up on the dock quarreling about the quality of the day's bait. She was lying uncovered on one of the bunks. Her skull was splitting. How very odd!

In the way of metapsychic spouses, she cast about for her husband's aura, but he was apparently nowhere nearby. She swore mildly, got up, and secured warmer clothing from a locker. After she had dressed, she went forward to the pilothouse.

And found Brett lying there. And screamed.

He was facedown, and his dungarees and jersey had been burned from his body. Most of the skin was charred and cracked, revealing a terrible red moistness beneath. Along the spine and the back of his neck and head the burning had been deeper, blacker. But along his body's dorsal midline there were seven curious white areas, patches of ash about the size of a palmprint, each one having the distinct outline of a different intricately drawn multipetaled flower.

Catherine Remillard's mind was lost to rational thought, and she did not really notice the patterns. She only screamed again and again and again, and the three fishermen came running, and the watchman, and eventually the Rye Township Police.

The Hydra was back in bed long before then, sleeping and sated and out of Fury's reach.

FROM THE MEMOIRS
OF ROGATIEN REMILLARD

Teresa and I stood on the tiny rocky beach of Ape Lake, surrounded by our collection of duffel bags and boxes, which now seemed very meager indeed. We watched the De Havilland Beaver disappear behind a wooded slope above Ape Creek, which drained the lake at its eastern end. When the buzz of the aeroplane engine finally cut off, I had to bolster my emotional screen to prevent Teresa from detecting the sudden panic that washed over me. I was no longer concerned about Paul or the Magistratum tracking us down; what frightened me was the isolation of this place, and the responsibility I had assumed by agreeing to hide here in the wilderness with an inexperienced, mentally unstable woman, who harbored in her womb a child marked for some awful Galactic destiny.

Forcing myself to concentrate on practicalities, I began to move our supplies off the exposed beach and into a patch of shrubbery, where they would be hidden from aerial observation.

The sky was indigo, except for a residual carmine radiance at the opposite end of the four-kilometer lake, where the sun had gone down behind the heavily glaciated crags of what would one day be called Mount Remillard. A single bright planet hung above the mountain's shoulder. The lake waters were pale opal blue, ruffled by the floatplane's dissipating wake. Across the water was a steep 1800-meter ridge that connected two anonymous peaks that I later christened Mount Mutt and Mount Jeff. This precipitous opposite shore was thickly forested with spruce and whitebark pine in its lower reaches and had sparse patches of dwarfed and battered krummholz trees and tundra vegetation at the higher elevations. Tree level at this latitude was about 1500 meters, but much of the lakeshore at the western end was barren moraine or ice-scoured rock. An arm of the huge Fyles Glacier formed a natural dam at that end of the basin, and small icebergs that had calved off its face were white specks on the distant waters.

Behind us little Megapod Creek chuckled as it flowed down from another ominous hanging glacier that nearly hid Mount Jacobsen; only the hulking summit of this peak, more than 3000 meters high, was visible. To the south, a delicate pink afterglow tinged snowfields covering Talchako Mountain, which was even higher than Jacobsen. We seemed completely hemmed by ramparts of rock and ice, alone in a secret oasis of alpine forest and high meadows, where the last flowers of summer still bloomed and milky water lapped the lichen-crusted boulders at our feet.

Teresa said, "How lovely." Her mind was smiling.

"It is that." I was casting about with my inefficient seekersense. "Uh—do you detect any critters?"

She sat down on one of the supply boxes, eyes shut, and concentrated. "Birds," she whispered. "Something small up the slope, among the trees. It may be a hare or a marmot."

"No Bigfeet? No bears?"

"No . . . Rogi, may I just sit here for a moment? I want to describe the place to Jack. He's very interested."

And something seemed to say: Yes.

I felt the hairs creep at the back of my neck and ventured a telepathic query: Baby? Jack? Is that you?

There was no response. Teresa had become pensive and inaccessible, and the baby's thoughts—if I hadn't imagined them—were doubtless linked to hers.

I picked up the duffel that held our sleeping bags, my little old dome tent, and the necessities I had set aside for our first night in the wilds. It was going to be dark soon, and the beach was too narrow and rocky to camp on. I decided to take a look at the cabin site, which was up the slope. From the air, the log structure had seemed much more dilapidated than I had remembered from my visit of eight years earlier. I thought I might as well find out the bad news right away.

I climbed up a dim trail that angled off to the right of the creek through a tangle of stunted mountain hemlock and Englemann spruce. The way was steep but short, and I came almost at once to a reasonably level little bowl-shaped clearing, where the log cabin stood.

The structure had originally been erected on a 4.5-meter-square foundation of cemented fieldstones, with a small set of concrete steps leading to the east-facing front door. The four walls remained more or less intact, although in places the cement chinking between the logs had fallen out. The north-side window from which I had watched the Sasquatch family still had glass. The pole roof had collapsed from the weight of too many winters' snows, scattering nearly indestructible silvery cedar shakes all over the rotted wood-plank floor.

The cabin interior was a jumble of moss-clad poles and broken rusty stovepipe sections. The crumbling bunks and the other rustic furnishings I remembered had mostly biodegraded into nature's green maw, but I did spot one corner of the iron stove peeping coyly from beneath a growth of scrubby willow that had made itself at home among the moldering floorboards.

I took a deep breath and told myself there was no reason to panic. I was simply going to have to repair the cabin before the snow flew, using our small stock of tools and whatever information on the subject might be found in our fleck library. I had never constructed anything more elaborate than a predrilled bookcase in my life, but in my veins flowed the blood of voyageurs, coureurs de bois, and ten generations of bushwhacking Franco-Canadians. There was also, in a pinch, the Family Ghost. I would manage.

I found a suitable spot for the tent and wasted no time setting it up and camouflaging it lightly with evergreen branches. Mosquitoes and other biting insects were beginning to home in on me in spite of my metacoercion, and pretty soon it would be impossible even for an operant to move around outdoors without a head net or plenty of insect repellent. There was just room inside the tent for two people to sit and heat tea water in my little portable microwave, and then doss down in sleeping bags atop inflated Mylar mats.

We would have to leave the rest of the equipment down on the beach for the night, since there was no time to build a cache. But none of the food was open and attractively odoriferous, and the local wildlife would probably take a day or two to move in and check us out. I figured the stuff would probably be safe. I would drape the more brightly colored bundles with my old camouflage tarps, on the off chance that personnel of the Megapod Reserve would fly over.

Only one other necessity required investigation. When I had arranged everything neatly inside the tent, I emerged and prowled slowly along the edge of the clearing farthest from Megapod Creek, looking for another trail that I remembered was somewhere in the vicinity. Sure enough, I found it partially obscured by a fallen snag, which I moved aside. The path wound through the thick growth of krumm-holz and shrubbery to another tiny clearing—and there fortune (or a certain Lylmik) smiled, and I discovered a roofless but otherwise intact little portable fiberglass latrine hut, of the type used in campgrounds all over North America during the late twentieth century. All I would have to do to put it into operation was dig a fresh pit nearer the cabin, drag it over, and stretch some plass on top to keep out the elements and the bugs.

I was whistling as I made my way back to the cabin site in the fast-fading twilight, heading for the shore trail to call Teresa. I could see her down below. And I thought: Tonnerre de dieu! The dear girl has actually thought to do something useful! She had gone a few meters to the outflow of Megapod Creek, where there was a clear dark pool uncontaminated by the floury glacial silt, and was kneeling there filling one of our collapsible 19-liter water containers.

Teresa stood up and turned again toward Mount Remillard, now a black silhouette against the purplish western sky. A light breeze had begun to blow, and there was a scent of evergreen resin and distant snow. The evening-star planet shone with uncanny brilliance in the pure cold air.

And Teresa sang to it.

I stood rooted to the spot, unbelieving. The voice that had sup-posedly been lost forever soared once again with the old magical richness that had enchanted audiences across the inhabited Galaxy. She sang to the star and to her child, and a flash of premonition chilled me at the same time that the beauty of the music wrung my heart.

Oh, Teresa. Let me be able to save you. Save both of you . . .

The cold wind strengthened and the song soon came to an end. She began to look about anxiously, and so I hurried down to her, sending on my farspoken reassurance that everything was ready for the night.

[10]

FROM THE MEMOIRS OF ROGATIEN REMILLARD, A DIGRESSION

The conspiracy that eventually led to humanity's Metapsychic Rebellion was a long time germinating.

For more than thirty Earth years there were only two rebels: the Soviet-born Anna Gawrys-Sakhvadze, a professor of physics at the Institute for Dynamic-Field Studies at Cambridge, and her sometime lover and colleague, Owen Blanchard, an American who eventually emigrated to the planet Assawompsett and became the first President of its renowned Academy of Commercial Astrogation.

In the twenty years that Anna and Owen were together at Cambridge, the inevitable subject of their pillow talk concerned the cowardly way in which their fellow Earthlings had surrendered their birthright of freedom to the benevolent despotism of the Galactic Milieu. Throughout many a long English night, after they had satisfied the demands of their bodies, the couple debated, analyzed, and ultimately condemned the Great Intervention of the Galactic Milieu as an immoral piece of meddling in the evolution of a sovereign race. By invading our planet in 2013 and thrusting Earth compulsively into their advanced civilization, the Milieu had violated some of the most fundamental tenets of human freedom. The Simbiari Proctors, who acted as agents of the other four nonhuman races during the long "educational" years that preceded our attainment of full Milieu citizenship, had severely restricted humanity's intellectual freedom, religious freedom, reproductive freedom, media freedom, educational freedom, and freedom of choice in matters of lifestyle and domicile. They had made a mockery of habeas corpus and the right to mental privacy. They had seduced human youth with visions of high technology and new worlds to win. They had virtually enslaved human metapsychic operants (Anna and Owen both had exceptionally high mindpowers) by limiting their career choices and by attempting to manipulate their motivation and loyalty. And always, lurking in the future when the number of living human minds attained a certain mystical "coadunate number," was the inevitable time when all human operants would be inducted into a mysterious mental state called the Unity, which a good many psychologists and theologians feared would submerge human individuality in a Cosmic Overmind.

I myself still shrink away from Unity four decades after the fact; but I am the perennial outsider, the last of the Metapsychic Rebels, too feeble a mentality to threaten the Milieu. And so I have been left in peace, granted immunity by the capricious Lylmik I call le Fantôme Familier, as a reward for serving as a cat's-paw . . .

From the earliest years of her academic career, Anna Gawrys-Sakhvadze had been happy enough studying the permutations of sigma-fields at Cambridge, which probably boasted more operants on its faculty than any other human university. But Owen Blanchard had been a promising concert violinist at the time of the Intervention, and the Simbiari testing program that had uncovered his coercive and creative metafunctions also decreed that he renounce music in favor of dynamic-field physics, a science vital to the entry of the Human Polity into full citizenship in the Milieu. In those early Proctorship days, Earth needed all the high-wattage brainpower that it could get. So Owen bowed to the inevitable and even came to enjoy designing hyperspatial drive mechanisms and then supervising the Department of Upsilon Studies. But when he played his violin for Anna, his resentment of the Milieu, and especially of the nonhuman Simbiari Proctors who had denied him the life he had chosen, gave his performance a fire that was almost diabolical.

At the time when circumstances eventually parted the couple, they knew that their treasonous opinions were held by few other metapsychic operants of importance. Open opposition to the Galactic Milieu was futile; operants did not even have the dubious option of escaping the twenty-first century through the time-gate invented by the eccentric Frenchman Théo Guderian, as "normal" humans did. If operants bowed to the Milieu's yoke, they might prosper and ascend to positions of honor and responsibility, while resistance to the dictates of the Simbiari Proctors brought professional disgrace, the ignominy of "open incarceration," or even the death penalty for sedition.

"We are two lonely rebels," Anna whispered when she kissed Owen goodbye at the Unst Spaceport. "But let us not give up hope completely. As the end of the Proctorship nears, humans may once again remember the nobility of self-determination. I shall keep a cautious eye out for other operants who share our beliefs, and you must do the same. Humanity can be free again, and it may be that you and I are destined to play a role in bringing about that freedom."

Deep in his heart, Owen Blanchard thought her dream of rebellion was hopeless. Once he reached the exuberant new planet he had been assigned to and became absorbed in the affairs of the fast-growing academy, he had no time for idealistic brooding. He worked hard building his institution into the best school for superluminal starship personnel in the Human Polity, he married and fathered two sons, and he nearly forgot Professor Anna Gawrys-Sakhvadze of Cambridge University.

Until he met Ragnar Gathen in 2050.

Gathen was a senior captain in the Civil Interstellar Force, the closest thing to a military space fleet that the Human Polity boasted during the years of the Proctorship. Sheer serendipity seated the two men side by side at a performance of *William Tell,* that operatic tribute to Swiss liberty. Between the acts, over drinks, Blanchard and Ragnar Gathen discovered they were both in their secret hearts rebels against the Galactic Milieu, both operants with growing political influence, and both likely to be nominated Magnates of the Concilium in two years, when the hated Simbiari Proctors finally stepped down and the Human Polity took control of its own destiny.

After assuring himself of Ragnar's sincerity by means of a mindprobe, to which the other man willingly submitted, Owen introduced him to Anna, who also anticipated being nominated as a magnate. Anna saw interesting possibilities in the new recruit, and he visited her often when he was on Earth.

Ragnar introduced his sister Oljanna, a spaceliner captain who shared his rebellious sentiments, to Anna's nephew Alan Sakhvadze, who was similarly inclined. The young people promptly fell in love and were eventually married.

Alan Sakhvadze, who also worked at the Institute for Dynamic-Field Studies, in a different department from Anna's, was a close friend and colleague of his cousin Will MacGregor. Eventually he converted Will to the anti-Milieu point of view, bringing the number of rebels to six. Neither young man was magnate material. But Will's father, Davy MacGregor, the son of the metapsychic pioneer Jamie MacGregor and an administrator of the European Intendancy, was. His metafaculties were so extraordinary that he was considered the only serious rival to Paul Remillard for the post of First Magnate.

Will was certain that his father entertained serious philosophical doubts about the mysterious concept of Unity, which the operants of the Human Polity would eventually be obliged to embrace. Whether Davy's doubts might lead him to repudiate the Milieu was problematical. No member of the cabal possessed the mental firepower to undertake a coercive-redactive mental examination of the great Davy MacGregor. If he was to be brought into the group, it would have to be accomplished by more subtle means.

Anna nevertheless found the conjecture about Davy very interesting, as did Owen and Ragnar. Three—possibly four—Magnate-Designates were strongly opposed to the exotic domination of humanity! Might there be other potential rebels among the nominees?

She herself knew of two possibilities. Jordan Kramer was a stalwart twenty-four-year-old psychophysicist and Magnate-Designate who worked both at Cambridge and at a research facility on Okanagon. Gerrit Van Wyk, a year older, was probably the most brilliant cerebro-energetic specialist in the Polity. Unfortunately, he was also a very low-powered operant and a notorious lush; in addition, he had a face like a frog and possessed a querulous and eccentric personality. The Milieu nominated him to the Concilium anyhow.

After the most delicate kind of backing and filling, the suspect pair were maneuvered into situations where Owen, the most powerful coercer in the group, could forcibly probe their minds. When the indignation of the probees subsided, they allowed themselves to be recruited, and subsequently indicated to the group that they were at work upon a revolutionary kind of psychoassay device that might ultimately be very valuable—or very dangerous—to the cause of human freedom.

The mind-reaming of the unlovable Van Wyk brought unexpected bonuses. He knew of two other highly placed operants with seditious propensities and suspected that a third might also be a closet rebel. The first was none other than the famous Hiroshi Kodama, Intendant Associate for Asia. The second was also an Associate, in the European

Intendancy. Her name was Cordelia Warszawska, and she was a prominent xenologist at the University of Cracow as well as a skillful politician . . . and a platonic friend of Davy MacGregor's.

The third suspect dredged from Van Wyk's quivering psyche was so unexpected and outrageous that no member of the little group would have dreamed of attempting to sound him out. His recruitment would have to be postponed until after the Magistratum withdrew its surveillance from him, since he was not only a Magnate-Designate but also a suspect in a murder investigation.

His name was Adrien Remillard.

The Intendant Associate for Asia looked out over the breathtaking view from the balcony of the summerhouse. The tray in his hands with its pitcher of beer and earthenware mugs was forgotten.

"Taihen utsukushii desu!" he exclaimed, and Inga Johansen came hurrying out from the kitchen to see what might be wrong.

"What is it, Mister—I mean, *Citizen* Kodama?" Like most Norwegians of the older generation, she had spoken English as a second language from childhood, so the Standard English prescribed by the Simbiari as the official Earth tongue had been no hardship for her.

Japanese was the second language of thirty-seven-year-old Hiroshi Kodama.

"Nothing at all. I beg your pardon for startling you, Fru Johansen." Hiroshi set down the tray on the heavily laden dinner table with an apologetic little laugh. "It was only this gorgeous vista of the fjord and the harbor below that suddenly struck me. When I arrived yesterday in the rain I never dreamed that you lived amid such splendor! The awesome gray cliffs so lightly touched with green, the water, such an incredibly luminous shade of aquamarine blue, the small white boats dotted about it like gulls. And the exquisite houses, so vivid a scarlet, with their somber black roofs."

"They are the rorbuer, the old fishermen's shanties that are rented out to vacationers. The cheerful color is traditional. Our islands are not always as sunny as you see them today."

She carried a bottle of aquavit that had been frozen into a block of ice and set it down beside a salver of tiny glasses. There would be toasts on this very special occasion. When her grandson had called her at her apartment in Trondheim, asking if he might borrow the ancestral home on remote Flakstad Island above the Arctic Circle for a get-together of his friends, the old lady had said, "Only if you let me cook you good Norwegian food!" Ragnar Gathen had laughed and agreed. She was a nonoperant, and all of their discussions would be in mental speech, so why not? He himself had not been to the house in Nusfjord since he was a boy; but when Owen asked him if he knew of an out-of-the-way place for the first "official" meeting of the rebel group, Bestemor Inga's summer place had come immediately to mind. The abrupt pull of nostalgia for the beautiful old fishing village, which he had not seen in eighteen years, also helped cement Ragnar's decision. He was American-born, and the planet Assawompsett, where he had lived most of his life, was a thriving and attractive world; but something deep in his bones insisted that Norway was his true home.

Fru Johansen now surveyed the table, hands on hips. She was a round-cheeked woman with white hair, and to honor her grandson and his important guests she wore the traditional costume of her birthplace in Trøndelag: a long dark skirt with a brocaded apron of green and gold, a red brocade bodice with a peplum, held together at the waist with silver clasps, and a white embroidered blouse adorned with two large silver rosesøljer, brooches with many glittering little concave bangles.

Hiroshi wore the sober dark blue suit he had arrived in, a fresh shirt and a bow tie, and the crisply starched white apron his hostess had insisted he don to protect his clothes.

"There! That looks very nice, I think. Thank you for helping me, Citizen Kodama. Now I shall check the oven, and perhaps you will see if the others are ready for dinner."

The Intendant bowed and hurried off down a hallway past the kitchen, a place of intriguing smells and considerable clutter, to the sitting room. Its floor and walls were of varnished light wood. Sitting in one corner on a stone slab was an ornate black cast-iron stove with a brass finial on top. Ragnar, Owen Blanchard, Will MacGregor, Alan Sakhvadze and his wife Oljanna Gathen, and Jordan Kramer had been out fishing together. They had changed into clean casual clothing and now lounged about, discussing the day's sport, on the settee and easy chairs, which were covered with well-worn chintz. Cordelia Warszawska, a tiny, sweet-faced woman notorious in the European Intendancy for not suffering fools gladly, was standing at a carved pine table in front of the open window, arranging a large bouquet of wildflowers she had picked.

Anna Gawrys-Sakhvadze had remained in the sitting room most of the day, catching up on the flood of physics literature that sometimes seemed to overwhelm dynamic-field studies. She had finally put the plaque-reader aside when her fellow conspirators joined her, and was now examining Fru Johansen's collection of antique wooden tankards, which stood on a wall shelf. She was seventy-one years old, of medium height and sturdily built. Rejuvenation had restored her thick red-gold hair, which she wore in a severe chignon at the nape of her neck, but it had not completely obliterated the web of tiny lines around her green eyes or refined her typically Slavic snubbed nose.

When Hiroshi entered the room radiating thoughts of their impending meal, Anna projected a mischievous thought at him on the conversational mode:

You must forgive me my friend for being amazed that a Japanese gentleman of exalted political rank would help in the preparation of dinner. But the apron looks very nice on you.

Hiroshi removed it with perfect aplomb as the others chuckled. He replied:

For a person of an older generation such a thing would have been unthinkable. We younger men are more flexible. Our women have worked with great zeal to raise our consciousness in such matters. [Image of his wife's dauntless face.] And besides Fru Johansen is a treasure trove of local lore. Do you know that these Arctic islands retain a moderate climate all year round because of the warming Gulf Stream? The Lofotens have been inhabited since immediate preglacial times. They were once reputed to be the home of supernatural beings. And the fabulous Maelstrom the deadly whirlpool celebrated by Jules Verne and Edgar Allan Poe is located off the tip of the island just south of here.

Cordelia Warszawska said: It doesn't surprise me one bit. The scenery is positively uncanny! Crags and mist on the one hand and on the other the sun lighting up the sea until it glows like some fabulous liquid gemstone. I half expected to be jumped by trolls as I hiked among the rocks picking these flowers.

Will MacGregor spoke out loud. "*Our* Troll stayed in bed all morning with a migraine, poor little sod. Do you suppose he's getting an attack of cold feet as well? And if so, won't it leave the rest of us in a fine bloody mess?"

Owen Blanchard said: *Will. Bag it.*

The younger members of the company laughed uneasily.

Alan said: Will was only joking.

Will said: Bedamned if I was.

"I think," Oljanna Gathen said aloud, "that we'd better up-screens and stick with an old-fashioned tongue-wag. Some of the heads around here could give colanders lessons, leaking their latent hostility. And we wouldn't want to hurt *anyone's* feelings and have them withdraw in a fit of pique, now, would we?"

"Oljanna's right," said Alan. Several others agreed with him.

Jordan Kramer kept his own mind clammed up, so the very serious doubts he had begun to entertain wouldn't leak out. It was the earnest young American Magnate-Designate's first meeting with the others. Jordy was the youngest of the group. The ideal of human freedom from exotic repression burned as strongly within him as it ever had; but some of his companions had begun to inspire qualms. Not Owen and Anna, of course; both of them were respected leaders in their fields, richly deserving of their nomination to the Concilium. Hiroshi and Cordelia also struck Jordy as being rock-solid, fully committed to human liberty, and psychologically mature. On the day's fishing trip, he had also decided that both Ragnar Gathen and his sister Oljanna were the kind of people he'd be willing to risk his neck with in a treasonous enterprise. But Alan Sakhvadze and Will MacGregor, who were in their early thirties, like the Gathens, were another kettle of fish altogether. Jordy wondered why they had been recruited. Both were undoubtedly excellent scientists who had done good work under Anna at the IDFS. But they had not been nominated magnates, and both were bitter at being passed over, so their motivation might not be completely free of taint. Alan was a quiet, almost colorless man who usually deferred to his outspoken wife, while Will was flamboyant and often tactless.

And then there was the most dubious member of the cabal—ironically, the one Jordy knew best—his own professional colleague Gerrit Van Wyk. Like all the rest of them, Gerrit had submitted to the secret new psychoassay device, which gave a much more accurate mental analysis than redactive probing by human operants. At the time of the testing he was proved loyal to the group. But would he stay that way when the going got tough? Will MacGregor evidently had his doubts. And so did Jordy himself . . .

"If our enterprise is to succeed," Oljanna was saying, "we'll need all the heads we can get. Especially the magnified kind! I move that we refrain from uncharitable cracks about any member of the group, even those of us that richly deserve being sneered at, unless said member is present and ready to defend his or her honor. Do I have a second?"

Ragnar Gathen said, quietly, "Second."

Will MacGregor uttered an impenitent snort. His hair was a fiery auburn in the sunlight streaming through the window, and his black eyes snapped from beneath thick tangled brows. "Think you've put me in my place, do you? I'll say and think what I please, and the devil with being *nice*, for I'm only saying aloud what the rest of ye think!"

He hoisted his rangy frame out from the depths of the overstuffed settee and pretended to examine the mica windows on the old iron stove in the ensuing silence. Then he looked around and grinned. "Ah, well. No harm done, and the atmosphere needs defrosting! So here's some news I was going to save for dessert: My dad's decided to run against Paul Remillard for First Magnate after all."

There were whistles and exclamations.

Cordelia asked, bluntly: "Why? It's a one-eighty-degree flip. Davy MacGregor knows Paul has a greater metapsychic armamentarium than he does, to say nothing of charisma enough to blast himself into a solar orbit. Davy is also Denis Remillard's bosom chum, isn't he? I thought you told us your father was determined to let Paul take the First Magnate chair by acclamation."

"Ah, but that was before the murder," Will said.

Jordy Kramer blinked. "I've been busy with a brain-booster project on Okanagon. But there was something about a killing in the Remillard family on the Tri-D . . ."

"It was an atrocity, and it was undoubtedly committed by a Grand Master operant." Will opened the fire door of the old stove and peered inside. It was full of kindling and ready to light. "When the news broke about the entire Dynasty and young Marc being suspects, my dad farspoke Denis immediately. You know: 'Say it ain't so, Joe.' Denis pooh-poohed the idea of any of his spawn being responsible for the crime. Said he knew their minds inside out. But yesterday Dad got word from a source inside the Magistratum that the exotic investigators are pretty well convinced that only a Remillard could have done the killing. There's really no solid evidence to back that conclusion, but it was enough to get Dad's knickers all in a twist. Three of Paul's siblings are now supposed to have been completely exonerated; but the other four and Marc are still very much under suspicion."

"Which four?" Owen Blanchard's voice was tense.

"Catherine, the wife of the murdered man, her older sister Anne, Adrien . . . and Paul. That's the main reason Dad has decided to run against him."

"Holy shit," whispered Alan Sakhvadze.

"Does he have a chance?" Oljanna Gathen asked. "Will the suspicions of the Magistratum be made public, so the other Magnate-Designates will know?"

Ragnar said to his sister, "That's very unlikely. The exotics *want* Paul for First Magnate."

"He's a gonzo champion of the Galactic Milieu, and he favors coadunation of our racial Mind," Hiroshi Kodama said in clipped tones. "Ask anyone who has heard his speeches in the Intendant Assembly in Concord. The Unity is like a Holy Grail to him."

Cordelia Warszawska turned away from her flowers to face the others. "Hiroshi is absolutely right."

"Right about what?" inquired a querulous voice. Gerrit Van Wyk, alias the Troll, came slouching into the room. His sparse blond hair was disheveled, and there were deep furrows between his eyes and angling beside his wide mouth. His mind-tone was that of a man with a skull spun of the most fragile glass filigree.

"Gerrit, dear." Anna was solicitous. "I see your migraine is better. It would have been such a pity for you to miss Fru Johansen's fine dinner."

"I might manage a bite," Van Wyk said ungraciously. He assimilated the news that Anna broadcast to him and blinked his slightly protuberant blue eyes. "Well well well! So the great Paul Remillard's a viable suspect in the murder, is he? And his son, too!" He uttered a cynical laugh. "I'd say it was to our advantage to make sure that as many Magnate-Designates as possible know about that. If Paul wins, we'll have to unveil the psychoassay device whether we want to or not and reopen the inquiry into the crime. Can't have a homicidal First Magnate, can we? Or even a First Magnate with a killer besmirching the family escutcheon. On the other hand, if Davy MacGregor wins First, our noble cause gets two significant boosts. We can keep our mechanical mind-probe secret for a while longer, ensuring that it doesn't get used on *us*. And with Davy leading the Polity, we can actually have open debate on humanity's subjection by the Milieu."

"That's our best hope," Owen said. "As the Human Polity becomes autonomous, those magnates who hold to our point of view might stand up and be counted under the leadership of a man like Davy MacGregor. Under Paul, the political climate would be much less favorable."

"There are probably plenty of other M-Ds who think that humanity belongs outside the Milieu," Gerrit sniffed. "And even more who think the Remillard gang is a pretentious collection of superior assholes. 'First Family of Metapsychology'! What a laugh. If those exotic nominators considered *nobility of character* rather than the mere size of the metaquotient, hardly a one of the Remillards would qualify for a Concilium seat."

There was an uncomfortable pause, in which all mind-screens of those around Van Wyk were tightly shut, while at the same time everybody had the identical, reprehensible thought.

Finally Anna sighed. "We will have to use every weapon at our command to help bring about Davy MacGregor's victory over Paul Remillard. Gerrit is right about the family being resented. When the seven of us who are Magnate-Designates go to Orb, we must be prepared for action. We will decide upon our strategy here tonight."

There were murmurs of agreement. Then Ragnar's urgent thought silenced them:

She's coming!

Fru Inga Johansen came into the sitting room, smiling shyly, her hands clasped in front of her apron. She said, "Vær så god! Dinner is now ready." And they all followed her out onto the balcony and for the next hour and a half forgot completely about the Galactic Milieu.

First there were toasts in aquavit—to a venture carefully left undescribed, to absent colleagues and well-wishers known and unknown, and to David Somerled MacGregor, Intendant Associate for Europe. After the "Skål" came beer chasers, and appetizers in the form of Lofotkaviar—preserved cod's roe—and smoked salmon shaved so thin as to be translucent, and succulent corned trout, all accompanied by rye rounds and local butter. As they wolfed these down, Fru Johansen carried in a tureen of steaming ølsuppe, ale soup, which was served garnished with tiny salt twists.

"Superb!" Gerrit Van Wyk beamed upon Ragnar's grandmother, demanding a second helping of the soup. He had hogged most of the corned trout, too. "And what will be our pièce de résistance, madame?"

"More fish, of course!" Ragnar cried, and he leapt from his seat. "The pride of the islands! I will help Bestemor Inga bring it in."

The entrée was a deceptively simple dish of breaded baked cod with grated goat cheese called Reine-torsk, served with a sauce of thick sour cream. Gerrit went into raptures over it, and all three of the large serving dishes were eventually scraped clean. Then came a råkostsalat of lettuce, cucumber, tomatoes, and cauliflower lightly tossed with mayonnaise and sprinkled with chopped dill.

Ragnar refilled the beer pitcher and Oljanna helped serve the fjelldessert, homemade macaroons sprinkled with multer—rare orange cloudberries, something like small raspberries, that grew wild in the cold bogs of the islands. Each serving was decorated with whipped cream.

As the dessert was devoured, the old lady rose and regarded them all with a smile that mingled fondness and the faintest tinge of reproach. "And now I will leave you to your discussions. There will be coffee and cookies in the sitting room, and the cognac and liqueurs. I am going down the road now to visit an old friend, and I will be gone for quite a long time. Forget about the dishes. I have one of the new ionic cleaners that will make short work of them when I return late this evening."

They all sprang to their feet. Ragnar said, "Tusen takk for maten, Bestemor! We will all remember this dinner for the rest of our lives!"

"Yes," Inga Johansen said sadly. "I think you will." And then she left them, and they all sat down again.

Oljanna broke the long, thoughtful silence. "Well, I suppose it's only logical that she might sense something of what we're up to."

"She will not betray us?" Anna's face had gone pale in the sunlight.

"Never!" Ragnar exclaimed.

"But she does not approve," Anna said.

Hiroshi Kodama sipped from his mug of beer, then set it down and stared into the foam-streaked depths. "She is like so many of the elders—those who remember the political chaos and worldwide privation and fear of the pre-Intervention Earth. To her, the coming of the Galactic Milieu was a miracle that saved our world from its own foolish pride and greed—perhaps from nuclear holocaust . . . Anna, only you and Owen are old enough to remember those times: When operants were persecuted, when energy supplies were dwindling, when the air and the waters and the land were so polluted by the waste of humanity that it seemed they never would be made clean. Think back to that day in 2013 when thousands upon thousands of starships materialized over the great cities of the Earth and told us that the nightmare was over—that they had come to Intervene and welcome us into their Galactic civilization."

"I remember," Owen whispered. His head was bowed, and now so was Anna's. Through the technology of the regeneration tank, both now looked fully as youthful as their fellow conspirators; but their mental overlay, with its indelible patina of memories and experience, would always mark them as elders.

"With the Intervention," Hiroshi went on, "there was immediate peace, immediate solutions to our ecological and economic problems. You two were perhaps among the few to question the coming of the Golden Age in those early years. The smallness of our group here attests that most human beings still feel as Fru Johansen does—that the way of the Galactic Milieu and its Unity are the only hope for us. If we—we rebels—attempt to point our race in another direction, we must think deeply about the opinions of our opponents. Could they be right? Could we possibly be wrong? Is our viewpoint that of a proud elite and theirs that of the great majority of humanity . . . ?"

"I have never had any doubts," Anna said, straightening in her chair and meeting Hiroshi's eyes.

But Owen Blanchard looked away over the fjord, to where the small pleasure boats played on deep, mirrored waters. "I have."

Ragnar Gathen said, "If we succeed, it will be because the majority agrees with us."

Cordelia Warszawska gave a humorless laugh. "Thus speaks the bluff and sturdy spaceman! But social change isn't quite as simple as that. Sometimes people don't know what's good for them. They have to be led, educated. Even compelled to do the right thing when the mutual good seems to conflict with their selfish interests."

"We operants are the ones the exotics have chosen to be the leaders," Gerrit Van Wyk declared. "It's a consensus of *operants* that we have to win, not normals."

"Only in the short run," Oljanna said. "Operants are still only a tiny percentage of the human race, even though our ranks are increasing. And all of you know that the coadunate number—the number of minds needed for Unity to be imposed—includes normals as well as us. When we are Unified, whatever that means, rebellion will be impossible. We'll somehow be—be engulfed in the exotic mind-set. At one with the Lylmik and the Krondaku and the Poltroyans and the Gi—"

"And the Simbiari," Will added. "Those fewkin' self-righteous green bastards."

For some time they all sat without speaking. The air was cool, for all the brightness of the sun, and when dusk came they would be glad to light the stove.

Owen finally rose to his feet. "Humanity won't be subjugated to the minds of exotic races! In the beginning, at the Intervention, we were overwhelmed by the benevolent aspects of the Milieu. It could hardly have been otherwise. But after forty years of the Proctorship, a few of us at least have recognized that the price we paid was too high. And for us operants, it will eventually be higher still, unless we do something about it . . . Come on, let's go find that coffee—and get down to serious business."

[12]

CONCORD, HUMAN POLITY CAPITAL, EARTH, 28 AUGUST 2051

They could have taken the subway tram and covered the distance in less than five minutes, but Paul suggested that the two of them walk through the rain-freshened capital gardens. There were things that needed to be said now, not later, and neither one of them wanted to sit around Paul's office until the time of the appointment, accepting commiserations from Tucker Barnes and Colette Roy on the family's double tragedy. Triple, when you counted Brett's weird demise.

Paul asked, "Were you comfortable in the hotel?"

"As comfortable as any prisoner could ask." Marc was expressionless. "It was kind of the Magistratum to allow me to have family friends for custodians."

"A professional courtesy. And Dr. Roy and Professor Barnes were glad to take the responsibility, to spare you being confined in an exotic detention facility. But such courtesies can extend only so far."

"I understand, Papa."

They descended the shallow steps of North America Tower and started across Canada Plaza. "I'm sorry I was unable to have breakfast with you. There was an early vote on the new 'American' planet proposal, and I've been scheduled for two weeks to do the summing-up speech in favor."

"That's all right."

The young mind's adamant screening was unperturbed. If Marc was apprehensive about the upcoming interrogation, no mental or physical clue betrayed his emotional state. He wore white slacks and a white rugby shirt with green, navy, and gold stripes. His hair, which usually stood out in a careless halo of dark curls, was neatly combed and sprayed. He asked casually, "How did the vote go?"

"The 'ayes' had it by a landslide. The new world will be called

Denali, after the highest mountain in Alaska, and a precedent-setting compromise amendment will allow unlimited immigration from Canada and Greenland and the Arctic areas of Europe and Asia after the initial wave of Yank settlers takes first dibs."

"So it's going to be a kind of bastard ethnic world rather than a true cosmop?"

"Looks like it. And that's just what the sponsors were hoping for. Aside from the rich mineral deposits, the place is more marginal in human preferenda than the typical cosmop planet. The landmasses are mostly polar, and the climate is severe. It's unlikely that Denali will ever attract a large enough population to warrant true cosmopolitan status. It certainly wouldn't repay any Milieu subsidization or immigrant incentive bonus plan. So it falls into the ethnic class by default. The 'American' ethnic label is broad enough to embrace the hodgepodge of settlers the planet will no doubt attract."

"Yukon gold-rush adventurer types?"

"Those and deep-sea fishermen. Its oceans are incredibly well populated with gourmet-class pseudocrustaceans. There's a certain je-ne-sais-quoi romantic charm to the planetary landscape, too—if you enjoy Old Man Winter wearing his wildest, most majestic face. Lots of neg-ions in the air and superb mountains. I liked the place myself when the committee checked it out. You may remember that survey junket your mother and I took in March."

"I remember. Mama said it was the best holiday you two had had in ages . . ." And very romantic.

Paul's mental aspect remained bland in spite of the unsubtle provocation. The illicit child had undoubtedly been conceived during the Denali trip, and Teresa had very likely worked the whole thing out in advance as carefully as blocking the stage moves in one of her operas. God damn her!

Or have mercy on her if she's dead . . . Please, God: dead.

Paul said to Marc, "Denali may not be your typical picture-book colony, but what ethnic world is? After all, the whole idea behind the concept is to encourage settlers with special solidarity to go out together to planets that are more difficult to colonize. And the Alaskans *did* scrape up the minimal seed-population requirement for ethnic planet status—with some surreptitious help from Minnesota and Maine and Wyoming and North Dakota. After I delivered my little rouser of a speech in favor of the amended proposal, and hinted that any IA who presumed to question the ethnic dynamism of those sourdoughs would end up lynched with a walrus-hide rope, most of the Assembly caved in and passed the resolution by a big majority."

Marc nodded soberly. "Sounds like Denali is going to be a great planet. I'd like to visit it myself."

"Funny . . . quite a few of the Intendant Associates said the same thing. And their subliminals all flashed SKIING in neon lights. Just like yours do."

Marc managed a wan smile. "I may not be doing any skiing for a long time, Papa."

"That," said Paul carefully, "is entirely up to you."

They walked under stately mutant elms that had grown to their full height of 40 meters in the twelve years since the establishment of Concord as capital of the Human Polity. Off to the west was a striking vista of the Merrimack Valley, and on the other side of the river lay Old Concord, the capital of the state of New Hampshire. The city had graciously agreed to change its name when the Human Polity capital was established in the Loudon Hills to the east of it. The most prominent landmark in Old Concord, easily visible to Paul and Marc in spite of the lingering morning haze, was the white dome of the venerable New Hampshire State House, where a stubborn and uniquely democratic legislature born in the year 1680 still met and prided itself on being the model for the regional level of Galactic government. Like so many Earth cities, Old Concord had been purged of all ugliness; its service, manufacturing, and commercial structures were either relocated underground or concealed in restored buildings of architectural importance, gathered from other parts of the state during the drastic population redistributions of the early twenty-first century. The revitalized city evoked the image of a peaceful eighteenth-century New England village while catering efficiently to the needs of a population living in the Galactic Age.

Marc said, "I can detect Brebeuf Academy with my mind's eye, over there behind Rum Hill. Funny. I couldn't wait to graduate in March, get out from under the thumb of the Fathers, do my first field trip on an exotic planet, start college. But now I really miss Brebeuf. We seniors were the kings of the cosmos. We thought we knew everything there was to know. Now all of a sudden we're bottom dogs again, college freshmen at large in an inhabited universe . . . and we realize that we don't know beans, and we're trapped like the rest of humanity under the biggest thumb of all."

There were very few other people on this particular path. Paul had been looking at the landscape as he walked, not at his son. They had come to a deserted enclosed garden with a large informal pool overhung by willows. Pink and white lilies dotted the surface of the dark water, which reflected not only trees and shrubs but also the delicate alabaster stratotowers of the North American and European Intendancies that seemed to pierce the sky on either hand. The path traversed one arm of the pool by means of large flat stepping-stones, and now Paul halted on the midmost stone and prevented Marc from going any further.

His hands rested upon the boy's shoulders, and Marc was forced to look into his father's compelling blue eyes. Paul was tall but not massive, with a very erect carriage and a natural grace to his movements that was almost Latin. His black beard was closely trimmed, and his hair cut Caesar-style to minimize its waving and already beginning to gray, in defiance of the self-rejuvenating genes. As usual, he was smartly and expensively dressed. His suit was khaki-colored silk noil, and he wore a black open-neck shirt with a flame-red scarf.

"You do understand," Paul said, "why it was necessary for me to report this affair—and your own role in it—to the Magistratum."

"But you didn't tell the Proctors what Grandmère Lucille and Uncle Severin planned to do, did you, Papa." Marc spoke very softly. "That they would have taken the baby without reporting the pregnancy."

"No. Their . . . desire to spare me, and avert the scandal at its source, was regrettable as well as illegal. But your grandmother's scheme came to nothing. Unlike your own unfortunate escapade. And your overnight disappearance automatically made you a suspect in Brett's murder as well."

Marc remained silent. His mind seemed open, but the deepest levels were utterly impregnable. As they had been throughout Paul's own assaultive mental interrogation on the morning following the alleged canoe accident.

Paul went on. "Two presumed criminal incidents that closely concern persons like me and your uncles and aunts, Grand Master metapsychics who are also high officials of the Polity and designated magnates, put your interrogation out of the jurisdiction of ordinary human law enforcement bodies. The matter *had* to be referred to the Magistratum. I was subjected to coercive-redactive probing myself and so were my brothers and sisters. You could not be exempted. Your metafaculties are too great, and your actions were too suspicious. The Magistratum must rule out a connection between Brett's murder and the disappearance of your mother and Uncle Rogi."

"I understand, Papa."

"What will happen to you today—" Paul broke off to reinforce his own faltering emotional barricade. "Dammit, Marc, you *must* allow the exotic interrogators to see the truth! Whatever it is. No matter who it hurts! We have a solemn duty—all of us who are privileged operants in training to serve humanity—to conduct our lives honorably. To obey and uphold the laws of the Galactic Milieu."

Without question?

For now . . . yes.

Some of the Milieu laws are unjust. Cruel. Inhuman!

SonmydearSon I know they may *seem*—

Papa I'm not the only one to doubt.

No. But doubting isn't the issue at hand. Action is.

You needn't worry. The interrogators won't find any incriminating data in my mind. The family honor is safe—

Paul cried out, "Damn you and your half-baked arrogance! Don't you realize that a Krondak Grand Master forensic redactor will be questioning you today?"

Mind-reaming me, Marc corrected. Out loud, he said, "Papa, nothing the Magistratum learns from me will damage your reputation or compromise your authority. You and Grandpère searched my mind three days ago, right after the drownings, and Uncle Severin and Aunt Anne and Professor Barnes all had their chance to turn me inside out later. All of you believe that I've told the truth. Now it's time for the exotics to satisfy themselves officially. They'll either believe me, too, and let me go—or decide I've broken their laws and pass sentence on me right here this morning. That's fine with me. Just let me get on with it!"

Because the longer we delay the more afraid I am.

"Marc, let me into your mind," Paul pleaded, gripping the boy's upper arms. "Into the secret place. I know we failed to turn you inside out. You were very good at hiding the inner thought-masking, but I know you concealed things from us. Let me see! Trust me! For the love of God tell me whether or not your mother and Uncle Rogi are alive!"

Marc's psychokinesis gently canceled the muscular tension of his father's hands, and he pulled free. "You know the answer already, Papa. You tore my screens down and looked for yourself. All of you did."

We did yes we *think* we did but if the drowning story's true why is there no grief Marc you can't not care you can't have killed her deliberately you did love her—

More than you did Papa.

Paul said, "That's not true!" Look in me. Look!

The boy shrugged, ignoring the invitation. Through his mind danced the fleeting images of many different women—all of them beautiful, all powerful operants, all infatuated with Paul Remillard.

"You don't understand," Paul said. "That . . . has nothing to do with love." The hint of empathy he had extended vanished like a snuffed candle flame, and once more the father looked down from his Jovian rampart. "You're too young to understand the complexities of male sexuality. You're too—[inhuman!]—emotionally detached."

"Uncle Rogi used to tell me that. I'm going to miss him."

Marc tell me ARE THEY REALLY DEAD?

The full force of Paul's coercion struck the boy. Marc stiffened convulsively and would have tumbled into the water if Paul had not caught him. No sooner had Paul struck than he retreated, frustrated again by the unbridgeable abyss that separated his own passionate nature from the icy profundity of the young mind's psychic core, those dark distances that could be concealing anything . . .

The father held the son in a desperate physical embrace while their minds remained walled apart. Paul said aloud, "I love your mother and I love you. If you've done what I think you have, I believe that your motives are good. I can't help you, but I'll do my utmost to salvage the situation. Do you understand?"

"Yes, Papa."

Paul let the boy go. Then they walked on across the stepping-stones and through the trees and came to another plaza that fronted a large gray building.

The Polity capital's departmental structures, unlike the magnificent office towers of the continental Intendancies, were modest in design.

This one seemed to be trying to efface itself by melting into the wooded hillside. Its stepped granite balconies dripped with flowering vines and other foliage, and the windows were deeply embayed and mirrored, so that they seemed part of the stone or the lush greenery. The building entrance, like the windows, was hooded and unpretentious. The double doors of massive carved oak were stained gray, with black iron fittings in American colonial style. A granite plinth on a small patch of lawn beside the steps held an identifying sign:

MAGISTRATUM OF THE GALACTIC MILIEU
EARTH PROCTORSHIP

The handsome bearded man and the tall boy walked up the steps side by side. Marc held the door politely for his father. Inside was a very small lobby with a polished black-and-white marble floor and richly paneled walls of chestnut wood. On either side of the room stood well-worn brown leather settees, each flanked by an occasional table and a brass Stiffel lamp. One of the tables had a bookplaque reader, the other a telephone without a viewer. The third side of the room, opposite the entrance, was inset with a featureless brushed-bronze door. Beside it was a viewscreen and a small bronze plate with an old-fashioned mammary push button that was labeled: INFORMATION.

Paul pressed the button.

The screen lit, showing the glistening green countenance of a male member of the Simbiari race. "Good morning, Intendant Remillard," said the exotic in unaccented Standard English.

"Good morning, Enforcer Abaram. I have in my custody the witness-defendant Marc Alain Kendall Remillard, who is scheduled to be interrogated at this time."

"You are three minutes early, Intendant, but this insignificant deviation can be readily accommodated by Enforcer Chief Malatarsiss and Evaluator Throma'eloo Lek—unless the witness-defendant prefers to wait out the interval."

"He does not," said Paul.

The bronze portal slid open, revealing two expressionless Simbiari in golden uniforms. "The witness-defendant will accompany these enforcers," Abaram said.

As Marc came forward, Paul said sharply, "When the questioning is completed, please bring the boy to my office in North America Tower. Immediately."

"This will be done," Abaram said, "if the action is feasible, pending the outcome of the interrogation. We will notify you promptly if the witness-defendant's presence is required elsewhere." The screen went black.

Marc stepped between the two exotics, and they about-faced. Then the door slid closed, leaving Paul standing alone.

When they had finished, and the boy was breathing normally again and his brain cycling in dreamless sleep, the two exotic redactors went into the adjacent parlor to escape the examination room's lingering aetheric stench of pain and terror.

Moti Ala Malatarsiss dug a handful of Kleenex from the platinum sabretache case that hung from her uniform belt, scrubbed her slimy palms, and dropped the green-stained wad into a wastebasket. Her complexion had gone an unhealthy olivaceous tan. She flung open a refreshment cabinet, filled a glass with carbonated water, and tossed it down in a single swallow.

Belatedly, she said, "My apologies, Evaluator, but I felt an overpowering need for rehydration. May I offer you a drink also?"

"Single-malt Scotch, if you please. Straight up."

The Simbiari Enforcer Chief seized a fresh bottle of Bunnahabhain and fumbled to open it. The bottle neck clinked as she poured sloppily, and she left sticky padprints on the glass. "Sorry about *that*, too." She thrust the drink into Throma'eloo Lek's extended tentacle.

The grotesque Krondaku blinked his primary optics in mild acknowledgment of his colleague's unusual state of flusteration. "A most peculiar and fascinating case, is it not? Once again the human race displays its bottomless capacity to astound."

The Chief refilled her own glass. "And this one is only a pubescent child!" She sipped with partially restored composure. "Let us go out on the balcony to discuss this, shall we? Disturbing resonances still propagate in here."

"As you wish," Throma'eloo sighed, slithering after her into the fierce sunlight through sliding doors opened by psychokinesis. Unobtrusively, he sent a restoring redactive impulse into the limbic system of his fellow interrogator, while on another level of his mind he was assembling a précis of the bad news for the Select Judicial Evaluation Committee back at Concilium Orb. A more primitive level of the Krondak consciousness deplored the excessive gravity, low oxygen partial-pressure, and intense ultraviolet radiation of the Human home planet. The booze was superb, however, and Moti Ala had remembered to bring the bottle out onto the balcony with her.

The Chief flopped into a deck chair, rolled up her silvery uniform sleeves, and extended her bare green arms to the healing sunlight. "Sacred Truth and Beauty, that's better!"

The monstrous Krondaku squatted in the shadiest spot, near the place where the balcony merged with the granite of an artificial cliff. A waterfall splashed down mossy stones and beaded Throma'eloo's warty integument with welcome moisture. He appropriated the Scotch and began a formal recapitulation.

"I understand now, colleague, why you requested my assistance in this apparently straightforward investigation. The metapsychic precocity of the Remillard line is, of course, a continuing topic of study amongst evolutionists of the Concilium. We were not aware, however, that an individual with the potential of this examinee had been born into the family. His ability to resist Simbiari-Krondak psychoprobing technique has disturbing implications. Of course, Marc could be unique. His father and the father's siblings are arguably the most powerful of human operants, yet our probing of *them* was readily accomplished. Nevertheless, I must point out that the blocking mechanisms that Marc used, virtually instinctively, are susceptible to program analysis and could, at least in theory, be passed on to and utilized by other humans of high metafunction."

"But we broke him . . . I think."

The Krondaku indicated qualified assent, simultaneously introducing a generous nip of Scotch into his buccal orifice. "I believe we have ascertained the truth of the drowning incident, at least, lamentable though it may be. The boy was clearly appalled by his mother's procreative risk-taking. Like many immature male Earthlings, particularly those of high intelligence and stunted affect, he represses sexual feelings for the female parent while at the same time craving the maternal consolations she vouchsafed him during his infancy, which she now denies him. In the human species, the hormonal imbalance of puberty exacerbates the aforesaid psychological turmoil. Thus we may see that, all unconsciously, Marc hates his mother for denying him and envies both his father *and* the unborn sibling, seeing in the latter, especially, a usurper of the love that he feels is owed to him—and also a metapsychic challenger. The boy's relationship with his father is complicated by the role-model factor. He has a powerful respect for Paul, at the same time that he is jealous of him. This is quite normal amongst humans. When Marc's mother revealed her illicit pregnancy, the boy's highest level of consciousness perceived a grave threat to both himself and his father—"

"While the deeper mental strata cogitated the situational potential for simultaneous revenge upon both parents and elimination of the sibling rival. Yes, yes, I agree with your assessment, Evaluator."

The Chief's face slowly regained its normal emerald hue as her hyperactive mucus glands simmered down. The area around her chair was now littered with used Kleenex, a situation that distressed the orderly sensibilities of the Krondaku. Before the Simbiari race had undertaken the Proctorship of planet Earth, they had been accustomed to blot up their excess bodily fluids with unobtrusive small sponges concealed in their clothing. Their stewardship of the Earthlings had proved so stressful, however, that the traditional expedient became inadequate without inconvenient wringing-out operations; and so Earthbound Simbiari had become addicted to Kleenex, which they carried in ornamental belt containers and rarely disposed of properly. They passed on the nasty new habit to their congeners throughout the Milieu (to the delight of human paper-product companies), and nowadays crinkled wads of tissue seemed to litter half the planets of the Orion Arm. Throma'eloo Lek, like many of his ancient and fastidious race, secretly deplored the lowering of standards but never would have dreamed of humiliating the Simbiari by reproaching them. Earth was the first Proctorship undertaken by that semiUnified race, and the project had shaken Simb courage severely.

"Is it your conclusion, then," the Krondaku inquired, "that the boy is innocent of double homicide by drowning?"

The Chief assumed a more dignified posture and refastened her cuffs. "Volition in the immature human psyche is not easy to pin down. But I believe our efforts show that Marc Remillard acted entirely through unconscious impetus when he brought about the drowning of his mother and the incidental demise of the aged male relative. Marc suggested the canoe trip in the first place, then neglected to portage around the rapids. However, there was never in his mind a deliberate intention to kill. I do not believe he has any complicity in the McAllister murder, either."

The Krondaku hesitated. "Let us postpone for a moment any deliberation on the boy's possible implication in that truly heinous crime. I would like to clear up the tag ends in the matter of the illicit pregnancy. Are you satisfied that Paul Remillard was unaware of his wife's condition and her determination to flout Milieu law?"

"My personal redactive examination of Paul Remillard immediately prior to his appearance before the Special Committee on Ethics convinced me that he was innocent of conspiring with his wife. What has puzzled me is Paul's equivocal reaction to Marc's original account of the canoe trip. His apparent *fear* that his wife was not actually dead."

"Neither Teresa's body nor that of Rogatien Remillard has been found."

"The Hartland rapids, in which the canoe capsized, have apparently trapped human victims among their dense and chaotically tumbled rocks before." The Chief rose from her seat, frowning. "Still . . . it would be most unsettling if thou and I shall have erred in our analyses of these affairs, my dear Lek. There were aspects of mentation in both the boy and his close relations that I could not apprehend at all. And the coincidence of the two fatal events happening so close in time is peculiar, to put it mildly. Yet there seems to be no connection between the deaths. No one but Marc seems to have been involved in the canoe incident, and the adult Remillards appear to be completely innocent of any involvement with that or the murder of Brett McAllister. The Magistratum has been obliged, as a result of these mental examinations, to exonerate Paul and his six brothers and sisters. Now it is the boy's turn to be discharged . . . And still thou seest that I am sorely dissatisfied."

The Krondaku's mind was reassuring in response to her anxiety-laden use of the second-person familiar. "The Lylmik, who selected the seven Remillard siblings to be magnates of the Concilium, would hardly nominate persons of dubious integrity. Marc is, I admit, a knottier problem. He is certainly an egocentrist, imperfectly adherent to Milieu ethics, and capable of almost anything. But I hardly think that a human stripling—even one as mentally talented as this one—has the metapsychic wattage to hoodwink a couple of old pros like thee and me, my dear Moti Ala."

"Thou hast not struggled amongst these barbarous folk for thirty-eight orbits as I have, Lek! It's been one nasty surprise after another . . . The Galactic Milieu laid a heavy burden of trust upon the Simbiari race when it gave us Humanity as our first Proctorship. All through these difficult years, I have often in the desolate hours of night fought back the growing conviction that we are inadequate to the task."

"Balderdash, Moti Ala." A tentacle patted her silvery shoulder, and she felt suffused by a cheering psychocreative boost to her chlorophyll.

"No, seriously, Lek. I must still ask myself why Paul was afraid that his wife was alive. And why I was unable to look deeper into this fear or find any explanatory data for it in the mind of Paul's son. It's *impossible* that humans should be able to resist our metaconcerted coercive-redactive probing! Yet . . ."

"It is impossible. As thou sayest. Only our Lylmik mentors surpass us in the deep-probe function. Art thou suggesting that we refer this affair to them—express our misgivings and petition for delay of inauguration of the seven Remillard magnates? . . . Or wouldst thou go further and request an extension of the Proctorship?"

The two of them, by unspoken consent, reentered the parlor. The Chief squared her shoulders and made her decision.

"No," she said evenly. "I would not go so far as that, Evaluator." She returned to the formal vocal mode. "You will notify the Select Committee on Orb that the Earth Proctorship Magistratum issues a pro tempore acquittal of both Paul Remillard and his son Marc, who have been adjudged not proven of contriving the deaths of Teresa Kendall and Rogatien Remillard. Paul is also adjudged not proven of conspiring to conceive an illicit child. You will notify the Committee that the investigation into the disappearance of Teresa Kendall and Rogatien Remillard will continue. We will maintain covert surveillance of the boy, who may have a synchronicitous relation to the crimes."

"I will transmit the decisions, Enforcer Chief. Meanwhile, we will expect to receive ongoing updates concerning the other case—the bizarre murder of Intendant Associate Brett Doyle McAllister. I confess I am both intrigued and mystified by the apparent draining of life force through intricate and symmetrical psychocreative wounds. The killing technique is curiously reminiscent of that of the so-called Vampires of Shigoomith-4, a preemergent race that most fortunately extirpated itself before attaining interstellar travel some forty-two Galactic millenaries ago."

"Chaos take your extinct vampires!" the Chief exclaimed with asperity. "We have no useful data whatsoever in the McAllister case. No suspects once the seven Remillards and Marc were acquitted, no motive, no clues, not even a confirmed mode of death. Nothing except the fact that the victim was married to one of the Remillard Dynasty—just as Teresa Kendall was."

"You still intuit that there might be a connection between the cases?"

"We shall keep open minds concerning the possibility."

"These enigmatic Remillards!" Throma'eloo uttered a great sigh. "So talented. So controversial. So . . . important. One can hardly forget that in one hundred and thirty-one days, this same remarkable family will be among the first humans to become voting members of our Concilium. The fact cannot help but color one's investigative judgment. If it were possible that members of the Remillard family had managed to conceal evidence during coercive-redactive interrogation, the very jurisprudence of the Milieu would require restructuring—taking for granted, as it now does, that the truth is always obtained through mental probing . . ."

Moti Ala Malatarsiss felt the finally admitted uncertainty hit her like a blow in the chops. "Thou *dost* think we ought to put it up to the Lylmik! Thou hesitateth to say so flatly out of a delicate regard for my ego, not wishing to undermine what thou perceivest to be my teetering self-esteem!"

"Poppycock, Moti Ala," said Throma'eloo. "Thou art valiant as ever—only perplexed by this admittedly discrepant situation."

"Right." The Chief's face began to glisten again. "So I've changed my mind. I want you to report the whole kit and caboodle to the Lylmik Supervisors. Let *them* decide whether to put their Remillard pets—or perhaps even the whole human race!—on hold until we find out what's going on here. At the least, I would recommend that the Human Polity be put on probationary status in the Concilium for one Galactic year—a thousand Earth days."

"I will do as you request, Enforcer Chief Malatarsiss."

Throma'eloo Lek opened the door to the examination room. The disruptions of the aether had completely subsided. The boy was still lying on the couch, sleeping, and in his sleep he smiled. The Krondaku flowed closer, placed one of his minor prehensorial appendages upon the lad's forehead, and tried to read the dream.

Marc's eyes opened. His obdurate conscious barrier was already in place. He stared at the hideous Krondak visage with perfect composure. "Am I innocent?"

" 'Not proven guilty' is the verdict we will submit," said Throma'e-loo Lek. "You have been acquitted. Do you feel able to walk?"

"Certainly." The boy was smiling again, and he got up off the couch easily. "It wasn't nearly as bad as I had been led to expect. Bad enough, though." The smile vanished and the gray eyes were suddenly cold.

The Krondaku let his redactive probe slide lightly over the boy's mental shield. It was perfect, an artifact worthy of his own race of metapsychic titans. Oh, yes—a conference with the Lylmik was indeed called for! He said aloud, "Do you resent what was done to you?"

"Wouldn't you?" Marc's voice was neutral. "I suppose I do concede the Magistratum's right to probe me. But not . . . the vehemence of the operation. You slipped a block into my memory, but I know that you caused me great pain and forced me to expose my innermost thoughts to you. I think this was wrong. Most humans still believe that the will of the individual should be inviolable, that no one but God has a right to know a person's most secret thoughts. But this is contrary to your Unity, isn't it?"

"No. You misunderstand. I suggest that you study the principle of Unity more carefully, even though you are still far too immature to fully apprehend this most sublime concept, which is the very operational basis of the entire Galactic Milieu . . . A mind immersed in Unity is at once sovereign and coadunate. And incapable of committing the kinds of offenses you were suspected of. Since your race is still of client status, noncoadunate and unUnified, we do not hold your will to be sovereign and untouchable. We are thus justified in having taken the most strenuous interrogatory actions in cases as serious as these."

Marc nodded coolly. "Thank you for explaining, Evaluator."

"You are welcome."

Marc turned to the Simbiari official. "May I go now?"

"Please wait in the lift area for your escort to North America Tower." Chief Malatarsiss was distant. "He will bring along your notice of acquittal."

"Thank you," said Marc. He left the room without haste.

The two exotics bade each other a perfunctory mental farewell, after which Evaluator Throma'eloo went out by another exit. The Chief went back into the parlor for more Kleenex to refill her platinum sabretache. For some reason, her face and palms had begun to sweat heavily again, and the next examinee was almost due.

SECTOR 15: STAR 15-000-001 [TELONIS]
PLANET 1 [CONCILIUM ORB]
GALACTIC YEAR: LA PRIME 1-378-470
[1 SEPTEMBER 2051]

Four entities of the Lylmik Supervisory Body were in a slightly edgy mood, having spent a considerable time deliberating over the disturbing data transmitted by the Krondak Judicial Evaluator, Throma'eloo Lek. Since no conclusion could be drawn without the input of Unifex (and It was absent on one of Its extraGalactic mystery excursions), they decided a distraction was in order.

So they translated themselves to the chamber where the bodies were kept, and debated actually trying them on. It was a daunting prospect.

"One realizes," Homologous Trend remarked with a touch of grumpiness, "that Unifex wishes to impress upon the entire Concilium the important status of the group of newly installed Human Polity magnates. But one might also question whether Unifex carries honorific condescension too far in requiring us Supervisors to assume the *actual material aspect* of humanity at the inauguration ceremony."

"One would have thought astral bodies would suffice," said Asymptotic Essence, viewing the four upright forms askance. They were displayed in transparent cases extruded from the softly glowing green walls of the room: two male and two female bodies, alarmingly substantial.

"By the Prime Entelechy, but they're ugly things!" said Eupathic Impulse. "Especially the males. And wouldn't one know that Unifex— doubtless exerting Its famous sense of humor—would assign *this* entity to *that* sex!"

Noetic Concordance, the poet, said: "This entity agrees with its feminine designation, having once acted as creative matrix in the generation of a new Lylmik person, the dearly loved Resolute Mandament. This event took place in Fa-Time, and the coercive instigator was none other than Homologous Trend."

"One admits having forgotten this fact," Eupathic Impulse said.

"Well, so did this entity," said Homologous Trend.

They all laughed.

Lylmik reproduction had ceased in Ti-Time, more than eight Galactic revolutions ago. It was generally agreed by the absentminded historians of the race that the tragedy had nevertheless had the happy consequent of initiating the Outreach from the Lylmik Twenty-one Worlds, which eventually led to the establishment of the Galactic Milieu and the beginning of coadunate mental evolution in the Milky Way.

"The long-ago reproductive event explains why Trend was assigned male and Concordance assigned female sex," said the logician, Asymptotic Essence. "But why is *this* entity, which has never acted as creative matrix, designated female? And why is Impulse, similarly innocent of coercive generation, called male?"

Concordance said, "Unifex contemplated our personalities when making Its sexual determinations. One presumes that Its selection is in some way justified."

"Oh, indubitably justified," Impulse said, displaying a tinge of exasperation. "It has certainly worn the human material form often enough on Its own Earthside perambulations—to the scandal of the entities here present. One might wonder whether honoring magnified Earthlings at the Concilium inauguration constitutes Its sole motivation in foisting these fleshy envelopes upon us."

The other three entities scoffed merrily at their colleague's misgivings. But then they resumed examination of the bodies themselves, and felt their confidence waver. The things were so dismayingly *solid*. Omega knew what would happen when one actually put a body on . . .

The individual Lylmik mind was normally invested upon the most diaphanous material substance, all but imperceptible to the physical sensing organs of Krondaku, Poltroyans, Simbiari, and Humanity. Only members of the hyperkeen Gi could readily differentiate the wispy molecules hosting the Lylmik psyche from those of the inanimate atmosphere. On occasions when, for courtesy's sake, a visible presence was called for, Lylmik were accustomed to assume illusory astral bodies of varying form. What Unifex was now asking of the Supervisors was something far more radical.

"Regard the lumpish, sinewy feet," Impulse declaimed. "The unsightly blemish of the umbilical scar. The vestigial pelt, with its inconvenient facial lushness in the male and the odd little patches here and there on the torsos of both sexes. Some of those ridiculous hirsute regions have associated apocrine glands, with secretions that will surely stink once the atmospheric bacteria get to work on them."

The other three entities cringed.

Impulse was taking a melancholy relish in its catalog of infelicities. "Note especially the inelegant design of the male reproductive organs—tacked on almost as an afterthought without regard to the artistic composition as a whole, vulnerable to injury, kinetically awkward—"

"One wears garments," Trend said. "We shall certainly do so at the inauguration, since this is the human custom."

Asymptotic Essence noted gently, "We are procrastinating. Shall we pluck up our courage and perform the experiment?"

"Yes," said the others.

And in an instant, the transparent cases dissolved and the bodies lived and breathed as the four Lylmik Supervisors became incarnate as moderately youthful men and women who were neither excessively beautiful nor noticeably plain. They were of differing racial stock, and the only indication of their exotic nature was the inhumanly brilliant aquamarine color of their eyes.

High thoughts to you, colleagues—and congratulations! You all look splendid.

"Unifex!"

Uneasy giggles filled the chamber. Eupathic Impulse discovered, to his horror, that an involuntary vasodilation had turned his pinkish face and countenance bright red.

The Lylmik overlord said, "The phenomenon is harmless, even susceptible to mental override. Let me pass on to you all certain physiological information that will assist adaptation." [Data.]

Impulse's blush faded as he applied the program that Unifex had transmitted. "One is thankful for that knowledge. And might one inquire which human form *you* will assume for the inauguration?"

"I think this one would be safest," said Unifex. There was a brief flash, and the overlord stood before them in the shape of a white-

haired, white-bearded, powerfully built older man, taller than his colleagues, with deep-set gray eyes. "And let's have clothes for everyone."
Another flash; and they all wore long tunics and softly flowing over-
robes of different subtle colors. "It is fitting, perhaps, that we have a
little practice session now."

"Very well," said the others.

Unifex was abruptly businesslike. "Then let us deal with the intelligence vouchsafed by Evaluator Throma'eloo Lek. If we were truly
human, we would be seated during our consultation."

A round golden table and five matching chairs appeared. Unifex
plumped himself down with careless familiarity, and the other four
followed his example, with more circumspection.

"The Krondak Evaluator presents us with two very disquieting
pieces of information," Unifex said, having instantly digested a synopsis proffered by the minds of his fellows. "The first involves a suspicion that the mind of the youth Marc Remillard, and perhaps also the
minds of his father, Paul, and certain other senior Remillards involved
in this investigation, have been able to resist mind-probes of the most
stringent type. One questions whether the boy may be guilty of the
murder of his mother and great-granduncle, and whether the father
and his siblings may be conspiring to conceal the crimes of the
son—or, less likely, may even be accomplices in those crimes."

"Shall we join in Quincunx to consider?" Trend asked. "It would
take only moments to farscan the entire planet Earth and ascertain the
whereabouts of the physical bodies of Teresa Kendall and Rogatien
Remillard—whether or not they are still alive."

"It isn't necessary," said Unifex. "I will tell you flatly that Teresa and
Rogi *are* alive. For reasons that I decline to share at the moment, we
will not inform the Magistratum of this fact, nor will we transmit to
it any new data concerning Marc Remillard's complicity in the disappearance of the pair. The boy is a technical violator of certain Milieu
statutes, but he has not committed murder or any other crime that
need concern us. His peccadilloes have justification in the Larger
Reality and can be ignored for now. We can tell the Earth authorities
to keep an eye on Marc, however, to see that he doesn't get into any
more scrapes before the Human Polity joins the Concilium."

Eupathic Impulse was struggling to subdue his rising indignation.
"May one inquire just how you formed this amazing judgment?"

"No," said Unifex.

"One objects! One is miffed in the extreme!"

Asymptotic Essence laid her hand upon the shoulder of her inflamed colleague and let calming redactive power flow through it. She said to Unifex, "We accept your reassurance, as we have accepted it so many other times, on good faith alone. But we regret that you do not feel inclined to confide in us."

Unifex shrugged. "In time, it will all be clarified . . . The second matter for consideration is the psychic vampirism implicit in the death of Intendant Associate Brett Doyle McAllister." He hesitated, and his high brow creased in a deep frown. "I have no input to contribute in this case. I suggest that we leave the matter in the capable hands and tentacles of the Magistratum. I *am* certain that there will be a satisfactory resolution, in time, and the perpetrator of the crime will be brought to justice."

Homologous Trend studied his own new hands. The fingers had interlaced, and the thumbs were busily twiddling. "You do not then foresee any barrier to the inauguration of the seven Remillards, in view of the grave questions raised by these two cases? Both Throma'eloo and Chief Enforcer Malatarsiss had deep reservations about the family's fitness for magnification. They even suggested that we might wish to consider postponing the termination of the Simbiari Proctorship and refrain from granting humanity autonomy and Milieu citizenship at this time."

Asymptotic Essence said, "There is a strong sentiment among Simbiari and Krondak magnates for continued oversight. For at least a one-year probationary period of the Human Polity Magnates of the Concilium and a moratorium on colonization of new planets by humanity. One intuits that the potential for metapsychic calamity still lurks within the Mind of this highly renitent people."

Trend, Impulse, and Concordance nodded in agreement.

Unifex declared: "Friends, there are destined to be scandals and disasters whenever Human Polity affairs touch those of the Milieu. What happens must happen! But in the end Unity will prevail out of chaos, I assure you of that. The Simbiari Proctorship must now end, and inauguration of humanity into the Concilium must proceed. One does accept the one-year probation period and the planetary moratorium. We'll wait a few days and then break it to the Earthlings tactfully.

I want any resentment over our action to have largely dwindled away before the majority of the Magnate-Designates begin to assemble here in Orb. We wouldn't want to cast a pall over the festivities."

The others bowed. "Very well. We will transmit this judgment to the authorities on Earth."

Unifex rose from his seat and gestured. Five containers of foaming amber liquid sprang into being, one in front of each entity. "Let me introduce you to another human tradition—the cup of fellowship. On important occasions, one proposes a sentiment devoutly to be wished and drinks to it. I shall do the honors: To the magnification betimes of the Galactic Milieu—and all *six* of its Polities!" He lifted his glass and drained it, then uttered a deep sigh. The others sipped dutifully.

"Well, I must be off," Unifex said. "We shall meet again at the inauguration! Do work out a bit with your new bodies between now and then, won't you? You will want to be at ease with their physical senses, voices, muscles, and other material paraphernalia before manifesting yourselves before the entire Concilium." Unifex's smile was a trifle sardonic. "There will be a bit of a commotion when we appear this way, you realize. One will want to be prepared. And now I bid you farewell."

There was again a flash as the overlord's human-body molecules disassembled and were dispersed into the matter-energy lattices.

The four sat for some time, drinking the beverage and contemplating. Finally Noetic Concordance said, "I perceived from the vestibular mind of Unifex that this liquid is called Labatt's beer. I rather enjoy the mild euphoria induced by the small alcoholic content. It diminishes anxiety impulses in the primitive human brain in a manner remotely analogous to the consolations of the Unity. Let's have some more."

Four full glasses appeared.

"*Really!*" Eupathic Impulse was slightly reproving, but not to the extent that he refused the second round.

Homologous Trend shared a more serious thought. "Unifex virtually conceded that the Remillard father and son did manage to deceive the Magistratum interrogators. We may note that the redactive examination of the other adult Remillard siblings was similarly inconclusive. The whole lot of them are probably capable of encrypting their secret thoughts." He raised his half-empty glass and watched the small bubbles rising in it. "It is worrisome that human operant metapsychics are revealed to be so strong-minded before being safely coadunated and drawn into the Unity."

Asymptotic Essence said, "We have been assured again and again by Unifex that humans have the highest mental potential of any race in the Galaxy. Why should we be surprised that truly grandmasterclass minds appear among them somewhat early in the psychoevolutionary sequence?"

"What is the coadunate number for humans anyhow?" asked Impulse. "One forgets these trivial details."

"Ten thousand million minds," said Homologous Trend. "They have seven and a half now. The race had nearly outstripped the planetary resources just prior to Intervention, and births had dropped drastically. Now, with the fresh population upsurge on the colonial planets, one projects coadunation around the year La Prime 1-390-150—what humans would call A.D. 2083."

"No time at all," Asymptotic Essence mused. She conjured her glass full again, and at a nod from Eupathic Impulse, replenished his also.

"One cannot help but think of the thousands upon thousands of evolving worlds that have passed under Lylmik scrutiny during the life of the Milieu. So many sapient lifeforms, obedient to the evolutionary paradigm, rising inevitably from biosludge to transcendent self-awareness—yet almost all of them doomed to dead-end at the precoadunate level through technological misadventure or natural disaster. Five victories in seven hundred and thirty Galactic millenaries! It seems so wasteful . . ."

"Evolution is wasteful," Trend said austerely, "if one is impatient for Omega. One would do better to look at the diminishing temporal interval between the achievement of coadunation by the five successful races. And if humanity does not falter, it will have matured its Mind the fastest of any. Perhaps we hover upon the brink of a veritable metapsychic explosion amongst ascendant intelligent races."

"Do you imply that the Human Polity might have a pivotal role to play in this problematic mental efflorescence?" Impulse did not bother to conceal his skepticism as he created a fourth beer.

"Well, I wouldn't want to go out on a limb," Trend hedged.

Impulse tossed down his drink and plunked the glass firmly on the golden table. Essence refilled it again. "*My* prolepsis hints that the Earthlings are more likely to foment disaster than they are to accelerate progress! They're wily, that's what they are. Wily!" He finished his fifth glass.

"There will be only a hundred of them raised to the Concilium," Trend pointed out. "How much trouble can they cause, being so greatly outnumbered in the vote?" His mind displayed:

Krondak votes	3460
Poltroyan votes	2741
Simbiari votes	503
Gi votes	430
Human votes	100
Lylmik votes	21
(with veto power)	

"We may just find out too late what Humanity is capable of!" Impulse exclaimed. "Don't say one wasn't warned!" He gave a sudden start, then looked down in surprise into his lap. "Oh! The body! What's it *doing*? Colleagues, help! This appendage has acquired a terrible will of its own . . ."

Trend got up, took his fellow male by the arm, and hurried him toward the door. He said reassuringly, "I have analyzed the phenomenon. You've simply had a bit too much to drink, and it produces this odd physiological effect. Don't be concerned. All one has to do is—"

The door slid shut.

Noetic Concordance and Asymptotic Essence exchanged glances.

"Perhaps we should take our bodies off," Essence suggested.

Concordance smiled. "In a little while. But first I think I shall take the tube to the observation lounge and look out at the stars with my eyes. Would you care to accompany me?"

"It would be an interesting experience. Perhaps we can invite the boys to join us."

Laughing, the two Lylmik women finished their drinks, adjusted their garments so that the folds fell harmoniously, and went out into the teeming Central Promenade of the administrative center. There were already fair numbers of Human Polity bureaucrats residing in Concilium Orb in anticipation of the inauguration, so no one took any particular notice of the pair as they strolled slowly along, chatting, and keeping their peculiar eyes modestly downcast.

[**14**]

FROM THE MEMOIRS
OF ROGATIEN REMILLARD

On the morning after our arrival at Ape Lake I woke shortly after dawn, left Teresa sleeping in the tent, and walked up the misty meadow to the margin of the woodland, where there was a fine view of the pale, eerie lake waters below. And there I seemed to feel the huge resonances of the place envelop me. I, the interloping alien tuning fork, was being urged to synchronize myself with the country's telluric vibrations—or even to sing, as Teresa had instinctively done, blending into the enormous and subtle harmony of lake and mountains and glaciers and the indomitable plants and creatures of the place.

Do not oppose, the soul of Ape Lake seemed to say, do not impose. Only abide.

I began to walk.

The grass was dew-drenched. The sun was still concealed behind the eastern ridge; but behind me, the hanging glacier of soaring Mount Jacobsen was a dazzling white shelf, poised above us like a line of frozen surf. I came to the steep creek trail that led down to the lakeshore. The stream was tiny, splashing through dark gray strata of shale or some other kind of mudstone that had cracked into thin slabs, oddly tilted to a vertical position by an ancient seismic convulsion. The pure cold stream, sliced apart scores of times by sharp blades of rock, almost seemed to sparkle with satisfaction when it reunited at last in a small cascading sheet and fell gently into the pool at the rock-strewn shore.

I strolled along the lake's edge for a short distance, then stood receptive and relaxed beside the expanse of calm milky water, listening with my mind's ear. I am not a poet, not a sensitive; I have never experienced cosmic consciousness, never joined in a true coadunation of minds, never experienced even the least hint of those awesome precursors to Unity that the young operants of the modern, post-Rebellion Human Polity yearn after and mind-whisper about.

But I did experience the essence of Ape Lake that morning.

The rearing mountains were a palpable sensation, like drumbeats deep in my bones. I tasted a tangy shrillness radiating from the surrounding icefields, sensed the defiance of the valiant, twisted little trees of this exposed shore, veterans of hundreds of years of storm blasts. I heard the distant thunder of an avalanche, the rush of a small waterfall tumbling down the slope on the other side of the lake. Most portentous of all, I perceived that I was watched by other minds— gentle, subrational, *operant* minds, whose contribution to the plenum of Ape Lake made it a part of planet Earth unlike any other. I felt amazed and grateful that these minds seemed quite willing to let me and Teresa and unborn Jack share their home with them.

My fears and misgivings seemed to evaporate along with the dew on the willow thickets. I prayed, which I hadn't done for some time; and then, loaded down with sacks of food, I climbed back up the trail to the meadow and began to make breakfast.

During our first week at Ape Lake, which coincided with the last week that caretaker personnel worked in the Megapod Reserve, Teresa and I refrained from any activity that would drastically change the appearance of the cabin site as seen from the air. And as it turned out, two vintage flying machines did pass over—a large banana-shaped turbocopter toting some kind of bulky load on a dangling cable, and a venerable Cessna floatplane. Both were far to the south, behind Mount Jacobsen, and heading northwest toward Megapod Reserve HQ at Bella Coola. The noise of their internal combustion engines gave us plenty of warning so that we could hide. I made a stab at farsensing the occupants of the aircraft but only managed to determine that none of them was operant.

One of the first tasks I set about was the digging of a new latrine pit closer to the cabin, and the moving and roofing of the johnhouse itself. Meanwhile, it was Teresa's job to gather and dry large quantities of moss and old-man's-beard lichen. Over the next week she gleaned twenty giant garbags full of this material, which we would need for log chinking.

Building a food cache came next. This was vital in a region where bears, wolverines, and other creatures with a taste for human victuals abounded. I didn't know too much about Bigfoot appetites, but I had a hunch the creatures might be even more of a nuisance than grizzlies if they pegged us as a free lunch stop, so I designed the cache accordingly.

The time-honored method, according to our wilderness references, was to find four stout trees that grew more or less in a smallish square, lop off the branches, then construct a high platform using the trunks as corner posts. The cache is accessed by a removable ladder. Unfortunately, our cabin site was on a northern slope, and the nearby trees were mostly stunted hemlocks or other varieties deformed by winter wind blasts and heavy snow. The best I could find were two fifteen-meter whitebark pines a stone's throw uphill of the cabin and close to little Megapod Creek. Their battered trunks were so wide at the base that I couldn't close my arms around them. However, they tapered drastically higher up and were barely adequate. I figured to make the other legs out of two logs buried upright in holes; but the ground was so rocky and hard to dig that we eventually settled for a triangular cache.

I used my old axe to cut down and delimb a suitable Engelmann spruce, leaving a few of the top branches for camouflage. (The more efficient woodzapper would have created clouds of possibly betraying steam, and we didn't dare use it until the first of September.) We hauled the log laboriously into position with the come-along hand winch. A pole tripod, with the come-along suspended, enabled us to raise the log and socket it in its pit, which we filled with rocks and soil. Later, we would fit the three supporting posts of the cache with conical collars made from flattened Spam cans in order to discourage squirrels, mice, and other marauding small fry.

I built the ladder out of saplings—deliberately making it too fragile to bear the weight of a Bigfoot!—and nailed the platform beams in place. I was amazed when Teresa volunteered to hammer down the trimmed poles of the cache floor and build its tarp frame.

"Oh, I'm not afraid of heights at all." She laughed. "When you sing Queen of the Night, you get hung from the stage flies as often as not."

So I left her to it, working fearlessly four meters above the ground and vocalizing like the Lark Ascending, while I got on with making the temporary shelter we would live in until the cabin was refurbished.

This shedlike structure, which Teresa dubbed Le Pavillon, was a simple framework of poles, lashed together with wire and guy-roped against the wind. It became a reasonably snug four-by-six-meter wigwam once it was roofed and draped with heavy plass sheeting, then thickly covered with evergreen boughs on top and on three sides. The fourth side, facing the cabin some three meters away, had the transparent plass exposed for lighting, and an overlapping flap door that could be tied shut. The floor was more plass sheeting, turned up at the edges and basted to the walls so that water couldn't run inside. I scattered dried grass underfoot for absorption and less slippery walking.

Le Pavillon was to be our principal dwelling place for the next four weeks. It was, of course, unheated; but so far the weather had been warm, with some brief periods of rain. After the first shower, I added a kind of lean-to porch at the door. This was roofed not with plass but with the old cedar shakes from the cabin, which we had carefully collected in order to reuse. I rescued the iron stove, set it up in the lean-to, abbreviated chimney poking out the side, and—presto! A nifty covered hearth. Once it was safe to make a large fire, we could cook and bake decent meals on the stove instead of living on trail rations reconstituted with water boiled in our little microwave. When the first frost killed off the blood-sucking insects, we'd be able to sit by the fire and toast our bones on all but the stormiest days, and even use the stove to dry clothing when the humidity was high.

The woodpile and chopping block were right beside the porch. After the cabin was repaired, Le Pavillon was going to become a wood-storage shed, easily accessible from the cabin a couple of meters away even when the snow was roof deep. I scavenged broken floor planks from the derelict building and whacked together benches and two rickety tables. I also made a few rough shelves, promising to do better on furniture later, when I could slice up fresh boards with the woodzapper. The little dome tent, which I moved inside Le Pavillon and placed at the far end, was the designated bedroom and the only true refuge from the ravenous blackflies, mosquitoes, and mooseflies that plagued us in spite of our coercion and our repeated applications of repellent.

We worked so hard during those early days (and fell asleep so quickly each night) that there was very little time left for simple socializing. Teresa was cheerful but very often lost in mystical communion with the fetus, who, it seemed, was keenly appreciative of the special ambiance of our refuge. In workaday matters, she was usually willing to let me take the lead, doing without complaint whatever jobs I assigned her. She was a strong woman with a ravenous appetite, and her condition seemed to cause her no physical discomfort whatsoever. Since there was as yet no outward sign of the pregnancy, I tended to forget all about it.

Seven days after our arrival we were sunburned, bug-bitten, and afflicted with a few minor scrapes and bruises—but we had shelter from the elements, a secure cache, and a few rude comforts. The old cabin had the rubbish cleared out of it and was ready for its new floor and roof. Now that the long-awaited first of September had come at last, we could finally work on our wilderness home without fear of being spied out. But first—a day of rest!

I decreed that we would celebrate the traditional American Labor Day holiday three days early that year. It was time for Teresa to relax, and time for me to explore. She had no desire to accompany me and tried to persuade me not to leave her alone; but I convinced her that it was necessary to know what resources the area had. Most important, we needed larger and straighter trees than the gnarled specimens growing around the site if we were to repair the roof of the log cabin properly and cut new floor joists and planks. I already had a pretty good notion of where I could find what was required.

"You *will* be careful?" Teresa's mind reflected quick-flicking disaster scenarios of me tumbling into ravines and ice crevasses, being chased by enraged Bigfeet, fending off slavering grizzlies and wolves, getting lost, suffering a heart attack.

"Of course I'll be careful. And you know we don't have to be afraid of any of the critters. Why don't you just play your keyboard and sing, or watch a good old movie on your Tri-D? You've worked hard and you deserve a rest. But hiking is *my* recreation. Has been for damn near a hundred years! If you feel lonesome, you can give me a mind-shout. I'm not going to go more than two, three kloms away. Just around the end of the lake to check out Ape Creek Canyon and the opposite shore."

She cocked her head as if listening, then broke into a brilliant smile.

"Jack agrees with you that there's nothing for me to be afraid of."

"Exactly." I kept my mental overlay solemn. "Well, wish me luck, ma petite. If I don't find some decent roof beams, we may end up spending the winter in Le Pavillon!"

I stowed a few necessary items in my old Kelty backpack, then hoicked it on and set off across Megapod Creek, heading for the eastern end of the lake. It was a marvelous sunny day, brisk with a light breeze. There were white cirrus streaks clawing up the azure sky over Mount Remillard, and I hoped that a cold, clear air mass was moving in on us. This hope was reinforced once I hit the bush, for the goddam bugs came at me in kamikaze squadrons, wild for what might be their last chance at a blood feast before a hard frost stopped their little clocks. I despaired at driving them off with my coercion and finally put on gloves and my head net.

There was a game trail a dozen meters upslope from the shore, which I was able to follow through an area of dense wooded growth. Then I came to a series of rocky meadows, where the alpine wildflowers made a beautiful season-end display. Scarlet paintbrush, lavender asters, and yellow daisylike arnica bloomed amid the last spikes of arctic lupine. There were plenty of ripe blueberries that could be used to make plass-baggie jam, and abundant black crowberries that I seemed to remember were also edible. I farspoke Teresa and transmitted a mental picture so she could check on the crowberries in one of the reference flecks, and also told her the good news about the blueberry crop. She was really an excellent cook, and our restricted menu of freeze-squeeze meals had been a sore trial to her, although she had never complained vocally. Her farspeech now came to me all scintillating with enthusiasm:

RogiIknowwhatI'lldo! I'll come pick some berries and *I'll bake us a PIE!* And make some decent bread instead of that awful bannock!

Sounds wonderful . . .

I went up onto a bold little promontory to survey country that was not visible from the cabin site. Beyond the rocky outcrop there was a large clearing extending down to the lakeshore. I saw no watercourse, but from the suspiciously lush dwarf willows and other rampant vegetation, I judged it to be a bog. As I tramped across it I discovered that I was half right: it was a kind of suspended water meadow—the flower-dotted surface quite dry at this time of year but pocked abundantly with holes a meter or less in diameter, having deep pools of peaty-brown water 20 or 30 cents below their overhanging grassy rims. It was necessary to step cautiously to avoid breaking through the treacherous areas of thin crust. I negotiated this obstacle course and passed into a dwarfed hemlock forest beyond, keeping an eye out for animal droppings or other signs of life. But there was nothing except the ubiquitous insects and one friendly whisky-jack, a bird that outdoorsmen with no sense of humor vilify with the name of camp-robber. The western race was a little grayer than the birds of my New Hampshire White Mountains, but its habits were identical. It followed me, announcing my presence and begging for a handout by means of noisy clucks and squawks and throaty whistles. I couldn't have asked for a better bear alarm.

Ape Lake's shape resembled that of a poorly baked croissant, about three kilometers long and one wide. The northern shore was a fairly smooth concave curve, while the southern, where the cabin stood, was irregular, with a couple of largish outwash moraines down at the glacier-dammed western end. An extensive grass flat at the lake's pointed southeastern terminus made a natural corridor between the heights of Mount Jacobsen on my right and Mutt-and-Jeff Ridge on the left. There was a region of thick forest at the corridor's far end that I decided to investigate later. Ape Creek did not drain through this gentle notch. Instead, the flat held only a meandering trickle that flowed into the lake. The Ape Creek outflow was a few hundred meters up the opposite shore, where an abrupt gash broke through Mutt-and-Jeff Ridge.

I followed the narrow white-mud shoreline across the flat, then walked over rocks until I came to a thick tangle of driftwood logs blocking the Ape Creek debouchment. With the whisky-jack yelling at me to beware, I crept across this mantrap with exquisite care, the waters of the creek rushing two or three meters beneath me. When I reached the other side, I climbed partway up a talus slope until I had a good view down Ape Canyon. Its walls looked as though they had only recently been cleaved from the living rock, and lacked any semblance of a shoreline. The creek waters crashed down a series of ledges, then leapt outward in a white, rumbling cataract that my farsight estimated to be a good 20 meters in height. There were smaller cascades further on. It seemed fairly obvious that Ape Canyon would provide no easy thoroughfare for either human or Megapod. When the big apes came visiting, they probably entered the lake basin through the notch . . .

I had finally reached my goal, the shore opposite the cabin. Beyond Ape Creek the terrain was very dicey going. Contorted spiky krummholz and tangled alder grew close to the water's edge, and behind them the slope was extremely steep. But I didn't have to travel much farther to find what I had been looking for. The brush thinned a bit, and there on the precipitate hillside I found a stand of fine straight Engelmann spruce trees. Numbers of them were ideal for boardmaking purposes, measuring more than 35 cents in diameter at the base; the smaller ones and the saplings would make perfect beams and roof poles. All I would have to do was zap down a sufficient number of trees, delimb them and trim them to size, and tumble them down the 40-degree slope into the water.

And then figure a way to get them across the lake.

I found a breezy rock to sit on, took off the head net and gloves, and shared my lunch of raisins and Velveeta-smeared bannock with the whisky-jack. (Neither Teresa nor I had managed to bake anything respectable in the microwave. Bannock, a traditional wilderness food made by mixing flour, lard, baking powder, and water, was fairly tasty when baked in ashes or fried over an open fire. Unfortunately, microwaves turned it into gray slabs with the consistency of plassfoam padding.) As I ate, I considered one solution to the log-transport problem after another.

Solution the First: Our hardware-store loot included tenpenny nails. These could be used to spike small log stringers to the larger timbers, forming them into narrow rafts. I could pole these along the V-shaped shore to the cabin, a distance of perhaps two kloms. It would be desperately hard work, but my arms are strong, and I could walk on shore some of the time, lining the rafts and playing Volga boatman. *Evaluation:* Practical, but very slow. And I'd surely get wet, and the water was ice cold.

Solution the Second: If I could rig a sail, the rafts could travel directly across the lake, less than half the distance of the shore route. No sweat for me, speed dependent upon the wind . . . which unfortunately prevailed from the west, straight down the lake, when it wasn't dead calm, as it had been rather often during our week-long stay. *Evaluation:*

I'd still get wet, and how the devil do you steer a 400-kilo log raft through deep water in a crosswind?

Solution the Third: Tow the rafts across the lake behind another boat. *Evaluation:* We didn't think to bring an inflatable, and I hadn't a prayer of building a canoe or dugout.

Solution the Fourth: Stop thinking like a deadhead normal, you klutz! Chop and slice the wood to size on this side of the lake, then use your psychokinesis on a calm day to push the individual pieces of lumber across. Even your lousy PK is strong enough to move floating wood. *Evaluation:* Eureka!

The whisky-jack laughed at me.

Feeling very pleased with myself, I finished lunch and then scrambled up the slope to cruise the trees and select appropriate specimens. Then I stood quietly among the doomed spruces and told Ape Lake that I would do my best not to scar the landscape if *it* would cooperate by keeping its waters calm during the transport phase of the logging operation. The local vibes remained tranquil, and I decided that the response was affirmative. Tomorrow I'd begin cutting with the wonderful new Matsu woodzapper, the laser device that had made chain saws obsolete—to say nothing of simple axes. With luck, I'd have the cabin in good shape inside of three or four weeks.

The day had lengthened into late afternoon. Across the lake, a small plume of smoke rose from the campsite. Teresa had fired up the iron stove for the first time, and perhaps even now she was beginning to cook us a civilized meal. I decided not to farspeak her; it would be more fun to be surprised.

I started back along the shore, feeling more vigorous than I had in years. Negotiating the Ape Creek logjam was easier the second time around, and when I reached the opposite bank I sat down and stared at it for a while. Providential, that mass of tangled timbers. Without it, I would have had a hell of a time crossing the strong creek outflow to my tree farm. Once again, my mind acknowledged the genius loci.

And my eyes, suitably cast down, spotted the gigantic naked footprint, twice the length of a man's, freshly impressed in the white mud along the creekbank.

[15]

HANOVER MUNICIPALITY, NEW HAMPSHIRE, EARTH, 4 SEPTEMBER 2051

Professor Denis Remillard sat on a stool at the greenhouse bench, preparing the last orchid plant.

A violent storm was sluicing the vicinity of Hanover, filling the air with thunder and lightning and ebullient ions, so of course this had to be the night that the several-times-postponed Remillard family conference was finally scheduled to take place—here, at his farm, in just a half hour or so.

When the more spectacular varieties in Denis's orchid collection came into bloom, he was accustomed to bring them into the house for Lucille to admire, or to use as decorations when she gave one of her famous dinner parties or other academic entertainments. Tonight's somber family gathering had nothing festive about it; but that was all the more reason, she had said, for some distracting flowers.

Lucille had wanted to select the orchids herself. Just as she and Denis were about to go out to the little semidetached greenhouse, she had a sudden brilliant idea—coinciding with the arrival of a massive cloudburst—and dashed heedlessly into the rain to her car. Her motivations and goal were artfully hidden, but she did fling belated mental reassurance at Denis as she roared away into the storm. She had just remembered something, she told him, something that might be an important clue in the disappearance of Teresa and Rogi. She would be back soon, and Denis was not to let the family conference start without her.

After fifty-six years of married life with Lucille Cartier, Denis had learned to be philosophical about his wife's volatile mood swings and abrupt flashes of creativity. He knew it would be futile to attempt to stop her or to demand an explanation, so he simply went about the business of fetching the orchids, and now and then thought to pray peace for the whole troubled Remillard family.

As the hour drew near for the seven children's arrival, Denis had already prepared and carried in two beautiful plants. One was a long spray of Phalaenopsis for the mantelpiece, delicate as pale yellow moths perched on a bough. The other was a huge specimen for the Chinese porcelain pot by the front window, an Oncidium ornithorhynchum bearing a cloud of dancing rosy-lilac blossoms of quaint birdlike form. There remained only one last plant to groom: the pride of his collection, a Fujiwara Azurine "Atmosphere" with a cluster of three splendid sky-blue flowers, each nearly 18 centimeters wide. It had just reached perfection, and it might help to raise the spirits of poor Cat, who had always admired it extravagantly.

Ironic that it was Uncle Rogi's favorite orchid, too.

Using a sterile knife, Denis cut away a few damaged roots, then swabbed the wound with fungicide. He inspected the plant carefully for pests, watered it, and set it into a decorative basket. Then he tidied everything up, washed his hands at the sink, turned out the lights, and stood quietly for a moment in the humid, fragrant dark.

Rain continued to batter the glass roof, but at least the thunder had stopped. Now and then a distant, silent lightning stroke illuminated the tossing maple trees outside. It had been one storm after another all throughout that dreary Labor Day weekend—not that the inclement weather had particularly discommoded the family. The recent tragedies had forced the cancellation of the traditional monster beach bash at Adrien and Cheri's house; and in its place, Paul had called again for the family conference that had already been put off twice—the first time because of the disappearance of Teresa and Rogi, and then once more when it seemed that the Magistratum might demand that Paul and his siblings be barred from the Concilium. No spouses and no members of the younger generation were invited to the meeting. It was only for the seven grandmasterclass children of Denis and Lucille. They would discuss Catherine's future, and what measures the family should take concerning the disappearance of Teresa and Uncle Rogi, and whether they should attempt to intervene actively in the apparently stymied investigation into Brett McAllister's ghastly death.

Denis brooded over the latter, as he had done all weekend, ever since a certain shocking notion had presented itself.

Dear God, he said to himself, it couldn't possibly have been *him* that did it. He's dead. You took him! Freed us . . . But the pattern of Brett's burns was identical I can't be wrong about that I'll never forget that horrible sight her poor burned body as long as I live! *But he couldn't have killed Brett.* He's dead safely dead God he's got to be but how else to explain it?

And Uncle Rogi . . . ! He certainly hasn't drowned. I can't be sure about Teresa but I'd *know* if that old rascal had turned up his toes. I love him too much not to know and I deepviewed the Connecticut River from hell to Hinsdale and found nothing nothing nothing . . . and even if the bodies got over the Bellows Falls dam they never could have made it past the Vernon so they *aren't there* no matter what Marc says the little wretch !!he knows!! and—

"God, you've got to let me know too!" he cried aloud.

But the sexternions of the Divine Concursus remained obstinately mum.

Standing there in the flickering, ion-charged night, fed to the teeth with mysteries, grief-bereft of his usual composure and self-command, Professor Denis Remillard did something very atypical. He lost his temper. Frustration channeled all his immense metapsychic power into a bellow of sheer rage directed along his uncle's intimate mode:

Rogi! Answer me! I know you're not dead. Farspeak me damn you vieux connard and tell me the truth!

And for the briefest instant—

Denis seemed to detect a minuscule response coded with Rogi's mental signature, a telepathic squeak, quite involuntary, from a mind unexpectedly pricked. It came from far to the northwest—

Denis flung himself mentally in the direction indicated by that eyeblink-brief trace. He soared across North America out-of-body, scanning, scanning for Uncle Rogi's familiar oddball aura, over the eastern mountains, the Great Lakes, the woodlands and high plains of Canada, the Rockies, the interior plateau of British Columbia, the coastal mountains, the fjords and rain-forested islands of the Pacific—

And found nothing.

Of course, nothing. Even if Rogi's paltry metafaculty had heard, if the old man was hiding with Teresa he would hoist mental barricades and lie doggo, mistrustful even of the man he loved like a son. Denis's tremendous seekersense, still imperfectly trained according to Milieu standards, could only flail about in helpless wrath, not knowing where along that attenuated, fuzzy-edged mental beacon-flash to look.

I'm going to find you Uncle Rogi! Sooner or later! You'd better believe it!

Denis returned. He commanded himself to be calm again.

And at once a thought impinged on his still receptive mind. But this time the telepathic hail was from nearby, and it was his wife and not his quixotic uncle who bespoke him. Lucille was back, calling from the living room of their elaborately refurbished farmhouse:

DenisDenis come inside I've found A CLUE!!

. . . a clue?

At the SouthStreethouse Paul's place went there looked again found— Denis COME IN AT ONCE it's Paul's egg landing in the driveway and Philip and Maury together—

Right. Coming.

And here's Anne. And Sevvy. And Adrien bringing Cat!

Yesyes I'm on my way.

He picked up the blue orchid plant carefully and used his PK to open the door to the passage leading to the main house. The powerful, precisely directed mindspeech of the seven Grand Master metapsychics who were his adult children called out affectionate greetings to Denis as he approached, and completely obliterated the dire aetheric reverberations of the storm.

PAUL: Here's Papa. *Now,* Mama, will you tell us what you've found out, or must we commit mental matricide? Are Teresa and Rogi alive?

LUCILLE: I think I have proof of it.

PAUL: Oh, Jesus . . .

DENIS: Come—everyone sit down. For heaven's sake, Lucille, take off your raincoat.

PHILIP: I'll hang it up, Mama.

LUCILLE: Oh, *damn* the raincoat! . . . You know I've been going through your house, Paul, trying to discover if any significant items were gone—things Teresa might have taken away—

PAUL: And you've had no luck because her rooms are a mare's nest. Teresa has three closets stuffed with clothes and enough musical junk to stock a small conservatory. The housekeeper always followed madame's instructions and never touched the personal things, so who could tell what items might be missing?

LUCILLE: [tartly] Certainly not *you.* You spend most of your time at the apartment in Concord. But never mind . . . The reason I found nothing earlier is that I was checking out the wrong kind of things!

I realized that this evening. What I should have been looking for were baby items.

CATHERINE: Of course!

ANNE: If Teresa did run away with Rogi, it was certainly in order to save the child.

PAUL: The cedar chest. The one in that dressing room that we always converted to a nursery . . .

LUCILLE: Yes. That's where she kept the baby things—the christening gown that Tante Margie made for you, Philip, that's been worn by all the children. And the shawl that Annushka Gawrys crocheted for Marc, and that silver dumbbell rattle that all your children teethed on . . . and the beautiful swansdown bunting that Colette Roy gave Teresa. The chest was all in a mess, and some minor items may have been gone—I couldn't be sure. But one important thing *was* missing. The bunting! Its protective wrappings had been torn open and left there empty inside the cedar chest.

VARIOUS: [Exclamations.]

PAUL: [dully] Alive. I knew it. I knew it all along. God! How could she do this to me? To all of us?

SEVERIN: That's hardly the question. She *has* done it, and artfully at that.

PAUL: Goddammit, Sevvy— !

DENIS: Your mother has more to tell us.

LUCILLE: She took the bunting, and that set my mind onto a fresh track. Teresa may seem rather blasé about her older children, but never where helpless babies are concerned. If she was planning to hide for the next four months in a place where winters are cold, she might very well have wanted certain specialized information about the environmental requirements of newborns. I realized that no one had thought to check the public database records—

MAURICE: That's right! The library! How stupid—

LUCILLE: —so I went down to the computer to see what materials had been accessed from the house on August 24, the day of the disappearance. There were no books on infant health listed, but someone had downloaded these . . . [Image.]

ADRIEN: *Skills for Taming the Wilds. Camping and Woodcraft. How to Build Your Home in the Woods. The Camper's Bible*—

PHILIP: *Walden!* Good grief.

PAUL: *The Collected Poems of Robert* fucking *Service?!*

MAURICE+SEVERIN+ADRIEN: "A bunch of the boys were whooping it up in the Malamute Saloon . . ."

ANNE: She's gone to hide up in the Yukon? Preposterous!

DENIS: Not necessarily the Yukon. But somewhere in that area. I have some brand-new proof of my own. [Recapitulation.]

VARIOUS: [Exclamations and expletives.]

DENIS: So Uncle Rogi is definitely alive, and Teresa is probably with him, and it seems a foregone conclusion that Marc conceived and executed the entire scheme.

PAUL: [groaning] He had to. Uncle Rogi doesn't have the expertise—or the balls—to engineer a stunt like this.

ADRIEN: Given the fact that Marc was only missing for a period of fifteen hours or less, they must have flown out of here.

PAUL: . . . If we turn this new information over to the Magistratum, I have no doubt that it would find Rogi and Teresa. Knowing Marc, we can be sure he created a fine mess among the Vee-route traffic records. But even if the flight can't be tracked, Papa's farspeech trace narrows the search area to a fairly reasonable size, one that can be marked off and combed methodically by Simbiari-Krondak teams working in metaconcert. It might take weeks for the enforcers to pinpoint my wife and Rogi. But eventually they'd nail them.

LUCILLE: *If* we turn over the information. Marc must have known that there was a good chance that Denis would scan out Uncle Rogi. He set up the canoe accident to give the family an excuse not to pursue the matter further.

ANNE: Our interrogation—and Marc's—by the exotics produced no evidence that we conspired, or that we knew Teresa and Rogi were alive. The family is legally off the hook.

SEVERIN: We'll be on again—at least Paul will be—when Teresa shows up on the front doorstep with the fruits of her crime wrapped up in Colette's bunting!

MAURICE: Four months from now . . . By then we'll all be safely magnified—

ADRIEN: We could call in all our political markers, pass a retroactive legitimizing bill for the child and pardons for the lot of us once the Human Polity has legislative autonomy. Human sentiment will be overwhelmingly on our side. The Repro Statutes are probably the most bitterly resented aspect of the Simbiari Proctorship, and the laws are bound to be modified.

PHILIP: May I point out that our future credibility—our personal integrity as officials of the Galactic Concilium—will be compromised if we conspire after the fact of a felony—

ADRIEN: Fuck it! I say, good for young Marc!

PHILIP: On the other hand, from a Milieu legal standpoint, the Reproductive Statutes violation falls under the jus civile category rather than the jus naturale, and it may be argued that from time immemorial humanity has held reproduction to be one of the sovereign rights of the individual—

SEVERIN: [groaning] Save it for the courtroom, Phil.

PAUL: This damned affair has me crawling the wall! Cat, you haven't made any comment yet. What would you do?

CATHERINE: I'm a human, a woman, and a mother. Need you ask?

ANNE: Poppycock! I'm human and a woman and a legal scholar, and I think Phil raises a perfectly valid objection. The Human Polity is going to be on probation within the Concilium for a thousand days, and during that time the five exotic races of the Milieu will be judging our race by its leadership. And we all know that's going to be *us!* Is this family willing to march into the Galactic Age papered with pardons like some gang of operant Nixons?

ADRIEN: [shrugging] It would be the Earthling thing to do! I don't think the Simbiari would be disillusioned, poor green bastards. Not after pushing broom behind the human circus parade for thirty-eight orbits.

MAURICE: I rather doubt that the Gi would be scandalized, either, given their racial penchant for reproductive enthusiasm. And the Poltroyans are inclined to clap their little purple paws and give three cheers whenever we put one up the Leaky Freakies.

DENIS: Paul, you're going to be First Magnate unless Davy MacGregor manages a major upset. Teresa is your wife, and the child is yours. So is the decision.

PAUL: . . . Let it be.

LUCILLE: [Sighs.]

CATHERINE: [embracing Paul] Bless you. All the problems will be worked out in time.

SEVERIN: Marc thinks he fooled the exotic interrogators, but you can bet your boots the Magistratum still has him under surveillance. We'll have to warn him to watch his step.

PAUL: We will *not* involve that boy any further in this family conspiracy!

ADRIEN: Seems to me he's already in above the eyebrows.

SEVERIN: If we don't tell the kid that we know what he's done, we're putting ourselves at risk. I for one wouldn't put it past him to make visits to his mother's hideaway between now and the time of the baby's birth. He could be followed by agents of the Magistratum, and we'd all be back to square one.

ADRIEN: Marc would put any trackers off the scent the same way that he deceived the forensic redactors who tried to mind-ream him.

PAUL: Not necessarily. If the Magistratum used a mechanical surveillance device rather than a living farsensor, Marc might not even condescend to notice it! That son of mine is lousy with raw power, but he still has a few things to learn about high-tech machinery. Sevvy's right about Marc being a danger. But taking him into our confidence . . . we'd end up actively aiding and abetting him! Aggravating the original crimes rather than passively acquiescing.

PHILIP: [dourly] A *nice* point.

ANNE: Positively Jesuitical.

VARIOUS: [Uneasy laughter.]

LUCILLE: I have a suggestion, Paul. In two weeks you'll be sending your new staff to Concilium Orb to deal with the preinauguration details and set up your office there. Send Marc with them! Get him off Earth entirely. Make him a junior member of your staff. Other Magnate-Designates are doing it. I know that Annushka Gawrys is bringing her nephew, Vasiliy. The child is even getting university credit for time spent as a Concilium page. We could arrange the same thing for Marc with the Dartmouth Department of Political Science.

ANNE: We'd have to keep a sharp eye on the young devil in the meantime. The safest thing would be to ship him off-world immediately. Tomorrow!

SEVERIN: Damn straight. And *you're* the perfect one to nanny him!

ANNE: Oh, no you don't, Sevvy—

SEVERIN: It's logical. You're a coercer wiz, you have low cunning and a suspicious nature—essential for coping with Marc—and you're the only one of us who's unencumbered with a family, who can drop everything and go. Your work in Polity Jurisprudence is all in your skull and a fleck library that you can tuck into your purse. Mama's scheme is our best shot—and Marc might actually turn out to be useful on Orb. He could use his mind-bending faculties to coerce suitably spiffy family accommodation out of the Concilium billeting flunkies.

PAUL: Annie, I think it would be for the best.

LUCILLE: Undoubtedly. Please, dear.

ANNE: Trapped like a rat.

ADRIEN: Well, thank God that's settled. [*Image of agenda.*] On to the next item of business.

CATHERINE: [Screenslam.]

PAUL: Cat, don't. You knew when you agreed to come here that we would have to work this out.

PHILIP: [gently] The project you and Brett worked on is sidelined for complete restructuring. It may take months to replace Brett—if he can be replaced. You must face it, my dear: you're no longer indispensable to that particular operation. You belong where the exotic nominators said you belonged—on the Galactic Concilium.

MAURICE + SEVERIN + ANNE + ADRIEN + PAUL + DENIS: *Yes.*

LUCILLE: You know in your heart that we're right, darling.

CATHERINE: You were *all* right . . . from the beginning. If I hadn't balked, Brett might still be alive.

VARIOUS: [Indignant horror.]

PAUL: Cat, for God's sake . . . !

CATHERINE: All right! All *right!* You win! The damned Dynasty always wins! I'll stop my puerile mourning for Brett, and admit that my project no longer needs me, and accept my responsibility to the Human Polity! Are you all satisfied?

PAUL: Thank you, Cat.

CATHERINE: And now for the love of Christ get on with the next order of business—the one all of you have been afraid to face from the start!

MAURICE: [uneasily] Um . . . can I get us all drinks first?

LUCILLE: Come and help me bring in tea and coffee, Maury. We need something to warm us on a night like this.

SEVERIN: Cognac in my tea, garçon, s'il vous plaît. The good stuff.

MAURICE: [following Lucille] Canuck Philistine! . . .

DENIS: [to Catherine] I understand why you did it, but I'm sorry about your hair.

CATHERINE: [smiling absently] No big thing. Brett liked it long, but it was always a bit of a nuisance to care for.

DENIS: I'm a little disappointed that you haven't noticed the blue orchid. I brought it in just for you.

CATHERINE: Papa, it's exquisite . . . And three blooms at once this time.

DENIS: You'll take one home with you.

CATHERINE: I couldn't—

DENIS: Certainly you will. I insist. [Cuts a flower with his penknife and places it in her hands.] There. I'll have Maury bring you a plass bubble to carry it in.

CATHERINE: I—all right, Papa. [Kisses him.] Thank you for—for trying to cheer me up.

ANNE: All of us loved Brett. But we can't afford the luxury of mourning. The only meaningful way to honor his memory is to bring his killer to justice.

SEVERIN: The damned Magistratum has been doing nothing but spinning its wheels since it put the family through their brain-grinder and came up empty.

ADRIEN: Do you know what the latest scuttlebutt theory is? That the murderer is a nonhuman! One of my colleagues in Exotic Affairs told me that the Proctors now suspect a metaconcert of disaffected Simbiari, since their own race is the only other besides humanity that's so poorly attuned to Unity as to be capable of murder. They postulate a metaconcert because no individual Simb has the mental wattage to have extracted the summa totalis of Brett's psychocreative energy in that crazy complex fashion.

PHILIP + ANNE + SEVERIN + CATHERINE: [Incredulity.]

PAUL: The theory is perfectly plausible.

SEVERIN: Bullshit. The murder was the work of a psychopathic human operant with a tantric lotus-ladder fixation.

ANNE: Thank you, Dr. Jung.

SEVERIN: [doggedly] The seven ashen chakras found on the body can have no other meaning. The police ought to be looking for some Oriental colleague of Brett's with a professional grudge.

PAUL: They did. No such person exists. Neither Brett nor Cat has any associates who could be classified as genuine enemies. And among those who are less than warm chums, none possesses high meta-function.

SEVERIN: Then the perpetrator was a random killer. The idea of a Simbiari metaconcert is absurd. What *rational* motive could our worthy Green Brethren—or anyone else, for that matter—have for killing Brett?

ANNE: The Magistratum was willing to believe that all of us had a rational motive . . . until they probed us.

CATHERINE: Only exotic imbeciles would think that my own brothers and sister would conspire to kill my husband just because I had refused the magnateship!

PHILIP: [quietly] But now you have agreed.

CATHERINE: Yes . . .

PAUL: The Magistratum still questions whether the forensic redactive probing of the seven of us—and Marc—gave any valid data at all! They suspect that we may be powerful enough to thwart the mind-ream technique.

ADRIEN: That's ridiculous. No human Grand Master is that good—

PAUL: Frankly, I wonder whether this Simbiari villain metaconcert theory might be only a smoke screen.

SEVERIN: While they continue to suspect us?

PAUL: Or Marc.

CATHERINE: My God.

PAUL: If any human being is capable of resisting Krondak-Simbiari mind-probing, it's Marc. God knows none of us can get through his deep screens. Not that I actually suspect him of having anything to do with killing Brett—

ANNE: We must mount our own investigation of Brett's death. Use every resource. It's the only way to clear the family name. Accepting pardons for helping Teresa have her baby is one thing—but an allegation of murder is something else.

ADRIEN: You know, Annie's hit the nail on the head. As usual! It's no secret that the new probation period for humanity was a direct consequent of the murder investigation. Krondak and Simbiari members of the Magistratum even tried to rescind our family's nominations because of Brett's death and Teresa's disappearance. All that saved us was the Lylmik veto.

PHILIP: Now, there was a curious thing . . . It might lend credence to the notion of a nonhuman faction attempting to discredit us. The Lylmik would put a stop to that, but they might be willing to let the Magistratum plod on and ferret out the Simbiari cabal on its own.

MAURICE: [reentering with Lucille] The Lylmik want the Proctorship ended. They want the Human Polity to take its place in the Concilium, and they want the most powerful operants of our race— that's us!—working *for* the Milieu rather than against it. This is why they've decided to ignore the scandals and push on with our inauguration.

ADRIEN: [ruminatively] Paul, you reported Teresa's illicit pregnancy to the Magistratum before Brett's death, didn't you?

PAUL: I notified Malatarsiss right after Mama called me. At 1346 hours on Thursday the twenty-fourth. Brett was killed at least fourteen hours later, in the wee hours of the twenty-fifth.

ANNE: So the exotic metaconcert theory is remotely plausible. Given a conspiracy in the Magistratum itself. We should also keep in mind that Cat's decision to decline the magnateship was the talk of Concord that afternoon.

CATHERINE: But . . . that the exotics should kill, just to impeach us and keep us from taking our Concilium seats. *Why?*

MAURICE: They might be looking ahead. Afraid that what the Lylmik say about humanity's mental superiority is true. Resenting it.

CATHERINE: The Galactic Milieu is supposed to be above dirty politics! That's what the concept of Unity is all about.

PAUL: The Simbiari are an imperfectly Unified race. Just as we will be someday. The fact that this theory is being taken seriously should indicate to us that a Simbiari conspiracy *is* within the realm of possibility.

ADRIEN: There's no way this family can initiate any private investigation of exotics. Not before the end of the probation.

PAUL: True . . . Shall we be content to leave matters in the hands of the Magistratum until then?

PHILIP+MAURICE+SEVERIN+ANNE+ADRIEN: Aye.

CATHERINE: What if the killer is someone else entirely?

MAURICE: You mean, some psychopathic Kundalini Yoga adept who murdered Brett with or without a motive?

CATHERINE: It *could* have happened . . .

PHILIP: All the more reason for us to postpone action. The Magistratum is aware of that possibility. Its enforcers can do a better job searching for such a person than we ever could.

PAUL: So we're agreed: we wait.

PHILIP ı MAURICE+SEVERIN+ANNE+CATHERINE+ADRIEN: Yes.

CATHERINE: Then that winds everything up . . . Mama, Papa, I know you'll understand if I leave now. Adrien, can we go?

ADRIEN: Sure, Sis. My egg is your egg.

ANNE: Let me remind you all of one thing! Tomorrow you will be part of an honor guard escorting me and young Marc to the Kourou Starport in Guiana.

VARIOUS: [Moans and catcalls.]

ANNE: Cheer up. You can all have Cayenne chicken and mango daiquiris at the Devil's Island Rendezvous after the dear lad and I pop into hyperspace. [To Paul] You'll have him ready? I checked the Orb flight on my wrist-com. We'll all have to take the shuttle from Burlington at 0635. Keep Marc in the dark until we're safe at the Kourou boarding gate, won't you, Paul? Just to be on the safe side. Tell him you're just seeing me off, and pack a bag for him on the sly. We wouldn't want him to disappear, or get sick at the last minute, or think up some extremely logical reason why he has to stay here on Earth.

PAUL: Will do.

[Denis helps Catherine wrap her orchid. She goes out with Adrien. Anne leaves. Lucille begins to collect cups and saucers. Paul helps her carry things to kitchen.]

DENIS: [on intimate mode] Philip. Maury. Sevvy. Please stay on after Paul goes.

PHILIP+MAURICE ı SEVERIN: ??? Certainly.

PAUL: [reentering living room] Well, I'll get along, too. Good night, Mama, Papa. Thanks for hosting the confab. [To his brothers] See you at Burlington, mes frangins. [Exit.]

DENIS: [after an interval] I have something to tell you three. It concerns Brett's murder. Perhaps we'd all better sit down again.

LUCILLE: [looking in] Et moi aussi!

DENIS: You may as well.

LUCILLE: [sitting] I knew you were up to something when you coerced Paul into leaving.

SEVERIN: [astounded] Papa! You mean, you can still—

PHILIP: Be quiet, Sevvy. What is it, Papa?

DENIS: I have one solid piece of information to put before you. The rest is only intuition . . . You all know what this is. [Image.] It's a depiction of the peculiar patterns of ash that were left along Brett's spine and on his head when his killer extracted his psychocreative lifeforce. Please compare that set of lotus patterns with this one . . . [Image.]

PHILIP: They are virtually identical.

DENIS: The second set was found on the body of Shannon O'Connor Tremblay. She was murdered in 2013—on the very day of the Great Intervention—by my younger brother Victor. Similar marks were found on the body of her father, Kieran O'Connor, who was also presumed to have been killed by Victor. I regret to say that an emotional block in my mind prevented me from making the correlation before this. [General consternation.]

PHILIP: But Victor acted alone! He shared his powers with no one, not even Shannon's devil of a father. There's no person he could have transmitted his—his *technique* to. And Victor's been dead for eleven years. We were all there at his bedside and saw him—felt him!—die.

DENIS: He died. After nearly twenty-seven years in a coma, encapsulated inside his own brain, unable to communicate mentally or physically with another living thing. He died. Yes . . . That's what we thought.

PHILIP: God almighty, Papa, are you suggesting—

MAURICE: —that Victor's mind somehow regained its potency—

SEVERIN: —that the contagion was passed on, that his diabolical ambition lives—

PHILIP+MAURICE+SEVERIN: —*in the mind of one of us?*

DENIS: I've asked myself if it was possible, if God could have permitted Victor's imprisoned psyche to reach out at the very end, after we'd prayed for him for so long . . . reach out either in love or in a last temptation—

MAURICE: Papa, I don't mean to be blasphemous, but God doesn't have a damned thing to do with this! The question is: Did Victor have the strength, right then at the vital-field dissolution, to break through his latency and take over another human mind?

PHILIP: Mama wasn't there at the deathbed. But all the rest of us and our spouses were. I think we can eliminate Maeve and Cecilia from suspicion. Since the divorce, Maeve has avoided the family. At the time of the Rye Beach barbecue, she was in Ireland, asleep in bed with her latest boyfriend. And Cecilia was off-world at a medical convention. That leaves me and Maury and Sevvy, my wife Aurelie, Adrien and Cheri, Anne, Paul, and Cat herself. Nine family members as potential tools of Victor—if he *was* capable of mind-transfer.

LUCILLE: No! No! You're talking witchcraft, not valid metapsychology! Such things can't happen! One mind can't be enslaved by another. The human personality—

SEVERIN: —can fragment. Multiply. You're a trained psychologist, Mama. You know that scores of separate personas can reside within a single diseased mind. An ordinary mind! Who knows what monstrous deviations might afflict operants? We can utilize the mental lattices to influence the very fabric of time and space, matter and energy! Who's to say what else we're capable of? The abnormal psychology of Homo superior is still being written. I'm writing a bit of it myself! *If* such a transfer were possible, the victim might not even be aware of it consciously—just as a patient with multiple-personality disorder is unaware of the existence of the other identities.

LUCILLE: Denis . . . do you think it could happen?

DENIS: I don't know. But you see why I'm afraid, don't you?

PHILIP: Good God, yes! Maury and I are probably the only ones besides you and Mama and Uncle Rogi who can remember what Victor was really like in his prime. The man wasn't a human being at all. He was . . . an evolutionary aberration.

SEVERIN: [quietly] *I* remember Victor quite well. The last time we saw him—before the Intervention, that is—was at the family Christmas party at Tante Margie's in Berlin in 2012. You were fifteen, Phil, and Maury was thirteen, and I was nine years old. Anne and Cat and Adrien were just little kids, and of course Paul hadn't even been born . . . Uncle Victor came in with his twin deadhead stooges, Uncle Lou and Uncle Leon, all loaded down with expensive presents just like always. And just like always, the operant relatives were polite and had their toughest mental defenses in place, and the normal ones were either fawning over the family black sheep with the Midas touch or else scared white. Only the littlest kids were glad to see Uncle Vic—the ones who were too young to realize that there was more to him than a big good-looking guy handing out incredible loot . . . That year, when I was nine, was the first time I *knew*. Vic didn't try to make mental contact, didn't really do a thing. But all the same, I knew. It was the mystery of evil coming home to me for the first time, and I was damn near petrified. Vic just laughed and gave me this fantastic rhythm programmer with one of the first of the brainboard interfaces. Right after Christmas I traded it . . .

MAURICE: Good thing. Those early brainboards had nasty possibilities. [A meditative interval.]

DENIS: [slowly] Boys, do you agree when I state that no known operant entity could have killed Brett in that manner from long distance?

PHILIP: I think it's a safe assumption. Even a grandmasterclass exotic operant—always excluding the Lylmik, whom we know so little about—would have had to be in Brett's immediate vicinity to initiate a psychocreative drain of such extraordinary complexity.

DENIS: The Magistratum probed all your minds and presumed you and your spouses innocent of Brett's murder. Aurelie and Cheri were exonerated because their metapsychic powers are too meager to have accomplished the killing, and they are completely incapable of resisting exotic mind-probe techniques. We can safely eliminate them from suspicion. But we know, and so does the Magistratum, that probing does not necessarily exonerate *us* . . . There are only four members of the family who I can be certain were nowhere near Rye Harbor when Brett died on that boat. You three and your mother. Severin was here in Hanover all the previous Thursday and throughout the night and early morning on Friday, the day of the murder. Lucille had called him up from Concord when she thought she'd convinced Teresa to have the abortion. Early Thursday evening, when your mother discovered that Teresa had disappeared, she called you two others up from the capital to help in the rough farscan search. The three of you stayed with her until the next morning.

SEVERIN: But Paul never went to the beach. He remained in Concord and came to Hanover late Friday morning—

MAURICE: Yes. On the evening of the beach party he was to make a statement before the specially convened judicial panel that would determine whether he should be suspended from the Intendant Assembly during the inquiry into Teresa's criminal pregnancy. When he was allowed to keep his seat, he decided against egging up to Hanover immediately. On Friday morning there was an important Assembly session debating the Denali colonization, and he had made his mind up that Teresa was only hiding and that she'd turn up . . .

DENIS: Paul didn't come to Hanover until long after Marc was found on the riverbank around 0630 Friday morning, when we had the first suspicion that Teresa and Rogi had been drowned. Paul says he was at his Concord apartment all night.

SEVERIN: But he had all the time in the world to egg over to Rye.

DENIS: Adrien and Anne and the wives didn't know about Teresa and Rogi's disappearance or any of the rest of it until I told them. That was after the police notified me of Brett's murder on Friday morning. I farspoke Paul to inform him and found him still in Concord, so he must be considered a viable suspect.

LUCILLE: Oh, my God . . . !

DENIS: And so are Adrien and Anne. Both of them came in from Concord on Thursday afternoon, as Cat and Brett did, wanting to escape the magnate madness that had broken out in the capital. On Thursday night Adrien and Anne were at the Rye beach barbecue with me and all the grandchildren.

LUCILLE: Adrien . . . Annie . . . Paul . . . It's not possible that one of them is a psychic vampire!

DENIS: Don't forget Catherine herself. If the aberration is locked away in the unconscious, she could be guilty.

LUCILLE: Denis—no!

DENIS: [calmly] Yes. A part of her mind could have resented being tied to Brett and the Child Latency Project. Catherine seems to have the smallest coercive component of any of you, the least ambition. She married Brett—a brilliant man, but her metapsychic inferior—against the advice of the family because she was deeply in love with him. But if she was invaded by Victor long ago, who can say what motivates her inner persona? Perhaps a kind of—of psychic time bomb lay dormant in her mind until the appropriate stimulus activated it.

SEVERIN: Marc is also a suspect. No one knows for certain where he was before he turned up on the riverbank at dawn.

MAURICE: But how could Vic ever have got to *him?* Marc wasn't there at the deathbed like the rest of us were. And he was only two years old! Papa, you postulated Vic acting out some kind of temptation scenario in extremis. But no one can tempt a two-year-old!

DENIS: Not an ordinary two-year-old.

PHILIP: Marc was there. Uncle Rogi brought him and Teresa to Berlin because Paul was flying Papa in from Johns Hopkins.

DENIS: Yes. Paul had tried to convince me that I was too ill to attend the Good Friday meeting. But some premonition told me it would be our last chance.

SEVERIN: Marc wasn't in the same room as Victor at the end, but he was across the hall with the nurse. And Victor was strong enough at his death to take Louis and Leon and Yvonne with him . . .

MAURICE: So he could have reached Marc.

DENIS: [sighing] Yes.

LUCILLE: [abruptly] But this entire notion is monstrous! That one of our family could be some sort of fiend in disguise!

PHILIP: Brett is dead. The ash patterns match those on a known victim of Victor Remillard. There must be some correlation. The modus operandi is too bizarre . . .

MAURICE: Papa, were the details of Shannon and Kieran O'Connor's deaths publicized? I certainly don't remember anything in the media at the time. Of course, the Great Intervention overshadowed everything . . .

DENIS: Uncle Rogi—who practically caught Vic in the act—knew about Shannon. He told me early the next day, and we led a handful of New Hampshire State Police officers to the closet in the hotel offices where Shannon's body was hidden. The ambulance attendants who took her body away would have seen the ash patterns. And later, so would the county medical examiner who did the autopsy. Who else? The employees of the funeral home who put her body in a closed coffin. Nobody else . . . Except for Uncle Rogi and me, everyone who saw the ash marks was nonoperant. There was no publicity whatsoever on the cause of Kieran O'Connor's death. As for the inquests—well, as Maury said, the Great Intervention was all that seemed to matter. Rogi and I agreed that nothing was to be gained by accusing Vic of killing Shannon. We had no proof, and he was in a profound coma. In the end there was an open verdict on her death. It wasn't even called murder! She had no close living relatives. Her estranged husband, Gerry Tremblay, claimed the body, and it was cremated. I suppose Gerry might have seen the ash patterns. But he's long gone, too . . . Victor remained comatose and was eventually remanded to the custody of the family because nobody could think of anything else to do with him except keep him in a private facility—and we were willing to take responsibility for him. He couldn't be tried for the gun battle on Mount Washington. He wasn't officially accused of anything, because his accomplices had mental blocks preventing their testifying against him. By the time the Proctorship looked into the case and officially pinned the attack on my brother, it was agreed that his medical prognosis was hopeless. We were free to pull the plug—if we wanted to.

PHILIP: And none of us has ever understood why you didn't, Papa. We thought we were joining with you in metaconcert to pray for Victor's natural death every year on Good Friday because you—because you couldn't—

LUCILLE: You all saw that Victor's body did not deteriorate. Even without muscle stimulation, and provided with only simple food and water, he retained the appearance of a healthy man. His nervous system functioned perfectly. His EEG traces showed normal sleeping and waking patterns and apparent cognition even though he was incapable of making any voluntary movement or communicating verbally or metapsychically. He lived, and apparently thought. What his thoughts were, whether he was sane or insane, no one could say. He was utterly isolated.

SEVERIN: Then why didn't you—

DENIS: Because while he lived, I could still hope that one day he would be sorry. That he'd feel remorse for what he had done. And it seemed obvious to me that he was not ready to die. He could have stopped his life processes by willpower alone at any time.

MAURICE: Good grief, Papa—!

DENIS: None of you children knew the true extent of my brother's sins. Very few people did. I'll have to tell you now, I suppose . . . but not tonight.

SEVERIN: [softly] He was a monster. But to condemn him to *that* . . .

MAURICE: Every year, every Good Friday you made us all visit him. We never knew the real reason why you joined us in metaconcert, why you focused our massed mindpower with your own coercion, subjugating us.

DENIS: [wearily] Would it have helped? To know that my poor brother had damned himself? We can only do it to ourselves, you know. And we make our own hell. But as long as he was capable of thought, not in physical pain—

SEVERIN: Imprisoned in the ultimate solitary confinement. Is *that* what you sentenced Vic to, Papa?

DENIS: I did what my conscience directed. What my religious beliefs required.

PHILIP: Oh, Papa. If only you'd told us the truth. You were mistaken! No matter what kinds of crimes your brother had committed, you had no right to—

LUCILLE: I concurred with your father's decision. It was a matter of hope. We are required to take charge of our lives. To make responsible choices. But we also face perplexities—times when there is no ready answer. Victor himself seemed to want to live, and we hoped for his eventual reformation. Your father did for his brother what he had a right to do.

SEVERIN: And now we all live with the result.

DENIS: Yes.

[A long silence.]

MAURICE: If somehow we could acquire—or design—a coercive-redactive probe configuration that would give us the *truth* when it was used on a Remillard . . .

PHILIP: The five of us, working in metaconcert. Using purely human parameters—not the half-exotic techniques of the Krondaku and Simbiari! We could probe the suspect family members and establish guilt or innocence for Brett's death. Use the Milieu's own mental evidence-gathering technique to support or contradict the inconclusive Magistratum interrogation sessions. It would be legally admissible evidence.

DENIS: I don't know. I just don't know. We're only beginning to understand the programming principles for precision human meta-concert. When I worked with you on Victor, I coordinated almost instinctively! I could try to design an infallible probe program, but I don't think I have sufficient skill. I doubt that any human does yet—not even Davy MacGregor or Ilya Gawrys. It would be best to wait until our Polity takes its Concilium seats, then request informal help from the Krondak Ministry of Evaluation. They wrote the damned book on mind-reaming.

PHILIP: Yes . . . that seems the best course.

MAURICE: And the safest. As long as there's a chance that a member of our family is a deliberate or unconscious murderer, the five of us will have to guard our minds and act with the utmost caution. If our Monster of Iniquity feels threatened, it might kill again. We still don't have the remotest inkling of its motive.

SEVERIN: Once we're all in Concilium Orb, we'll surely be safe. No operant murderer would dare to try anything in a cerametal beehive crawling with exotic Grand Masters and Lylmik Supervisors. We might even be able to resolve this thing before we return to Earth— if Papa will agree to work out a probe program with the Krondak Ministry of Evaluation while we're all there.

DENIS: Your mother and I aren't Magnate-Designates, and we certainly can't tag along with you ahead of time, pretending to be part of your staff. I'll come to Concilium Orb when the rest of the family guests do, and meanwhile I'll do my best to work up the skeletal probe configuration. I promise I won't try to play Sherlock Holmes or flush out bogeypersons ahead of time if *you* won't.

PHILIP+MAURICE+SEVERIN: We agree.

DENIS: Then I think we'd better say good night.

[Parents and children embrace. Philip, Maurice, and Severin leave. Lucille and Denis stand at the front window, watching the rhocraft loft into the sky. Small clouds speed before the moon. The rain is over.]

LUCILLE: It's *none* of them. I know it.

DENIS: We can hope.

SECTOR 15: STAR 15-000-001 [TELONIS]
PLANET 1 [CONCILIUM ORB]

GALACTIC YEAR: LA PRIME 1-387-497
[28 SEPTEMBER 2051]

On the morning after their arrival at the world called Concilium Orb, Anne Remillard and her nephew Marc went out for breakfast to La Closerie des Lilas, an "open-air" restaurant across the square from the little Hôtel Montparnasse, where they were staying until more permanent accommodations for the family could be arranged.

The orbicular wedge within the great hollow planetoid built by the Lylmik already had over thirty different enclaves set apart for humanity, each one simulating a distinctive district on Earth. They featured appropriate landscaping, typical ethnic commercial, cultural, and artistic amenities, and characteristic residential areas. Some enclaves bustled, and some were quiet; some were tasteful, and some were gaudy; some were urban, while others imitated the inhabited countryside and housed people in tiny villages. The enclaves were of differing sizes, separated from one another by carefully tended parklands and forests that underwent "seasonal" variation, by rockeries that looked much like mountains, by desert gardens, jungles, simulated tropical lagoons, waterways, and lakes. Over all stretched an illusory sky, which brightened and darkened in the 25-hour cycle of the Galactic day, showing the star patterns and the single moon of Earth at night, and changing varieties of clouds during daytime. Rain fell when and where it was appropriate; and in the Boreal Forest separating Scandia and Baltica enclaves, and in the Alpenland, Yakutskaya, and Himalaya enclaves, there was occasional snow. Most of the plantlife was living and authentic. Most of the fauna, except for some domesticated species, was bionic. Everything was kept clean and tidy by automated mechanisms.

The new human Magnates of the Concilium, their immediate families, and their operant assistants might live in whatever enclave they wished during the periods that the Concilium was in session, and they could return to their home world or continue to reside in Orb while the Galactic governing body was in recess. Although there were only one hundred human Magnate-Designates now, it was expected that many more would be raised to the Concilium in years to come, until humanity was represented proportionally, as the exotic races were. The human enclaves would expand and multiply as the need arose.

All of the Magnate-Designates in the Remillard family except Paul and Anne had requested beach houses in Paliuli, a Hawaiian-style paradise that was fast becoming one of the largest and most popular enclaves in Orb. Paul had asked for a place in Golden Gate, the Lylmik evocation of sophisticated San Francisco, situated near Orb's Central Concourse and meeting chambers. Anne thought she might like a Parisian-style apartment in Rive Gauche, which was why she had chosen to stay in a hotel in that enclave.

Marc thought Rive Gauche was too suffocatingly quaint and whimsical for words, and he found it inexplicable that the normally sensible Anne would even consider living in such a kitschy place.

Although his aunt ordered only café au lait and a couple of croissants for breakfast, Marc insisted that he was starving after more than three weeks of mediocre shipboard meals on the CSS Hassan Bashaw. With adolescent perversity, he turned up his nose at all of the elegant French items on the Closerie's menu and scandalized the waitron by demanding corned-beef hash—fried extra crisp—with poached eggs, a slice of fresh papaya with lime, banana-walnut bread, and a pitcher of Mexican chocolate.

"Those are hardly the specialties of the house," the prim, middle-aged waitron began. She was dressed like a nineteenth-century serveuse, in keeping with the décor of the establishment.

"But you can get them, can't you?" Marc's face wore the mocking one-sided smile that had driven Anne to distraction during their long voyage from Earth. "All the food in Orb comes from a central provisioning depot, and you can have any Earth edible imaginable sent to your kitchen within five minutes. If I wanted to, I could order witchetty grubs or sheep's eyeballs or bison hump-ribs or poi."

"Marc . . ." Anne said wearily.

"Well, couldn't I?" the boy demanded.

"Yes, m'sieu." The waitron, like all human service personnel in the huge artificial planet, was a nonoperant; but she knew a rebellious brat when she saw one, and her attitude changed instantly, becoming sweetly patronizing. "Of course we will be delighted to prepare what you have ordered. It is unsettling to be so far away from Earth, isn't it? Poor little fellow! We must do our best to ease your homesickness. Would you like your witchetty grubs on toast?"

"No," he growled. "Just the other stuff."

"Very well." And she patted Marc on his head, winked at Anne, and swept away.

Face flaming, the boy stared at the tablecloth. In the everblooming mutant lilac bush behind him, a robotic bird began to warble. Other human patrons of the outdoor restaurant filled the air with the hum of their verbal conversation. The aether, as everywhere within Orb, was pervaded with the most serene and benevolent vibes.

Marc felt like puking.

"Don't you think it's about time you and I declared a truce?" Anne asked him.

He raised his eyes. "A truce?"

"You know very well why we wanted you off-Earth."

"Yes," he snapped.

At the embarkation, when Paul had abruptly handed Marc his carry-on bag and credentials, and the entire family had focused their coercion on him, the boy had offered no resistance at all. Helpless in the multiple grip of the Grand Master adults, he had simply looked his father in the eye and said, "You may regret this." Then he had turned away and followed Anne onto the starship without another word.

Now she said, "You're going to stay here in Orb at least until January, until after the inauguration. You can continue to brood and sulk like a silly child if you wish, but I had hoped you would accept the family's decision and be of some help to me while you're here. There's a great deal to be done in our offices before the others arrive in December."

He stared at her and she stared back at him, yielding not a mental micron, until he finally lowered his eyes. Like her younger sister Catherine, Anne was tall and blonde; but where Cat was as impetuous and passionate as Lucille, Anne embodied the icy intellectualism of

Denis and had always been her father's favorite. There had been sibling jokes about her springing fully armed from Denis's brow rather than being born normally like her five brothers and her sister. Anne had taken the jests to heart while still a young girl, obtaining a small statue of Pallas Athene, which she made her mascot and still kept on her desk in Concord. Marc had asked her once what the goddess symbolized, and she had replied, "The victorious mind."

Marc was not particularly close to his uncles and aunts. But early on he had recognized a certain affinity between himself and this calm, efficient woman who had always spurned any kind of emotional involvement. For some reason it was to Aunt Anne, rather than his own parents or Uncle Rogi, that he had turned as a nine-year-old boy puzzling over the mystery of human sex. She had explained it with brisk clarity, putting it into perspective for the nuisance it was to those who were dedicated to a higher life of the mind. Sex distracted you from important matters, she explained. It was only biochemistry, a mere animal drive; nevertheless it had the potential for devastating a person's reason, and so it was never to be trusted. (Marc had not understood how this could possibly happen; but Aunt Anne had only laughed grimly and said, "Wait!") She told him that she had chosen not to marry or have children or seek any other kind of close relationship with another person because her work for the Milieu and operant humanity must take precedence in her life over mere private gratification. At the time, Marc had thought her example noble and admirable and well worth emulating; but he had been very careful not to let *her* know how he felt.

Anne had been the first Remillard to be appointed by the exotic Proctors to the North American Intendancy and to the Assembly of Intendant Associates, the Human Polity's quasi-independent legislature. She had also been the principal political mentor of her younger brother Paul from the very beginning, guiding and advising him in his swift ascent to Intendant Associate, encouraging him to aspire to the First Magnate chair when the Human Polity was accepted into full voting membership in the Galactic Concilium. After Anne herself achieved the rank of Intendant Associate, she dared to speak of her own secret ambition to the rest of the family: she wanted to be no less than Planetary Dirigent—the chief operant executive—of Earth, after the Simbiari Proctorship ended.

His aunt's dream had further overawed Marc, and he had continued to admire her uncritically . . . until this enforced trip from Earth to Orb. Furious at being shanghaied and fearful about what would happen to his mother and Rogi, the boy had shut himself up inside his inviolable mental fortress, hardly speaking to Anne during the voyage and even distancing himself from her physically, insofar as that was possible on a rather small starship. There was plenty of time to think during his self-imposed isolation, and one of the things he brooded over was the murder of his Uncle Brett McAllister. Using much the same logic as Denis had, Marc deduced that Anne—together with her sister Cat and her brother Adrien—was a principal suspect.

And so was his father.

In his solitude, thinking about unnatural death and trying to suppress the very genuine fear that had taken root within him, Marc also puzzled over something that had mystified and disturbed him for nearly eleven years: the passing of Victor Remillard. His recollection of the events on that Good Friday in 2040 had the vivid accuracy of perfect memorecall. As a precocious toddler, he had been curious about the family ritual he had been excluded from, and so he had extended his ultrasenses into the adjacent bedroom and experienced the deathbed scene almost as fully as the adult witnesses had. What young Marc had seen and felt had been quite incomprehensible to a baby's understanding. Even now it defied complete analysis. But things were becoming clearer to him as he grew more closely acquainted with the shadowy aspects of his own mind and the minds of other superior metas.

However, there was still no answer to the principal question: Could a dying mentality, energized by evil ambition, find sanctuary in the mind and body of another? Everything Marc knew of psychology and theology denied that such a thing was possible. But *something* had happened at Victor's deathbed; and whatever the dying man had done was done with the conscious or unconscious assent of the mind—or minds—invaded. The notion that Victor, or some agent of his, must be involved in Brett's strange death had come upon Marc in a synchronicitous flash, having nothing to do with logic, and all the more distressing because of that . . .

Aunt Anne was looking at him now with those pale, cold eyes of hers that also held a surprising intimation of foreboding.

"*Will* you work with me, Marc?"

His gaze slid away. As subtly as he could, he projected grudging resignation, a slight cracking of the mental shell that she had perceived as completely indomitable. He projected adolescent uncertainty, and a desperate need to trust in some reliable adult. He projected the merest hint of his old admiration for her.

"I'll—I'll do my best, Aunt Anne."

She reached out one hand and touched his own, smiling a little. "Good. And I'll try to help you, too, Marc."

Then the food arrived, and the French waitron was very maternal and jolly when Marc apologized for insulting the restaurant's cuisine. He confided wryly to her that he was only a Franco-*American* and a poor excuse for a gourmet, but he hoped to visit all of the ethnic enclaves of humanity while he was in Orb and educate his taste buds.

She laughed pleasantly. "And you must try exotic food, too! Except for the Krondak kind, of course, which contains too many petrochemicals and unhealthy alkaloids. The cuisine of the Gi is really delightful—like feasting upon the most subtly perfumed desserts and salads—while Poltroyans do wonders with seafood and strange meat dishes, and the Simbiari devise the most delicious candies imaginable. The Green Ones are only partially photosynthetic, you know, and do amazing things with sugars. Then there are the Lylmik. Just think! You may actually *meet* one of the rare beings here. Those who have done so say the experience is unforgettable. One realizes that they do not eat. Some say they subsist upon the music of the spheres, but I suspect that is nonsense."

Marc said, "I'm looking forward to my stay here very much. I've heard that visiting the exotic enclaves of Concilium Orb is like taking a quick tour of the inhabited Galaxy. I'll be the envy of my college classmates when I get back to Earth. Everybody's heard the fabulous stories about Orb and wants to come here, but of course it's off-limits to tourists—even operant ones."

"How long do service personnel contract for?" Anne asked the woman curiously.

The server sighed. "Only three hundred days for most jobs. I hope they change that eventually. I would love to re-up when this tour is finished, even though my husband can hardly wait to get back to Paris. But life is so much more exciting here, especially now that humanity will be taking its place in the Concilium." She lowered her voice. "And salaries in Orb are triple those of the Human Polity worlds, and of course we normals have the same shopping privileges that operant bureaucrats do. We can also use the same artistic and cultural and recreational facilities as the magnates and their operant assistants—if we want to."

"*Do* you want to?" Marc asked.

The woman eyed him shrewdly. "Not always, no. And we are very glad to be able to live in our own nonoperant neighborhoods within the ethnic enclaves. One is always most comfortable amongst one's own kind, n'est-ce pas?"

Marc said, "Mais naturellement, madame. Vous m'en direz tant."

She uttered a happy cry. "You *do* know French after all, young Franco-American! Épatant!"

"Only a little. My great-granduncle taught me."

"And is he here with you?" the smiling woman inquired.

"No." Marc looked away, his face now expressionless.

The waitron tucked her big tray under her arm and began to move away from their table. "Eh bien. Bon appétit, and have a nice day."

For many minutes, Marc and Anne ate in silence. When she had finished the second of her croissants, she said, "If there was a very good reason for it, you could call your grandfather on the subspace communicator and arrange for a head-sked on intimate mode. His farspeech would have no difficulty reaching the four thousand light-years from here to Earth."

"Why would I want to talk to Grandpère?" Marc finished the last of the hot chocolate and licked the foam from his lips. It had been served in an incongruous large cup of thin china, but it was whisked perfectly, with honey and vanilla and a hint of cinnamon.

"I know you're not that close to Denis. But if there was any . . . serious family business you had to discuss with someone on Earth, any matters you had to arrange, he would be the one to call on."

"I'll keep it in mind." Marc pushed the empty cup away and laid his knife and fork parallel across his plate. "Will we have to begin work right away?"

Anne smiled. "Not really, although I do want to drop in at our offices today. What did you have in mind? Sightseeing?"

"I'd like to check the place out. Just prowl around. Twenty-three days in the gray limbo didn't do my nerves any good."

"I can certainly vouch for that!" Anne consulted her wrist-com. "We've been invited to dinner tonight at 1930 hours by Kyle Macdonald and his wife Mary Gawrys, over in Lomond Enclave. You remember them, don't you?"

Marc nodded. "He's the science fiction writer, she's the European IA. Uncle Rogi told me that he introduced them. I tried some of Macdonald's plaques, but the stuff was pretty wild and implausible."

"I hope you'll keep your literary criticism to yourself at dinner. Now: If I let you run loose today, will you promise to work on the Paliuli housing tomorrow? It's going to be very difficult to get anything decent on the beach. I've heard the Russians have tried to hog all the best places."

Marc's gray eyes were alight. "Just let me have some time to myself today, and tomorrow you can ask me anything!"

Anne laughed. "Off with you, then. Just don't get into anything you can't get out of."

He flung his napkin onto the table and almost upset the wrought-iron chair as he sprang to his feet and hurried off across the terrace. There was a tube entrance a hundred meters away from the restaurant, next to the boulangerie, and he forced himself to slow down and walk to it, turning once to wave over his shoulder to Anne, who was drinking another cup of coffee and watching him with an expression that betrayed considerable anxiety. Then he plunged down the steps into a glowing glassy gut that was a shocking departure from the folksy charm of the French enclave. He caught an inertialess capsule almost immediately and headed for the outermost level of the colossal cerametal planetoid—and the Orb Spaceport.

For over four hours, Marc sat quietly on a bench in the Human Terminal, letting his farsight and other ultrasenses roam, absorbing all of the formalities of departure to be certain that he would make no mistakes. He studied the ticketing procedure, the quarantine setup, the rather casual way the smaller private superluminal craft were boarded, even the way the exotic ground crews serviced the ships of the Human Polity in the docking bays.

This time he was ready to break whatever laws it took to get him back to Earth. But how to do it?

He could easily coerce his way on board a big passenger ship and brainwipe the coercees—provided none of them was masterclass. But when he disappeared, Anne would be bound to send out a subspace squawk on him, so that was out. He could use his creativity to disguise himself or go invisible, then stow away; but she'd still have the Magistratum waiting Earthside to check out arriving ships from Orb, and a Grand Master exotic cop would see through any attempted mental camouflage of his like a plate-glass window.

Okay, what was left?

Use his coercion to hijack a very small ship. One of those executive hoppers with a crew of three. There was a Caledonian jobbie over in Bay 638 that checked out as a likely prospect. Disable its communications and beacons. Mind-fuck the crew just short of imbecility once they put the ship on course, popping in and out of hyperspace. Sleep only while the ship was traveling its catenary in the gray limbo. And none of your bunny-hopping 180 df this trip; push the displacement factor to 250 or even higher. *He'd* have no trouble taking the pain of tight-leash translations through the upsilon-field. If the crew wonked out from overload, they'd be that much easier to handle. With luck, he could get home in two weeks, long before they'd expect him. He'd load up with food and get gone to B.C., and hide out with Mama and Uncle Rogi until it was safe to resurface.

If he pulled the trick off artfully, the family would probably even continue to cover up for him. Buying off the owner of the hijacked exec hopper and the crew would cost a bundle, but that was no big deal for the family corporation. Provided he didn't kill anybody.

He got up from the bench and bought himself a large Pepsi-Cola at a refreshment bar. Then, sipping it through a straw, he strolled casually to the feeder tunnel that would take him to Bay 638. The small-craft facilities were much less crowded than the main terminal area and the noncrew people hurrying along the tunnel tended to be earnest-looking business types in sober suits, carrying briefcases, or rumpled scientists meandering along, thinking great thoughts on declamatory mode. There were no young people about, and several passersby eyed him curiously as he stopped at the observation window overlooking Bay 638 and stood there drinking his Pepsi.

The display beside the access door told him that the ship was CSS Roderick Dhu, a twelve-passenger De Havilland S-211 out of Grampian Town, Caledonia, owned by Guinness PLC. Its EDT was about one hour from now.

Perfect! And the spacecraft was even a lineal descendant of the antique Beaver floatplane that had carried him, his mother, and Uncle Rogi into the Megapod Reserve!

"Seems almost like fate, doesn't it?" an adult voice remarked.

Marc whirled about, his heart pounding. He had been aware of no one approaching him, sensed no aura. But he had company. Standing close behind him was a very tall elderly man with a neatly trimmed white beard and a patriarchal halo of snowy hair. He wore floor-length blue garments in a style that Marc could not immediately identify as typical of any ethnic group. His eyes had a preternatural brightness, set deep within dark sockets.

Marc suspected immediately that he was not human. The mental signature was totally absent, even to a third-level probe delivered at point-blank range. But what kind of exotic was he? The Krondaku were known to assume illusory bodies sometimes, especially when they undertook sociological research or other work among humanity that depended upon an unobtrusive or nonthreatening presence. A Krondak Grand Master would be able to suppress his aura beyond the reach of any human-generated redactive probe . . . and the Magistratum had a disproportionate number of the frightful, supremely intelligent beings on its roster.

The cup of Pepsi trembled in Marc's hand as he turned, his mental screen strengthened to the maximum. "Excuse me. What did you say?"

"I said nothing special. I implied a great deal."

Marc grinned and shrugged. "Sorry. I don't understand. I was just looking this ship over."

"Wondering whether the crew would use this access door or the one down in the bay to board her. The answer to that is: neither. They've just been notified that they can't return to Caledonia today after all. A small problem with the environmental system. But you needn't start looking for another ship."

"Oh," said Marc. Oh, Jesus—the exotics were on to him. He had been so sure that his secret thoughts were beyond their reach, so sure that he'd pulled the wool over their eyes during the interrogation. But they'd only bided their time! Some giant brain had been reading his mind, probably from the moment he arrived in Orb, and knew all about—

"Your scheme to pinch the ship. Oh, yes. It would probably have worked, too, if you were able to control the coercive-redactive ream precisely enough to avoid permanent mental damage to the crew. I'm not sure you're up to that yet. But the point is moot. There's no need for you to go back to Earth. The two of them will survive without your help."

"Who will?" he whispered. But he knew.

"Off we go," said the disguised exotic briskly. "Don't waste time."

A heroic form of metacoercivity took hold of Marc. He had never experienced anything like it. He wasn't a child hurried along by a stronger adult; he was a mosquito borne along by a gale. As he walked helplessly alongside his captor, heading back toward the main terminal, Marc managed to look more carefully at the face of the person beside him. "Do—do I know you?"

The tall man laughed but did not answer the question.

"What do you want?" Marc asked.

"I want you to take a hike, kiddo. Get the hell out of this terminal and don't come back until you're ready to go home."

"Am I under arrest?"

"No. Providing you haul your young ass out of here and don't try pulling a stunt like this again. You do, and I'll see that you come down with the galloping shits and spend the time from now until Inauguration Day in the hospital. The *pediatric* hospital. You'll like it. The bed gowns have Walt Disney characters printed on them."

Marc was dumfounded. This was a *Krondaku?* He sure as hell didn't talk like one! But whoever this guy was, he was no Enforcer of the Magistratum. He was somebody else—playing games! Somebody who obviously knew all about Mama and Uncle Rogi . . .

Marc felt the anger that had blazed within him drain away. A sudden, awful suspicion gripped his heart. "Are you *him?* Vic . . . ?"

"I have nothing to do with Victor Remillard or his creatures," the being said. "But you're quite right to keep the possibility in mind. They pose a rather serious threat to the good order of the Galactic Milieu. They're damn near as dangerous as *you.*"

The two of them had entered the busy terminal. Marc's mind spun as he was compelled to walk directly to the tube entrance. His mind began to shout: *Who are you who are you who are you?* He was aware that the telepathic scream went no further than the boundary of his own skull.

Side by side, the disoriented boy and the tall man stood waiting for a transport capsule. In one last futile attempt to break the coercion, Marc had managed to drop his nearly empty cup of cola, scattering bits of crushed ice all over the capsule platform.

"You'll find out who I am eventually," his captor said. "Just remember what I told you. I wasn't joking about incapacitating you if you make trouble . . . Here's your capsule. It's been very interesting talking to you face-to-face, but now—get lost."

A big hand took hold of Marc's shoulder with a painfully strong grip and thrust him unceremoniously into the open hatch. "I'm sending you to Carioca Enclave. Colorful as all get-out, but don't lose track of time and turn up late for dinner, or your Aunt Anne will be more than a little pissed. Au revoir, kiddo."

The hatch slammed, and the capsule shot into the glowing purple rho-field of the tubeway, whisking Marc away at 6000 kph. Unifex's smile faded, and he shook his head. Then with a gesture he cleaned up the ice and the rest of the mess and went back into the terminal. He had decided to have a Pepsi himself before he dematerialized.

[17]

FROM THE MEMOIRS
OF ROGATIEN REMILLARD

I said nothing to Teresa about the telepathic bolt from the blue, that furious farspoken blast on my intimate mode that Denis had broadcast over the entire planet Earth and God knew how many parsecs of interstellar space, calling my name. The thing hit me with the impact of a punch in the stomach and I had responded with an involuntary mental grunt. But I clammed up immediately thereafter, and I was certain that Denis hadn't been able to fix my position . . . yet. Many times during the following weeks at Ape Lake I lay half awake, momentarily expecting my mind's ear to hear the precisely directed mindspeech of my foster son, telling me that his seekersense had found our hideout at last. But it didn't come, and I finally convinced myself that Denis wouldn't find us, and neither would anybody else—not until young Jack was born, and the Remillard Dynasty was safely inaugurated into the Concilium, and Teresa and I were safe from the clutches of the law, and we all lived happily ever after.

It took two months for us to finish repairing our rustic home and get it ready for winter. The tree felling and carpentry were made almost pleasurable by that miracle machine the woodzapper, which I thanked God (and Matsushita Industries) for almost daily as I worked on the cabin and its furniture. When I was a youth, I had used a device called a chain saw, which was a wonderful improvement over chopping or sawing wood by hand. But even small chain saws were awkward and dangerous to use, were fueled by petrochemicals, and needed frequent sharpening. In contrast, the woodzapper was a lightweight wonder. In place of the chain saw's oval guidebar, it had a business end that looked something like the capital D frame of a large hacksaw, but without the blade. When you switched the thing on, a thin bar of coherent golden light closed the gap. This photonic beam (so the instructions assured me) "would slice through the most dense varieties of wood like tofu." And it did, too, exploding the cells of green wood with a great blast of steam and yielding a smooth raw surface that seemed almost to have been sanded. Dry wood had a residual thin layer of charring after being zapped, but I used hardly any of that in my construction.

Notching logs was a breeze with that sweet little woodzapper, and one of the most tedious parts of log-cabin making—cutting boards— was almost like slicing bread. You could debark a log with the zapper as quick as peeling a carrot, and cut and split billets of fire-wood as fast as you could wave your arm. The only thing you had to remember was to wear the protective face shield and gloves, and keep your bare skin out of range of the cloud of hot sawdust. The device was powered by one of the ubiquitous small D-type fusion cells that had been part of the Milieu's answer to Earth's energy hunger, and it was guaranteed to operate for some two hundred hours before need-ing a fuel refill. I loved that woodzapper dearly, and it worked like a charm up until the fateful day of 19 October, when I forgot to press the STANDBY button after knocking off work. The overnight tempera-ture outside on the porch where I had left the zapper fell well below freezing, turning the D-water inside the machine's integral fusion unit to ice and ruining it. Fortunately, the construction work was nearly finished by then; but from that time on I had to split firewood with an axe.

The flights of migratory birds began early in October, and often at night we would hear them calling as they winged southward, especially when the moon was bright. The geese and tundra swans hooted and blatted and honked as they flew; but the trumpeter swans made glorious music, like an airborne squadron of French-horn players, and sent Teresa into raptures. She managed to reproduce their calls with her electronic keyboard and composed a "Swan Sonata" that sounded rather good to me—although she deprecated it as too derivative of Sibelius and Rachmaninoff.

On 21 October the first feathery flakes of snow fell, whitening the heights of Mount Mutt and Mount Jeff across the slowly freezing lake but accumulating less than a couple of centimeters around our cabin. The sun came out immediately afterward, creating a sparkling wonderland until most of the snow melted; but I was in no mood to join Teresa in her celebration of the beauty of it all. The first appearance of the white stuff only served to remind me that I had forgotten to bring snowshoes, and without them we would be unable to move away from the cabin when the really heavy snow arrived.

I made two stout wooden snow shovels at once, then consulted the reference flecks for a suitable snowshoe pattern. The ones I had used back home in New England had been of the classic Maine pattern, wide and quite large, with long tails, having ashwood frames and rawhide webbing. (Decamole would not be invented for another fifty years.) The Maine shoes were devils to use in brushy or steep terrain, which Ape Lake had plenty of, and I decided to make the more compact, rounded style called "bear paws" instead. The only flexible hardwood available for the frames was a kind of shrubby willow. I feared that the thicker sticks would break under my weight once the wood dried, and so I lashed together four much narrower withes with wire to give the outer framing and crosspieces the extra strength of lamination, then webbed them with stout cord. This webbing would be much less efficient than rawhide, which was nearly indestructible and did not stretch; but so far we had seen neither moose nor caribou in the region, and only the hides of these large animals would have been strong enough to make suitable babiche thongs.

I expected to have to use the improvised shoes only in the immediate vicinity of the cabin, digging us out after storms and doing chores. It never occurred to me that those crudely made snowshoes would one day make the difference between our living or starving to death.

In the early weeks, when it seemed that we had all the food in the world, the only animals Teresa considered fair game were the snowshoe hares. These creatures, which were brown-furred when we arrived at Ape Lake and became pure white except for black-tipped ears as the season advanced, were at first very numerous on the lightly wooded slopes above the cabin and easily taken in wire snares. Teresa not only caught and cooked the hares; she also skinned them to a special purpose.

After I completed the new floor for our home, Teresa had made floor mats from part of the ten meters of wide wool duffel cloth we had bought. A couple more meters of the stuff were earmarked for childbirth supplies, and there was enough left to make a single narrow mattress pad for each bed. But she fretted that we might not be warm enough, even with our sleeping bags and the down comforter and the pads, when the temperature dropped far below zero. Then she happened to read in one of the woodcraft references how the Indians had made robes by weaving strips of rabbitskin. She decided to make fur blankets in the same way, and set about immediately snaring the unfortunate snowshoe hares without mercy, extending her trapline in all directions. Her scheme eventually yielded two sizable blankets (fragile but luxuriant) and a small fur robe to wrap the baby in.

From September until late October we dined on sautéed hare, roast hare, hare cutlets, civet of hare, hare pie, southern-fried hare, blanquette of hare, ragout of hare, hare ravioli, fricassée of hare, hasenpfeffer, pasta with hare sauce, and hare soup with bannock croutons. Finally a diminishing bunny population and the increasing awkwardness of her pregnancy brought her trapping career to an end. To this day, the mere mention of any dish containing rabbit turns my complexion green.

In its finished state, our cabin on Ape Lake was about 4.5 meters square. Teresa had rechinked the old log walls tightly with moss and mud. The new roof was constructed on a framework of log beams which I had hoisted into place with the come-along, suspended from a three-legged tripod. I nailed close-set poles onto the beams, overlaid them with plass sheeting for waterproofing, then nailed down a second layer of stringers and poles chinked with moss. Teresa and I capped the whole lashup with the old shingles, plus some new ones I had made. I was bound and determined that *this* roof would not collapse, no matter how heavy the snowpack. The roof overhung a small porch that ran along the eastward-facing side of the cabin. I cut more poles and enclosed most of the porch with a windbreak so that snow would not blow in each time we opened the door.

Here is a diagram of the interior of the birthplace of Saint Jack the Bodiless:

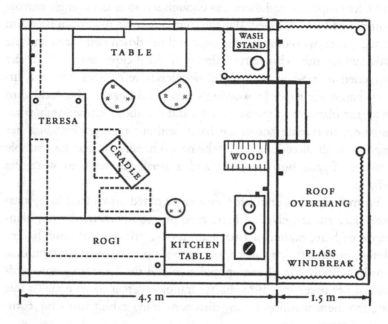

APE LAKE CABIN
October 2051

Both bunks were wooden frames with rope-webbing "springs," the longer one being mine. They stood high above the floor for the sake of warmth, and we stowed items underneath them and on shelves built above.

Teresa had patiently scraped most of the rust off the cast-iron stove with grit, and we stood it upon a shallow bed of small stones covered with glacial-silt "cement." Fortunately, the stovepipe sections were sound, as were the damper and roofplate. Being familiar with the dire effects of carbon monoxide in small shelters (a second cousin had perished that way in an ice-fishing shack on Lake Winnipesaukee), I sealed the pipe joints carefully with Pyron duct tape.

We discarded the earlier, crudely made furniture, and I managed to make some rather nifty new pieces with the woodzapper before its untimely demise. It could be manipulated with considerable delicacy once you had a bit of practice. A large table and the smaller kitchen worktable were fastened to the walls and had shelves above them. Most of Teresa's musical things were stored beneath the large table, as was the sophisticated little hydrogen-fueled fusion power-supply (incompatible with the woodzapper, alas!) that operated her equipment, the stereo unit, the Tri-D, our two lamps, and the microwave.

I crafted two "uneasy" chairs, which Teresa fitted with moss-packed pads on the seat, arms, and back. A stool near the beds also served as a nightstand. I built a slew of wanigan storage boxes (we had brought in all our food from the cache), more shelves, a washstand, a woodbox, and a cradle—which was nothing but another box on tall legs. Our bathroom was the small area adjacent to the front door, where I hung the old Porta-Shower pouch from my camping equipment. Teresa curtained it with cotton flannelette from the bolt we had brought. The single window, facing the lake, had a movable shutter hinged at the top that we sometimes lowered over the glass at night and when the wind blew strongly from the north. I was very proud of the shutter hinges, which I had to whittle with a jackknife. We had found serviceable iron hinges and a latch for the front door buried beneath the derelict cabin floor.

Our cabin acquired a family of wood mice as soon as we brought food inside. The wretched little creatures lived under the new floorboards and became terrible pests, attacking our food supplies and even shredding one of my wool socks to make a nest . . . until a beautiful little ermine—snow white with a black tailtip and black eyes—showed up and made short work of them. The ermine was ridiculously tame and eventually came to treat our cabin as his private stamping grounds. I was surprised at his friendliness, for I thought all creatures of the weasel family were vicious. Teresa called him Herman and gave him bits of Spam as a reward for exterminating the mice; and when she played her keyboard and sang softly to unborn Jack late in the evening, the little beast would lurk behind the woodbox, listening, with its beady eyes aglitter.

The cabin was complete by 23 October. I had mounted the snowshoes, the axes, the saw, and the rifle on the wall outside—which gave the place a fine coureur de bois air—and above the door, on a peg, I stuck up a bear skull I had found, for a totem. We looked forward to showing the cabin off to Marc when he arrived with the additional supplies of food. Ape Lake was beginning to freeze over already, but I assured Teresa that the antique Beaver aeroplane would be able to land and take off just as easily on skis as it had on floats.

That final week in October was our first opportunity to really relax. Now that there were no more construction noises, the place reassumed its mantle of profound peacefulness during the day as well as at night. We had a brief Indian summer when it was warm enough for us to potter about in our shirtsleeves—blissfully free of the insects, who had died with the first hard frost, along with the woodzapper.

On the twenty-ninth we undertook one of Teresa's favorite hikes, moving westward along the southern lakeshore as far as the lateral moraine of Ape Glacier, where a brawling torrent dropped steeply down Mount Jacobsen. The moraine stream had shrunk since the last time we had seen it, two weeks earlier. The glacier that fed it was congealing with winter cold, and soon our own little Megapod Creek and all the other cascades rushing into the basin would dwindle away, and we would have to take our water from the lake.

On our Indian summer walk we saw only the friendly whisky-jack birds, some spruce grouse, and the trail of a small wolf in some unmelted snow beneath the gnarled trees. We always kept a sharp eye out for the elusive Bigfeet, but we had found no footprints other than the single one I had seen. The only other trace of the primates had been a faint, rank stench occasionally borne toward us from the foot of the lake on the rare easterly breezes. I remembered Arôme de Sasquatch from my previous encounter with the creatures and had alerted Teresa to its significance, but no Bigfeet had ever appeared.

When I awoke on the morning of 30 October, our cabin was very cold. The bucket of water on the unlit stove was skimmed with ice, and I cursed under my breath as I made up the morning fire with stiffened fingers. Outside, clouds of deep gray hung low, and snow was sifting down thickly through the dead-calm air. These flakes were unlike the tentative, feathery ones that had fallen earlier; they were small, and one had the impression that they intended to keep on falling for a good long time. There was already about 15 centimeters' worth on the ground outside, and I could see that the lake was frozen at last from shore to shore, a level expanse of purest white.

I let Teresa sleep on. When the fire was going well, I bundled up and slipped outside. The snow shovels were ready on the porch, and it was an easy matter to clear paths to Le Pavillon and the latrine. I brought quantities of split dry and green wood to the porch (one required the first for proper cooking and the second for maintaining heat), then took the smaller axe and an empty bucket with a rope on it from the porch and went down the path to the shore. The ice round about the little rock jetty I had built was only a couple of centimeters thick. I broke it easily and scooped up a pailful of milky water. Now that the silt-laden streams had ceased to flow, the lake water would begin to clear. I stood looking out over the lake for some time.

There was no sound except the gentle hiss of falling snow. I could smell woodsmoke and frosty air. I was well dressed for winter in a down parka, heavy polypro pants, and felt-lined Pak boots. Up the slope behind me, the comfortably furnished little cabin was slowly warming, and in a few minutes I could go up and make a breakfast of scrambled powdered eggs and fried bacon and coffee, and share it with Teresa. Her fey mannerisms and innocent carelessness no longer troubled me. Keeping her out of trouble and advising her in the ways of the wilderness made me think of the time more than eighty years before when I had been the best friend and metapsychic mentor of baby Denis. He had depended upon me in order to survive, and so did Teresa now. Having been a loner for so long, I had forgotten what a great satisfaction it was to be needed by another human being.

Two, actually.

After breakfast Teresa would do the dishes and get the sourdough bread ready to rise. She might put beans on the back of the stove in the Dutch oven, where they would cook all day. If I felt like it, I could watch an old movie on the Tri-D or read a plaque-book or wash my socks. Teresa might practice silently on her keyboard, using the earphones, or sew baby clothes. Then we might play poker, using dry beans for chips, and the greasy old deck of miniature cards that I always kept stowed in my Kelty pack's lower right pocket. Or she might work on one of her musical compositions while I brought my plaque-journal up to date; I'd neglected it, working twelve or fourteen hours a day getting the cabin finished.

Time had raced by. Next week would mark the halfway point in our sojourn at Ape Lake. Teresa was healthy and happy, full of a naïve certainty that Jack's birth would rekindle Paul's love. The prodigious fetus was seven months alive, apparently thriving and learning about the world through ultrasenses and through his mother's borrowed faculties in the mysterious way unborn operant babies do.

And I was surprised to realize that I was enjoying life immensely. I was fit and strong again, feeling like a forty-year-old, and of the six bottles of 151-proof rum I had bought in Williams Lake, five and a half remained.

When he showed up in the Beaver with the rest of our food, Marc was going to be mighty proud of his old Uncle Rogi.

[18]

HANOVER, NEW HAMPSHIRE, EARTH
31 OCTOBER 2051

The Great Enemy had unexpectedly accepted an invitation to speak at a symposium on Milieu politics at Dartmouth College, and there was to be an informal dinner party for him and two other distinguished symposium speakers at the President's House on that same evening—on Halloween.

It was too good an opportunity for Fury to miss.

Who would pay any attention if the Hydra prowled the landscaped grounds around the college president's mansion on this festive New England night of nights? All of Greek Row was throwing impromptu bashes. Half the undergraduates were roaming around the campus in costume, as were the town youngsters—most especially the operants—playing trick-or-treat and having no scruples at all about ringing the president's doorbell and the bells of the frat-sor houses. There was a certain risk, bringing Hydra into the open; but it just might be possible to put Davy MacGregor out of the game now, right here on Earth, rather than waiting until the Magnate-Designates were assembled on Concilium Orb.

Fury had decided to risk it.

The night was crisply chilly and clear, and it was nearly 2130 hours before the Hydra arrived. It flitted across the moonlit lawn toward the President's House with Fury watching from above. The windows of the stately Georgian-style dwelling were all ablaze, and the front door was flanked with sheaves of cornstalks and a collection of glowing jack-o'-lanterns. There were three groundcars parked along the drive, together with a small rhocraft having both Polity Capital and Lothian registration. MacGregor lived in Edinburgh when he wasn't on deck down in Concord at Europa Tower.

<So you're finally here. It took you long enough.>

FurydearestalmightyFury don't be mad I'm sorry I came asfastas I could putmyselftogether—

<Never mind. You feeling in top shape?>

Oh yesyesYES!

<I may be able to let you do it tonight sweet little Hydra.>

Do it? You mean really DO IT AGAIN?

<If conditions are favorable. Only then! I'll have to decide and *you* will have to obey.>

Yesyesyes but *please* letme pleasepleaseplease IT WAS SO WON-DERFUL IT MADE ME GROW!!

<Silence! *Absolute* mental silence from now on! Everyone at this dinner party except the president and his wife are powerful operants. If you're detected—if anyone gets the least notion who you are and what you're up to—you're to zorch on out of here screened so tightly you're bugfucking invisible! Do you understand?>

[Assent.]

<Study the metapsychic armamentaria of *both* MacGregor and his wife Margaret Strayhorn while they're finishing their meal. Then come to the front of the house and wait in the shrubbery near the library windows until I give the word.>

[Assent.]

Three little children in costume came romping up the drive, giggling and squealing. They were nonoperant and had no idea that the Hydra was watching them from the shelter of the bushes. The children rang the bell, and one of the president's adolescent daughters opened the door.

The youngsters yelled, "Trick or treat!" The president's daughter dispensed candy bars, which the kids tucked into their loot bags. Then they dashed away to try the Sigma Nu Delta house.

Thoughtfully, Fury followed them for a few minutes with its far-sight, mulling over the startling new idea that had occurred to it that afternoon.

Davy MacGregor was going to be a far more formidable opponent than Brett McAllister had been. Fury's own cautious appraisal during the political symposium had confirmed certain suspicions: Over the past year—and especially since his second marriage, nine months earlier—the Great Enemy had changed and had probably become too strong for the still inexpert Hydra to damage significantly—much less kill. Davy MacGregor had been transformed from a morose and aging widower of sixty-five into a rejuvenated operant stalwart. He had gone into the regen-tank before Margaret Strayhorn had finally agreed to marry him, and now he once again looked like what he had been in his youth, the champion caber-thrower at the annual Caledonian Games, tall and dark-haired, with snapping black eyes and a snowplow jaw decorated at the sides with archaic dundreary whiskers. Davy was also deeply in love with this new wife of his; and romantic passion, as so often seemed to happen among humans, had augmented his already powerful creative metafunction. But there were other ways for Fury to deal with the Great Enemy besides the obvious one.

The new wife herself presented one attractive option.

Socorro Ortega was very good at her job, which was officially listed in the employment roster of Dartmouth as "First Lady to the President of the College." She was compensated with a salary equivalent to that of a full professor and worked a good deal harder than most academics did, serving as the official hostess (and unofficial mother confessor) of the institution, as well as being the president's wife and the co-parent of their children. More often than she liked, she was also called upon to defuse potentially disastrous social situations, among which this Halloween dinner for the operants certainly qualified.

Ordinarily, the first lady had no qualms about entertaining the human metapsychic elite, though some highly educated "normals" did have. Why, nearly a tenth of the Dartmouth faculty were operants, and most of them were sedulously agreeable people who would never dream of condescending to nonoperants. But human metas nonetheless possessed the same frailties as the rest of the race, and therein lurked the challenge that Socorro Ortega had faced—and bested—tonight.

Her husband, President Tom Spotted Owl, had once been a student of Davy MacGregor's in Edinburgh, before the Scotsman (who was the only son of the famous Jamie MacGregor and a celebrity in his own right) had given up the teaching of xenopsychology to serve in the

European Intendancy. When an important speaker at the symposium on Milieu politics had fallen ill the day before the event, Tom had prevailed upon his old mentor to egg up from Concord and fill in, and so both of the principal candidates for First Magnate of the Human Polity, David Somerled MacGregor and Paul Remillard, lectured on their personal political philosophies on the same day. The result had been a public-relations triumph for the college, heavily covered by the media. The next afternoon, which was Halloween, a mated pair of distinguished psychopoliticians of the Amalgam of Poltroy had joined the two human Magnate-Designates on a brilliant (and often contentious) panel that was bound to keep the dovecote of political science aflutter for months to come.

It was Tom who had decided at the last minute that Davy and his wife Margaret must also attend the little informal dinner at the President's House that was being given for the two Poltroyans, who were newly installed visiting fellows at the college. The first lady had agreed; but without thinking through the more subtle repercussions, she had decided that Paul Remillard should be invited, too. Paul was not an old friend of Tom and Socorro's, as was Davy MacGregor; neither she nor her husband was particularly fond of the dashing Intendant Associate, whose media popularity and fierce loyalty to the Galactic Milieu were somewhat at odds with his reputation for sexual adventurism. But the college could not afford to snub Paul, either. He was one of Dartmouth's most famous alumni, and he would expect to be invited to the dinner if MacGregor was.

And so the invitations to MacGregor and his wife were conveyed by the first lady personally to Seuss Auditorium, where the symposium was being held, and were accepted. But when Socorro went in search of Paul, she happened upon the two Poltroyans in the participants' lounge and blithely mentioned the expanded guest list for dinner. To her dismay, she met with distressed hemming and hawing and finally a "sudden indisposition" on the part of the female exotic that precluded their attending the dinner after all.

The president's wife was no mind reader, but she was an experienced diplomat. She quickly ascertained through a sympathetic third party what the problem was: Paul Remillard's inseparable female companion all throughout the symposium had been none other than that puta callejera Laura Tremblay, the wife of Paul's perennially cuckolded colleague, Intendant Associate Rory Muldowney! It was common knowledge that Paul and Laura had been intimately involved for more than a year. The two Poltroyan academics (especially the female, who was a keen devotee of human opera) had been scandalized by what they considered to be Paul's insensitive behavior following so closely upon Teresa Kendall's tragic death. It was instantly obvious to Socorro why the exotics had abruptly declined to attend the dinner she had planned in their honor. They were afraid Paul would bring along the lovely, round-heeled Laura. And he *would*, too—if Socorro did not find a way to outwit him.

¡Caracoles! Was Dartmouth College to insult the kindly (and anthropophilic) Poltroyans merely for the sake of Paul Remillard's insatiable cojones?

Then a brilliant thought struck Socorro. Instead of a dinner for eight, the Dartmouth president and first lady would host a dinner for ten. Socorro quickly phoned Lucille Cartier, begged for her help in the emergency, and obtained it. Later, when the first lady finally managed to corner Paul alone and give him his invitation, she mentioned that she had also invited his parents, and "wondered" demurely if he would like to bring his godmother, Dartmouth's Emeritus Professor of Human Genetics Colette Roy, as his dinner companion. Socorro and Tom were *so* fond of Colette, and they had not seen her in quite some time . . .

After an instant's hesitation, the outmaneuvered Paul had agreed. Whereupon the first lady had recontacted the Poltroyans, begging them to reconsider, mentioning casually that Paul would be squiring the venerable Professor Roy. The exotic couple reaccepted with alacrity, and Socorro was finally able to tell Tom that all was in order.

From the beginning, the dinner party had every indication of being a notable success. Paul and his rival for the office of First Magnate put aside the political differences that had provoked fireworks at the symposium and confined their audible conversation, at least, to innocuous chitchat. Denis Remillard was happily renewing his old friendship with Davy MacGregor and charming the socks off Margaret Strayhorn. The diminutive mauve-skinned Poltroyans, looking almost like bald-headed Earth children costumed for Halloween in their bejeweled exotic robes, turned out to be hilarious raconteurs of exotic political shenanigans. And Lucille, whose faculty parties had been legendary when Tom Spotted Owl was no more than a lowly assistant professor of political science at Dartmouth and Socorro a doe-eyed undergraduate from Campeche, had been lavish in her praise of Socorro's recent redecoration of the President's House.

It was, the first lady thought happily, going to be a night to remember.

In the plant room, where the dinner was in progress, Tom and Socorro and their eight guests were seated on white iron chairs around a large round glass-topped table. Brightly colored chrysanthemums and asters growing in black Oaxaca pots were combined with great stoneware vases of flaming maple leaves to make a display around the diners that almost, in Lucille Cartier's opinion, crossed the bounds of good taste.

Or am I just being bourgeois? Lucille thought. Or could it be a touch of indigestion? (The fish had been so terribly spicy.) But everyone except for her seemed to be enjoying the dinner tremendously. The panel with Davy and Paul and the Poltroyans this afternoon had evidently been a smashing success, and there wasn't the least hint of enmity between the two men tonight. Why, then, did she have this feeling that something awful was about to happen?

The first lady had arranged a meal in a pre-Conquest Meso-American mode. The exotic couple, Fritiso-Prontinalin and Minatipa-Pinakrodin ("Call us Fred and Minnie"), and the visitors from Scotland had gone into raptures over the fish in annatto-pepper sauce, the mole de poblano, the tortillas, rice, frijoles, and the accompanying guacamole sauce. Denis and Paul made positive pigs of themselves, especially over the Mayan-style fish, which Socorro had prepared herself from an old family recipe. But Lucille had only toyed with the highly spiced food, having felt unaccountably queasy all during the day because of the maliferous vibes that seemed to pervade the aether. When she and Denis had suddenly received the invitation to dine at the President's House, Lucille had almost declined; but she had not wanted to let Socorro down, and she was also curious to meet Margaret Strayhorn, a powerful operant whom Davy had recently married, after being widowed for over thirty years. Lucille had steeled herself and accepted.

But now she bespoke her son Paul, seated at her left, on his intimate mode:

Darling can you manage a quickie redact of your poor old mother? I'm feeling just the least bit delicate in the head and tummy.

[Sympathy.] Is that better?

Much. Are you aware of any peculiar disruptions in the mental lattices today? Sunspots or supernovae or anything?

No. I'm only rather surprised that Davy and I are getting on so well. He came at me hammer and tongs during the discussion this afternoon. The audience just loved it, too—especially when Davy castigated me and the other North American Intendants for not taking a stronger stand against the thousand-day probation period summarily imposed by the Lylmik. There's nothing the academic crowd likes better than to see a bigwig politico savaged with style by one of their own. Even one of their ex-own! Davy MacGregor seems to think that if the Remillard family members had withdrawn en masse as Magnate-Designates, then the Human Polity would have been admitted to the Concilium without condition. We Remillards are suspicious characters in exotic eyes, you see, holding back Galactic Humanity through our dynastic hubris.

Oh my dear. But that's so unfair! The Lylmik never *asked* you to resign.

On the contrary. It was made quite clear that the Remillards were to remain on the roster of the Designated and I was to continue my campaign for First Magnate—

"Our dessert tonight will be something very special," Socorro Ortega announced, as the dinner plates were being cleared away. "They are sapote-pietos, tiny blue persimmons that my sister picked earlier today in her garden down in Mérida, in the Yucatán, and sent to me on the XP shuttle to Boston. I hope you'll all enjoy them."

There were dutiful exclamations of appreciation from around the table. Lucille found the sweetness of the little fruits to be almost cloying, but she ate them resolutely while the Poltroyan called Fred, sitting on her right, told her how much he and his mate were going to enjoy being visiting fellows at Dartmouth College.

"The countryside with its sugar maples is extraordinarily beautiful now," Minnie said, her ruby eyes twinkling with enthusiasm. "I can scarcely think of any other place in the Galaxy where the changing of the seasons proclaims itself so vividly." She sat on the opposite side of the table, between Tom Spotted Owl and Davy MacGregor, looking almost doll-like next to the burly Native American and the rangy Scot. Both Poltroyan sexes had hairless heads, but the females painted their shapely purplish skulls with elaborate designs in gold paint. "We are also greatly looking forward to winter here, which will be so much more like the climate on our native world. Fred and a colleague actually did pre-Intervention research in this region of Earth, and he jumped at the chance to return here."

Fred said, "Our twin daughters will be joining us on campus beginning with the winter term. They've enrolled in several music courses, and they're eager to try human winter sports."

"How nice that your family can join you," Denis said. "Dartmouth has its own skiing facilities, you know. Both alpine and cross-country. And there's a college ice hockey team, and toboggan races, and dogsledding and skating, and even an ice-cycle racing event on the frozen river that my grandson Marc has been dying to enter. But he's only a freshman, and so he'll have to wait until next winter."

"Ice-cycle racing? I don't believe that I am familiar with that particular sport," Fred said.

Paul Remillard frowned into his dessert dish. "It can be quite dangerous, and that's undoubtedly why my son wants to participate. The motorcycles are high-powered, heavily built machines, and the wheels are shod with steel spikes to grip the ice."

"Love's Oath!" Fred exclaimed. "This son of yours must be a very brave lad."

"Foolhardy might be a more apposite term." Paul nodded pleasantly to the Poltroyan and turned away to converse with Margaret Strayhorn on his other hand.

Fred leaned close to the kind-faced Colette Roy, who sat at his right, and spoke very quietly. "Didn't I hear that one of Intendant Remillard's sons was—*oof!*" Too late, Minnie had delivered a sharp mental caution to her mate on his intimate mode.

But Colette only sighed. "That's the boy, I'm afraid. After he was acquitted, Paul sent him on to Orb for prudence's sake."

"The young man is said to be—uh—amazingly talented in the

higher mindpowers," Fred persisted, in spite of his mate's anxious looks, "as is his distinguished father, of course. Is it true that Intendant Remillard was the first human to be educated in the womb by means of the preceptorial techniques of the Milieu?"

Colette Roy nodded. "I had the honor of making the suggestion."

"Which is why you're my godmother," Paul said, showing snow-white teeth in a flashing smile. "With your work cut out for you, trying to keep me sinless and worthy!"

Denis said quickly, "Lucille and I had considered our family to be complete when we had six fine operant children. But Colette insisted that we make one more baby and teach him in utero more or less the way you Poltroyans teach your fetuses."

"I learned about the technique quite by accident a month or so after the Intervention," Colette said. "One of the Poltroyans in the local liaison group was pregnant. I'd had a hysterectomy years earlier after the birth of my son, so I put the proposal to Lucille and Denis. It seemed a marvelous research opportunity."

"Funny thing," Denis added. "My Uncle Rogi had made the very same suggestion to me less than a week earlier. God knows where *he* picked up the notion. He's only an antiquarian bookseller."

"The Milieu has cause to be very grateful to your vision, Dr. Roy," Fred said. "The book that resulted from the—uh—cooperative researches of Lucille Cartier and Denis Remillard proved to be seminal in human metapediatric studies."

"We humans have so much to thank Poltroyans for," Margaret Strayhorn said warmly. "You've always been so friendly and sympathetic to our race of primitives. You—you *humanized* the Galactic Milieu for us during the difficult Proctorship years. If we had had only the other exotic races as examples of Galactic citizenship, we might not have been able to persevere, to hold on to the belief that humanity really belongs among the coadunates of the Milieu. You're a rather daunting lot, you know."

"It seemed unfortunate to many of our people," Fred said, "that the Simbiari were appointed your Proctors rather than us! But one does not question the decisions of the Lylmik."

"Oh, yes one does," muttered Davy MacGregor.

Minnie, sitting next to him, smiled sweetly and said, "Humanity's ultimate mental potential is much stronger than ours, Intendant Mac-Gregor. We would not have been such stern taskmasters to you as the Simbiari, and no doubt the Lylmik took that into account."

"It's very fashionable to put down our Green Brethren," Colette said with some asperity. "I myself believe that the Simbiari did rather well at a thankless job—and at least they're humanoid. Would we rather have had those Krondak monsters riding herd on us?"

Several of the humans at the table winced.

"They proctored our Poltroyan race," Fred said. "Our legends say that we barely survived the terrible experience and achieved coadunation. We have empathized with your own racial distress because we feel closely related to you, having experienced an evolution that largely parallels yours, even to the aggressive impulses that once ruled us. This is why we have been eager to mitigate the severity of the Simbiari Proctorship whenever possible and to share with you our fetal educational techniques and other useful data. So you would not make the mistakes we made long ago when the Krondaku proc-tored us—"

"Or even fail," Minnie put in, her pretty little face somber, "as did the seventy-two luckless emergent races entrusted to our Poltroyan Proctorship."

"What happens to those who flunk out?" Tom Spotted Owl asked.

"They are isolated," Fred said sadly, "denied the superluminal trans-port system that makes travel among the stars practical. The gray limbo of hyperspace is patrolled by the Lylmik to ensure that the quarantine is kept. Most civilizations do not endure long after failing coadunation."

"This so-called coadunation." Denis leaned forward, his blazing blue eyes fixed on the male Poltroyan. "It actually *prevents* aggressive behavior and guarantees altruism?"

"After a time, yes. Once a race reaches its coadunate number and is thoroughly matured, the racial Mind as a whole attains Unity and rejects malignant aggression just as any highly complex system rejects disorganization. In an imperfectly Unified race such as the Simbiari, a certain number of—uh—maverick individuals may still be capable of antisocial behavior, but not the vast majority. The four elder races of the Milieu, being perfectly coadunate, also partake wholemind-edly of Unity—and this renders us incapable of any serious social sin.

Of course, we still manage to commit personal transgressions. Pride, despair, frivolity, that sort of thing."

"Fascinating," said Margaret Strayhorn. "And how amazing that we humans were brought into your Milieu while we're still so imperfect! Even with the new probationary period imposed upon our Concilium magnates, we're being given far more than we deserve."

"It was one of many decisions of the Lylmik in your favor," Minnie said, "in which we Poltroyans have always concurred without reservation."

Fred shrugged humorously. "And which the other coadunate races always opposed! But there you are."

Everybody laughed.

Davy MacGregor lifted his glass of Rioja Reserva. "Here's a toast to kind Poltroy! And to its reproductive physiology, so similar to ours, and its fetal education techniques, which we were able to borrow. But for them, we humans would have had to adapt the methods of the Simbiari."

"And for the next eight months," Margaret added, her face triumphant, "Davy and I would have had to pretend I was carrying a suboperant tadpole."

Everybody called out congratulations amid laughter, and they all drank to the Amalgam of Poltroy and to the embryo.

"Immature humans and Poltroyans may matriculate at Dartmouth," said Tom Spotted Owl solemnly, "but tadpoles, never." More laughter broke out.

"If everyone has finished dessert, perhaps we can have our café de olla in the living room," Socorro Ortega suggested. She explained to the Poltroyans, "The caffeine beverage is flavored with a spicy bark called cinnamon, and an aromatic semirefined sucrose called brown sugar is added to taste."

"It sounds delicious," Fred said. "The more sugar, the better!"

"He puts maple sugar in his soda pop," Minnie confided to Socorro, shaking her head. "And jam on his scrambled eggs, and he dips fried onion rings in honey."

But the president's wife was unfazed. "The next time you come to dine, I'll make a real treat for Fred: candied jalapeños."

As they all rose from the table and began to move slowly out of the plant room, Paul fell in beside Davy MacGregor and his wife. "Will you and Margaret and Will be traveling to Concilium Orb on the CSS Kungsholm with us, by any chance?"

"Why, no," Davy said. "That ship leaves on the seventeenth of November, doesn't she? The three of us and Will's wife are leaving day after tomorrow on the Aquitania. The ship's a bunny-hopper, though, and we actually arrive at Orb four days after you do, on sixth December."

Margaret Strayhorn gave a self-deprecating laugh. "I'm afraid I can't take ships with a high superluminal displacement factor. Even slow-track translations through the superficies into hyperspace make me feel dreadfully seedy, and now that I'm gravid I'll probably be even worse. It's a good thing that human magnates don't have to meet in Orb more often than twice a year—an Earth year, that is. Otherwise Davy would have to go along without me."

Davy MacGregor put a proprietary arm around his wife. "Not fewkin' likely."

Denis laughed. "Still on the honeymoon, I see."

"Now and for aye," growled Davy. "It wasn't the bloody regen-tank that rejuvenated me, it was Maggie. And I'll not be separated from her by the Concilium or Auld Clootie himself!"

Margaret shook her head in mock exasperation. She was tall and raven-haired, only thirty years old but already an Intendant Associate for Europe, like her husband. She had not been nominated to the Concilium, which seemed not to bother her in the least. "Davy, you are a darling idiot. What am I to do with him, Lucille?"

"Denis turned the magnateship down," the older woman said quietly. "It's hardly a disgrace." She left unsaid the fact that Paul would now probably be unopposed for First Magnate if Davy *had* declined. Only the son of Jamie MacGregor was deemed to be as fit as Paul Remillard to be humanity's first spokesman in the Galactic Concilium.

The dinner guests followed Socorro and Tom into the magnificent formal living room of the President's House, where chairs had been grouped around the great fireplace. A middle-aged woman in a dark dress and white apron was bringing in a coffee urn, and the president's daughter followed with a big tray of cups and saucers.

"This is Susan O'Brien, who made the mole de poblano we enjoyed tonight," Socorro said, "and her helper is our daughter, Maria Owl, who has been keeping the trick-or-treaters from storming the fort."

The guests all murmured appreciatively as they acknowledged the introductions. The president and first lady showed Davy and Margaret and the Poltroyans some of the antique treasures that graced the room, including the portrait of the second Mrs. Daniel Webster, an exquisite small sculpture by Jadwiga Majewska, and a number of pre-Columbian artworks from Dartmouth's collection that were on loan to the house.

The doorbell rang.

"Drat," said Maria Owl, who was serving the coffee. "Won't those kids ever give me a break?"

"Why not let me take care of them this time?" Margaret volunteered. She started for the front hall before Socorro or Tom could protest. "We have nothing quite like this at home in Scotland. It would be a pleasure."

"Oh, would you?" Maria said. "The candy bars are in a basket on the table by the door. One treat for each trickster, and if it's students, don't let them bully you into handing out more."

Margaret laughed. "No fear."

Although the outside porch lights were bright, the hall itself was rather dimly illuminated by a small crystal chandelier. Margaret Strayhorn picked up the basket and opened the heavy door.

Five children who looked to be ten or eleven years old stood there in an expectant line. There was a colonial miss in a domino mask, a Bugs Bunny, a heavily made-up witch, a pirate with an eye patch, and a clown-faced tramp. Margaret was charmed—and simultaneously surprised to note that all of the children were operant and their minds thickly screened.

"Trick or treat!" the youngsters said.

And Hydra struck.

Margaret Strayhorn was a strong-minded woman, especially in the metafaculties of coercion and creativity, and she had the advantage of a split second's worth of guarded surprise just as the Hydra focused its initial drain upon her crown chakra. This saved her life.

As her hair burst into flames Margaret gave a single piercing scream. At the same time she instinctively mustered her entire creative quotient into a self-preserving barricade. An instant later, she crumpled to the floor. The mental defense had drained all her strength.

By that time the others had come rushing into the entry hall. The front door was wide open on empty blackness. Margaret lay on her side with both arms crossed in front of her face, as if still warding off her attacker. The top of her scalp was scorched and smoking in a peculiar radially symmetrical pattern, as if some diabolical agent had momentarily impressed upon it an incendiary brand.

Stunned with horror, Davy MacGregor dropped to his knees beside his wife and lifted her burned head. "Maggie! My God, Maggie!"

Her eyes opened. The pupils were so widely dilated that they seemed black pits. "I saw it," she whispered. "It would have killed me, but I got a wall up and deflected its first strike. And then . . . it went away."

"What did?" Denis cried.

"I don't know," Margaret Strayhorn said helplessly. "I don't know."

<Cretin! Imbecile! You gave her a chance to cry out!>

ForgivemeforgivemeOdearFuryIdidmybest—

<Yes. All right . . . Damn! I never thought she'd be that quick. Are you safely away and well hidden?>

Yes. [Panic regret anger yearning BROKENHEARTED WEEPING.]

<Fool! *Stop that!* Do you want to attract the attention of *normals?* . . . that's better. Smile. Laugh. Act ordinary. And now, as quickly as you can, back where you belong!>

But Fury I FAILED. And . . . she *did* see me.

<She saw the Hydra itself?>

No . . . just *us*.

<She's in shock. She won't remember anything useful. I can reinforce that redactively. She won't be able to make sense of it. She'll only remember opening the door, not . . . what was on the other side of it.>

[Misery. Deprivation. Insecurity. Impending disassembly.]

<No! Pull yourself together! Much of the blame for tonight's failure is mine. I underestimated Margaret Strayhorn. I took for granted that her mental assay file was accurate. It doesn't categorize her as a master, but it's only too clear from this fiasco that there must be subjacent masterly components to her mind that were activated in response to your attack.>

She was so quick . . . I never thought she'd be able to scream or prevent the insertion of the crown chakra drain. I was going to paralyze her with the first stroke, then pull her into the bushes. Afterward I would have incinerated her body completely—just as you told me to do. No one would have suspected that I did it. But now—

< The burn has the lotus pattern. Both Denis and Paul Remillard will know what that means . . . Well there's no helping it. I still believe that my strategy involving Strayhorn is the correct way for us to dispose of the Great Enemy. Her death would totally devastate him. >

But HOWFuryHOW? I'm not strong enough to take her!

< You need more coaching that's all. I can take care of it during the trip to Concilium Orb. Those boring weeks in hyperspace can be put to very productive use. And by the time we're there— >

[Sigh.] Will it hurt as much as the other lessons Fury?

< Oh yes. *More* if you ever hope to become strong enough to subdue masterclass minds and take what rightfully belongs to you— what the Milieu would rob you of. You'll have to endure a good deal to build up your strength. Unless you've changed your mind . . . >

NO! Goddamfuckshit NO! I'll do anything! I want it! All of it!

< [Laughter.] That's my sweet Hydra. But remember: *you cannot succeed without my help.* You must do things my way even if that way is difficult. >

I'll do anything! Dearest Fury you made me and you made me so very happy. I'll do anything you say. Just let me feed on lifeforce again. Let me grow. Please.

< Go home. Margaret Strayhorn's injury is readily treatable. She won't let this stop her from accompanying her husband to the inauguration. By the time *you* reach Concilium Orb you'll be ready to try again—and this time you won't fail. >

[19]

FROM THE MEMOIRS
OF ROGATIEN REMILLARD

I awoke on the morning of 21 November with a throbbing skull from the hangover of the Western world, but no guilt at all. If ever a man had a good excuse for getting shitfaced, c'est moi.

Marc had told me that he would coerce Bill Parmentier to fly him back to Ape Lake between the first and fifteenth of November with more food. But though the weather remained unaccountably perfect, so that supplies could have been dropped to us even if the lake ice would not yet take the weight of the ski-shod Beaver, Marc had not come.

As the food ran low, we had tried to trap more hares; but Teresa's earlier massacre had exterminated those in our immediate vicinity, as the absence of tracks proved. Ape Lake had very little other accessible winter wildlife aside from mice, our good friend Herman the Ermine, and a few spruce grouse. We had tried one of the latter, and it looked tempting coming out of the Coleman oven, roasted to a turn and accompanied by spicy apple rings. But the meat tasted horrible, permeated through and through by the skunky flavor of the spruce needles the bird had been eating.

I suppose we might have gagged it down if we were actually starving to death—but neither of us was that far gone yet, and so the bird was given to a grateful Herman, and we ate our last tin of sardines spread on biscuits, with peanut butter and biscuits for dessert. Later, upon consulting one of the reference flecks, Teresa learned that she should have prepared the bird by parboiling it and dumping out the malflavored water several times. The next time she cooked a grouse she followed the technique, and the result was edible—but just barely.

During the week that had just passed, I tried no less than twenty times to bespeak Marc telepathically—and damn the consequences if my feebly powered, imperfectly beamed thoughts slopped out from intimate mode and were overheard. But there had been no answer, which led me to two possible conclusions: either the boy was far out of range of my farspeech, no longer on the planet Earth . . . or he was dead.

My natural Franco pessimism opted for the latter. I feared that the Magistratum had discovered that our canoe accident was faked and that Marc had been an accomplice in Teresa's disappearance. The Simbiari Proctors might never squeeze the whole truth out of that valiant young mind, but that wouldn't stop them from pronouncing him guilty of compounding a felony and accessorizing after the fact. Their meting out of punishment was customarily swift. The family would have been helpless to save him.

Nevertheless, day after day, as my own hope dimmed, I kept on burbling to Teresa that her son was bound to show up tomorrow for sure. I tried to suppress my growing panic, commanding myself to keep up a cheerful front for Teresa's sake, all the while thanking heaven that the one operant trick I was good at was keeping my thoughts well screened. But finally, on November 20, without my knowing it she inventoried our remaining supplies. At supper she quietly told me that we had less than three weeks' worth of food reserves left if we ate very sparingly, and we would have to resign ourselves to the fact that Marc was not coming.

"I suspected as much," said I. We had dined on pasta and Velveeta with leftover pease porridge on the side. Most of what remained in our larder of staples was simple starches. We did have fair amounts of spices and condiments left, and plenty of tea and freeze-dried coffee and dried fruit, but almost no protein.

As she uttered the fateful words, I stared down at my tongue-polished plate in despair. I momentarily considered emulating the noble Captain Oates on Scott's fatal Antarctic expedition: I would take a hike out into the snow, telling Teresa that I might be gone some time, and simply never return. But even as the fantasy played itself out in my imagination, I realized that my death wouldn't save her. She would still be out of food before Jack's birth, and what would become of her and the child then? The strongly coercive members of the family who might be able to penetrate the Megapod Reserve tracelessly and take her and the baby home and hide them would by that time be 4000 lightyears away on Concilium Orb, attending the inauguration. Even if they became aware of her need, it would take them two to three weeks to return, and long before then Teresa would have starved in the wilderness, or else she would be compelled to reveal herself to the Magistratum.

"It's not hopeless, Rogi," she said. "You have the rifle. You can go hunting."

"There's nothing left to hunt around the lake but small game, and the high-powered rifle bullets would blast them to shreds. I could certainly trap what's left of the hares and grouse, but you expend a lot of energy moving around outside when it's very cold. I don't think I'd be able to bring in enough small critters to keep us both going."

Teresa had leaned across the supper table and bestowed that dazzling smile of hers upon me. "Why then, you'll simply have to go off away from the lake and find something *large.*"

It was at that point that I decided the only useful thing to do was get drunk . . .

Huddled deep within my sleeping bag on the morning after, with my head on the verge of meltdown, I could hear Teresa moving about the cabin, humming an intricate operatic aria as she whipped up something that was probably flapjack batter. The bacon and powdered eggs were long gone, and breakfast was now usually fried cakes, oatmeal, or cinnamon-rice with raisins and a bit of reconstituted milk.

The ambrosial smell of coffee seeped through the thick layer of down and bunny fur covering my face. I heard her footsteps approach, ventured to use my broken-down farsight, and saw her with my mind's eye, holding a steaming cup.

"Rogi, dear, don't worry," she said. "You'll find some kind of big game. And if we have lots of meat, we can eke out the other things."

I sat up, taking the coffee and cradling it in my shaky hands. "All I have is two boxes of ammo. And I don't know a thing about hunting. My sport is backpacking, and I've always believed in live and let live. In rugged mountain country like this . . . dieu de dieu, I don't know! I'd have to hike down to a lower altitude——"

"Of course!" she agreed brightly. "You see? You're thinking positively already. Now get up, dear. I've got the plaque-reader all loaded with Alan Fry's *Wilderness Survival Handbook.* It has an excellent chapter on hunting that you can read while you eat breakfast, and I'll find some other books for you, too."

I groaned and rolled out of the sack. Books! But they'd helped me to rebuild the cabin and make snowshoes, and they'd taught Teresa how to snare and skin hares and cut the skins in a spiral to make the furry "yarn" for her rugs, and I'd learned from a book that it was necessary to keep the rifle out in the cold to prevent condensation of moisture and rusting when it was brought into the warm cabin, and Teresa had read somewhere that both dry and green firewood would be necessary for cooking and heating, a piece of practical lore I had never heard of. There were scores of other bits of information that we had gleaned from the fleck library and made good use of.

So I would read, and then I would pray a whole lot, and then tomorrow I would go a-hunting.

We had chosen for our refuge one of the most glacierbound areas in North America. In almost every direction about Ape Lake, precipitous mountains and impassable icefields hemmed us in. There were only two feasible exploration directions for me to consider. The first was the Ape Creek corridor, which trended eastward into the deep interior of the Megapod Reserve. The second was a northwestern route beginning at the opposite end of the lake. It skirted the tongue of the vast Fyles Glacier, descended to the valley of a fairly large river called the Noeick, and eventually reached an arm of the sea.

Recalling the cascades of Ape Creek, I thought at first that the other, northwestern route would be better. Ape Lake was at an altitude of 1400 meters. After traveling only 14 kilometers northwest, I would have descended 850 meters to the heavily forested river bottom, where there would certainly be wintering elk. Killing a single one of those large animals would solve our food problem completely—provided I could haul the meat back up to Ape Lake.

But a study of the durofilm topographic map we had swiped from Bill Parmentier revealed those crowded-together contour lines that always ring alarm bells in the mind of the cross-country hiker. The route was extremely steep, and there was almost no forest cover that might harbor animals until I reached the river itself. Furthermore, traveling along that exposed and barren way would take me out of the snow shadow of Mount Jacobsen and into the teeth of the howling storms that swept in from the Pacific.

The other possibility, a route leading from the eastern end of the lake down Ape Creek Canyon, showed the green tint of forest every centimeter of the way into the valley of the north-flowing Talchako River, some 18 kilometers distant. In most stretches along the canyon, the contour lines were reasonably far apart. Now that the temperature stayed well below freezing both day and night, the creek would surely have dwindled and frozen just as the other streams had, making it easier for me to descend. On the other hand, the canyon route would not take me down to as low an altitude as the other path would. Nevertheless I finally decided that I would have a better chance of finding a sizable animal sooner, going that way. What sort of game I would find in the interior was anybody's guess; but the winter was not yet far advanced, and I hoped for a late-prowling bear, or perhaps a deer or two.

I prepared to leave early on the following morning. I transferred a small mountain of firewood to the vicinity of the porch for Teresa's convenience and ordered her to melt snow for water, rather than chancing the steep trail down to the lake. She prepared a dozen fat oatmeal cakes filled with dried fruit for my rations. I also took some packets of soup mix, which had little nourishment but would provide me with something other than hot water and tea to drink. In my backpack I carried a plass tarpaulin and lots of plass garbags, a little pot to boil water, the small axe, my biggest knife, the whetstone, a hank of rope, the ammunition, and the dome tent. I lashed my sleeping bag and pad to the pack frame and put a firestarter and Teresa's Swiss Army knife with its saw blade into my pocket. When she wasn't looking, I filled a spare canteen with the high-proof Lamb's Navy Rum.

"How long will you be gone?" she asked.

"As long as it takes. Don't try to farspeak me unless there's an emergency. If they're still searching for us, that might give you away."

She nodded, her face calm. She was wearing an oversized buffalo-plaid wool shirt, jeans let out at the waist, and unlaced boots over heavy socks. Her dark hair, once so sleek and shining, was lank now from being washed with soap, and pulled back into a ponytail. But otherwise pregnancy had made her bloom, and she looked so beautiful and young and vulnerable that I had to turn away from her quickly so she would not see my eyes brim up.

She kissed me on the cheek as I put on my backpack and said, "You'll succeed, Rogi. It can't end this way. Jack is positive that he's going to live and accomplish great things. That means we will, too."

I tried to laugh. "Cocksure little beggar, that Jack."

"Oh, yes. His ego is extremely healthy. I've already had to lecture him about the perils of pride and self-absorption. It's difficult for Jack to understand that I'm a separate person with an independent life— not simply a loving receptacle who exists only for his convenience. The very notion that other people will someday interact closely with him still frightens him. He—he tends to equate nonmaternal minds with danger. You can understand why."

"Well, I'm no threat. I don't know why he's too shy to even say hello to me."

"While you're gone, I'll try to teach him that it's a human survival trait to socialize. To be friendly. He and I have so much to thank you for. I'll try to get that idea across to him, too."

My gloved hand rested on the door latch. "If I'm not back in six days, I want you to farspeak Denis."

Her eyes widened. "No!"

"You must," I insisted. "But you can't wait too long, or he'll be off-world on his way to the inauguration. Denis might be able to think of some way to save you. He has an incredible mind, Teresa. Because he's such a self-effacing man, people tend to forget that. Even his own children do. But his metaquotient in some faculties is even higher than Paul's. He's a better coercer, for certain, and I know he strongly disapproves of the more tyrannical aspects of the Proctorship. He might be willing to stick his neck out for you and Jack if you convinced him of the baby's mental superiority."

"No!" she cried. "Denis is too cold! Those eyes of his frighten me. He'd think only of the family, just as Lucille did. I can only trust you and Marc!"

"Marc's not coming back." My tone was bleak, final. "And I may fail."

Both her hands were clasped tightly over her abdomen, and she had shut her eyes against a sudden flood of tears. "You won't fail! Go, Rogi. Go now. I'll be waiting for you."

I shrugged, opened the door, and stepped out into the overcast winter morning. It took me a few minutes to put on my snowshoes.

Then I took the Winchester down off the wall, loaded it, hung the rifle over my shoulder, and set off. The temperature was somewhere not too far below freezing. The smoke from our chimney rose only a few meters before flattening out, which meant that the atmospheric pressure was low and some kind of bad weather was on its way. The snow was about 30 cents deep, and I mushed along easily over the frozen lake toward the Ape Creek outlet. Dark clouds hid Mount Jacobsen completely and seemed to race on ahead of me, but I never thought of turning back. Having the wind at my back seemed a good omen, and if it did begin to snow heavily, I'd simply hole up in my tent and wait for it to stop.

Five hours later, after I had managed to descend a couple of very steep kilometers into Ape Creek Canyon, the blizzard started.

From the lake, I had climbed down steplike terraces of rock that had formed cascades when the creek was high. Now only a little water still flowed beneath the ice crust. The canyon widened abruptly at a point where a nearly frozen waterfall dribbled into a pool. This lay in a brushy clearing, with terrain that was much more level than the upper part of the canyon. Scattered around the basin were tumbled rocks, looking like huge sleeping beasts partially mantled with snow. Thickets of leafless alder mingled with the spires of tall subalpine fir and spruce at the forest's edge. It must have been an idyllic spot in warm weather. With a storm beginning to roar down the canyon, I found it much less appealing.

The falling snow thickened rapidly to the point where the landscape began to dissolve into amorphous white. I knew I could go no further until it stopped. The temperature was dropping rapidly and the wind blew harder and harder. I slogged back among the large trees, found a reasonably sheltered place, and trampled down a spot. Then I took off snowshoes, gun, and pack, and set up the dome tent, which had an integral floor. I heaped loose snow around it so that it would not immediately blow away, then spent a bad five minutes searching for the snowshoes and the Winchester, which had been completely buried by blowing snow while I worked.

Zipped inside my shelter at last, I did what any sensible Canuck would have done: I crept into my sleeping bag, had a good nip of rum, and went to sleep.

For some reason, my slumber was as deep and restful as a child's. I don't remember my dreams, but they were innocuous. Every now and then I would half waken to the roaring of the gale in the trees and the sharp hiss of snow against the taut fabric of the tent, then drift back to sleep again. In time, the sound of the wind became muffled and the snow hiss stopped, and I knew that the tent was buried. But not to worry: the little screened window at the back was open a little at the top for ventilation, and loose snow has plenty of air in it. So I slept on and on . . .

. . . Until utter silence woke me up.

It was pitch black inside my shelter and the storm was over. I had slept with most of my clothes on, and if anything, I was too warm. The felt liners of my Pak boots and my mitts were shoved down in the bottom of the sleeping bag along with my food sack and water canteen. I retrieved the lot, put on my damp parka, ate a soggy oatmeal cake blind (ugh!), and drank some water. Then I began to dig myself out, since nature called. The snow had drifted more than a meter and a half deep, but it was so soft it was easily pushed aside. A snowshoe, plied with care, made a good shovel. I stomped and scraped a ramp, peed into a snowy alcove, put the snowshoes on, then moved onto the fresh snow surface.

Up there it was bitterly cold. To my surprise, the night sky was bright. The aurora borealis glowed overhead like enormous curtains of green and scarlet light. As I watched, enthralled, they rippled and even seemed to rustle, and then a great expanding lance shape of white radiance thrust up from behind the ridge on the opposite side of the canyon, piercing the colored draperies. It was followed by another beam, and then a third and a fourth, like celestial searchlights. I gave an exclamation of awe. The trees now cast sharp shadows on the new-fallen snow, and the entire little basin was lit up as though a full moon were shining.

And not 15 meters away, on top of a great heap of nearly snow-free rocks, I saw something move. Something large.

I stood petrified. And then I caught a faint whiff of a pungent animal odor—and the thing on the rocks stood upright on two legs, the aurora silvering its shaggy pelt. It was huge, a good half-meter taller than I, and I knew in an instant what it was.

Careful to make no sound, I ducked back down into the tent, seized the rifle, and shook off my right mitt. Flipping off the safety, I crept back up the snow ramp, lifted the weapon to my shoulder, and lined up the sights. The creature was still there, facing away from me, looking as tall and as massive as a grizzly bear.

But it wasn't a bear. It was a member of an endangered species: Gigantopithecus. The Bigfoot. The largest primate that had ever lived. A creature that was telepathic, as I was, but with a mind still innocent, as mine decidedly was not. As I drew a bead on the Megapod, I completely forgot all the high-minded musings that had occupied me when I first came to Ape Lake. I thought only of how much meat that great frame carried—meat that would keep Teresa and Jack and me alive.

I would have killed it. At that range, even a duffer like me wouldn't miss. And I had no qualms of conscience at all. It was an animal and I was a desperate human being, the most dangerous species in the universe. But just as my finger was tightening on the icy trigger, the aurora burst into a fantastic display of purple and green and white shapes, like multicolored ghosts gliding about the sky.

And the Bigfoot raised its arms, and my mind heard it utter a formless telepathic cry of wonderment and joy.

Slowly, I let the barrel of the Winchester sag. The sky phantoms danced above us and the stars sparkled and the great creature crooned its silent hymn from the rocky eminence. I tried to lift the rifle again, then gave it up and snapped the safety back on. The small sound echoed in the crisp cold air like a cracking twig, and the Bigfoot swung around abruptly and looked at me.

I waved.

It vanished.

Sighing, I returned to the tent, had another oatcake and a snort, and went back to sleep.

The next morning, it was snowing again, but lightly. I 'shoed over to the rocks where I had seen the giant ape and found nothing, not even tracks. Perhaps the thing had a den deep inside the pile.

"Snooze in peace," I told it. "Reason tells me that you're groceries, but my heart says, 'Nay, nay.' One simply cannot eat a fellow operant."

After breakfast, I packed up and continued my journey down Ape Canyon.

Below the little basin, the bed of the creek steepened once again. With the snow much deeper now, I had to proceed with greater care and much more slowly. So far, I had not encountered any formidable obstacles to travel—but I hadn't seen any game trails, either, except for the tracks of something that might have been a mink or a marten in a place where the creek had a small area of open water.

It snowed dismally on and off all day long, accumulating another ten cents or so. Ape Creek curved in a northerly direction now, skirting the little peak I had named Mount Jeff. I might have traveled four or five more kloms downstream by the end of the day. I found a place where there were wind-scoured rocks, pitched the tent, and built a fire. The oatcakes were not much more palatable warm than they had been cold, but a potful of hot chicken soup warmed my belly nicely. I lay in my sleeping bag at the open door of the tent, sipping the rum drop by numbing drop, watching the fire die and the snowflakes sift gently down. As boozy contentment took hold of me, I wondered if I was going to die. Freezing to death is supposed to be an easy way to go. Much easier than starvation. Lucky me. Poor Teresa . . .

But then I snapped out of my morbid reverie, remembering that I had not decided to accompany Teresa to this place of my own free will. I was ordered to do so by the Lylmik entity I called the Family Ghost, who had said that my participation in the adventure was necessary.

Necessary! To what? To the thing's cosmic chicanes, of course. I was quite certain that Teresa's unborn child was the key factor in my spectral hassler's schemes; this meant that she would live to see Jack born. It was logical that I would probably live as well, so that she would not have to go through her ordeal alone in the dead of winter. Un point, c'est tout, Oncle Rogi! The luxury of freezing to death was not to be mine after all.

Still, I was getting mighty tired of clambering down this canyon. The farther away from Ape Lake I went, the more trouble I'd have returning. One more goddam blizzard, and I might not be able to get back at all . . .

"Mon fantôme!" I called out. "Are you there?"

The last flaming chunk of wood in my campfire subsided into the ashes. Only embers remained, making little sizzling sounds as the snowflakes pelted them.

"Ghost! I know you can hear me. It's getting colder and colder, and this rock-scrambling on snowshoes is pooping me out. I'm only a poor old man—a hundred and six years old! If I go much farther, I'll have big trouble hauling back any game I find. You shag me out some kind of edible critter tomorrow—you hear me? No more fooling around. You want me to do this job you handed me, then gimme a break! Big game! No shit! Tomorrow! Right here! Without fail!"

Feeling much better, I capped the rum canteen, zipped the tent flap, and slept.

In the morning, it was very cold and cloudy, but the snow had stopped. When I went down to the creek for water, I discovered that something had been there before me. Tracks led upstream on the opposite bank, and I could see a thin plume of smoke or steam arising from a stand of small fir trees about a hundred meters away.

I got the Winchester, crept up my side of the creek, and spotted him browsing among the firs. Aim for the front of the body, where the vital organs are, the *Wilderness Survival Handbook* had said. And the book even included a line drawing of an animal with a bull's-eye on it for the sake of idiots like me. I slipped off the safety, took aim at the proper spot, and fired.

The young bull moose dropped dead into the snow.

It must have weighed upwards of 450 kilos. Even if I made a sled, it was going to take several grueling trips to get all the meat back home. But what the hell. I'd done it! Giddy with success, I got out the axe and the knives and the tarp and the plass bags, and tried to remember what the book had said about butchering. I was a little hazy on the details, but I figured I'd manage somehow.

Before I started, I chanced one triumphal telepathic shout, imperfectly directed along Teresa's intimate mode:

Foodgloriousfood!

And another thought-beam pierced my brain like a tiny dart, smack between the eyes:

Gotcha Uncle Rogi!

Denis had finally found me.

[20]

SECTOR 15: STAR 15-000-001 [TELONIS]
PLANET 1 [CONCILIUM ORB]

GALACTIC YEAR: LA PRIME 1-387-566
[6 DECEMBER 2051]

On 4 December by Earth reckoning, Anne Remillard had requested—no, ordered!—that Marc do his family duty by tourist-guiding small groups of his newly arrived cousins about Concilium Orb, orienting them to the legislative center of the Galaxy. She had delivered this stunner with oh-by-the-way casualness as the two of them were leaving the Human Polity office block on Monday, heading for the tube station along with a great mob of operant human bureaucrats.

"But what about my *real* work?" Marc had protested. "I'm not finished with the research correlating GPPs of the cosmop worlds with their crime rates."

"Junko can finish it."

"But I'm supposed to be acting as a legislative page, doing important work for you and the other family magnates—not wet-nursing gangs of gawking juvenile relatives!"

Anne was adamant. "Young man, until your father or someone else requests your inestimable services, you are still *my* page, and you will do as I say. After two days of rest, your cousins are all recovered from limbo lag and spoiling for something to do, especially the young ones. There's no reason why they should waste time sailboarding and lying on the beach in Paliuli when they could be furthering their education."

"Why *me?* There are regular tours for the families and friends of the new human magnates—"

"I know you've been spending every spare minute prowling this exotic beehive. Make some good use of what you've learned. Your uncles and aunts and your father and I are going to be much too busy with the inauguration preliminaries and other Concilium affairs to spend much time with the children, and your cousins will learn much more from you than they would from a canned tour."

Most of the Remillards had arrived on the CSS Kungsholm, which had docked two days earlier, and all of the families except Paul's had settled in at tropical Paliuli. Only Denis and Adrien remained behind on Earth to take care of last-minute business. They would be joining the others just before Christmas. Lucille had insisted upon taking charge of Marc's motherless younger siblings during the space voyage and was still supervising them in Paul's big apartment in Golden Gate, bossing the nanny and the housekeeper about. She had also appointed herself Paul's official hostess, to his well-concealed chagrin, and had arranged for herself and Denis to take an apartment right next to Paul's.

"Show your cousins around in small groups," Anne said, as she and Marc descended the escalator into the tube station. "Not more than six or seven kids at a crack. Five days with each bunch ought to give them a useful overview of the human and exotic enclaves, especially the latter. Do an especially good job showing them how our nonhuman compères behave in simulated natural settings. And don't forget to take the youngsters to the visitors' gallery in the Concilium chambers so that they can experience legislative procedures."

Marc groaned. "I'll be running fifty-pence tours from now until New Year's!"

"The Galactic year is a thousand days long. And we are now"— Anne allowed herself a small smile as she paused to consult her wrist-com—"only on Day 566. You'll be back home on Earth long before then."

Marc looked at her with a startled expression, his annoyance wiped away by a sudden new thought. "Back home . . . Aunt Anne, do you know what Papa and the others are planning to do?"

"About what?" Anne inquired blandly. She had turned aside into a refreshment bar once they reached the lower level. "Buy you a ginger ale?" She fed her credit card into the small machine on the bar and punched up an Anchor steam beer for herself.

Marc nodded to the drink invitation but otherwise kept his mind well guarded. He did not reply out loud but projected to her on her intimate mode twin portraits of his mother and Uncle Rogi.

"We've not yet held a family memorial service or a requiem," Anne said, pressing her right thumb on one corner of the tab display and then scanning it swiftly with her wallet for a receipt. "You can have masses said for them yourself if you want to do something special."

"You know very well that's not what I mean." The two cold beverages popped out of a hatch in front of them. Marc picked his up and began to drink in apparent unconcern. The bar was crowded with humans and exotics, and Marc and Anne were squeezed in between a tall Gi daintily sipping a cocktail of frangipani nectar and a stout little Poltroyan chugalugging a stein of crème de menthe.

Anne said to Marc on intimate: *If you have questions about Teresa and Rogi ask your father if you dare but do it very ADROITLY because this entire Orb is supposedly bugged by Lylmik surveillance machinery.*

I can't ask Papa. I haven't been able to get him alone since he arrived. All he's interested in is scrounging for votes and fooling around with Laura Tremblay the damned HYPOCRITE he's supposed to be such a high-and-mighty great leader and statesman and he's going to be First Magnate for Christ's sake and he doesn't even care about his wife and unborn child—

SHUT UP.

You know I'm right! You hate that part of him too.

You're mistaken.

I'm not! Whyareyoulying?Tellme!Whydoyouallstickupforhim—

TO SURVIVE.

Whatthehell's that *supposed to mean?*

You'll find out soon enough—

I want to know what the family is planning to do about Mama!

"Well, we'd better be getting along," said Anne, smiling sweetly at Marc as she finished the last of her beer. "I'm going to the theater tonight with Ilya and Katy, and *you,* my lad, are going to spend the evening preparing a tour schedule for my inspection first thing tomorrow. You can start the tours immediately."

Marc leaned toward her with apparent casualness, still sipping his drink. Then without warning his gray eyes locked onto hers, and Anne felt the initial grip of a near-indomitable coercion.

Jesus! When had he mastered *this* maneuver?! Before the boy could insert the redactive component of the mind-ream and peel her open like a tangerine, she lashed back at him with a stunning mental riposte. It rocked him physically as well as cutting him loose from her.

Marc was flung against the Poltroyan standing next to him and began to choke on his ginger ale.

"Oh, dear," Anne exclaimed, reaching out to her nephew with an air of anxious solicitude. "Did I jostle you? Did some of your drink go down the wrong pipe? Shall I slap you on the back?" *Don't you ever try to ream me again you arrogant young shit.* "Here, take my handkerchief, dear. I'm so sorry!" *Of course I know what you did with Teresa&Rogi we ALL do we know EVERYTHING except where you stashed them and we're going to do our best to salvage the situation but YOU STAY OUT OF IT DO YOU UNDERSTAND?*

Marc apologized to the exotic he had bumped, then said to Anne, "That's okay. I'm just fine now." *And what about the attack on Margaret Strayhorn? What's the family going to do about that you* know *one of us had to be responsible—*

How did you find out about that?

Grandmère was leaking like a sieve the day she arrived. It must have been preying on her mind during the trip out. Davy MacGregor's wife had one of those weird psychocreative drain-burns exactly like the ones that killed Brett a Victor burn—

YOU WILL DISCUSS THE MATTER WITH NO ONE YOU WILL UNDERTAKE NO INVESTIGATIONS WHATSOEVER I AM DEADLY SERIOUS MARC DO YOU UNDERSTAND ME?

. . .

The adults in the family will deal with it. And it's NOT certain that one of us was responsible.

Don't make me laugh! It could even be Papa! And Strayhorn and MacGregor are due to arrive in Orb day after tomorrow. What if the damned Victor-tainted mind goes for her again?

If it does and if the Magistratum investigating team decides that a Remillard is behind both attacks then we might all find ourselves for the chop—at least as far as membership in the Concilium goes. We're doing our best to cope with the matter—

Hah.

Damn *you Marc! Do you want me to sling you onto the slowest bunny-hopping crate I can find? One that'll get you back to Earth in time for Dartmouth summer break? If you don't keep your nose out of this affair I'll do it so help me God. We can't have ham-handed* adolescents messing around. This matter is too important and too dangerous. For all of us.

. . . I'll lay off. [Affirmation.]

"Now, about the guided tours for your cousins." Anne took Marc's arm and steered him out of the bar and onto the tube platform. "Would you like to take the youngest children first? I won't ask you to cope with anyone under the age of nine. We'll let their parents decide what to show *them,* but you can have a free hand with the older kids. What do you think?"

"Whatever you say, Aunt Anne."

A minute later, the inertialess capsule for Golden Gate arrived, and he got on without saying another word to her.

He performed his duty with perfect efficiency. Tuesday he Papa-Goosed seven peewees around the human enclaves, enduring their puerile questions and their imperfectly screened dumb remarks about the way so many people native to one part of Earth always thought some other part was more desirable and wanted to live there. Today he was trying to keep his temper as the same group argued about which exotic enclave they wanted to see first. He should never have offered them a choice.

The roster of juveniles included Uncle Phil's third son Richard, who was ten; two of Uncle Maury's brood—nine-year-old Roger and prim, eleven-year-old Celine; and four others who were also eleven: Uncle Sevvy's youngest, Quentin; Aunt Cat's blustery son Gordon; Parnell, the second-born of Uncle Adrien and Aunt Cheri; and Marc's own younger sister Madeleine. (His frail little brother Luc, who still hadn't recovered from the painful upsilon-field translations of the trip out, would be joining a later group.)

Gordo had sneered when Marc suggested that they begin the exotic itinerary with a Simbiari enclave. "Who cares about how the Green Leaky Freakies live? They've been treating us like dogshit for forty years!"

"Watch your mouth, Gordo," Celine said. "They could be listening."

"Ooo, mercy! I'm scared *poopless!*"

"C'mon, Marc," pleaded Cousin Parni. "We'd rather see those crazy lagoon islands where the Gi sexify!"

"Better yet, the big tankfuls of gunk where the Krondak monsters do it," Quint added, his eyes glittering.

"Do what?" inquired innocent little Roger.

His big sister Celine said, succinctly, "Copulate."

"That sounds nifty," said ten-year-old Dicky. "I bet it'd beat those elephant seals we saw mating one time in Argentina. Krondaku must weigh twice as much. And they have tentacles!"

"Boys." Maddy sighed, rolling her eyes heavenward. "*I* want to see a Poltroyan Wintergrove, with the cute little houses nestled among the giant tree roots, half buried in snow. I want to go inside a Poltroyan home and see if they really have jewels all over everything. Their houses are supposed to be the most gorgeous things in the universe. Let's go there first, Marco."

The three older boys jeered.

Gordo said, "Sure we'll go there first, Maddy. Anything for Marco's darling little baby sister."

"We've all seen Poltroyan stuff a million times on the Tri-D," Parni put in scornfully. "But they hardly ever show anything about the way the Krondaku live. Probably don't want to scare us poor Earthworms to death."

"I vote for the Krondaku, too," said Quint. "I've heard that sometimes even *real people* screw in their aphrodisiac goo-pools, right along-side the exotic Bloboids."

Gordo's eyes bugged out. "You're kidding!" He turned to Marc. "Humans would be poisoned wallowing in that stuff, wouldn't they?"

"No," said Marc austerely. "The liquid in the Krondak connubial vats is mostly glycerin, with a small amount of imidazolidinyl urea and traces of isoyohimbine, tetrahydroharmine, nicotine, and other psychoactive alkaloids."

"Son of a bitch," breathed Gordo.

"How many of you guys want to start with the Krondak octopussies' enclave?" Parni demanded.

All of the boys raised their hands, while the two girls scowled.

Marc sighed. "You won't like it much. Krondak domicilia are great big clinkery black things made out of lava, like a dark coral reef, with holes in the rock for the family dwelling units. The Krondak gravity preferendum is half ours, so you keep bouncing around, scraping your head on the rough passageway ceilings. And they like their atmosphere cold and damp and so high in oxygen partial-pressure it makes you giddy."

"We want to see a Krondak enclave first anyway!" the boys chorused.

"Especially the woo-vat," Gordo said.

"All right," said Marc. "But you runts better be polite and tactful. We're not visiting a zoo, you know. The Krondaku are the most influential race in the Milieu, aside from the Lylmik. They're not just big ugly brutes. They're smarter than we are, and they'll be forming judgments about humanity from observing the behavior of you filthy-minded little puny-prongs."

"We never asked," Madeleine said sweetly, "to be dragged into their precious Galactic Milieu. If they don't like us, it's just too bad for them. Shall we get started, Big Brother?"

When they stepped out of the transport capsule into the Krondak enclave of Lurakal, the youngsters gasped and instinctively huddled together. The place was crowded with huge many-armed creatures of nightmarish form, and Marc and his charges were the only non-Krondaku there. The tube station had pocked and pitted black walls that seemed roughly carved from a substance resembling coal or obsidian. All of the surfaces gleamed with beads of moisture, and there was a peculiar tangy odor resembling that of machine oil in the chilly, vapor-laden air. The reddish tinge to the ambient illumination made the children think of evening light filtered through storm clouds.

Marc's young cousins had seen members of this awesome exotic race in person before; but always in a human setting, where the impact of the horrifying, supremely intelligent entities could be mollified by the presence of friendly adults of the children's own species. Back on Earth, a young human mind could easily dismiss the Krondaku as a frightful aberration that would soon be gone; but here in their own enclave, the monsters lived and moved and went about their business in a world where only they could be at home, where human beings were the exotic interlopers, yearning desperately to be somewhere else.

The group bounded along awkwardly after Marc in the low gravity, ascending the station ramp, shivering from the abrupt drop in temperature, and too overawed even to speak. They emerged upon what appeared to be a raw volcanic shore, where an artificial lake of some thick transparent liquid rippled sluggishly. The landforms round about it featured sharp promontories, looming rock pinnacles, and scattered inshore stacks and jagged islets of some dark mineral like basalt. The Krondak enclave had a twilit crimson "sky" full of swift-moving black clouds. The odor of volatile hydrocarbons was pronounced, and a biting wind blew, raising sullen wavelets on the lake, whose boundaries were lost in mist. Tendrils of vapor streamed and roiled from each small island's summit and from the eminences on shore. The rough rocky flanks had myriad openings that glowed green, blue, or vermilion within. Only gradually did the young Earthlings become aware that what appeared to be barren volcanic formations were actually amorphous apartment structures inhabited by the Krondaku.

The cousins gaped as they watched the commuting exotics. Some surged out of the lake and descended into the tube station, while others flowed up from the tunnel to vanish sedately into the waters, evidently swimming to the island of their choice. Except for the wind whistling softly among the crags and the lapping of the waves, it was very quiet. The Krondaku were capable of vocal speech, but long aeons ago they had chosen to communicate mostly by telepathy. None of the great invertebrates acknowledged the presence of the visitors by so much as the twitch of an accessory eyeball. The aetheric charge of the enclave was entirely benevolent; but every one of Marc's young companions still felt vaguely threatened.

After about five minutes, a Krondak individual of exceptionally large size came gliding up to them, swiveling bright blue primary optics from one young face to another. The being transmitted a grave farspoken speech of welcome, introducing herself as their hostess, Loga'etoo Tilk'ai. She carried a satchel, which she opened after concluding her telepathic remarks. Plucking forth Abercrombie & Fitch hooded jackets with this tentacle and that, she distributed them among the chilled Earthlings.

"I have summoned a surface vessel," Loga'etoo Tilk'ai said aloud in a peculiar voice reminiscent of a talking kettledrum, "which will convey us to my personal domicilium, located less than a kilometer offshore. There for the next three hours you will receive a superficial but rewarding introduction to Krondak domestic life."

"It will be our pleasure," said Marc. The younger boys were trying valiantly to conceal their despair, while the girls wore superior smiles.

"My own three beloved larvae have done careful research on human dietary needs and will prepare luncheon for you as an educational exercise," Loga'etoo continued, expanding her befanged buccal orifice in the Krondak equivalent of a smile. "I know you will be forbearing if their efforts show occasional amateurish lapses in culinary technique. I will make quite sure that none of the food served to you is poisonous or completely unfit for human consumption."

"I'm quite certain it will be delicious," Marc said, administering coercive prods to the petrified cousins.

"Delicious!" they parroted.

Loga'etoo indicated her approval. "After the meal, I will conduct you to the Lurakal Exhibition Hall of Krondak Science and Natural History, which you may already have discerned a few hundred meters further along this attractive esplanade. There you may improve yourselves amongst full-sensory experiential analogs of Krondak anatomical evolution, planetary morphology and ecology, and overviews of our technological progress covering the past two hundred and fifty thousand Earth orbits."

"Can—can we see a connubial vat?" little Roger asked timidly.

"Certainly. There is one just adjacent to this tube station. Would you care to visit it before we embark for my domicilium?"

"Yes, please!" the other cousins chorused, their faces brightening. None of their minds showed any trace of the earlier prurient fatuity, however. Even Parni, Gordo, and Quint were subdued.

"This way, then," Loga'etoo said. "Do be cautious in your ambulation. Our diminished gravity is usually perceived by humans as pleasurable, but it may also be unexpectedly hazardous in more restricted interior spaces."

She moved off with surprising speed. In an environment that artificially simulated their own, the Krondaku displayed none of the ponderous lethargy that afflicted them on strong-gravity worlds. The children bounded and leapt along after their exotic hostess, who led them to what looked like a large hole in a raw lava cliff. It was actually the entrance to a Krondak house of worship, and they had to endure a tour of the eerie sanctuary—which seemed to be little more than a bare cavern illuminated by flickering orange grease lamps—before she finally conducted them to an open shaft in one alcove of the temple, where a cage elevator waited. They plunged downward into utter darkness, coming to an abrupt stop in a dimly lit little cave.

Leaving the elevator, Marc and his cousins followed the Krondak female as she slithered down a dank tunnel with many side branches. In addition to signs written in exotic languages, there were occasional notices in Standard English that read:

TO THE CONNUBIAL VAT — ALSO KNOWN AS THE
"POOL OF THE MONSTERS"

Since coming to Orb, Marc had visited the Krondaku fairly often; but he never had any desire to see one of their trysting spots, and he felt increasingly ill at ease as he bounced cautiously along behind Loga'etoo. That men and women would experience an enhancement of their erotic response as they cavorted with lascivious invertebrates was a notion he found as repellent and incomprehensible as the other irrational aspects of human sexuality.

The cousins, on the other hand, were quickly recovering their earlier high spirits. Marc was aware of secret mental exchanges going on among the eleven-year-olds, and he supposed that the silly little fools were once again giggling and indulging in callow vulgarity. Finally the group reached a cul-de-sac with two doors. The sign on one said: VIEWING CHAMBER. The other said:

CONNUBIAL VAT ENTRY
ATTENTION, NON-KRONDAK ENTITIES!
PLEASE DO NOT ENTER
WITHOUT THE APPROPRIATE RESPIRATORY
EQUIPMENT IN PLACE
ALL ACTIVITY IS UNDERTAKEN
AT THE RISK OF THE PARTICIPANTS

Loga'etoo opened the door to the viewing chamber and gestured with a tentacle for the children to go in. They found themselves in a black-rock grotto, almost entirely filled by a dark pool. The vibes of the place were strange—scary and thrilling at the same time—and the air temperature was no longer chilly but pleasantly warm. All of the illumination came from deep within the pool, where indistinct large shapes that glowed with shifting, throbbing colors were languidly adrift. Racing swiftly and erratically among the great shining masses were a few smaller ones.

Loga'etoo's mind spoke: We will move to a place where we will be able to survey the scene beneath the surface. Please do not speak. Many Krondaku hold their sexual congress to be sacred, as do certain humans.

Marc trailed after the others as they descended a narrow ramp. At the bottom was a great transparent window similar to that found in some Earthside aquariums. Now it was possible to see more clearly the Krondak couples, conjoined at the ventral surfaces and suspended in the dense liquid. Their huge bodies, so shapeless and hideous on dry land, had a strange rippling grace when afloat. The tentacles of the mated exotics curled and uncurled in rhythmic mutual motion, and what had once been mere ugly warts on the blotchy Krondak integument were transformed into multicolored luminescent organs pulsating in slow synchrony to the sexual tempo.

And the other, smaller lovers, the bright conjoined darters weaving in and out of the slower dance of the mated Krondaku like writhing double flames, were human.

Marc caught his breath as one golden-glowing pair soared in close to the window. He found himself fighting for self-control as the corona of their ecstatic aura momentarily touched his mind and aroused him. (The younger children, all prepubertal, felt only a fleeting sense of joy.) The lovers were nude, their bodies glorified by an intricate pattern of yellow light that overlay a deeper blue glow. They were beautiful and at the same time grotesque, for their faces were entirely hidden by breathing masks, with bulging eye lenses that blazed with blood-red radiance. They carried no air tanks, nor any other apparatus that would inhibit their freedom of movement.

There were three human couples sharing the connubial vat with the Krondaku. The psychoactive alkaloids in which they swam were absorbed through the skin, stripping them of their mind-screens along with all the rest of their inhibitions, so that their mental signatures were readily accessible. One man and woman were Ilya Gawrys and his wife Katy MacGregor. The second pair were Katy's brother Davy MacGregor and his wife Margaret Strayhorn.

The third pair glowed with more intensity than the others, and their movements were more frenzied and complex. The man was Marc's father, Paul Remillard, and the woman was Laura Tremblay.

"Thank you, Loga'etoo Tilk'ai, for this interesting experience." Marc whipsnapped his coercion at the mesmerized minds of his cousins and sister and forced them to turn away from the window. "But we'd better be moving along now. The children have so much to learn about your race, and so little time."

< Yes my sweet Hydra? >

They're *here* Fury! They must have come in on a starship today.

< Excellent. She must still be semiconvalescent from your attack on Halloween and hyperspatial translation will have weakened her as well. Take care of her as soon as possible. >

I'm already making my plans.

< After you've drained the lifeforce dispose of the body completely in a solid-waste destructor. There should be a farewell message. Like this: [Image]. You must force her to write it after the crown chakra is drained destroying her willpower. Is that clear? >

Gotcha! OGodGodGOD I can hardly wait!

< A lot depends upon you Hydra. I'll be watching but *you* must do this important job. Don't fail me again. If you do . . . I may have to find another helper. >

NONONOnono!

< You'll do it tonight? >

Tonight. Without fail.

Davy had been right, as usual. All of the lingering traces of her trauma, to say nothing of the weariness after that interminable journey from Earth, had been washed away as they made love for hour after fantastic hour in the Pool of the Monsters. Margaret's erotic tastes had never leaned toward group sex, and at first she had balked when Ilya and Katy proposed the perfect remedy for what ailed her.

"But there's nothing crass about it," Margaret's sister-in-law had said, with gentle seriousness. Katy was a tiny woman with delicate features whose rejuvenated form was as frankly and deliciously plump as that of an archaic Venus. "In the Pool of the Monsters, you're so wrapped up in your love that you have no sensation at all of being part of an orgy. The mating Krondaku and whatever humans are there seem only to be dream images made of colored light. The exotics drift around slowly like monstrous star clusters, and the humans are golden meteors, and the only input your mind receives from them is beauty and harmony."

"And besides," the saturnine Ilya had put in pragmatically, "the humans wear masks. One effectively becomes *something else* before entering the connubial vat . . ."

Davy had urged that they give it a try, and finally she had agreed. There had been another, oblivious pair of human lovers already in the pool when the four of them arrived; but to spare Margaret's lingering squeamishness, Davy had blanked out their identities with a psycho-creative screen, so she had no idea who they were. Not that it would have mattered.

For nearly eight hours she and her husband had experienced un-flagging bliss. When it was over (Ilya and Katy and the anonymous human pair having long since departed) and he led her out of the pool, they took off their masks and together showered off the last traces of the psychoactive liquid. Margaret was surprised to discover that she was not exhausted at all, but invigorated and—yes—almost unable to believe that the amazing experience had been real.

Davy had taken her then to their new apartment in the human enclave called Ponte di Rialto. There were some formalities of arrival to be taken care of; so Davy went off to deal with them, leaving her to do a leisurely unpacking of the luggage they had abandoned so precipitately at the spaceport earlier in the day, when Ilya and Katy, who had welcomed them to Orb, had hatched their therapeutic scheme.

Margaret pottered around, still in a state of postcoital languor. After she had put their things away, she found out who their neighbors in Rialto were and admired the view of the so-called Grand Canal from their balcony window. She was surprised to note that the gondoliers poling along the watercourse were living nonoperant humans, not robots. Then it occurred to her to check out the apartment's kitchen, since cookery was one of her minor passions.

It was well equipped, if not very large. Virtually any sort of fresh comestible could be summoned up from the Central Distributory of Goods to the little domestic convenience station built into one of the kitchen walls. There was a solid-waste disposal system there as well, much more efficient-looking than the complicated ones at their flat in Concord or at the Midlothian country house. The machine evidently recycled nothing but seemed simply to convert all refuse to its elements. No doubt the accumulated dust and gases were then reassembled by the arcane creativity of the mysterious lords of the Galaxy into tomorrow's fresh muskmelon, Ryvita, or leg of lamb—to say nothing of lipsticks, pocket handkerchiefs, and other smallish items, which could also be ordered up from the extensive menu of the Distributory.

Margaret checked the contents of the kitchen cabinets and was happy to see that they had an ample supply of both Darjeeling and Spiderleg teas—respectively the favorites of herself and Davy. She put a china teapot full of water into the microwave to boil and sat down with a note-plaque to make a grocery list.

And then the back doorbell tinkled.

Come in! she said absently, using the declamatory mode.

The door opened and then closed again. Margaret looked up with a puzzled frown and then burst out laughing as the cloak of invisibility fell away.

"Well, of all things! Whoever are you lot—a welcoming committee?"

"Yes," said Hydra.

This time, its attack was swift and efficient.

But before her mind was destroyed she was able to utter a formless farspoken scream of agony on her husband's intimate mode—together with one single intelligible word:

Five.

Paul came back to the apartment in Golden Gate very late, long after Marc was in bed and nearly asleep. Lucille was still there, playing five-card draw with Herta, the operant nanny, and Jacqui, the nonoperant housekeeper. Jacqui was ahead by seventeen dollars. The two metas would never have dreamed of using their farsight to view the cards. Marc heard his father dismiss the two employees and ask Grandmère to stay for a moment. His voice had an abnormal timbre.

Marc came fully awake, his farsenses alert.

Paul's composure was so shaken that he neglected to use Lucille's intimate mode, blurting out the terrible news en clair, in ordinary mental speech:

It's Margaret. The Magistratum reached me at Laura's place with the news. I rushed right over to Davy's apartment in Ponte di Rialto but he wouldn't see me. He wouldn't see me—

Paul fortheloveofGod *what's happened?*

Margaret . . . she's dead.

Oh no—

There was a suicide note. Handwritten. She said she couldn't take the pressure—Davy's nomination to the Concilium, his candidacy for First Magnate. She also said she couldn't bear to bring up their unborn child in a world dominated by nonhumans. And then she evidently shorted out the fail-safe switch on the waste decompositor. And climbed in.

[21]

FROM THE MEMOIRS
OF ROGATIEN REMILLARD

Denis did nothing.

Or rather, he did nothing to harm either me or Teresa.

Once his seekersense had zeroed in on me, he could use EE—excorporeal excursion—to view me fully in an out-of-body trip and talk to me mentally in that precise, unhurried way of his without fear of exotic eavesdropping. He calmed my panic, reassured me that he had no intention of calling in the Milieu gendarmes, told me what had happened to Marc, and even advised me to get a move on butchering my moose, since a much larger winter storm was heading my way from out in the Pacific Ocean and would probably hit Ape Lake within forty-eight hours.

"Well, then," said I, feeling cocky as all hell once it had sunk into my mind that I was not about to be handed over to the law, "perhaps you'd be so kind as to consult your library and tell me the best way to cut this monster up into steaks and chops tout de suite. I'll be damned if I can remember what the books said."

Yes, I can do that easily.

"If there's another blizzard coming, maybe I just better whack off a haunch or something and get on home and leave the rest of the animal here to pick up later."

Denis said: That might not be such a good idea. Wait a minute while I look up the procedure.

I sat there on my heels while the Nobel Laureate and Emeritus Professor of Metapsychology, who was at that moment in his office in Hanover, called up the reference on his computer. I had no doubt that he would find what he was looking for in Dartmouth's extensive database. After a few minutes, he said:

You can't just leave the moose carcass. Either scavengers will get it, or it will freeze into a rock-hard mass that you could never cut up later.

No . . . you'll have to bleed and skin the animal now. Remove the entrails and salvage the edible organs—heart, liver, and kidneys, at least. Then cut up the rest of the meat as quickly as possible into smallish portions and cache most of them for your later trips.

"Listen, it would take me two days just to build a cache!"

You don't have to build anything. Just hang the meat up in trees. How cold is it there?

"We forgot a thermometer."

All right, I'm farsensing your ambient atmosphere and comparing its temperature with that in my office . . . About minus sixteen Celsius. That should freeze your meat quickly enough to retain its quality if you cut the pieces smaller than two or three kilos. You won't need the entire moose carcass, of course. Only about a hundred kilos of meat and fat, if you and Teresa and the baby intend to return to civilization immediately after the birth . . . But wait: You really can't come out of hiding until the pardon is pushed through. Humanity will no longer be wards of the Simbiari Proctorship after the inauguration, but their arm of the Magistratum still has legal jurisdiction until the Human Polity reconvenes. I'll have to consult Anne on the legalities—

"No!" I shouted wildly, shaking my knife at the gray sky. "Don't you dare tell anybody we're alive! Not Anne, not Paul, not even Lucille!"

Rogi, they already know.

"Oh," I said, deflated.

He explained how the family had found out, and why they decided to do nothing about it.

"If Paul did agree with the others not to press the search for us," I said, "then I don't care whether you consult with him or any other family member you please. Just try to figure out a way to get us home as quickly as possible without having us land in some exotic jail."

I will. But it will have to be after the birth, when the child is legally a separate entity from his mother.

"You and all the rest of the family will be on Concilium Orb when the baby's born, and it'll take weeks for you to get back to Earth—"

Don't worry about it, Uncle Rogi. Paul and I will find a way.

"Okay. I'll salvage all of the moose I can, and we'll have food to last until spring. We'll get awfully sick of venison stew, but we'll survive."

We'll get you out of there long before that . . . H'mm! I've found an interesting book in the data bank entitled *Moose on the Table*, by one Swede Gano, with recipes. I can farspeak them to Teresa. By the way, exactly where is she?

I hesitated, then realized it was ridiculous not to answer Denis's question. He could body-scan the area and find her easily enough now, even without my help. And of course, I really did trust him. "She's in a cabin at Ape Lake, about six or seven kloms up the creek. But will you let me break the news to her about you finding us? She's—she's a little leery of you, Denis. Not to make too big a point of it, but you do come on strong without realizing it. You wouldn't want to upset her."

No. I understand.

"You could take a look at her and let me know if she's all right, though. I can't scan through rock worth a damn."

I'll be glad to . . . She seems fine. And so is the—*Jesus!*

"Denis! What's wrong?" My stomach had done a backflip as he cried out in shock. For at least two minutes he was silent. Then I felt a kind of mental shiver, and he said:

The baby. My God, the baby.

Oh-oh. "He sort of screens himself when I'm around, so I haven't really experienced him yet, if you know what I mean. I take it you got a peek at what his mind's really like."

Rogi, I touched that fetus for the merest instant, with my lightest probe. And he locked on, traced my position, rummaged through his mother's memories to identify me, said, "Hello, Grandpère," and slammed down the strongest screen I've ever encountered in a human mind. Even stronger than Marc's. I'm—I'm completely at a loss.

"Well, well." So was I. "So the little guy's really got the watts, has he?"

He's got *something* extraordinary . . . I won't try to touch him again. I've got to think about this. I'll leave you now—

"What about this damned moose?" I cried. "At least send me a meat-cutting diagram so I know where the frigging tenderloins are."

Denis said: Of course. I'm sorry . . . [Image.] There. Complete instructions for butchering. Uncle Rogi, I'd like to talk to you later at more length. I'll return to you this evening after you've made camp.

And he signed off abruptly.

It was my first inkling of the kind of reaction young Jack would provoke among other human operants. Especially a certain type of operant.

Shrugging, I got on with my job, and an unbelievably messy one it was. Of course, I had no way of hoisting the carcass, and it was only through the kindness of the Family Ghost that I had downed it near the creek, where there was a small area of open water I could use for washing the meat. Thanks to Denis's instructions, I knew enough to open the creature's neck blood vessels before beginning; and I also knew the great trick for skinning—which involves slicing the hide very carefully over the belly to avoid puncturing the innards, and cutting a circle around the anus and then tying it closed with string, so that shit doesn't come pouring out all over everything when you remove the entrails.

The skinning and gutting of the massive animal took me over three hours, and the cutting of the meat another two. I ended up soaked with blood, and when the last rump roast and the last bag of flaky body-cavity fat was either hanging high in the trees near the creek or ready to be packed, I looked like a slaughtered, half-frozen thing myself.

I built a roaring fire, rinsed my gory mitts and my parka exterior in the icy water, and let them steam more or less dry while I broiled exquisite cubes of moose liver à la mode sauvage and stuffed myself to the eyeballs. Then I packed the rest of the now frozen raw liver in a plass bag to take back to the mother-to-be. I was also taking the well-rinsed heart and kidneys, the tongue, and of course the pendulous nose—or muffle—which I knew from my youth was a notable delicacy when boiled. To this load I added about fifteen kilos of loin and chuck meat, together with plenty of the fine white fat, which is a nutritional necessity. I had decided against making a sled. Time enough for that on the next trip. I needed to return to the cabin as quickly as possible, and that meant toting everything on my back.

With about two and a half hours of daylight left, I started off for Ape Lake and Teresa and Jack, carrying enough food to keep us going for at least two weeks.

Denis bespoke me again as I lay me down to sleep in the canyon on that frigid, starry night. This time, since I was not distracted, I could see as well as hear him. With his blond hair flopping boyishly over his unlined brow, and his rueful altar-boy smile, he looked to be in his early thirties rather than his actual age of eighty-four. You might have guessed that he was a computer technician, or the manager of a supermarket, or a graduate student, or even your friendly neighborhood egg-bus driver—just as long as he didn't look you squarely in the eye. Denis was usually careful not to do that; there was a code of etiquette among the grandmasterly coercers to the effect that Thou Shalt Not Absentmindedly Sandbag Innocent Bystanders. In the vision, he was staring at me directly; but I was far beyond his compulsive range, and so those devastating blue eyes appeared to reflect only loving concern. Which may have been all that was in Denis's mind at the time.

Once again he reassured me that he would not give us away to the authorities. I asked him why, and he said:

I'm not quite sure myself, Uncle Rogi. Perhaps I don't view Milieu ethics in quite the same light as more dedicated humans do. I'm afraid that I've come to believe that the welfare of my family—and the human family, in the larger sense—is more important than any Galactic civilization. It's reprehensible of me, but there it is.

"I'm reprehensible, too," I admitted. Just my nose stuck out of the sleeping bag. I was completely exhausted, I ached all over from wrestling and chopping up the moose, and my stomach was beginning to feel collywobbly from all that liver. "Is that why you declined to serve as a Magnate of the Concilium?"

That, and other reasons.

"I think even Lucille was shocked when you turned it down."

Denis laughed, then said: She had been looking forward to the social aspects of magnateship. Giving parties on that level would have been a considerable leg up from our little faculty shindigs here at the college.

"Poor Lucille. Well, at least you get to attend the inauguration."

Yes. You should see the incredible dress she got for the ceremony. All black and green and silver beads. She's left Earth already, along with Paul and most of the others and their families. They're scheduled to arrive in Concilium Orb on second December Earth date. Only Adrien and I are still here, winding up some work. We'll be taking off in about two weeks, and we'll get to Orb in time to join the family for Christmas.

"About Paul . . . Denis, Teresa is convinced that having this superior baby will patch up the troubles between them."

I'm afraid she's indulging in wishful thinking. You know that the marriage has been on shaky ground for years now. Teresa's criminal pregnancy and her collusion with Marc in his scheme to fake her death were the last straws for Paul. He'll never divorce her, and he'll go along with the family in seeking a pardon for her. But that's about it.

"Merde . . . But what's done is done. Would he farspeak her from Orb, do you think? Reassure her on the baby's behalf, at least?"

I can ask, but I doubt he'd want to speak to her. Look at things from Paul's point of view: She deliberately set in motion a chain of events that will eventually do great damage to his prestige and that of the family. What's more, her disappearance also helped influence the exotics to impose a thousand-day probation on the Human Polity's full admission to the Concilium.

"What the hell does that mean?"

It means that, given cause, within that period they can summarily rescind our full voting membership in the Galactic Milieu and reinstate the Proctorship for an indefinite period . . . or even abandon us.

"Abandon——! You mean cancel the Great Intervention?"

They probably wouldn't bring all the human colonists back to Earth. The planetary resources could never accommodate them. But the Milieu could fix up Mars or some of the asteroids for the overflow population and cut us off completely from any intercourse with their confederation.

"Oh." I thought about that for a bit. "But they could hardly take back the scientific goodies they've already given us—the superluminal drive and the new energy technology, especially. We already have a whole generation of human scientists who know as much about that stuff as any exotic does. And the metapsychic advances can't be canceled, either."

Denis said: No.

"We've been told again and again that the Milieu doesn't wage war. That their Unity—whatever it is—precludes any hostility between rational entities. But operant human metas are getting more numerous and more powerful every year, and we're supposed to have minds that will eventually surpass those of the exotic races. When we really get geared up, *could* the Milieu prevent us from retaking our colonial planets without fighting us?"

I don't know . . . I don't know.

"Maybe," said I, "getting out of the Milieu wouldn't be a bad thing at all! Sure—we'd have some problems after we cut loose, but eventually we'd be better off than before. It's a big goddam Galaxy."

For a long time, Denis was silent. I could see him in the study of his gentleman's farmhouse, sitting before the fire with one hand over his eyes.

Then: Why did you do it, Rogi? Go along with Marc's crazy plan?

"It wasn't so crazy. Both Marc and Teresa were convinced that the baby was a supermind—"

But *you* weren't, were you! You're too sensible to fall for an unsubstantiated notion like that. Why did you endanger your life, helping them?

I no longer gave a damn. I was beginning to feel very sick. That damned moose was getting postmortem revenge. Subliminally, I said to Denis: Just go away and let me alone. I'm feeling rummy in the tummy!

But he refused to take the hint. I muttered, "Denis—you wouldn't believe me if I told you."

Try me.

I sighed. My guts churned. "Do you remember the night of the Great Intervention?"

?? Of course. But what's that—

"Just before Vic's men started attacking the chalet on Mount Washington, I mind-hollered a message to you. I said I had been told to tell you and your metapsychic colleagues to renounce violence, to unite in a metaconcert of goodwill. And if you did, I said, then beings from the stars would let our poor little planet out of its Galactic Coventry and come to help us. Do you remember that?"

I . . . thought you were hysterical. Even so, your idea was a good one, and it crystallized notions that I had held for some time.

"I wasn't hysterical. A Lylmik has been talking to me for years."

Rogi—

"Shut up. You asked to hear it, and you're going to, by damn! This Lylmik told me that the exotics needed my help. Our family was pivotal, they said. Pivotal in the goddam destiny of the goddam world.

From time to time this Lylmik gave me orders. Like telling me to take a hand in your mental education when you were a baby. Some kind of exotic in disguise saved me when Vic came after me, ready to turn me into a zombie like poor Yvonne and Louis and Leon. Exotics meddled with my life at other times, too, forcing me to do things. And the Lylmik who talked to me—I've always called him the Family Ghost— farspoke me on the day last summer that Marc came back to Earth convinced he had to save his mother and her unborn child. The Lylmik quite flatly ordered me to help them."

Uncle Rogi, the Lylmik don't work that way! They're aloof, almost cosmically disinterested entities, who concern themselves with only the most long-range aspects of Milieu policy. They almost never participate in ordinary Galactic affairs—much less try to manipulate a mere human individual.

"Try to manipulate . . . ? Hell's bells, the goddam Family Ghost nearly drove me nuts before the Intervention, pulling my strings! Then it lay doggo until now, except for making me introduce Mary Gawrys and Kyle Macdonald. You might want to think about what plans it has for *them!*"

Do you have any proof of all this? Why haven't you ever said anything before?

"Ah . . . I knew what you'd say. I was given permission to tell you about their Intervention scheme, but I wasn't going to be laughed at. As for proof, they gave me a cute little magical talisman. The Great Carbuncle. You remember it."

Your *key-ring fob?*

"Don't knock it. It's a genuine twenty-five-carat red diamond, pol- ished spherical. It's something else, too, but I'm not sure what."

This is incredible. Do you have the thing with you?

"Damn right. Never go anywhere without my lucky charm. And the Family Ghost is hanging around, too. Who do you think delivered the fucking moose? . . . Not that I'm complaining. It was a beauty. That liver was the tastiest thing I've had in years. But I think I might have overeaten just a little."

Et maintenant t'as la chiasse, non?

"Maybe. Why didn't you warn me when I was stuffing myself? Now I'm going to have to get up and go, and it's damned cold out there!"

Uncle Rogi, has this alleged Lylmik given you specific information about Teresa's unborn child? About its future role in the Galactic Milieu?

"Ohhh . . . Denis, go away. Leave me alone. Withdraw your EE. I'm sick. And I'm going to get sicker. If you've any sense of decency—"

Yes, of course. I'm sorry. But I'll be back, Uncle Rogi. I want to hear more about your Family Ghost.

"Go!" I croaked, and started struggling frantically into my half-frozen outer clothes.

I made it outside in time, but just barely.

The rest of the night was an intestinal nightmare, and I remember very little of the next day's journey up the steep ledges. I suspect the Ghost helped me along, for my poor body retaliated against the sudden influx of rich food with an even more sudden outflux. I couldn't even retain the oatmeal cakes. I didn't dare make camp at dusk. If I stopped hiking, I'd knew I'd never start again.

Viewed partially through my ultrasense, the snow seemed to glow once night fell, and I was able to see well enough. It was impossible to get lost. All I had to do was keep crawling up Ape Canyon, and eventually I would make it home. My guts finally calmed down, although I was still unable to even think of eating any food. The cold was diabolical, and after a while I couldn't feel my feet. I slogged on mindlessly, grasping saplings to pull myself up the steep incline, sometimes even having to use a rope, trying not to trip over my snowshoes or fall down too many times beneath my back-breaking load.

And then, when I was starting to hallucinate, seeing Teresa, dressed in her Queen of the Night opera costume, come toward me with a steaming chalice of hot tea with brandy and honey in it, I finally reached Ape Lake. Up there on the flat ice, the Arctic wind blasted straight into my face with full-gale force. I groaned aloud. Less than a kilometer to go—but I couldn't possibly make it. I fell to my knees on the windswept ice, tried to get up, and failed.

Lying there, with my face turned away from the howling wind of the rapidly approaching storm and the terrible weight of the pack off my shoulders, I was too far gone even to think of appealing to the Ghost. I felt that I was beginning to warm up at last. I would sleep for a little, then continue on. Teresa wouldn't mind waiting a while longer. Just a little while . . .

I saw her face. So very, very beautiful.

But was it really Teresa? Or was it another woman, a woman from long ago with strawberry-blonde hair and eyes of a blue so pale that they were almost silver, a woman who had once awakened me to love, whom I had also awakened, whom I had pledged myself to and then stupidly rejected, love poisoned by my wounded pride.

Was it Teresa, or was it—

Teresa Kendall's grandmother, Elaine Donovan.

Is that you, Elaine?

It's me, Rogi.

What are you doing here?

I've come for you.

That's thoughtful of you. But I can't get up, you know.

Yes, you can. *Come.*

All right. All right, Elaine.

Come with me. That's the way. *Come.* It's not far to go.

Elaine! I didn't dare speak to you at Paul and Teresa's wedding. I hoped you didn't see me, there on the stage of the Met, in the mob. But I saw you and knew that I had never stopped loving you. Oh, Elaine.

Come. Come with me.

You looked so young. They said you had been one of the first to try the rejuvenation technology. I'm glad that I never saw you old. Elaine, Elaine! Now you need never grow old. And here you are, with me.

Come. It's only a little way now, Rogi. Dear Rogi.

Elaine, do you love me, too?

Come. Come.

But do you love me?

Come!

Elaine—are you dead? Are we both dead? *Where are you taking me?*

Come . . .

I opened my eyes and saw the beams and close-set poles of the cabin ceiling. It was night and the lamps were on. I was on my bunk, warm at last, my body inside a down sleeping bag, my head wrapped in soft white fur. My face was painful. So were my feet. The stove roared softly. I could smell coffee and freshly baked sourdough bread—

And roasting meat.

None of it made any sense. I closed my eyes again and seemed to open them almost instantly as the cabin door swung wide, admitting a blast of icy air and swirling snowflakes, then slammed shut.

"Elaine?" I mumbled.

There was a multiple thud as heavy things hit the floor. A bucket of snow and an armload of wood. She came running to me, making little mewing sounds of concern when she realized she was exuding cold. She stepped back and peeled off her snowy outer garments, dropping them in front of the stove.

Not Elaine. Teresa.

"You're awake! Oh, thank God. You've slept for nearly twenty hours! I thought you'd gone into some kind of coma. How do you feel? I brought back all the meat you were carrying before the storm hit us. It's wonderful! Can you smell it roasting? And I have your pack and the rifle and all your equipment safe, too. It took me three trips down the lake to bring it all, and then the blizzard started, and it's been continuing ever since. Oh, Rogi—we were so worried!"

"How did I get back here?"

She came to kneel beside the bed. Her hair, escaping frowsily from its ponytail after being crushed beneath her parka hood, was dark and not strawberry blonde. The eyes, watering slightly from the intense cold outside, and perhaps from some other emotion as well, were hazel green and not silvery blue.

"I heard you out on the lake. Your mind was calling very loudly, and I knew you were in dreadful trouble. So I dressed and took a flashlight and went after you. Once I got down the slope and onto the ice, it wasn't too hard going. The wind had blown away most of the deep snow. I found you near the Ape Creek outflow, nearly covered with drifted snow, and took off your pack and your snowshoes. You were conscious, but you seemed to be delirious. You called me by my grandmother's name."

"I remember."

"You—you were too weak to get up. I knew you'd freeze to death if you stayed there, so I began to drag you along the ice. But I was able to go only a little way before I had to stop. You were too heavy and I didn't know what else to do . . . so I asked Jack to coerce you."

"Coerce me!"

She nodded. "And he did, and you walked the rest of the way and fell onto the bed." She smiled and shrugged. "I undressed you and warmed you up, then went out for the meat and equipment before the blizzard began. And that's all there was to it."

I lifted my arms to her and she hugged me tightly, and I whispered, "Thank you. Both of you."

She took one of my hands and guided it solemnly to her distended belly. "I've explained to him very carefully all that you've done for us. How good and unselfish you are. He won't hide from you anymore. If you want to, he'll speak to you. He'd like to learn to love you."

I said: Baby? Jack? Ti-Jean? . . .

The cabin and its furnishings seemed to fade away, and I was surrounded by a strange light of the deepest carmine red. I heard a symphony of sound: a double-time beat played on two giant tympani, an accompanying fluid rustle adorned with small peeps and squeaks, slow periodic gusts of wind. I tasted something that was sweet-salty-bitter, felt lapped in warmth, comforted, shielded. My own heart seemed to catch on fire as the other mind touched me, came joyfully into me. I saw him and he saw me. His eyes were enormous and wide open and aware. He was serenely afloat, tiny hands clasped, a perfectly formed unborn baby boy. Perfect. Perfect . . .

He said: *Rogi!*

And let me know him.

[22]

SWAFFHAM ABBAS, CAMBRIDGESHIRE, ENGLAND, EARTH, 7 DECEMBER 2051

Adrien Remillard had had no idea why Professor Anna Gawrys-Sakhvadze was so anxious to see him. She had farspoken him in mid-morning, New Hampshire time, and asked him to have dinner with her that evening if it was at all possible.

Adrien was rushing to complete his portion of an extensive revision of his father's textbook *Metaconcert Structure and Template Programming*— its looming deadline being the reason he and Denis had stayed behind on Earth when the rest of the family left for Concilium Orb. He definitely did *not* have any time to spare for a chin-wag with an old family friend. Not even one so beloved as Dotty Annushka, so named by Adrien when he was a toddler unable to pronounce "doctor" and she was a visiting fellow at Dartmouth's physics department. Anna adored the seven Remillard children with the fervor of a woman unable to have any of her own, and as a frequent guest she had introduced them to homemade Russian ice cream and other unforgettable ethnic treats.

Adrien pleaded the press of urgent work when she called. He had only three days left to finish his section of the book before he and Denis were scheduled to leave Earth themselves. Couldn't he and Dotty Annushka get together when they were all in Orb, when there would be all the time in the world for lengthy discussion? Or perhaps whatever was on her mind could be talked about right now.

But Anna said: I must see you in person immediately Adrien. Please I beg of you I would not make such a request if the matter were not of the most paramount importance.

So he took off at once in his egg, and three hours later met her for a quick supper at The Windmill. The pub was not far from the Institute for Dynamic-Field Studies, where Anna worked, situated in a little village northeast of Cambridge. Although she greeted him with a hearty Russian hug and kiss, her rejuvenated face had a drawn look. She was clearly very much keyed up and apprehensive, betraying deep anxiety in spite of determined efforts to shield her emotional state. She would not talk about her "important business" in a public place—especially not one like The Windmill, filled with operant scientists champing sandwiches and cottage pie and swilling old ale. The discussion must wait until they went to her laboratory after the meal. There, she told him, they could converse behind the secure shelter of a mindproof sigma-field and be sure that no one on Earth overheard them.

Adrien's eyes widened at that. He said: For heaven's sake Dotty!

But she would say no more until he finished eating. Then they went out of the cozy pub into the winter night. A bitter wind was blowing off the frozen fens, but it was only a short walk to the IDFS complex. Following Anna's instruction, Adrien had left his rhocraft in the crowded car park of the pub.

When they were away from the center of the village, Anna said, "Do you know that Davy MacGregor's wife has died?"

"Yes. Paul farspoke the news to Papa, and he told me. It's a terrible thing. Margaret and Davy seemed so happy together. I understand that Davy is devastated by her suicide."

Anna took Adrien's arm as they crossed the road and entered a side lane. "Davy farspoke me early this morning with further details of the investigation. The Magistratum did find incinerated human elemental remains consonant with a woman of her mass, including gold and alloy metals equal to the weight of her wedding ring. And her aura is extinct, as far as the Krondak comparators can determine. She certainly isn't within a thousand lightyears of Orb. The Magistratum is prepared to declare her legally dead, but the verdict will remain open."

"But she left a suicide note—"

"The note was in her handwriting and had her fingerprints and DNA traces on it. But Davy is convinced that she never would have taken her own life. He thinks she was coerced to write the note, then was murdered in the same mysterious way that Brett McAllister was—by the person who attacked her at Dartmouth on Halloween. Davy told me he suspects that the killer is a member of the Remillard family. Perhaps even Paul himself."

Adrien halted in his tracks, looking down at the Russian physicist.

She wore a long faux-fur coat and hat, which combined with her stocky build to lend her a roly-poly teddy bear aspect that belied the brutal words she had just spoken. This dear old woman had known him and his family for over forty years; but she was more than a friend—she was also the Director of the Department of Sigma Studies of Cambridge University, and not one prone to vaporous fancies.

Adrien asked, "But what motive could any of us Remillards have?"

"Some Magnate-Designates of my acquaintance believe that the only conceivable motive for Brett's murder was his opposition to his wife's serving on the Concilium. Once he was dead, Catherine acquiesced. And now we have Davy as the only one opposing Paul for the position of First Magnate. Davy is too powerful an operant to attack with impunity. But this murderer—if Davy is right and Margaret *was* murdered—might well have thought that Davy would be so distraught with grief after Margaret's death that he would give up the candidacy. You know, of course, that Davy's own mother was murdered by an anti-operant fanatic years before the Intervention took place. And losing his first wife Sybil just after Will was born crippled him emotionally for thirty years."

They began walking again, and soon they entered the IDFS complex, with its scattered large buildings. The east wind raked the expanse of frost-silvered grass and strummed the leafless black poplars lining the drive.

"This murderer can't be one of my family," Adrien said. "I'd stake my life on it."

"Would you?" Her tone was as cold as the rising gale. "No doubt the Magistratum would agree with you. They subjected all of you to mental probing after Brett McAllister was killed, and they were forced to exonerate you."

"Nevertheless, you say that Davy believes that a Remillard killed his wife and Brett. Has the Magistratum taken any cognizance of his notion?"

"Davy has accused no one . . . officially. He may be wild with grief, but he still has sense enough not to precipitate a scandal that might disrupt the Concilium Inauguration. Nevertheless, you must agree that if the two deaths are connected, the Human Polity is placed in a frightful position. The Remillards are called the First Family of Metapsychology for a very good reason: all of you have positions of influence and power. And if one is a calculating killer—"

"No one in my family could have done such a thing! I know them too well."

"My dear Adryushka, you are hardly without prejudice." Her tone softened. "And perhaps, as you say, Davy's suspicions are unfounded. But if he is right, it is my considered opinion that there is only *one* Remillard whose innocence is utterly unassailable. One who could not possibly have killed Margaret—and by implication, did not kill Brett, either. You."

!!

"No one could have coerced Margaret Strayhorn to write a suicide note over a distance of 4000 lightyears—much less coerce her to jump into a waste destructor. You were here on Earth when she died—ergo, you are not the killer." She smiled at him. "Besides, I *know* you, my dear little Adryushka that I dandled on my knee! I know you are goodhearted and honest and unselfish . . . I know you do not blindly accept the dictates of the Galactic Milieu as Paul and Anne do, and you are not quite as bedazzled by your younger brother's undoubted brilliance as your older siblings often are."

Adrien only shook his head. They walked on for a while in silence. Then he asked, "Why did you want me to come here?"

"I must put a very important proposal to you. One that . . . I had intended to postpone speaking of until much later. But circumstances have changed, and it is appropriate to present it to you now."

"What is this proposal?"

"First, let me tell you that there has been a great scientific breakthrough at Cambridge, which the exotics are as yet unaware of. The discoverers have kept it under wraps, feeling it would not be politic to reveal it until after humanity has been granted full Milieu citizenship and exotics no longer control the law enforcement bodies. I will tell you about it very shortly, so there is no need for you to coerce it out of me."

Adrien was stung by her evident mistrust. "Dotty Annushka—do you really think I would do such a thing?"

"I wasn't sure," she replied calmly. "If you were more loyal to the Milieu than to your own human race, you might."

They pressed on without speaking and without communicating mentally, Adrien at a loss to understand Anna's imputations against his siblings. And what was this about a mysterious breakthrough? It was a serious breach of professional ethics not to publish news of important scientific discoveries immediately. If Anna, normally so conscientious, had colluded in a cover-up, she must have had an extraordinarily good reason for doing so. What in hell was going on?

At last, when Adrien was nearly half frozen in his light windbreaker jacket, they reached a wing of the extensive Sigma Studies Laboratory. Anna doffed a glove and put her thumb on the heated lock pad of a side door. It swung open. Inside, the mock-medieval structure was warm, silent, and brightly lit, its corridors deserted.

"No one is working here tonight," Anna said. "I made certain of that. Being the director of an establishment has advantages as well as responsibilities."

They came to a door marked EXPERIMENT IN PROGRESS— ABSOLUTELY NO ADMITTANCE, which she also thumbed open. Beyond was a rather small, windowless room clogged with equipment and haywired power cables. The air carried a faint odor of ozone, and the floor looked as though it hadn't been swept in weeks. In the center of the room, where there was a cleared space, two rickety old wooden folding chairs stood before a small, very businesslike control console. A piece of apparatus suspended from an electric hoist hung about two meters above the console.

Anna slipped out of her furry coat and tossed it aside. Beckoning Adrien to join her, she sat down on one of the chairs and began working at the controls.

"Is this the new ultrathoughtproof sigma generator?" he asked, indicating the gadgetry that dangled just above his head. He sat down beside her and let his deepsight tour the circuitry of the device at lightning speed. It was very compact and obviously more sophisticated by several orders of magnitude than the mechanical privacy screens that had already been in use for many decades in the Milieu. None of those was secure against the probing of a Grand Master operant human, a Krondaku, or the more powerful minds among the Simbiari. Before Adrien had finished analyzing the new generator, the lights in the room suddenly went dim and it seemed as if they sat inside a dome of darkly transparent glass.

"The field is quite gas-permeable, so we can't possibly suffocate," Anna said, taking her hands from the control pads and sitting back with a suddenly relaxed air. "And as you see, it's not light-opaque like the earlier screens. No more claustrophobic feeling." She reached out and tapped the superficies with one knuckle. "Impermeable to solids and liquids, though, and alleged to be proof against the thoughts of even a Grand Master like you. Care to give it a test? There's a coffee machine on that bench in the corner. See if you can PK it into operation. Do your best, my dear. I could use a cuppa."

Obediently, Adrien exerted his psychokinetic metafunction, a faculty much prized by operant children but unappreciated by Milieu intellectuals, both human and exotic. An adult—especially a powerful adult—who used his PK blatantly risked being labeled a case of arrested development. Still, the odd bit of mental prestidigitation sometimes had its uses.

But not, evidently, inside Anna's newly designed sigma-field.

"That's very good," Adrien conceded. "Tried to hit the button on Mr. Coffee with every erg I could crank, and got nowhere. Is this screen your great scientific achievement?"

"Good heavens, no." She was staring at him with a strange expression that combined hopefulness and fear. "The existence of this new sigma technology is well known in the field, if not to the general public. No, our truly important breakthrough is something quite different, not even officially connected with the IDFS. I will tell you about it—show it to you—after we have discussed the reason why I asked you to come to England."

Heroically, Adrien restrained his impatience. "Very well."

Anna's hands, bare of rings and with the nails cut short, were laced tightly in her lap now. She stared at them as she began to speak. "I am, I suppose, a moderately important person. I have made a few good contributions to dynamic-field physics, and I have exerted a certain professional and public influence that must have impressed the exotic preceptors, since they have nominated me to be a Magnate of the Concilium. Still, if I should die tomorrow it would be no great loss. There are at least five others in this institute who are as deserving as I of the honor the Milieu has seen fit to bestow on me."

She lifted her eyes to meet his and continued quietly. "And I *would* die, my dear Adrien—that is, I would take my life—rather than reveal the secret I intend to share with you tonight. I know in my heart that you would not do anything to harm or compromise me. But if you betray me, I will have no other recourse than death. I tell you this so that you will know the depth of my commitment. A commitment . . . that I think you will want to share."

Alarm surged up in Adrien's mind. What the hell was she leading up to? Her mental barriers had abruptly fallen, and something unusual and very dangerous waited just beyond her passive vestibulum, daring him to inspect it. But he could not. Whatever this great mystery was, the responsibility for revealing it would have to be hers.

"No, Annushka. You'll have to speak. I won't take this from you."

She nodded. "Very well . . . A long time ago, you were at a large party. Everyone was drinking heavily, and thoughts that ordinarily are kept carefully sequestered were flying about like the proverbial bats out of hell. The burden of those thoughts was resentment against the Simbiari Proctorship, against the exotic domination of Earth—even though we humans had agreed, in principle, to endure whatever hardships were necessary to prepare ourselves for full citizenship in the Galactic Milieu. You were as drunk as the rest, and you spoke your mind with considerable vehemence, saying that we might be making a great mistake accepting the constraints of a civilization engendered by exotics. You said, among other things, that we were still ignorant of the very *essence* of the Milieu—that ineffable Unity so prized by the nonhumans, which seems so contrary to human nature and to our cherished sanctity of the individual."

"I did say that," Adrien admitted. "And I still have the same doubts. But lately I've been too busy with other matters to stew over them. And some of the studies by our xenologists and philosophers have led me to believe that Unity might perhaps not be the bugaboo it seemed to be. But—"

Anna held up a restraining hand. "What would you say if I told you that there exists a small group of highly placed operants, including myself, who are convinced that humanity's future best interests lie *outside* the Galactic Milieu?"

Adrien said quietly, "I think I might agree with you. In the short term, we need the exotics very much. In the long term . . . why shouldn't we be independent? Especially independent of this troubling Unity thing! I admit that I don't understand it, but it scares the hell out of me. It seems to have a different effect on different races, and it's certainly a more subtle thing than the hive-mentality analogs the nonoperant alarmists are so afraid of . . . I'm an American, Annushka, and we value our liberty above almost everything else in the world. Anything that threatens that freedom goes against our national spirit, which is why our people gave the Simbiari Proctorship such a hard time. What those exotics did whipping us into shape was nothing more or less than despotism—exerted with the best possible motives. I've had to ask myself if the Unity might be tyranny of a worse kind—something that we wouldn't even recognize as an abridgment of liberty. A kind of slavery that we'd *welcome,* that would make us very peaceful and contented, transforming our minds into something that isn't human at all. And we'd never realize what had been done to us, because we'd already be happily caught in the trap. Forever."

Anna took both his hands in hers. He was still her little Adryushka, keen as a razor, always questioning, never quite willing to take anything at face value. His hair, disheveled by the windy walk, was a dark tangle, and his rather plain face with its small mustache was pale and strained. He was only forty years old, a loving husband and father, with extraordinary talents and a long life of public service lying ahead of him. Did she have the right to ask him to be party to a conspiracy against an organization that had given humanity the stars?

But their little group needed him so badly—especially now, on the eve of humanity's admittance into Milieu citizenship. He would certainly be part of the Human Polity's inner circle of power, one of the operant elite. He, more readily than any of the rest of their little cabal, would be able to determine whether the Milieu and its Unity were as dangerous as her instincts prompted her to believe.

"Adrien, my dear, I have an invitation for you. I will only extend it once. This is why I called you here, so I could make this offer to you before you became a magnate—so, if you wished, you could take the oath to uphold the Milieu with a mental reservation and feel justified in conscience if later you decide to repudiate that oath. If you refuse my invitation, you will have a very perilous secret to keep, and my life will also be in your hands. I will not permit myself to be used to confirm the existence of anti-Milieu operants, much less betray them."

She took a deep breath, released his hands, and sat up straight in her chair. "Adrien, would you consider joining with me and with others—

other Magnate-Designates—whose sworn aim is the liberation of humanity from the Galactic Milieu? We plan no immediate rebellious activities, nor do we advocate violence. We intend to bring about the severance in a lawful manner when the time is fully ripe, and with no harm done to the exotics. Will you join us?"

He had lowered his head as she committed herself. Now he faced her squarely again. "Anna, in my heart, I've always believed that human beings must be allowed to pursue their own destiny, in freedom. The whole Unity question has bothered me for years. I never dreamed that there was organized operant opposition to the Milieu. Now that you've told me that there is, and that the movement has your support, I feel strongly inclined to join you. But I have to warn you about something that may make it impossible for your people to accept me. We Remillards *are* different from other operants. Stronger—especially in coercivity and redaction and creativity. Even the exotics are beginning to suspect it. *They can't get the truth out of us by mind-probing.* We're too powerful. The Milieu Magistratum bases its entire jurisprudence upon the infallibility of the Krondak-Simbiari technique of mind-probing—but we're above it. This is why . . . you may be right about one of my family being a murderer. I wasn't being straightforward with you before. The forensic mental examination of our family members after Brett's murder supposedly exonerated us. In reality, it proved nothing, because we are all capable of concealing our innermost thoughts from the strongest probes the exotics are able to inflict. We've admitted the possibility among ourselves that one of us might be a killer, and we're trying to deal with it. You say that you're satisfied I'm not a murderer. But if you accept me into your group, you can never be certain of my loyalty! I'm sure you've probed the motivations of each other, but you'll never be able to mind-ream me. So probably it would be best if I decline your invitation, with grateful thanks, before you disclose any compromising information, such as the identity of your associates. I'll never reveal anything of this conversation we've had tonight—most especially not to any other Remillard. But I don't see how you and your friends can risk having me as part of your group."

"I am already aware of the difficulty you just mentioned. The Remillard Dynasty and its preeminent mindpowers are seen by my group as part of the overall problem . . . However, we need ascertain only one thing of you: Are you or are you not telling the truth when you respond to our pledge of loyalty? We need not probe your invincible mind for detailed information. All we need is a single indication of affirmation or denial."

He laughed sadly. "You couldn't even be sure of getting that."

"Yes we can. My other secret—the scientific breakthrough that I spoke of earlier—is in Cambridge University's Department of Cerebroenergetics. Two of my fellow conspirators have finally developed the first true mechanical mind-probe. They did not want the Simbiari Magistratum to have this additional weapon to use against humanity, so they agreed to suppress the discovery until after the end of the Proctorship."

"Good God! And it would even work on somebody like me?"

"The psychoassay device is crude as yet. It indicates only 'truth' or 'nontruth,' as primitive lie detectors in use long ago attempted to do. Our machine works on completely different principles, of course, analyzing the total brain-wave spectrum. None of the operants we have experimented upon—and several of them have been Grand Master coercers—have been able to defeat it."

She opened the door to a compartment in the base of the console and took out a black box of modest size. Attached to it by a cable was a device resembling a baroque headset, which she handed to Adrien. He examined it with fascination.

Smiling, she lifted her hands in a wry Slavic gesture. "My—my fellow Metapsychic Rebels and I have all submitted to this mechanical inquisitor within the past month. I have been instructed to ask if you will do so as well."

"Willingly."

"Let me put it on you, then."

After some minutes of adjustment, the headpiece was finally in place, with a number of very fine needles sticking uncomfortably into Adrien's scalp. "It will render you unconscious for a brief moment," she warned. "This happens as the reading is taken. The effect is harmless."

"Go ahead."

She stood before him, the black box with its controls and display held in one hand while the other poised above the device's keypad. He felt a preliminary tingle as the thing was energized. Then:

"Adrien Remillard," she asked softly, "are you willing to rebel against the Galactic Milieu, putting the welfare of the human race before that of a Galactic civilization?"

"Yes," he said.

And a thunderclap of blackness seemed to crush him.

When he came to himself, Anna was smiling with tears in her eyes as she removed the device from his head. A moment later, she switched off the sigma-field. The dome of transparent dimness vanished, and several men and women suddenly entered the little laboratory and gathered in a nervous, expectant group.

Adrien grinned at them as he fingered the residually painful needle pricks. "My fellow conspirators, I presume."

He knew three of them already. Both Hiroshi Kodama and Cordelia Warszawska were prominent Intendant Associates, and Alan Sakhvadze was Anna's nephew, who worked in rho-field research at the IDFS.

Anna introduced the others. "Owen Blanchard is an upsilon-field researcher and President of the Academy of Commercial Astrogation. Jordan Kramer and Gerrit Van Wyk are psychophysicists at the university, largely responsible for the development of the device that just treated you so unkindly. Ragnar Gathen is a senior captain in the Civil Interstellar Force. There are two more of us, who could not be here tonight. One is Ragnar's sister Oljanna, pilot of the superluminal starship CSS Schlaraffenlande, on which we are all scheduled to embark for Orb in a few days. She is also Alan's wife. The other member of the group is Will MacGregor, Davy's son, who is already in Orb with his father. We have high hopes that Davy himself may someday be willing to join us. In the meantime, we are all campaigning on his behalf in the contest for First Magnate, since he is known to be sympathetic to our prohuman point of view—if not to our ultimate aim."

"We are most gratified to have you with us," Hiroshi Kodama said, bowing as he took Adrien's hand. "May we hope that you will also become a champion of human rights in the Concilium? Those of us who are Magnate-Designates have vowed to promulgate racial autonomy in open debate with pro-Milieu humans such as your brother Paul just as soon as it is prudent to do so."

"Well, I'll do my damnedest," Adrien said. And then he paused for a moment as a startling thought entered his mind. "But . . . the person we *really* need in this fight won't be able to join the group for quite a few years. And I'm not talking about Davy. I know someone whose mind is better than Davy's—better even than Paul's. And he's prohuman to the core of his soul."

"Who might this paragon be?" Cordelia Warszawska asked, a trifle dubiously.

"He's only a kid now," Adrien said, "but when he grows up—watch out, Milieu! I'm talking about Paul's son Marc. What a leader *he'd* make for this rebellion of ours!"

[23]

SECTOR 15: STAR 15-000-001 [TELONIS]
PLANET 1 [CONCILIUM ORB]
GALACTIC YEAR: LA PRIME 1-387-584
[24 DECEMBER 2051]

The four members of the Lylmik Supervisory Body, wearing their material bodies and also cloaked in mental disguise, walked unnoticed among the crowds on the Central Promenade of the planetoid. People of all races had come out to celebrate (or do ethnological research), and the first impromptu Christmas Eve in Orb was acknowledged by almost everyone to be a great success.

"One wishes that this Supervisory Body had thought to have the Concilium inauguration a bit later in the Galactic year," Noetic Concordance said, her handsome ebony face showing a trace of regret. "We showed a lamentable lack of sensitivity in scheduling it so that the poor humans would be obliged to be away from their home worlds during one of their most important holidays."

"Well, the Poltroyans and the Gi have atoned for our inadvertent solecism," Homologous Trend said. He neatly dodged a group of merrymakers being pursued by a white-sheeted figure topped with the skull of a horse, which was doing its best to bite people.

"Trust those two races to be perfervid sentimentalists," said Eupathic Impulse. "But one must admit that the gesture was an admirable one under the circumstances, and it must have involved a considerable search of the ethnological data banks."

"What a surprise to find this fantastic scene sprung up overnight on the Promenade!" said Asymptotic Essence, shaking her head in bemusement. "But one seems to recall that the element of surprise is traditionally part of the Christmas season. The humans certainly seem overjoyed at the gesture. Especially the little children."

The entire circular park area surrounding the great Galactic Concilium Chamber had been transformed into a holiday fairgrounds dedicated to the Earth celebration, and the Poltroyans and Gi had outdone themselves in making the spectacle as cosmopolitan and authentic as possible. There were even fireworks going off near the Simbiari concourse. The most prominent exhibition was a grove of gigantic Christmas trees, each done in a different human national style, fancifully decorated and sparkling with lights.

"One recollects that the illuminated tree with its ornaments was originally a German custom," Noetic Concordance remarked. "But by the time of the Intervention, virtually every ethnic group on Earth— even non-Christians—had adopted some variant of it, together with the celebration of Christmas itself, which was transformed from a purely religious commemoration into a secular holiday embodying the universal elements of gift-giving, feasting, conviviality, and family togetherness."

Prancing troops of goggle-eyed Gi, dressed in red or green velvet tunics trimmed with white fur and wearing pointed hats with white pompons, circulated among the crowd of tree-admirers handing out candy canes, Satsuma oranges, cookies, sugarplums, fruitcake, gingerbread men, marzipan fruits, and other goodies.

"Look, Mamushka!" cried one little girl, who had just been given a sugar pretzel by a simpering Gi. "It's *Big Bird!* Just like on the Tri-D!"

"A favorite nursery school fantasy character, one assumes," Trend murmured to his colleagues. "How thoughtful of the Gi to put clothes on for the festivities, even if it makes the dear things look sillier than ever."

"One is what one is," said Asymptotic Essence. But the others had not failed to notice that she had arranged the straight black hair of her body's head into an elegant coiffure for this evening's jaunt and created a striking Oriental dress of emerald hue to complete the effect.

"By the Prime Entelechy . . . !" Eupathic Impulse pointed to an elaborate assemblage of Poltroyans which had attracted a particularly large crowd of spectators in an area just beyond the trees. "What would one call *that?*"

"One perceives that this is a reenactment of a Neapolitan presepio," Noetic Concordance said, after a fast consultation of Orb's historical records, "an ornate folkloric interpretation of the Nativity manger myth. Such scenes are popular among practicing Christians, particularly the Italians. This particular style includes anachronistic Italian villagers of Earth's eighteenth century, mixed in with the angels, the Three Wise Men, and the other traditional figures. The originals were sumptuous miniatures, often hand-carved by the nobles of Naples themselves and dressed in beautiful costumes enhanced with real lace, precious metals, and jewels. The Poltroyans have simply—er—scaled the presepio up a bit, turning it into a tableau vivant."

The four Lylmik entities moved on through the crush of spectators, now and then accepting some item of Christmas food from Gi or Poltroyans in costume. Most of the latter were dressed as diminutive avatars of Santa Claus.

"If one looks about," Concordance said, "one may discern Poltroyans dressed to represent a multitude of different aspects of the elderly male giver of gifts. The French personage is called Père Noël, and in Britain he would be known as Father Christmas. Over yonder we see an exemplar of Grandfather Frost, traditional to Russia and the Ukraine and often assisted by a female dressed in white, sometimes called the Snow Maiden. The Chinese character is named Old Man Christmas. Some Japanese favor Santa Claus, while for others the gift-giver is the jolly god Hoteioshō, who is said to have eyes in the back of his head, so he can see if children have been bad or good . . ."

"Kurisumasu o-medetō!" cried the lavender-faced Santa-kurosu, mistaking Asymptotic Essence for a Japanese woman and giving her a little orange.

"O-sewa-sama deshita!" Essence said, bowing.

"That interesting variant over yonder is known in Poland as the Star Man," Concordance continued, "perhaps representing the survival of a pagan deity adopted by Christians through association with the star of Bethlehem . . . In many nations, Saint Nicholas, a generous ecclesiastic, is the yearly gift-giver, and he may or may not be associated with the Christmas celebration. Sinter Klaas, the Dutch Saint Nicholas, from whom the now archetypal Santa Claus was derived, is depicted by that entity over there wearing the bishop's costume. Note that he is attended by a shadow figure, in this case called Black Peter, who once would have delivered punishment to bad children rather than gifts. The motif of punishment contrasted to reward is a common one in the gift-giver myth, although in modern days all human children are considered to be 'good' at Christmastime. In parts of Germany, Austria, and Switzerland, gifts are distributed by an angelic impersonator of the Christ Child himself, Christkindl or Kris Kringle, also accompanied by a demonic sidekick. And look there: In the Scandinavian countries, Christmas presents come from gnomish creatures such as those, called Julnisse, Jultomten, and Julesvenn, displaying a more obvious derivation from non-Christian traditions."

The four Lylmik Supervisors paused at another well-attended theatrical spectacle, a quaint dwelling situated amidst artificial ice and snow, from which numbers of Poltroyans dressed as elves carried gaily wrapped presents to a waiting sleigh harnessed to eight small quadrupeds.

"The one in the red suit, white beard, and black boots is the most typical representation of Santa Claus," said Concordance. "So numinous and so well publicized has this originally North American figure become that he is rapidly replacing the other gift-givers in most parts of the Human Polity. He has, of course, no religious significance whatsoever."

Suddenly the small children in the crowd began to shout with excitement.

"Look there," Homologous Trend pointed out. "That elf character is bringing out another robotic animal to harness up ahead of the octet. What an unattractive thing! Is it meant to be a mutant? No, it can't possibly represent an actual creature . . ."

"That," said Concordance with a sigh, "is Rudolph the Red-Nosed Reindeer, the invention of a minor American writer named Robert May. The Infinite only knows why the beast has become firmly ensconced as part of the Christmas myth. One would not dream of boring one's fellow entities with the bathetic fable of Rudolph, which is basically a distortion of the Ugly Duckling motif. Let it suffice to say that human children's fondness for Rudolph indicates an inherent darkness in their psyches."

Nonsense! said a cheerful mind-voice, with which they were all too familiar.

"Greetings, Unifex," said the four Supervisors.

The oldest of them all, wearing human disguise with considerably more flair than his fellow entities, joined them from among the noisy throng, where the Poltroyan elves were now leading the children (and many of the human adults) in a Rudolphian carol of excruciating banality. With his twinkling gray eyes and rosy cheeks, his smartly barbered white beard and hair, and his well-cut maroon three-piece suit with a sprig of holly in the buttonhole, Atoning Unifex might have served as the prototype for Santa Claus as boulevardier. He even flourished a matching top hat.

"Shall we move on?" Unifex suggested. "The music is much better further along the Promenade, where the Brits and the Germans have got together with some Gi wassailers."

"One hoped you would soon make an appearance," Impulse said, his face gone stiff as he tried to prevent the balky musculature from betraying intimations of disapproval. His face was Caucasoid, and he was dressed in a fashionable cape and suit of gunmetal and coral lumasheen. His fellow male, Trend, who was brown-skinned, wore a lounge suit of charcoal worsted with a pink shirt and a paisley tie. "Two urgent matters require the consideration of this Lylmik Supervisory Body," Impulse continued, "but with the First Supervisor incommunicado—"

"I've had business of my own to attend to. But I'm ready to give you my full attention right now . . . My, isn't this a grand Christmas fête? One must remember to congratulate the Gi and the Poltroyans."

They paused before an open-air stage, where *The Nutcracker* ballet was being staged by human dancers, accompanied by an orchestra of exotics. Unifex frowned slightly as he studied the performance. "The Maurice Sendak setting? Yes, I think so."

"Please!" urged Impulse. "There has been another ghastly murder. Margaret Strayhorn, a Magnate-Designate and the wife of David Somerled MacGregor, was killed by some unknown entity right here in our own Orb. A note, written by the deceased, stated that she was committing suicide. The Magistratum has declined, with good reason, to confirm this verdict."

Asymptotic Essence said, "There is a well-founded suspicion that a person who made a previous attempt upon Margaret Strayhorn's life did in fact finally kill her. And the perpetrator of the earlier attack utilized the same peculiar lifeforce-draining technique seen in the murder of Brett McAllister."

"Are there any viable suspects?" Unifex asked, not taking his eyes from the stage, where the terrible Mouse King was menacing Clara.

"Officially, no," said Homologous Trend. "Many humans believe that Orb is full of mechanical surveillance equipment. As we know, this is not so. We have no way of knowing exactly how Margaret Strayhorn died. The Krondak Judicial Evaluator in charge of the case suggested that certain members of the Remillard family resident in the planetoid at the time of the killing be interrogated rigorously. We vetoed this on the grounds that insufficient evidence exists to warrant the drastic procedure, which would seriously violate the sovereign dignity and prestige of the examinees."

"Quite right," Unifex agreed.

Asymptotic Essence allowed a grimace of frustration to touch her porcelain features. "And besides, the forensic redactors probably wouldn't get the truth out of the Remillards anyway."

"Also true," said Unifex. In the ballet, Clara had hurled her slipper at the Mouse King, and the toy soldiers were finally winning the battle. "Then what's your problem?"

The four of them exuded astonished disapprobation.

"One knows very well!" Essence exclaimed shrilly. "One is being deliberately obtuse! One is once again subscribing nodally to a proleptic peculiarity in the human sexternion! Why does One persist in treating us in this dreadfully arrogant fashion?"

Unifex patted the outraged entity gently on her shoulder. "One really must not let the female hormones in one's physical body contravene straight thinking. What are you suggesting—that we Lylmik should take over the investigation? And perhaps psychocreatively dissect the brains of the Remillards to see whether any of them had a hand in the murder?"

"It seems to be the only way one might resolve the impasse." Essence drew away from the overlord's touch, pretending to adjust her green gown. "Here we have a crime of the utmost gravity, committed right under our virtual noses, and we can't do a thing to assist the Magistratum in nabbing the perpetrator!"

"No," Unifex agreed. "We can't. I'm irrevocably opposed to Lylmik intervention at this time. Be assured that forbearance is the best course. One is certain of it."

"David Somerled MacGregor decided yesterday that he would not withdraw as a candidate for First Magnate," said Trend. "His life could also be in danger, if the motivation for Margaret Strayhorn's murder involved discouraging him from opposing Paul Remillard. This is the other important matter we wished to consult you upon."

"There is undoubtedly a risk of further violence," Unifex admitted. "But Davy is a Grand Master coercer. If he keeps his wits about him—and he will—the killer won't be able to touch him. Trust me."

The four entities retreated behind mental barricades, but they could not control the reproachful expressions their faces assumed. In the ballet, the orchestra announced the transformation of the homely toy nutcracker into a handsome prince.

"We must trust," Noetic Concordance declared, in a resigned tone, "even though it is plain to us that One knows the identity of the killer."

"And One isn't going to do a thing about it!" cried Asymptotic Essence.

Unifex calmly regarded the two Lylmik in female form. "There are times when inaction is necessary. For the good of the Greater Reality."

Essence, her black eyes blazing, said: "But poor Margaret is dead, you coldhearted creature!"

"Yes. And poor Davy is alive. For now, that suffices." He turned and began to walk away. "I always felt that the choreography of this pas de deux lacked a certain je ne sais quoi. I think I'll catch the last of the *Messiah* before Cardinal Bogatyrev begins midnight mass."

Marc tracked down his younger sisters and little brother at the Greek Christmas simulation, where Poltroyans hideously costumed as Kallikantzaroi—subterranean goblins—were laying siege to a family of human actors attempting to enjoy a holiday meal in a mid-nineteenth-century cottage. The little horrors were hairy and deformed, and came riding in on misshapen small robot horses and gigantic chickens. Their leader, who arrived limping on foot at the end of the demonic procession, had a grotesquely swollen horned head with a lolling tongue and red eyes, and disproportionately large genitals. He introduced himself to the squealing juvenile spectators as Koutsodaimonas and vowed that he was going to deflower all of the young girls inside the cottage— and then the ones in the audience as well.

Marie and Maddy giggled, while young Luc growled, "I don't see what *this* has to do with Christmas."

A gang of Kallikantzaroi swarmed onto the cottage roof and went down the chimney. Once inside the house, they terrorized the residents by pissing into the hearth fire and then jumping onto the backs of the adults and forcing them to caper about and dance madly.

"In Greek folklore," Marc explained aloofly, "it was believed that the world was supported by a great tree. These demons supposedly work all year long to cut it down but are finally thwarted by the birth of Christ—or perhaps originally by the nativity of some ancient god— at which time the tree repairs itself and grows strong again. The frustrated imps surge up from the underworld and try to take revenge upon humans during the Twelve Days of Christmas. But they are always driven off by the appropriate folk magic."

The "children" of the besieged homestead were attacking their ugly little tormentors with brooms and sprays of hyssop, driving them out the door. To stem the chimney invasion, a great log was dragged into the fireplace, where it was stoked to produce demon-inhibiting smoke and flame. Once the house was free of the pests, the "mother" of the family distributed Kallikantzaros buns, dipped in wine.

These were also passed out to the audience, to the frustration of the demons. They were eventually driven off completely by a human actor costumed as the village priest, who sprinkled holy water all about and led the family in singing Greek Christmas carols.

"Okay," said Marc peremptorily. "You've seen it. Now come along with me. Papa wants us."

"Aww," said Luc. "We were going to go over to the Mexican display and break a piñata." He was a wan, fair-haired ten-year-old, whose peculiar aura still hinted at the congenital abnormalities that had been alleviated by extensive genetic engineering and microsurgery. The ordeal had left him vulnerable to injuries and to diseases that most humans were now totally immune to.

"And I wanted to see the next performance of *A Christmas Carol*," said Maddy.

Marie sighed. "I suppose we've got to go to midnight mass with the rest of the mob."

"You got it," said Marc, urging them along with his coercion. "Let's haul pétard."

The four of them went through the Christmas Tree Grove to a crowded plaza, where six churches representing various rites of Christianity seemed to have sprung up miraculously in place of the exotic gardens that had been there the day before. (The buildings would disappear, together with all the rest of the Christmas pageantry, on the Orb equivalent of 26 December.) The plaza was full of human and nonhuman carolers as well as worshipers streaming in for the services, and in its center was a Nativity scene in the traditional Provençal style. The seven siblings of the Remillard Dynasty, together with their many children, such spouses as there were, and Denis and Lucille, had gathered near the crèche. Paul stood apart from the rest, engaged in animated conversation with his close friend Ilya Gawrys. Paul and most of the other adults wore formal dinner clothes. There was going to be a réveillon for them and their political allies at Uncle Phil's Paliuli beach house after mass. The kids, who weren't invited, were stuck with a luau supervised by the various nannies.

"There's Papa," Marie said, without enthusiasm. "Do you suppose Uncle Ilya and Aunt Katy will be going with us to mass?"

"I doubt it," said Marc. "They'll be with their own relatives, if they go at all. Papa's probably just campaigning again. It really rocked him when Davy MacGregor announced that he was still running."

The sight of his father dampened Luc's earlier pallid enthusiasm and caused him to cling to Marie's hand. "It—it doesn't seem like Christmas Eve at all. I wish we were back home in New Hampshire."

"You should be grateful for all that the Poltroyans and Gi did for us," Marie reproved him. "I've never seen a Christmas spectacle like this anywhere! *Especially* not in New Hampshire."

"That's not what I mean," the little boy mumbled. "What good is all this stuff without Mama?" Tears sprang into his eyes.

Marc said gruffly, "Don't cry." But Luc only stood there with his head down, still holding fast to Marie.

Marc took a deep breath. Did he dare to risk it? Paul would be livid if he found out. But Papa didn't even seem to *care*, and it was Christmas Eve, for God's sake, and Luc, the poor little rug rat, was really on a downer and probably going to start blubbering . . .

He spoke on their collective intimate mode:

You guys. I'd like to tell you something. But you'll have to keep it to yourselves. No matter what! I don't think anybody'd try to probe a bunch of nitbrains like you but if they did—or if you leaked it—the whole family would be so deep in la merde we might never get out.

Marco! WHAT?

(God damn I must be leaking myself!) Look I'll tell you if you let me put a block into you afterward. Just a mild one that'd inhibit you from inadvertently spilling the beans in dreams or something. Will you let me?

Luc said: Will the mind-block hurt?

Marc said: No.

Maddy said: Will it keep us from talking about the secret among ourselves?

Marc said: No but you'd better watch your asses if you do.

Marie said: Last time you blocked me I couldn't even remember the damned secret you wanted me to keep!

Marc said: I'm getting better at it now . . . You all agree?

Maddy said: Is this secret *really* a good one?

Marc said: The best.

The younger trio said: Okay.

So Marc told them nearly everything. Marie and Luc wept softly for joy at the news that their mother was alive and about to give birth to a new baby brother. But Maddy said: I suppose the Human Polity will pardon Mama—provided that Papa and not Davy MacGregor is elected First Magnate. But *I* think it was a very selfish and foolish thing for her to get pregnant.

"Screw you," said Marc aloud, and slapped the mental block into all of them.

Fury! Fury! Can you hear me?

< Yes my dear Hydra. >

Teresa Kendall is alive! And she's carrying a baby with a supermind!

< I know. >

But . . . don't you think that could be IMPORTANT?

< The thought had crossed my mind. I presume you are entertaining the notion of seducing this wonder child and making him one of us. >

Well . . . it's pretty obvious now that we're never going to get a handle on Marc the way *you* hoped. But from what he said this kid Jack is even more metapowerful than him some kind of genetic sport too carrying lethal genes so he might end up more of a physical basket case than Luc and if that's so he might feel *we've* got something he could *use!*

< H'mm. I admit I never thought of it quite that way. I would have preferred to recruit Marc though. His powers are extraordinary enough and his temperament is eminently suited to our long-range goal. >

I hate his guts. He's an arrogantfrigidprick! He'd never approve of the goal any more than he'd approve of the nervebomb. (Andby-thewayit'sbeenalongLONGtime&whatareyougettingMEforXmas?)

< Hydra Hydra Hydra. What am I going to do with you? >

[Petulancy. Bloody-mindedness.] You don't really love me. You want HIM and you don't care that he'd push me around and this obscene baby Jack who knows what kind of a person he'll be and whyohwhy can't it be just *YOU&ME?*

< You are the most special person of all. My firstborn and best-loved. But we need others. I've explained that to you. This is only the beginning for us. We're preparing the groundwork for our glorious future [embrace] and later on when it's safe . . . Santa will bring you a nervebomb. Now—are you satisfied? >

Nervebomb! NervebombnervebombNERVEBOMB!! YesFuryyes . . . and if you want me to take care of Davy MacGregor just say the word I know I could take him he's still all soppy inside—

< NO. You are to stay away from him! Before Strayhorn died she transmitted a hint to him regarding your identity. >

[*!!!Panic!!!*]

< [Exasperation.] A hint only nothing concrete you fool be calm be calm wouldn't I have warned you if there was any real danger? >

. . .

< Of course I would have. What we must do now is be patient. You've done your work well but we must let the situation ripen a bit now before taking the next step. You won't hear from me for a little while— >

You're going away again? *Woe* . . .

< Now now. Concentrate upon building up your strength. You're nowhere near what you can be what you WILL be my darling Hydra no not yet you have a long way to go but O THE JOY when you reach the goal! When we reach it together! >

Yes. Isupposesoyes . . .

< Good night my sweet Hydra and Merry Christmas. >
You too Fury. I'll hang up my stocking and leave milk and cookies.

Five.

Davy MacGregor stood among the crowd on the side of the crèche
opposite the Remillard tribe and studied the lot of them with a dark
and baleful eye. With him were his son Will and his platonic friend
Cordelia Warszawska.

Five, Margaret had said, as she died. Five.

"Hiroshi has been working on M-Ds who are members of the Asian
Intendancy," Cordelia was saying, "and he is very confident that you
will gain a majority of their votes. So many of them have an inherent
prejudice against nepotism, and if Paul is elected he will undoubtedly
install members of his family in the steering committees—if not in the
Directorate itself. The European Intendants among the M-Ds are also
solidly for you, and if only Earth's Zone Intendants voted, you would
probably win. But the swing votes will undoubtedly come from those
Magnate-Designates who are not home-world elected—those nominated from the colonies, and the at-large M-Ds from the ranks of
science, the arts, and the smaller categories."

"If only the Magistratum had been able to find something implicat-
ing a Remillard," Will mourned. "Anything! But they haven't a clue—
not in the two killings and not in the Dartmouth College attack on
Margaret. And to think we once believed that the exotics were damn
near omniscient!"

"They're no such thing," Cordelia said. "Especially not nowadays,
when human operants are finally learning how to use their powers to the
fullest. The exotics have been reluctant to admit publicly that some of us
can screen them out and resist their probing, but it's true all the same."

"Especially of those damned Remillards," Will said. "But just wait
till the Human Polity gets its franchise! Our own Magistratum will
have the—"

Don't even think it, you fool! Cordelia admonished.

Will retreated precipitately behind a mental barricade, flushing to
the roots of his auburn hair.

Davy, who knew very well what his son was thinking, said quietly,
"Unless we want to be even more totalitarian than the Simbiari Proc-

torship, we'll have to put strict legal limitations on mental probing. *Any* kind of probing. Certainly the process will never be used casually—for investigative fishing expeditions. And there is no solid evidence whatsoever linking any Remillard to the crimes in question."

"Then we may never find out who killed Margaret!" Will said.

His father looked away. He, like his son, had inherited the rangy Highland physique and beaklike nose of Jamie MacGregor. But where Will also had his grandsire's flaming hair and impetuous temperament, Davy was swarthy, and his demeanor more dour and studied.

"There is one clue," he now admitted to Will and Cordelia. "I said nothing of it to the Krondak Evaluator because I'd blanked it out in my grief, along with Margaret's dying cry. She said a single word, you see. It seemed to make no sense then. But I've been worrying it in my mind for a while now, batting it about and tearing at it and trying to sift out the nuances of her meaning as I replayed it in memorecall. And I think I may have finally got it . . ."

"For God's sake, Dad!" Will cried. "You have a clue and you've said nothing . . . ?" Cordelia touched the younger man's arm, silencing him with her coercion.

Davy was looking away, over the crèche with its naïvely charming santons, to the dense group of people on the other side. Clustered proudly together now amid their children and spouses, exuding their inimitable aura of power and consequence, were the seven members of the Remillard Dynasty: Philip, Maurice, Severin, Anne, Catherine, Adrien, and Paul.

"As Margaret died," Davy said, "she cried out the word 'five.' I've pondered her meaning and come at last to the conclusion that she was describing her murderer. But he wasn't a single person at all. He was a meld of five minds—a metaconcert."

"Of course," breathed Cordelia Warszawska, her eyes widening in sudden comprehension. "And if the same metaconcert killed Brett, it would help explain the extraordinary amount of psychocreative force that had to have been exerted to drain the lifeforce in that unique way."

The church carillons started chiming, and a chorale of exquisite Gi voices began to sing the "Cantique de Noël." Almost at once, the exotics were joined by those humans in the crowd who knew the French lyrics—including every one of the Family Remillard.

"What we must determine now, somehow," Davy MacGregor concluded, "is: *which five?*"

"Peuple à genoux," caroled the exotic choristers, "attends ta délivrance. Noël! Noël! Voici le Rédempteur!"

"No one could sing that song like Teresa Kendall," Davy MacGregor said. He seemed to be staring blindly at the great star that now shone above the crèche. "But she's gone, too, poor lass. What a hell of a Christmas."

Cordelia was Jewish and Will was an agnostic, but that didn't stop the two of them from each taking one of Davy's arms and drawing him along with them into the throng streaming toward the Protestant Rite church.

"Noël! Noël!" the humans and exotics sang. And the bells rang out.

APE LAKE, BRITISH COLUMBIA, EARTH
25 DECEMBER 2051

Jon Paul Kendall Remillard had philosophical difficulties with the concept of Christmas. That the scraggly little evergreen tree his mother was trimming was a midwinter hope symbol was easy enough to understand from the explanations and mental images Teresa offered. But the notion of God creating a body for himself to wear—and even Creation itself—bothered Jack.

He said: It seems a very strange and unnecessary thing for God to do. To become human so that we'd love him rather than fear him. If he's truly a Supreme Being then it follows that he has no need of any other entity to ensure his own happiness. Especially entities that are so imperfect by their very nature that they will inevitably befoul an otherwise orderly creation. I can understand God creating the physical universe for fun. But why create other minds when you *know* they're going to mess things up?

"I believe famous human thinkers have debated those points."

Teresa was fastening diminutive candles made of moose tallow to the Christmas tree, which was hardly 60 centimeters tall. Each candle had a kind of saucer clip of aluminum foil to fasten it to the branch, but if one wasn't careful either the foil or the soft candle would crush. She had already spoiled three candles by working too fast, trying to have the tree finished before Rogi got back inside after his wood-splitting. The festive dinner was almost ready to put on the table.

"I seem to remember that the theologians [image] of early times were quite positive that God had no absolute need to create other thinking persons," Teresa said. "This is perfectly ridiculous, of course, since the theologians were willing to concede that he *had* done it and must have had a good reason. Now, unless we're ready to admit that a Supreme Being can be capricious or wishy-washy [grotesque images], it follows that he needed to do it. He did need us."

But what prompted God's need of us?

"Love," said Teresa.

The fetus said: That's irrational.

"Exactly. I don't believe anyone has ever *reasoned* out a satisfactory answer to God's need of us. Those religions outside the Judeo-Christian [image] tradition rarely hit upon the notion of a loving God at all. As for natural philosophy, loving-kindness would not be an attribute that one would logically deduce that a Big-Bang-Creator-God [image] would have."

Hardly.

"But love is the only motive that seems to make any sense. Without it, you have the Creator-God as a game player trying to assuage his cosmic boredom, caring about us only as game pieces [image]. That is to say, not caring very much! Now, if God wanted us to know that he created us out of love, he'd have to *tell* us, since we couldn't figure it out for ourselves. He'd have to get directly involved with us, rather than let us tick along obliviously the way the evolving nonsapient universe does [image]."

I suppose so . . .

"There are any number of ways he might have done this [images]. But put yourself in God's position and try to decide the most *elegant* way to get involved with your thinking creatures. The way that is at once most difficult and unlikely but has the potentiality to succeed in the most magnificent manner imaginable."

Not the easiest way?

"Heavens, no! What would be the satisfaction in *that*? I can sing 'Happy Birthday to You' [quotation], but I get more satisfaction doing the mad scene from *Lucia* [quotation], even if it tires me out terribly."

I understand.

Pinching and twisting, Teresa affixed one little candle after another, pausing now and then to straighten those that leaned out of true. "God's most elegant way of involving himself with us would have to be a scandal to the stodgy-minded and a delight to minds that have a sense of humor and of adventure. As his mind does."

God can laugh?

"Of course, dear, and feel sorrowful, too. A Supreme Being without those attributes wouldn't be supreme. Grim and joyless people try to pretend otherwise, but their arguments are unpersuasive."

Explain to me how God became directly involved with us.

"It has happened differently on different worlds in the Galaxy. On ours, *I* believe that the primary involvement happened through the Jewish people and the Christians. It's a long story, and you'll really have to read it in the Bible [image]. That book is a fascinating account of human moral evolution, with historical and deeply mythic truth all mingled in a wonderful mishmash. It's a literary treasure as well as the word of God, and some parts of it are profound, and some are fascinating and some are poetic, and some are even a bore, and parts of Saint Paul make me want to scream. I'm sorry that I haven't read the whole thing myself, but you can pull bits and pieces out of my memories. Different religions interpret the Bible in different ways, but we Catholics believe that when the mentalities of one single key tribe of extremely intelligent people [image] were finally mature enough to grasp the concept of a loving God, God simply spoke to them." She laughed. "Well—perhaps not *simply* [image]."

And the tribe accepted his messages and passed them on?

"Some members did. Others kept slipping and sliding back into primitive notions of angry gods that constantly needed to be appeased with blood sacrifices and other rubbish [image]. God had to keep coaxing them and smacking them down the way a loving mother has to do when her children are naughty [image], and—well, you must read the Bible and discuss it with people who know more about it than I do. Your Mama is a very poorly educated person, especially in religious studies. I'm probably explaining this all wrong. When I was in school and college, all I really was interested in was music . . . Now, where did I put that foil? I forgot to make a star. You can't have a Christmas tree without a star [image]."

Is love the motivation for all creation, then?

"I imagine so. Mental lattices within our normal Reality can't exist without the other five kinds, and vice versa. If God wanted to make minds to love, he had to make the whole cosmos. And it is quite lovely, most of it [images]."

But to create for the love of it seems so odd!

"Of course it does. It really makes no sense—in a rational view of the universe. And yet every artist knows the truth of it. And every healthy adult human knows that people who are in love want the whole world to be as happy as they are. If you are God, loving yourself or even *being* Love in some mysterious fashion, and there aren't any other minds to share happiness with—then you make some."

So one may conclude that God does need us?

"Most of our coreligionists today believe it's true . . . Damn! These two candles are bound to set the tree on fire if they sag just the least bit. I'll have to move them again!"

The fetus persisted: And the problem of the created minds being imperfect? And sometimes evil?

"I think that has something to do with advanced chaos theory, which I've never been able to make head or tail of. You must ask your big brother Marc to explain it after you're born. There's also some principle to the effect that it is much more glorious to make something wonderful out of imperfect parts. The very imperfection of the individual elements—even when there's actual evil involved, as there often is in human affairs—challenges God to greater creative heights."

What a strange idea.

"There's an old proverb that says: 'God writes straight with crooked lines.' Human history is just full of crooks and twists and twines [images]. One would think anarchy or barbarism or the lowest common denominator would have triumphed ages ago. But it hasn't. All the messes and atrocities and disasters have somehow been woven into a construct that looks better and better every year—at the same time that some things look even worse! The world you're going to be born into is a wonderland compared to the world that existed only forty years or so in the past [images]. That's because most people have easier lives in the Galactic Milieu than they did before the Great Intervention. But even so, there are still persons who are discontented or who are villains, and situations that are evil or tragic. Nevertheless we children of God continue to evolve and improve on every level, almost in spite of ourselves. That also has something to do with nonlinearity and chaos. And God's love, too."

The fetus said: That is very mysterious. Contrary to common sense! . . . Why do I find the concept pleasing?

Teresa only laughed. "Do you like the Christmas tree?" She had just installed the star and now moved back a pace or two to study the effect. The little spruce stood on the table in front of the window. It was trimmed with origami cranes made of foil, tiny oatmeal cookies, and gnomes made from pine cones and wire; sculpted hard-baked dough colored with cosmetics formed their tiny heads, hands, and feet.

Jack was tactful: You've worked so hard on the Christmas tree. Uncle Rogi is sure to like it. It will be interesting to see all the little fat-cylinders burning at once. Hazardous—but interesting.

Teresa spread a silk scarf in front of the tree as a festive tablecloth, then set out plates, cups, forks, and spoons. "We'll light the candles when we have dinner. The tree is not going to burn up! Rogi and I will watch it carefully. And after we eat, we'll give each other these gifts. The things wrapped in cloth lying under the tree."

Mama, why do you give gifts at Christmas?

"It's a tradition. Wise men [image] gave gifts to the infant Jesus. To Baby God. And he is God's gift to us." She checked the tenderloin roast, which was "resting" in preparation for being carved, and then used the whetstone vigorously on the big knife.

Jack said: That's the biggest paradox. Even greater than Creation. It was quite unnecessary for God to become human and teach us his love in person. I can see why some Earth religions deny that it happened.

"You've been rummaging in my mind again . . . Yes, Incarnation is quite absurd. But you must admit it would be an excellent way to catch our attention! And so madly elegant. It's also much easier for us to pray to and love a God-made-man, who would be more likely to understand our human difficulties, than to try to love an almighty Big-Bang-Creator. Why should *he* care if my roast is overdone or if I live long enough for you to be safely born?"

The fetus said: I would like him to care.

"Ah!" Teresa went waddling across the room to grope under Rogi's bed, where he had hidden the last of the rum. "Now we're moving into psychology! An incarnate, loving God takes on significant mythic overtones that appeal to the deepest levels of the human psyche. To that almost instinctive part of us called the collective unconscious."

I have not yet had any experience of that.

"You will," Teresa laughed, "when you really begin to socialize."

I—I wish I did not have to. Even letting Uncle Rogi know me was very frightening at first. There are dark parts to his mind. And I saw darkness in Grandpère Denis's mind as well, before I shut him out.

"You mustn't fret about it. All people have good and bad in them. I do, and so do you. This is one reason why a loving God is such an amazing consolation. He has no dark about him at all. God must know all there is to know about us—and yet he loves us anyway. He only wishes us well, even when we're wicked or when we deny him. We would never have guessed *that* about him in a million years, if he hadn't told us. It's mysterious beyond belief . . . Now let me see: The soup and the rice are keeping warm in covered pots behind the oven, and I have plenty of boiling water for the drinks, and the dessert is—"

Did God become incarnate for the other Milieu races?

"All of them except the Lylmik seem to think that he did. And Milieu anthropologists—or whatever they call themselves—tell us that many of the more primitive races in the Galaxy have Incarnation myths very much like ours. Of course, none of this is *proof* of God's Incarnation. It can't be proved. But I believe it, and so does Uncle Rogi, and your Papa and brothers and sisters, and billions of other entities. That kind of belief is called faith."

She pressed both hands against her enormously swollen abdomen, closed her eyes for a moment, and summoned the image of her unborn child. "I have faith in God's love just as I have faith in your great future, Jack. There are many things that frighten me and other things that make me very unhappy. But if I can just hold on to faith, I won't give in to despair. I *won't.*"

Mama—

But at that moment a booted foot began to kick loudly against the door, and Teresa hurried to open it for Rogi. He lurched in, weighted down by a great quantity of wood and enveloped in flying snow and Arctic air.

"Woof! This ought to keep us warm for an hour or two!" He dropped the frozen load, which overflowed the woodbox, and began to shuck off his outer garments. "Something smells mighty good in here."

"Roast moose tenderloin larded with garlic-salted moose fat. Moose consommé with moose-marrow dumplings and carrots. Rice with moose-and-mushroom gravy. And rum raisin tarts made with moose-fat shortening." She busied herself at the stove, pouring hot water into two cups, then added other ingredients while Rogi sat on the stool close to the stove, removed his boots, and wiggled his stockinged toes to restore their circulation.

Teresa held out a steaming drink, which Rogi took and sniffed at with incredulous delight. "Hot buttered rum? But I thought all the margarine was long gone."

"One thinks ahead," said Teresa solemnly. She lifted her own cup. "A la bonne vôtre, mon cher ami. And merry Christmas."

"Joyeux Noël to you," Rogi said, "and to Ti-Jean."

They touched cups, drank, and kissed each other lightly. Then she made him sit down at the table and begin carving the roast, while she brought the rest of their meal and lit the candles on the tree.

"Don't worry. I have a bucket of water and a wet cloth handy. We won't risk a conflagration." She slipped into her place. She had turned off the two powered lamps, and the two of them sat for a moment side by side with private thoughts, looking at the tiny dancing flames and their reflections in the frost-encrusted window and drinking the aromatic rum.

"It won't hurt him, will it?" Rogi asked after a while. "The liquor?"

Teresa shook her head, smiling. "It's well watered, and he's old enough to handle a little bit . . . aren't you, baby?"

The fetus said: It alters my consciousness. Curious! I'll study the matter.

Both Rogi and Teresa laughed. And then they asked a blessing and began to eat.

Teresa unwrapped Rogi's gifts to her.

"I have another one, too," he said, "but it's out on the porch because it's not quite finished, so I only put a picture of it in this package along with the other things."

Teresa stared at a thin slab of wood with a drawing on it, and four peculiar little objects. The artwork showed a simple inverted double-V frame with a thing like a small pack hanging from it. The wooden items looked rather like miniature dumbbells, six or seven centimeters long, with shafts nearly as narrow as toothpicks. Rogi demonstrated how one of the rounded ends was integral with the shaft, while the other could be pulled off with a tug, revealing that the shaft's end was sharply pointed.

"Those," said Rogi proudly, "are primitive safety pins. We forgot to bring any. These are made of hardwood, and they took me forever to whittle. Now you won't have to tie knots in Ti-Jean's diapers."

"How marvelous! And the picture—is it a baby swing?"

"Sort of. The woolen duffel-cloth pouch will have an internal padded frame when I get it finished. It's a papoose carrier. You either hang him up and set him swinging—he can watch you that way—or detach the carrier and put it on your back. It has straps."

Teresa embraced Rogi and kissed him. "What wonderful presents!" She got up from her chair. "Let me give you a refill of the hot buttered rum, while I get *your* present ready."

She handed him his drink. The candles on the tree had long since guttered out and the ordinary lamps were glowing on the table amid the remnants of their meal. Teresa directed Rogi to reverse his chair, so that he faced the beds. She turned the two lamps down to their minimal setting and put them on the floor in front of him.

"These are footlights!" she proclaimed. She hung long lengths of flannelette from the overbed shelves down to the floor, nearly hiding the beds. "This is the backdrop! And the stereo is ready with a very specially edited fleck. All that is needed is for the performer to don her costume in her sumptuous dressing room—namely the bath alcove— and then the entertainment will begin."

She handed him a cloth-wrapped object before she disappeared into the tiny curtained cubicle next to the front door. "This is going to take me a few minutes," she called. "Better put some wood on the fire! It wouldn't hurt if you cleared the table, either. But first open the introductory part of your present."

Mystified, he unwrapped another flat piece of wood, which had an ornamental border drawn around it, featuring vaguely Slavic motifs, and in the center a carefully lettered announcement:

◙ ◙ ◙ PROGRAM ◙ ◙ ◙

◙

SNEGUROCHKA—THE SNOW MAIDEN

A Tale of Springtime

◙

Opera in a Prologue and Four Acts by N. Rimsky-Korsakov
Libretto by the Composer from a play by A. Ostrovsky
French Translation by P. Halperine and P. Lalo
(for the Delectation of the Audience of One Frank)

STARRING: TERESA KENDALL

L I V E !

with the recorded voices and music of
Artists of the Metropolitan Opera

"Well, I'll be damned," said Rogi.

He had seen the opera once, on the night of Teresa and Paul's wedding, but he later admitted to her that he was completely distracted and remembered almost nothing of it. What could Teresa be planning to do now?

He cleared the table and replenished the fire. Then the musical overture began, and Rogi settled back in his chair. Outside, the winter wind hummed and hooted among the eaves. His stomach was full, the little cabin was warm, and the aroma of the hot rum went to his head, befuddling his senses in the most pleasant manner imaginable. The orchestration pouring from the small speakers was lush, romantic, full of flutes and horns calling like birds in April. But there was an ominous tone to it, too, a frisson of strings that seemed to hint that winter's power still reigned supreme, and spring might have come prematurely.

Rogi felt himself relaxing, his eyes closing . . .

He saw a bleak and frostbound woodland, and beyond it a frozen river. On its opposite bank was an ancient Russian walled town. The moon was setting, and dawn had broken. Cocks crowed. As the heavens brightened, it seemed that millions of birds winged through the air toward the forest, finishing their long journey from the south. A little faun sat on the root of a hollow tree, watching the spectacle happily. He sang that Spring would be arriving at any moment.

And then she came, carried down in a green-and-golden chariot drawn by swans and geese, surrounded by other colorful singing birds. She began to tell Rogi a strange musical story.

Spring had once fallen in love with King Winter and borne him a daughter, the lovely Snow Maiden, Snegurochka. But Winter kept the girl in his power, taking her away each springtime to the dreary Northland that never thawed. Now that she was sixteen, the Snow Maiden longed to live with human beings, away from her coldhearted father's domination.

Suddenly the landscape that Rogi imagined was swept by a brisk snowstorm, and King Winter himself strode into the scene. Spring pleaded with him to let the lovely little Snow Maiden go free.

Winter agreed but gave a grim warning: If the girl should ever fall in love and have that love returned by a mortal, the jealous sun god Yarilo would slay her—for love and the sun's warmth were akin, and both were forbidden to the Snow Maiden.

Then Snegurochka herself appeared.

Rogi realized that his eyes were wide open, and the illusion—could Teresa be creating it?—was suddenly penetrated by a living person. She was dressed in white robes trimmed with snowy fur and seemed to sparkle with silvery frost crystals.

And Teresa was singing—really singing again, as she had in her prime—her marvelous living voice somehow blending seamlessly with the recorded orchestra and the other singers. All the magic that had seemed to be lost forever was restored, and Rogi sat paralyzed in the midst of its glory, almost unwilling to believe that it was not part of the illusion.

The Snow Maiden rejoiced that she was to be allowed into the human world. She had seen a young man and fallen in love with him and the songs he sang. The very sound of his voice made her heart melt. "Melt!" cried King Winter, and warned her of her fate if she should have her love returned. But she could think only of the happiness that lay ahead of her.

Winter went off to his icebound lair, and Spring transformed the woods. The tiny Ape Lake cabin seemed to open wide into a huge green meadow full of flowers, and the delighted Snow Maiden was caught up in a mob of happy villagers, who danced and sang and welcomed her and took her home with them.

And the imaginary curtain fell on the Prologue . . .

Teresa stood there between the two glowing lamps, smiling at Rogi. Her splendid white gown and headdress were diminished, Cinderella-like, into ordinary cotton flannelette trimmed with the fur of snowshoe hares, with spangles and snowflakes cut from shiny foil. But she was still beautiful, still full of triumphant magic.

"Do you like the opera so far?" she asked.

"C'est fantastique!" Rogi cried. "But how are you projecting the illusion? I didn't think your creative metafunction was up to such elaborations."

"It's not. But Jack's is."

"The *baby* . . ."

"He finds the sets and the appearance of the other characters in my memories, and he realizes them. And now . . . Act One!"

Much later, Rogi would again not be able to recall too much of the opera's fairy tale plot; what he did remember was the haunting figure of the Snow Maiden, the girl begging her mother, Spring, for the very thing that was bound to kill her, which she declared she could not live without. Spring answered her daughter's plea. Snegurochka fell in love at last with a man who dearly loved her. She was about to be married along with the other village maidens at the yearly spring fertility festival.

But then came the most disturbing part of the fairy tale. The villagers sang a grain-planting song, in which a ransom was required if there was to be a good harvest:

Nous vous donnerons une jeune fille.
Et nous serons un de plus,
Et nous serons un de moins.

We will offer you a young maiden.
And there will be one more of us,
And there will be one less of us.

The Snow Maiden then sang a dazzling aria proclaiming her love. "Mon coeur," she cried, "mon sang, mon être tout entier s'embrase et brûle!" My heart, my blood, my entire being is set aflame and burns!

And a beam of sunlight suddenly pierced her, and she melted away in death.

Her bereaved human lover drowned himself in despair, unpersuaded when the local Tsar told him that the Snow Maiden's presence among the people was an affront to the sun god Yarilo, who would have withheld his light and warmth from the land had Snegurochka continued to live.

Yarilo himself then appeared atop his sacred mountain, holding in one arm a sheaf of grain and in the other a glowing human head, and the people saluted him with a final hymn.

When the opera was over, Rogi applauded until the palms of his hands hurt. The enceinte diva, completely exhausted and with tears of happiness coursing down her cheeks, slumped into his arms and had to be laid on her bed, costume and all.

"You've overdone it," Rogi said, trying to hide his alarm.

"No, no. I'm fine. It all went beautifully. I sang, Rogi! I *sang.*"

He eased the Slavic diadem off and propped one of the moss-stuffed pillows under her head. "You were tremendous! And that finale—I'm not sure that I understood the meaning of it . . ."

Teresa closed her eyes. "The fairy tale is a borrowing from an ancient Slavic religious rite. In order to placate the sun god and ensure that good weather would prevail and the grain would grow, the people would sacrifice a maiden. Too bad about her—but ever so satisfactory for the rest of the people, who got to survive and prosper and dance in the sunshine."

She opened her eyes and looked at him calmly. "Aren't you glad we don't have gods like that anymore?"

[25]

SECTOR 15: STAR 15-000-001 [TELONIS]
PLANET 1 [CONCILIUM ORB]
GALACTIC YEAR: LA PRIME 1-387-597
[6 JANUARY 2052]

He was dancing with his cousin Adrienne, a girl his own age whom he considered the least loathsome of his young female relatives. Marc had always loved dancing (which surprised everyone except his mother), and he was very good at it, except when his partners attempted to inject romantic overtones. Sex, that great nuisance, was the last kind of distraction he wanted out on the dance floor. The dance offered a safe relinquishing of personal power to the irrational. Perfectly attuned to a like-minded operant partner such as Adrienne, Marc was able to surrender his precious self-control for brief intervals without feeling threatened, and his guarded features would relax in a one-sided smile of rare sweetness.

The eldest daughter of Adrien Remillard and Cheri Losier-Drake was a tall girl, plain-faced and usually brusque and authoritarian in her manner. In her secret heart, Adrienne thought her cousin Marc was the handsomest, most excruciatingly adorable boy in the entire universe. But she would have died rather than let him know it, so when he asked her to dance, she hid behind her sternest mind-screen and feigned bored indifference. He seemed to appreciate that. The band went into the jazz-waltz dissonances of "I'm All Smiles," and she whirled away in his arms, so consumed with hidden ecstasy and oblivious to her surroundings that she almost missed the entrance of the Lylmik.

But Adrienne's ultrasenses were never completely off-line, even when she was semiorgasmic. They zeroed in on the unusual auras of the latecomers to the Human Polity Inaugural Ball without any volition on her part, and she stiffened, and the spell of the dance was broken.

"It's *them!*" she whispered, staring aghast over Marc's shoulder.

He didn't miss a beat, but his gray eyes lost their abstraction and were instantly wary. "By God, you're right, Addie. All five of them, and not wearing any simple Greek-god robes this time, either. They're spiffed to the teeth."

"What do you suppose they're doing here?"

"God knows. They might just want to socialize."

The furor that had attended the appearance of the incarnate Lylmik at the Concilium inauguration that afternoon was nothing compared to the astonishment now sweeping the ballroom. Earlier, many of the Earthlings had not fully appreciated the unprecedented honor granted their race when the five Supervisors materialized upon the Dais of Presiders in the Concilium Chamber wearing human form. The reaction of the exotic First Magnates and their congeners had been mixed: The Krondaku were mildly taken aback, the ecstatic Gi hovered on the brink of cardiac arrest (but adroitly eschewed the ultimate gesture), the Poltroyans uttered involuntary whoops and squeaks of appreciation, and the Simbiari were scandalized to their toewebs, reminding each other waspishly behind imperfectly woven thought-screens that the Galactic mentors hadn't condescended to honor *them* in such a dubious fashion when the first Simb magnates were inaugurated.

The Lylmik had presided over the brief ceremonial installation of the new human magnates. They had watched as Paul Remillard was elected First Magnate of the Human Polity by a small margin. They listened as Paul addressed the entire Concilium on behalf of humanity, and then applauded gravely as the Simbiari Proctorship was formally dissolved and all Earthlings were finally granted citizenship in the Galactic Milieu. (The probationary period of one Galactic year was diplomatically left unstated.) With the formalities concluded, the Lylmik Supervisors vanished, and everyone thought that was that.

Invitations to the Human Polity Inaugural Ball had been extended to every Magnate of the Concilium, with the expectation that only a few of the nonhumans would accept. The Krondaku had no tradition of dancing on dry land and sent polite regrets. The straitlaced Simbiari thought dancing was inane; they also knew very well that the humans didn't really want their ex-Proctors at the ball, so all except a handful of luckless high-ranking officials who felt obliged to show up and mingle also declined. The Gi would have loved to come, but their own parties inevitably climaxed in exuberant displays of communal licentiousness, and they thought it the better part of interspecies etiquette to pass. The kindly little mauve-skinned Poltroyans enjoyed dancing to human music, so fair numbers of them did accept.

And now bore witness to the phenomenon.

The jazz waltz played on to its conclusion, but many of the dancers left the floor to gape and whisper at the newly arrived Lylmik. The five Supervisors seemed not to notice that they were causing a sensation. Nodding and smiling and often pausing to give the dignified operant greeting, palm to palm, they mingled with the crowd and chatted. The venerable leader wore classic white tie and tails; his Caucasoid male comrade sported a fashionable jumpsuit of glittering green Nebulin; the third male, whose features had an Amerind cast, was attired in the black formal costume of a Latin caballero, with a ruffled shirt and scarlet faja. The two Lylmik in female guise were even more spectacular: the African wore a turban and caftan of cerise set off with heavy gold armlets and necklaces, while the Oriental's costume of turquoise and white silk brocade dripped with pearls.

The orchestra began to play "Dindi," a delicate Brazilian classic by Antonio Carlos Jobim, and the Lylmik did an even more astonishing thing: they asked humans to dance with them.

The Supervisor dressed as a caballero stepped out with Lucille Cartier, and the dapper fellow in the Nebulin bowed over the hand of Laura Tremblay. Davy MacGregor, wearing the kilt of his clan and a velvet jacket with silver buttons, found himself dancing with the Asian beauty, while Paul Remillard, his urbane composure shaken for only an instant, squired the statuesque Africaine.

Marc and Adrienne almost jumped out of their skins as a voice spoke behind them:

"I think I shall take this charming young lady away from you, my boy."

Marc whirled about and found himself face-to-face with the person who had foiled his attempt to stow away on a starship back to Earth. Sitting in the spectator gallery of the Concilium Chamber and watching the mysterious robed figures on the Dais of the Presiders, the boy had not recognized his nemesis. But now the Lylmik overlord named

Atoning Unifex towered over him and Adrienne, resplendent in his archaic black-and-white formal wear.

"You!" the boy exclaimed. "You're a Lylmik!"

"More than that," said the exotic, with a charming half bow. "I am *the* Lylmik." His deep-set eyes held the boy with irresistible coercion. "Before I dance with Addie, I have some further instructions for you, young Marc: Comport yourself with docility and good sense. When you are finally allowed to return to Earth, render to your father your strict obedience and respect in the difficult times to come. No matter what you may think, he is deserving of them."

Adrienne was struck dumb. They *knew* each other!

"And . . . what about the others?" Marc asked.

The Lylmik made an airy gesture. "You need not be concerned about their accommodation and comfort. That is all being taken care of. Later, you must assist the young one to the best of your ability." He turned to Adrienne, who was nearly paralyzed by awe, and brushed the backs of her fingers lightly with his lips. The inhuman eyes that had glittered with irony when he spoke to Marc were now gentle, almost sad. "How very lovely you look tonight, ma petite. No—you are more than that, dear Addie. You are beautiful! Shall we dance? I would like this to be a night you will remember all your life."

Homologous Trend danced with Lucille Cartier, and they were an amazing sight—the Lylmik with his chiseled copper features and dashing Latin garb, and the petite matriarch in a glittering cape of black, green, and silver beadwork with meter-long bead fringe, and a spectacular chapeau with bead plumage and multiple antenna-like filaments springing from the brow.

"May I compliment you on your ensemble, Professor Cartier," Trend murmured. "It is beyond question the most gorgeous attire at the ball."

"And the heaviest," said Lucille, giving him a radiant smile. "The beaded gown and the cape weigh fifteen kilos, and the hat weighs nearly five. If I didn't exert my PK every single minute, I'd collapse. Why I always end up choosing gowns like this I don't know! But I'm having the most marvelous time."

"One is delighted that you are temporarily distracted from the family problems."

Lucille locked onto the Supervisor's turquoise eyes. "You Lylmik know all about them, do you?"

"Not everything, Madame Professor. But enough. And we would like to help you. The Remillards are of great importance to the future of the Galactic Milieu, and we have been very disturbed by your recent . . . tragedies."

"How kind." Lucille was screening her mind as if her life depended upon it, realizing at the same time that the Lylmik was undoubtedly scanning her like a book-plaque. "Does your solicitude go so far as revealing who was responsible for the murders of my son-in-law and Margaret Strayhorn?"

"Unfortunately, no. I have no useful data on those crimes. But I might be able to suggest a solution to another matter that distresses you."

Lucille lifted a single eyebrow.

Homologous Trend danced her across the ballroom and indicated a Poltroyan male and female who were conversing with Denis Remillard.

Lucille frowned. "Why—it's Fred and Minnie! I didn't think they'd be here. Neither one of them is a magnate."

"Their attendance was specially arranged. But unlike the Magnates of the Concilium, who have business to transact before they can depart from Orb, the two Poltroyans will be leaving for Earth tomorrow in their private starship, so that they may minimize their absence from the classes they teach at Dartmouth. Their craft travels at an extremely high displacement factor. They should arrive on Earth in two weeks. I realize that you would prefer to remain here to supervise the—uh—motherless children of your son Paul. But if your husband Denis should wish to return home with the Poltroyan couple, they would be delighted to accommodate him. Denis will also find that both Fritiso-Prontinalin and Minatipa-Pinakrodin are extremely sympathetic to humanity's difficulties with the Milieu Reproductive Statutes."

Lucille stared at her Lylmik dancing partner with blank astonishment.

"Many Poltroyan ships have both superluminal and subluminal

capability," Trend continued patiently. "They can travel quite easily in planetary atmospheres, and they can penetrate the relatively weak force-fields generated by human security devices with impunity. And without trace, if such a maneuver is desirable."

Lucille danced in the Lylmik's arms for some minutes, her mind spinning. Finally she was able to whisper, "Would Fred and Minnie be willing to risk it? Or are you telling me that they have your *permission* to . . ."

"You Remillards are very important to the future of the Milieu," Homologous Trend repeated. "All of you."

Davy MacGregor was normally an awkward dancer, but with the lissome, silken-gowned Asymptotic Essence in his arms he was a man transformed. She was exerting metaredactive healing upon him, of course, assuaging the lingering grief of his bereavement with matchless expertise—while he was aware only of their two bodies swaying together, and her gentle smile, and the oblique, glowing eyes so incongruously set within her classic Oriental features.

He smiled at her. "You're redacting me, aren't you."

"Do you object?"

His gaze slid away from hers, and the smile faded. "I want to remember what was done to Margaret. Remember her. I loved her, and I intend to find the person who killed her and see that he's punished. The hurting—" He paused, and she finished the thought for him.

"You think it will aid your resolution. But you are wrong. It would only distort your judgment. However, the point is moot, since you are not the person who will be responsible for the apprehension of your wife's killer. That task belongs to another. You have a different job to do, which will require your complete attention."

"So you do concede that Margaret was killed! That she wasn't a suicide!"

The redactive energy exuded by the Lylmik suppressed his emotions without subtlety now, chilling his righteous anger, calming the fresh upsurge of pain. Davy was incapable of resisting. The crime would not be discussed. Not now.

They danced.

After a time, Asymptotic Essence said, "You have not even asked what your new job is to be."

"Whatever you Lylmik want," Davy said, dully.

"You are to be appointed Planetary Dirigent for Earth."

"Good God . . . I never dreamed . . ." *No! I don't want it!*

"The office is traditionally given to one who does not want it. One who will not be corrupted by it—or broken by it."

Davy began to laugh softly, bitterly. "You don't know what you're doing. I'm not right for it. I'm a MacGregor, Lord help me, and we've been a wild ilk from time immemorial, and I'm not diplomatic at all—"

"You have been chosen."

"I even have doubts about humanity's belonging to the Galactic Milieu! About the Unity thing. I don't understand how my race can submerge itself in an Overmind and retain its integrity. And I've plenty of company there, you know! Not all human operants think like Paul Remillard, believing that a permanent mind-linkage to exotic races is the greatest idea since sliced bread!"

Asymptotic Essence said, "Their conversion must follow your own."

"And how am I to be convinced that Unity is our destiny?"

"You may start by studying the works of a French philosopher who investigated the foundations of the concept many years ago, during your mid-twentieth century. His name was Pierre Teilhard de Chardin. By profession he was a paleontologist."

"I've never heard of him," said Davy MacGregor.

"Paul Remillard has. Which is neither here nor there."

"Then why didn't you Lylmik appoint Paul as Earth's Dirigent? Or another of his bloody dynasty?"

The Oriental woman shook her head. "Oh, no. Paul has his appropriate task, and you have yours."

"And God help us both," muttered Davy.

"We Lylmik will help you as best we can. You will have to coerce God yourself."

The two of them danced on without another word, and when the music ended, Davy bowed stiffly to Asymptotic Essence and stalked away.

Laura Tremblay nearly fainted with the excitement of it all. A Lylmik Supervisor! One of the Galactic overlords! Dancing with her!

Whatever would Paul say?

And then she happened to look over the glistening shoulder of Eupathic Impulse and saw whom the Lylmik disguised as a statuesque black woman was dancing with . . .

Paul.

Suddenly the giddy thrill evaporated, and Laura knew what was about to happen, and she was filled with terror. The Lylmik were going to separate them! She was certain of it. Paul was First Magnate now, and these inhuman creatures had picked out some other woman—no doubt some *worthy* intellectual, with superior metapsychic powers—to be his new wife.

But they wouldn't get away with their rotten scheme! Paul would find a way to counter them. Once she had divorced Rory, they'd be free to—

"It will do you no good," Impulse said.

She looked up at him, open-mouthed. Laura Tremblay was a lovely woman with transparent skin, dark-lashed blue eyes, and a proudly curved Celtic nose. Hair of frosty blonde was drawn severely back from her temples with a pair of golden combs. Her gown was black velvet, adorned with a single living orchid of pale yellow at the right shoulder. She said, coolly: "I don't know what you mean."

The entity that was not a man only smiled. "You may think that your marriage to Rory Muldowney has broken down irretrievably, that not even your mutual love for your three young children can hold you together—"

"It's true!" she said fiercely, trying without success to work up the strength to pull away from him. But she could not. They danced on to the gentle Latin beat. "Rory knows that we're finished. That I'm determined to go to Paul. He's resigned to it."

"Paul will not marry you," the Lylmik said gravely. "Our prolepsis reveals that he will never marry again."

"Prolepsis? What—what does *that* mean?"

"We can see what you would call the future. Not all of it, and not always clearly. But the prolepsis regarding you and Paul is quite incontrovertible."

"I love him and he loves me! He's told me that he does."

"Your first statement is undeniably true," Impulse said. "The second is doubtful—if by 'love' you mean a devotion transcending the self. Paul finds you charming and sexually desirable, a consolation during this very difficult period in his life. But he will never pledge himself to you or to any other woman."

What do you know about human love you BASTARD? You THING?

"One knows that love is mysterious. That it means different things to different human entities. That it can exalt and magnify, and also degrade and destroy. That it cannot be coerced. That it is sometimes spontaneous and sometimes learned. That it is born, lives, and sometimes dies. That it is an extension of the metacreative faculty, fulfilled only by bearing fruit. That it is akin to divinity but capable of malefaction. These things one knows. Wearing this human body, one continues to learn new and surprising things about love with almost every passing moment."

Laura Tremblay was calm again, resting easily against the Lylmik's shoulder. The music was drawing to an end, its sweetness touched with melancholy, and the dancers swayed more languidly. "Do you know how love can hurt?" she asked him.

"Not yet," Eupathic Impulse admitted. "But given time, even that is possible."

"And will you Lylmik be wearing human form on other occasions?" Paul asked Noetic Concordance.

"You will not see us so accoutred again until the human race attains Unity. If it does."

"Ah," said Paul. "What a pity. You're the most exquisite dancer I've ever partnered."

"You flatter me. My grasp of this art form is entirely theoretical. I have never danced before. The experience is pleasurable, however."

"I'm very glad to hear it. There are any number of simple pleasures available to the incarnate. As you may already have discovered."

The African beauty laughed richly. "I think, First Magnate, that you hover on the brink of impertinence."

"With such an august entity as a Lylmik Supervisor? I wouldn't dare!"

"I think you would dare a good deal, and not always wisely . . . But I am not here to chide you but to offer our congratulations. You gave a very inspiring speech to the Concilium following your election. Your remarks concerning the solemn obligations of operants toward non-operants were particularly memorable."

"Thank you. I meant every word of it."

"I wonder if the majority of your fellow human magnates share your idealism and devotion to the Galactic Milieu?"

He flashed his famous smile. "We're an uncoadunate race, but I think most of us are trying our damnedest. The Proctorship years were rough. There's a residue of resentment among all humans—operant and non—because of the price we had to pay for Galactic citizenship. But most of us realize that we were hopelessly unfit to join your confederation as equals when the Intervention took place. We were socially and morally immature. We still are, for that matter—but we're looking a hell of a lot better than we did in 2013."

Concordance laughed with him, then said more soberly: "You won't have an easy time of it during the thousand days of the probation. The other Polities—especially the Krondak and the Simb—have expressed grave reservations about the assimilability of the Human Mind into our Unity."

"And what do you Lylmik think?" Paul asked.

"The Supervisory Body concurs in finding humanity unique. Your mental potential is so great that it justified bringing you into the Milieu in advance of your sociopolitical maturation. But the Intervention was a calculated risk. It is also possible that you might destroy us."

"That's ridiculous! We're metapsychic infants compared to the other races, and your scientific achievements are so far beyond ours that it's—"

"With every passing year, the overall human metaquotient rises and more operant children are born to nonoperant parents. And your science advances at an even faster rate. By the time your population achieves the coadunate number, you will have surpassed the other Polities in virtually all aspects of technology."

"We won't surpass *you*."

"No . . . but the Lylmik are different. We are ancient, static, sterile.

Our minds are only minimally enmeshed with matter. We oversee and guide, but we cannot grow. The Galactic Milieu was our creation, but we will not survive to know its consummation. That falls to others."

"Are you implying that *we humans* have been chosen to be your successors?" Paul was incredulous.

"That is not a certainty. The exercise of the proleptic faculty is more an art than a science, and its manifestation is chaotic. The entity named Atoning Unifex decreed the Intervention and maintains that your ultimate Unification is . . . probable. But we are certain of this: there is no future for humanity outside the Milieu. Now that you are part of us, you can never secede and go your own way. If you leave us, it will be because you have been expelled, and the consequences will be more disastrous than you can possibly imagine."

They danced, keeping their thoughts scrupulously private, as they had from the start. Finally the music ended, and Paul said abruptly: "Tell me one thing, if you can, before we say goodbye. Did a Lylmik ever act as a kind of guardian angel to my Granduncle Rogi?"

Noetic Concordance shrugged delicately. "What makes you ask?"

"It was something my father mentioned in passing."

"I have no information to give you on the subject. But it does seem very unlikely, doesn't it?"

"Quite," said Paul. "Thank you very much for the dance."

"It was my pleasure," said Noetic Concordance. "Farewell."

Fury watched from above. Matters were progressing very satisfactorily, in spite of the fact that the silly Lylmik had made Davy MacGregor Planetary Dirigent. The Great Enemy! Empowered!

That would have to be rectified in time.

Unifex said: You aren't going to win.

< You can't be certain! I stand outside your prolepsis! >

That's true.

< And you can't touch me. Admit it! The great manipulator isn't so omnipotent after all. I'll do as I please. I'm a *necessary* factor in the cosmic equation. The negative factor! >

Don't play games. I'm not God, and you're no devil. We're minds in opposition . . . and you don't even know who you really are.

< No. But I know what I want to do. What I *will* do! >

You won't win. Your creature is flawed, and by yourself you're no more able to coerce Reality than I am.

< We'll see about that. You may be right about the creature. I faced certain limitations there at the inception. But there are other fish in the sea, to quote a human cliché. >

And other fishers besides thee and me, Fury. Keep that in mind as you do what you must do. Au revoir.

[26]

FROM THE MEMOIRS
OF ROGATIEN REMILLARD

On 5 January the baby "lightened," slipped downward in Teresa's abdomen in a preliminary move toward birth. Jack became frightened at this first sign that his tenure in the womb was about to end; and to reassure him, his mother spoke to him aloud and telepathically for hour after hour in one of the most amazing dialogues I have ever heard. Saint Jack the Bodiless was canonized not by the Catholic Church but by the acclamation of the Galactic Concilium. But if the Church *had* done an official investigation of his life and personal philosophy, and if I had agreed to have my chaotic memories tapped by Church experts, and if the experts were able to retrieve from me Jack's final prenatal conversation with his mother, it would have been a significant part of his dossier.

I cannot quote it verbatim in these Memoirs, any more than I can quote the later, even more portentous colloquies between Marc and Jack (and the Entity assisting me with my writing has declined to augment my own faculties of remembrance). But essentially, it was at this time that Jack first came to grips with the concepts of pain and prayer, and their potential usefulness in the nurturing of higher levels of consciousness. As he was born in pain, Jack first learned to pray.

Teresa knew instinctively that the birth process was going to hurt the baby, both physically and mentally. Human evolution had not yet progressed to a point where a fully rational and operant fetus could be delivered naturally without trauma. None of her other babies had been as mentally advanced as Jack at the time of birth; but even so, they had suffered considerably. After they were born, a natural amnesia had set in, and this, together with instinctive positive redaction from their mother, had seemed to heal them.

But Teresa was by no means certain that Jack would forget. He was obviously very different from her other children, and for this reason she decided to cope with his upcoming ordeal in a special way.

Jack had had very little experience as yet with pain. But he knew discomfort now that the "lightening" process had begun, and he didn't like it. The idea that the unpleasantness would become progressively worse understandably frightened him. Before, he had felt in control of his intrauterine world; but now the uterus had taken control. It was not only going to eject him from paradise, but it would also hurt him in the process.

Teresa told him exactly what lay ahead of him. She also explained how the pangs of birth were known to help even ordinary babies, in a purely physical way. The squeezing forced fluid from new lungs, so that they would be better prepared for the first breath of air. The shock of bright light, the sudden chilling, and the unaccustomed handling he would experience were stresses that actually had been proved to benefit healthy newborns. As they raged against the deprivation of uterine comfort, there was a feedback to the brain that enabled the babies to better adapt to life in the outer world.

Jack, because he was already rational, would suffer mentally as well as physically during his birth. But Teresa told him she was certain that if he *prayed* with complete trust, the pain would bring him strength. If he exerted positive coercion upon both himself and God—which was what "prayer" meant—then the birth ordeal would be in the end a triumphant experience for him, just as similar ordeals had been for mature humans all throughout history. Enduring the pain in the proper frame of mind could enhance his life in some mysterious way.

Birth, she explained to Jack, was a great transition—the first of many he would eventually pass through. He was about to lose forever the sheltered dimness, the suspended comfort and total security of the womb. He would come out into a world of light where there were opportunities for great joy and satisfaction, for individual types of accomplishment impossible for fetuses dependent upon their mothers. In this new world, suffering was commonplace—not because the Creator had maliciously planned it so, but because of the limitations of the physical universe and the imperfections of living things. Teresa warned her son that he would not only suffer at birth but also know pain of many different sorts during the independent life that lay ahead of him. It was part of being human.

But pain, she said, was a peculiar thing. Only higher living things had evolved the ability to suffer, and the higher the creature, the more intense its hurts might be—and so pain must have survival value. She explained to Jack some of its more elementary useful aspects, then went on to discuss the more difficult side of it. Intense pain could be, and perhaps most often was, degrading to the spirit of rational beings. However it might also be transformed by directed willpower—prayer —into a thing of great value, something that might enhance a person's own self-worth if he suffered for love of himself, or something that might magnify the worth of the great Mind of the universe if the person was able to suffer for love of others.

Jack had already begun to assimilate, with her help, the abstract concept of an incarnate God. Now she attempted to amplify the divine absurdity to include the notion of God freely choosing to suffer and die in order to achieve a higher goal.

Teresa was no theologian, but she was (in spite of her protestations to the contrary) an educated woman and also a very talented artist who had endured much to enhance that art. Her own ability to love both her husband and her children was seriously flawed by the demands and distractions of her singing; but the roles she had played had taught her well the extreme lengths to which love could drive the lover: to murder, to suicide, to madness, and even to greathearted sacrifice of one's own life and happiness.

Teresa told Jack that suffering for the love of others was a concept he would have to learn about more fully later, when he was more mature. Now it could only be an abstraction to him, except perhaps for his imperfect understanding of what his mother and his Uncle Rogi had endured for his sake.

Suffering for love of himself, on the other hand, was an opportunity no other unborn child—with the exception of an incarnate God—had ever experienced. This kind of suffering could teach him things about his own soul. It could strengthen him and expand his conscious mentality in an extraordinary way.

"Bearing children and giving birth to them is a great ordeal for the mother," she told the child in her womb. "But if she does it in the natural way, fully prepared and unafraid, then it's not a horror at all but an exaltation. At the instant the child's head is born, the discomforts of pregnancy and the difficult labor are completely forgotten, and the mother's nervous system responds with a flood of ecstasy . . . And I hope it may be the same for you, my dear little son." Jack said only: I will think about this.

When he was asleep (fetuses do sleep, even precocious ones), she confided to me that Jack was particularly fearful that birth trauma might interfere with his intellectual and metapsychic functioning, which he called his High Self. (His Low Self was the animal part of his mentality.) He was afraid that if he was "badly disturbed" and lost control during the ordeal, his Low Self and High Self would be somehow disconnected, leaving him dangerously exposed to . . . something.

"The poor thing is only a baby," I pointed out. "All very well for you to urge him to pray and be strong—but what if he can't manage? This 'High Self/Low Self' talk of his reminds me of something I read about Native American initiation ordeals. If you panic, the demons can get you! I suppose Jack's demons would only be subconscious ones—"

"I told him that we would guard him, Rogi." Teresa was quite serious. "That we would stay alert and keep his mind safe from outside threats if he should become vulnerable." She eyed me in that oddly trusting way of hers. "I have no idea what he perceives this threat to be. It must be some monster of the id. Surely no hostile external metapsychic influence could touch him here . . . could it?"

"I don't see how. Coercion can't operate at long range. Neither can the harmful types of redaction or creativity. The most that could happen is that one of the family could watch the birth: you know— through EE."

"I'm sure Jack's fears are irrational—as you said, he *is* only a baby!—but we must respect them. If Denis or even Paul should farspeak you, don't give any hint that I'm about to give birth. No one except you and I should witness my baby's first experience with pain."

Obscurely troubled, I agreed.

The weather had turned clear, and so hideously cold that when night came we heard trees exploding in the forest around us as freezing sap burst the wood fibers. Several of the roof timbers exploded as well, startling us out of our wits. When we awoke the next morning, the front door was covered with thick hoarfrost from top to bottom.

Previously, it had never frosted more than halfway up. A long time later, I questioned Bill Parmentier as to the possible temperature on that day, based upon my environmental observations, and he had shrugged. "Mighta been thirty, forty below, maybe. Not really all that cold for these parts. Just a bit brisk."

Naturally, that was the day young Ti-Jean, my great-grandnephew Jon Remillard, had to be born.

"Do you realize that today is the Twelfth Day of Christmas?" Teresa said, after she announced that her labor had begun. "Epiphany. A very auspicious time for Jack's manifestation! But the Bigfeet will have to stand in for the Magi." She laughed. "Be sure to farspeak them the big news after Jack arrives."

The baby's response to the beginning of labor was to virtually suspend communication with his mother, telling her that he needed to marshal all his mental resources to prevent, if possible, the separation of his two mystical selves. Teresa did not seem particularly worried about his withdrawal. Her mental state was one of great exhilaration—almost euphoria—because her most difficult pregnancy was over at last. She told me she had an overwhelming desire now to see her son, to hold him in her arms and kiss him and nurse him, to experience the body as well as the mind of this child whose gestation had been so perilous.

Both of us had been able to visualize the fetus with our ultrasenses, and we knew he was normally formed, in spite of what the dire genetic assay had predicted. But we wanted to see him, to be *sure*.

During the morning and afternoon hours, when the contractions were still far apart, Teresa continued with her cooking and cleaning and other household chores, stopping only to close her eyes and breathe in a completely relaxed manner when the pangs came. She explained to both me and Jack that this first stage of labor involved the dilation of the cervix, the birth canal.

After I'd performed my usual hewing of wood and drawing of water, she put a childbirth fleck into the plaque-reader and demanded that I absorb every awful detail, so I'd know what to expect. She reminded both of us that she had already borne four babies using the techniques of natural childbirth, without any recourse to chemical or mental anesthetics or any unusual medical intervention. (But she said nothing about the stillbirths or the abortions, nor did she mention

Marc's twin, Matthieu, who had died in utero under very peculiar circumstances.)

According to Teresa, there was no need for us to worry overmuch about the "unsterile" conditions in our log cabin. Newborns were usually quite tough, and she herself was perfectly healthy. Only ordinary precautions of cleanliness were called for. She took lengths of flannelette and wool that she had prepared and baked them in batches in the Coleman oven, and she boiled a knife and some string and wrapped them in a clean cloth. A pailful of boiled water was covered with a foil lid and left ready near the stove for washing mother and baby after the birth. She had me bring in a large quantity of sawdust from the woodcutting area. Chopped-up lumps of this were laid to thaw on the floor beneath the lower half of the bed. (Teresa discreetly left me in ignorance of the sawdust's function. So did the damned maternity fleck.)

When she began to approach the later stages of labor, she had me stoke up the fire until the stove was aglow and the log cabin's inside temperature approached that of a normal civilized room. Then we got her bed ready. She was going to lie with her head where her feet ordinarily were, in order to give me, the amateur accoucheur, more room to maneuver in. We arranged the folded air mattress and the pillows, first covered with plass and then with the wool duffel cloth, to form a slanted backrest. She would give birth in a half-sitting position, which was the most comfortable. On the half of the bed where the rope springs were exposed, she placed a pair of long wool pads she had made. They fitted into the bedframe rather like two small mattresses, with a slight gap between them down the middle of the bed. A large piece of sterile flannelette was laid atop the pads, making the bed's lower end look more normal.

Teresa showered in our little bath cubicle, using warm water with a bit of chlorine bleach in it, and then put on her long Snegurochka undergown, warm from the oven. Facetiously commanding me to avert my eyes, she got into bed with the back of the gown hoicked up and made herself comfortable. The upper part of her body rested against the folded mattress and pillows, but from the rump down she lay on the pads, with the front of her gown drawn modestly over her knees, and her feet, with clean socks on, braced against the foot of the bedframe. She faced the north window and the large table, where the lamps were turned on at low intensity and all of the birthing supplies had been laid neatly out.

"Now cover me up," she said, after pausing to endure a contraction. "First, the big flannelette sheet."

I laid it over her reverently.

"Now my down comforter, with the excess rolled up against the wall. For God's sake don't let it drag on the floor in that damp sawdust."

"Yes, ma'am. But the sawdust is really pretty clean."

"It is *now.*" She gave a great contented sigh. "Oh, that's better. Now all I have to do is wait. And when the time comes, all *you* have to do is help me the way I tell you."

And avoid giving way to panic!

I grinned, putting on my best air of confidence. "Are you sure it isn't drafty—uh—underneath?"

"Trust me. Everything is just fine."

I pointed wordlessly to the swell beneath the covers and lifted my eyebrows.

"He's . . . quiet," she said. "I can sense his distress at the contractions. It's his head, after all, that's dilating the cervix. Poor little baby! It will be much harder on him than on me. But there's no helping it. An ordinary baby would feel very little discomfort, and he'd forget it immediately. But the birth process just doesn't take rational fetuses into account."

Late in the evening, Denis farspoke me the details of the Conciliar Inauguration, including Paul's election as First Magnate. Mercifully, he didn't mention the warm cordiality so evident between Paul, presumed by all except the family cognoscenti to be a widower, and the lovely Laura Tremblay; nor did he discuss with me the murder of Margaret Strayhorn. (I was not to learn anything about the exploits of the being called Hydra until after my return to civilization.)

Denis wanted to know whether the birth was imminent and asked whether Teresa would farspeak with him or Paul after Jack was born. I lied brazenly, saying that there was no sign of labor as yet. I told Denis that Teresa was asleep, and that she still was afraid that farspeaking would betray her to her enemies, and so she probably would prefer not to attempt it. I said I would continue to be the conduit of maternity news. This seemed to satisfy Denis. Concilium Orb was so far from Earth that he would be unlikely to attempt casual EE. Even for a Grand Master, using the ultrasenses across a distance of 4000 lightyears was no trivial operation, and I didn't think Denis would add to his exertions by trying to view us, as well as speak telepathically, unless he had a good reason to do so.

When Denis had finished with me, I reassured Teresa, who had been hiding anxiously behind the strongest mental screen she was able to conjure up. But her refusal to farspeak her kindly and solicitous father-in-law, who would probably play an important role in her upcoming reappearance and legal battles, worried me. And then there was Paul. He was just as expert as Denis—perhaps even more so—in fine-beaming his thoughts so that no Magistratum monitor would pick them up. If Teresa really loved him and hoped for a reconciliation, she would have to respond to his telepathic call. When she continued to demur, I told her I was afraid that she had an entirely different reason for avoiding Paul.

But she only laughed at my clumsy attempts to bring her marital estrangement out into the open. "I'm not bitter about Paul's behavior over the pregnancy at all, Rogi. I understand that his first loyalty had to be to the Milieu and not to me. I *did* commit a serious crime. But now that it's turning out so well, I feel it's best that we wait to discuss it. Farspeaking would accomplish nothing. What we must say to each other, we should say face-to-face. I want to show Paul his perfect little new son as a fait accompli. Put Jack into his arms. Then he can't help but be as proud of us . . . as we are proud of him."

"He'll be damned proud," I asserted stoutly, "and now that he's First Magnate, he'll move heaven and earth to do whatever it takes to get you off the legal hook!"

She turned her head away. "I know. Once Paul *meets* Jack, everything will be all right again."

I busied myself making Teresa a cup of tea and then sat beside her on the stool while I rubbed her back and told her some of the details of the inauguration that Denis had passed on to me.

She asked, "Was the election for First Magnate close?"

"Fifty-nine votes for Paul, forty-one for Davy MacGregor. Closer than the family had expected."

"How strange . . . I'd thought Paul was a shoo-in. Not that Davy isn't a sweet person and a brilliant statesman. I've always liked him and his wife."

"There's going to be an inaugural gala—a banquet and a ball with celebrity entertainment. Lucille is all ready to do her metapsychic grande dame routine, and her gown will probably be a smash. Marc's going to wear his first white tie to the ball, and Denis is confident that he'll be the designated dreamboat of the younger adolescent female set."

Teresa laughed with genuine pleasure, then caught her breath abruptly. Her eyes widened. "Rogi! The waters!"

"You need water?" I leapt to my feet, alarmed. "Cold? Hot?"

"No, dear," she said gently, shifting about in the bed. "The amnion, the membranous bag full of fluid that Jack floats in. It's broken."

Perspiration shone on her brow. She gasped, then uttered a peculiar guttural cry.

I hovered at her side, terrified. "What should I do?"

Her eyes were closed, and she gripped the edges of the bedframe with whitened knuckles. Again she made that peculiar grunting noise.

She whispered, "Put on a fresh shirt. Scrub your hands to the elbows. Rinse them in water that has a little bleach added."

"Yes!" I cried, stumbling about the cabin. "Yes! Just take it easy. It won't take me two minutes!" Hold on, Jack! Not so damned fast, for God's sake—

IT HURTS! IT HURTS!

"Oh, Jesus," I wailed.

It wasn't Teresa in pain; she was pushing and straining, her mind closed in upon itself in utter concentration. The one hurting was Jack.

—the amniotic fluid that had cradled and protected him for nine months was now draining away with the rupture of the enveloping membrane.

—his delicate little body was squeezed by the fierce contractions of the powerful uterine muscles, now coming at two-minute intervals.

—and he was being propelled forward, centimeter by centimeter, headfirst through the crushingly narrow birth canal, the plates of his tiny skull and the marvelous brain within compressed, deformed.

—and with his mother distracted and withdrawn, he appealed to me.

IT HURTS . . . Uncle Rogi it hurts so much I can't do the thing Mama wanted help me pleaseplease helphelphelp—

"I will, I will!" I cried, kneeling beside the bed, putting one hand on Teresa's covered belly. She still lay beneath the comforter. I let my mind merge with that of the fetus and felt his agony, his terror. I seemed to see a bright fragile globular thing that pulsated with pain, threatening to shatter. And there in the scarlet dimness lurked something else, which would pounce if the bright globe broke and would devour the precious being that had been inside. The monster was there, but it had only limited faculties. I was a match for it! In some way I took hold of Jack's shining hurting mind, enclosed him and steadied him. I dredged up strength for both of us from God knew where. Somehow I shared my own experiences with suffering. Somehow I helped.

And abruptly, Jack withdrew from me, safe and in control again.

I was back in the dimly lit cabin with the Arctic night wind moaning outside. Teresa was still grunting at regular intervals and bearing down valiantly with each contraction; but the fetus was no longer crying out. He was exerting his metapsychic faculties in a new way, incomprehensible to me. He was *growing.*

I got up from my knees and stripped off my grubby wool shirt. A newly washed one hung on the line above the stove. I scrubbed my hands and lower arms and put the fresh shirt on, then checked over the birth supplies on the table: the folded clean cloths, the sponges made from wool duffel, a larger piece of material that Teresa had designated as the birthcloth, the sterile knife and string.

Teresa said calmly, "Rogi, I've soiled the bed. It's normal. I want you to take away the comforter now. Fold the sheet up over my stomach and lift my nightgown, and bring me a cloth dampened with clean water so I can wipe myself. Then slide the shitty cloth out from beneath my legs. Hold it by the edges when you gather it up, and burn it in the stove. Then bring another clean cloth and put it down."

I gaped at her.

"Hurry, dear." Teresa smiled encouragingly at me, but there were tears in her eyes for poor Jack's pain. "Do as I say, Rogi! The head is on the perineum." She gave another heroic grunt. Her face was deeply flushed and she was drenched in sweat.

I did it. There was a mess of fluid and a few feces on the cloth. I took care of things briskly.

"No, don't cover me up again," she gasped. "Can . . . you see him?"

I crouched down. Her feet were braced hard against the bedframe and her knees were spread wide. With no embarrassment, I checked the vulvar opening. Something was there. With each fresh contraction it advanced—then retreated a bit when the thrust ceased. But it came forward a little farther each time she bore down. Finally the entire top of the head was visible, like a cork in a wine bottle. It was slightly bloodstained and coated with a pasty white substance.

"I see him! He's coming. But there's blood and stuff all over him—"

"Okay," she gasped. "Okay . . . now!"

She gave a loud, orgasmic shout. I seemed to hear another cry ring in my mind, equally joyous, and at that moment the baby's entire head came free. His eyes were closed. His skull was pathetically misshapen—

She was looking down at him, her hands cradling the poor little head. "He's all right," she managed to say. "The distortion . . . normal. Get . . . birthcloth. Lay it . . . between my legs. No, further away . . . get ready to catch him . . . slippery . . . *aaaah!"*

With her second ecstatic cry the baby's head turned to one side. Tiny shoulders emerged, together with a great gush of clear fluid that soaked the flannelette and the pads and dripped into the sawdust under the bed. I took hold of Jack under his wee arms as the rest of his body slithered out quickly, together with more liquid, stained pink with blood. He was *very* slippery. His body was bluish beneath the cheesy white coating. The umbilical cord was a bright sky-blue color, and throbbing. The baby did not seem to be breathing.

Without thinking I lifted him by the ankles and smacked him on the bottom. He opened his mouth and spat out fluid. His little chest heaved. He turned pink almost immediately.

And began to squall and wriggle.

"Look! Here he is!" I babbled. "It's Jack! And he's breathing!"

I would have done it on my own!

"Put him down, dear," Teresa whispered. She was smiling now. "On the birthcloth. Get the knife and the string. Do you remember what to do?"

"You bet." Trembling, the great accoucheur tied one string tightly around the cord about two centimeters away from the baby's belly. Then tied another string a ways away. Then (cringe!) cut the cord.

"Wrap him up in some clean flannelette and give him to me."

I did as she said, and she took the wailing little thing and held him to her breast, crooning softly. His head was already starting to look more normal. I stood there at a loss, a "What next, Coach?" expression on my face.

Thank you. That's much better. Mama. Uncle Rogi.

Both Teresa and I burst into tears.

She rocked him in her arms, singing telepathically at the same time that she wept for happiness. The baby's mind had become completely inaccessible, shut away from all human intercourse except at the animal level, the superintellect having throttled back into oblivious infancy after savoring its triumph. Jack was breathing strongly, his heartbeat was even, and his head with its wisps of dark hair rested against his mother's breast. The yucky white stuff on his skin, Teresa informed me, was a normal coating called vernix which would easily wash off later. In minutes Jack had fallen peacefully asleep, his tiny mouth still fastened to the nipple.

I told Teresa about my excursion into the infant's mind, and about the "monster" I had apparently perceived hiding there.

"You must have imagined it, Rogi. Or else it was a construct of his own unconscious. His Low Self threatening the High Self in some strange manner."

I shrugged. "Well, maybe."

"Perhaps it was symbolic of all the difficult tasks that lie ahead of him. When he wakes there'll be all those new stimuli to process. The next few days will be very difficult for him. Poor Jack! His mind may be highly advanced and self-aware, but it's trapped inside a helpless infant body. It didn't bother him while he was safe in a symbiotic relationship with his mother, but now that he's out on his own, he'll have a lot of adjusting to do." She winced. "Oh-oh. Here we go again. It's the afterbirth. Now this is what you do . . ."

I attended Teresa as she passed the placenta. This was an unattractive fleshy mass like a thick, veined pancake with the umbilical cord attached to its middle. Along with it came miscellaneous bits and pieces that Teresa said were the membranes that had enclosed the fetus, and a fair amount of blood. The fluids were mostly soaked up by the sawdust. Teresa directed me to burn the afterbirth, the soggy sawdust, the bed pads, and the most badly soiled cloths. She herself swabbed Jack off, dressed him in a bellyband, a diaper, plass overpants, and a little terry-cloth suit, then stowed him in his swansdown bunting and cradle furs while she washed herself and put on a fresh nightgown. She lay down to rest on my bed, with him tucked into the sleeping bag beside her and both comforter and fur blanket piled on top. The cabin was cooling off rapidly; during the past hectic hour, I had forgotten to stoke the fire. I told her she must sleep in my bed, closest to the stove. We would switch bunks. "And why don't I make us some strong tea?"

"There's better than that for us. Look in the corner of the bath alcove."

Mystified, I went to check. And there was the split of Dom Pérignon that had been part of her original bag of "necessities," resting in a bucket of half-melted snow. I let out a cackle of appreciation, popped the cork, and poured the champagne into teacups. Laughing like loons, we toasted Jack's arrival and wished an early end to our other travails.

"I'm afraid my bedspring ropes are rather messed up," Teresa said, grinning over the rim of her cup.

"Big deal. I'll put a plass sheet over them tonight and weave a new spring tomorrow if I can't wash them clean."

She nodded. Her face was radiant. She looked like anything but your stereotypical exhausted new mother.

I said, "I didn't expect you to be . . . in such good shape. Afterward."

"Some women feel pretty decent, others are knocked out. I feel like I climbed a mountain and fell down the other side. But tomorrow I'll be fine. Cook your breakfast."

"Good God. And that's all there is to it?"

She laughed. "I'll bleed for a while, but I have pads ready. If I don't get an infection or hemorrhage too badly, I should be in fine shape inside of a week. But I intend to be a right layabout for the next six or seven days, eating and sleeping like crazy and nursing Jack. You'll have your work cut out for you, bonhomme, waiting on me hand and foot. I'll cook the breakfast tomorrow because right now you look worse than I do."

"I feel like *I* gave birth to the kid. My hands are still shaking!" I extended a batch of quivering digits. We were sitting side by side, she in my bed and me in one of the chairs I had dragged over. "Do I get to be godfather?"

"You get to baptize him."

"What . . . ?"

"Tomorrow. The circumstances are unusual, so it's quite justified. And it's the way I want it."

I took refuge in the cup of champagne. "Whatever you say."

We sat in peaceful silence for some time. The cooling stovepipe clicked and the Great White Cold crept in through the planks of the cabin floor and nipped my feet in their wool socks. Then there was a distant explosion.

"The trees are starting to pop off again," I observed. "Going to be another really cold night. Think I'll visit the outhouse and get us some more firewood before I turn in." I checked my wrist chronometer, which I had stashed out of the way when scrubbing up. "Almost midnight."

"We did a good job." She finished her champagne.

"Damn right."

I took her cup, and she settled back to sleep. The baby beside her had not made a peep, either vocally or mentally, since she finished bathing him. But now that all the excitement was over, I became aware of unfamiliar vibes pervading the atmosphere of our little cabin—weird and wonderful and quite different from any human aura I'd ever experienced before. I figured they had to be coming out of Jack.

I looked down at the tiny face, which was now pink and attractive. Perhaps he would grow up to be the greatest human mind ever! I said to him: Que le bon dieu t'bénisse, Ti-Jean.

Then, aching in every muscle, I put on my Paks and layer after layer of outer clothes and wrapped my lower face in a muffler before pulling the parka hood tight. When it was really cold, exposed facial skin would freeze in less than a minute.

"Back in a jif," I told Teresa, and went outside.

The aurora was crazily blazing, and every bare twig and branch was encrusted with glittering rime. The crystalline world was flooded with pale rainbow light. My heart caught in my throat at the beauty of it.

Thank you, I said. Thank you so much. Now let them live. Let it all work out for the best.

Then I crunched off into the cold-flaming night.

Both the woodshed and the latrine were on the west side of the cabin. I didn't bother looking into the shadowy gnarled trees farther over to the east, beyond the door. If I had, I might have seen the creatures that made the big footprints I found in the snow the next morning, right by the window.

One of them, I have since been told by a reliable source, had gray eyes.

27

APE LAKE, BRITISH COLUMBIA, EARTH
22 JANUARY 2052

Denis had farspoken Rogi on the day after Jack's birth, telling him that he was on his way back to Earth and would be coming to take the two of them and the baby away from Ape Lake. He would hide them, he said, in a more salubrious place until the Dynasty was able to repeal or modify the Reproductive Statutes and procure retroactive pardons for Teresa and Rogi.

The two of them spent the next two weeks very quietly. A new series of storms swept over the Coast Range, dumping deep snow upon the cabin so that it was almost buried to the eaves. Rogi always managed to shovel the roof clear, and he traveled easily to the cache of moose meat and to the lake on snowshoes. But the routes to the latrine and the wood supply in Le Pavillon were now snow tunnels, and he worried about how the chimney would draw if the cabin was buried much deeper.

Jack almost always behaved like a normal infant, nursing and sleeping and watching the two of them with solemn eyes during his periods of wakefulness. He spoke mentally mostly with his mother. Rogi gathered that he was hard at work processing a monumental batch of new sensory data input and had little time for social conversation. Jack intensified the bonding to his mother once he had "formally" identified her as a being separate from himself. And when Rogi baptized him, the infant bonded to the old man as well, somehow seizing upon the memory of Denis's long-ago christening and judging that Rogi, too, was an appropriate person to love without qualification.

The sun rose tardily during winter in the northland, and Rogi and Teresa usually did, too, conserving their body energies against the ever-deepening cold. She kept the cradle close beside her bunk, and when Jack indicated telepathically that he needed nursing during the night she would simply take him into bed with her and put him to the breast without really waking up. Rogi, in a similar state of somnambulism, would rise at night several times to restoke the fire. Even so, in the morning the door would be frosted from top to bottom and the water in the bucket frozen nearly solid. The adults found that they could sleep ten or eleven hours at a stretch; the baby slept twenty hours out of every day. They all seemed to be in a state of semihibernation, recuperating from the tension of the time before Jack's birth and marshaling their strength for whatever was to come.

On the evening of 21 January, Teresa and Rogi finally broke the news to the baby that Denis was on his way and they would probably be leaving the cabin the next day. Teresa spent a long time reassuring Jack that the change was necessary and good, but he was frightened at the prospect of meeting other persons and living in a new place. She tried to make a game of it by having him designate which things he would like to take away with him. He chose the swansdown bunting, the swing–papoose carrier that Rogi had made, and Herman the Ermine, who had fascinated Jack with his antics.

"No, dear," Teresa said. "Herman can't come. This is his home, and he would be unhappy going with us."

This is my home too! Jack said, his tiny face crumpling with woe. And he began to cry dismally.

"Not really." Teresa cuddled him against her shoulder. She and Rogi together projected images of the big house in Hanover in an attempt to show Jack what his real home was like. They showed him images of his father and his brothers and sisters and grandparents, new minds he would be able to bond with; but the only other person who seemed at all acceptable as a love object was Marc, whom Jack remembered very clearly. Paul and the others were equated with danger.

Jack finally fell asleep, and Teresa put him into his cradle with a sigh. "This is going to be very hard on him, Rogi. We probably won't even be able to go to the New Hampshire house."

The old man shrugged. "Denis only told me he'd find us a safe place." He was packing Teresa's musical equipment and the few other things they were going to take. "Jack will just have to learn to adapt. Other babies do. You can't raise the little nipper in an isolation chamber. He's supersensitive, and change will seem awful to him at first, but he'll get over it. I get vibes from him that tell me he's a lot tougher than we think."

Teresa began to rummage through her clothing. She held up her improvised Snegurochka headpiece. "Do you think we could find room for this and for the rest of the costume in our baggage?"

Rogi grinned. "Hell, yes. Someday you and Jack ought to do a repeat performance of the opera for the whole family. It could become a Christmas tradition!"

Later that evening, when the bundles were packed, they retired to their bunks, feet to feet, with the wind hooting down the stovepipe.

Teresa said, "I don't want to leave here, either."

"I know. I know exactly how you feel. And him, too. This place has been good to us, keeping us all safe. But Denis is right about taking us out of here. You need to get back to civilization, where you can wear clean clothes and take regular baths and eat fresh fruits and veggies and get some decent exercise. God knows how much deeper the snow will get here before the spring thaw. And what would happen to you if I got sick or broke a bone?"

"You're right. I was only thinking of myself. I'm sorry, Rogi. I keep forgetting what a terrible responsibility the two of us have been for you."

He made a growling sound deep in his sleeping bag. "Fool girl. I haven't enjoyed myself so much in years. And that includes hunting the moose! I'll be bored out of my mind back in the bookstore."

They laughed together and then went to sleep, lulled by the wind.

Mama! the baby's mind screamed. Both Teresa and Rogi woke with a start.

A thing [image]—*a terrible big thing!*

Rogi struggled to sit up in his bunk. It was pitch black except for the dull glow around the edge of the stove door. He squinted at his wrist and blearily made out that it was 0523 hours.

A THING!

"Rogi, what is it?" Teresa was petrified. She snatched Jack from his cradle and clutched him tightly. The cabin was like a deep freeze.

Rogi pulled his wits together. He could see well enough in the dark once he exerted his ultrasenses, but Teresa was very poor at that particular mental trick, and her agitation made things worse. Neither could she identify the farseen image that the terrified infant was projecting—something huge, silvery, and elongate that apparently hovered silently only a few meters above the smoking chimney pipe of the cabin.

But Rogi knew what it was.

"Easy! Easy, you two. It's only Denis, come to get us. And damn my eyes if he hasn't come in a Poltroyan orbiter!"

The old man flung himself out of bed, lit a lamp, and hastened to pull his clothes on over grubby long johns. Jack was wailing softly. Teresa put him back in his cradle and began to dress. No sooner were the two of them decent than something shocking happened.

There was a knock at the door.

Rogi stamped his feet into his Paks, ran his fingers through his greasy silver curls, and straightened up. He strode to the door and yanked it open. There stood a human in a full environmental suit with the helmet closed, and a lilac-faced Poltroyan male in a heavily bejeweled fish-fur parka and mukluks. They entered in a swirl of frigid air and ice crystals and slammed the door behind them. Jack abruptly stopped crying.

Denis lifted his visor. "Hello, Uncle Rogi, Teresa. Meet my good friend Fred."

"Enchanté," said the Poltroyan, stripping off his elaborate mittens. He shook Teresa's and Rogi's hands, beaming genially, and waved to Jack.

"We've come to take you away," Denis said. "Let's not waste any time. Fred's vessel is field-screened, but I'd like to land you two on Kauai while it's still night in the islands."

"Kauai!" Teresa exclaimed joyfully. "We're going to my folks' old place?"

Denis nodded. "It's all arranged. You and Rogi and the child will stay there until the mess is resolved. There's no longer any danger of a search by the Magistratum. The Human Polity is finishing up its preliminary work on Orb, and in a week or so everyone will head for home. There'll be debate on the Reproductive Statutes, and a lot of tap-dancing by the family lawyers once the Intendant Assembly reconvenes with the new magnates seated, but Paul plans to introduce a resolution granting you a retroactive pardon as soon as possible."

"And when can we go home?" Teresa demanded. "*Really* go home?"

"I can't be certain. Perhaps as early as March if the Dynasty can get

you bail or push through a general amnesty for Repro Statute viola-
tors." Denis's gaze moved for the first time to the cradle with its furs
and silent tiny occupant. "He's still well?"

"Perfectly," said Teresa.

"I see he's already learned to erect a mental barrier."

"He could do it in the womb," she said.

"Remarkable . . . It seems your illicit pregnancy is completely
vindicated after all."

She met his eyes without flinching. "I always knew it would be.
Little Jack's body is flawless. There is no congenital deformity and no
physical dysfunction as far as I can tell. His mind is . . . superior. I
should warn you that he doesn't think like an infant. You might think
of him as a precocious nine-year-old."

"A very *innocent* precocious nine-year-old," Rogi added. He began to
stoke up the fire for the last time.

Denis took off his gloves. The wan lamplight gleamed on his silvery
suit as he approached the cradle and looked down at the tiny baby.

Hello Grandpère, Jack said.

"Good morning, Jack. Are you ready to travel?"

I will be. Soon. I must be fed and changed. Will you and Fred mind
waiting for a few minutes?

"Not at all," Denis replied.

The baby said: I am going to try very hard not to be afraid. I hope
you won't be angry if I cry a little when something new startles me.
It's a reflex action I have very little control over as yet.

"I understand." Denis reached out one bare hand toward the baby's
pink cheek. "May I touch you?"

With your hand? Yes. But not with your mind.

"Oh, Jack," Teresa sighed. She made an apologetic gesture to Denis,
who smiled with apparent understanding and withdrew his hand after
a brief pat.

The baby said to Denis: I don't think I will be able to love you.

"You don't know me," Denis said equably. "Later, you may change
your mind. You have a great deal to learn, you know. Especially about
other human beings like yourself."

Are there others like me?

"Of course!" said Teresa, with mock indignation. She began to
bustle about, getting a washcloth and clean diaper and gown for him,

warming them first on the stove since the temperature in the cabin was still well below zero Celsius. She told Denis and Fred that the baby wouldn't mind the brief exposure to the cold as she changed him. Even ordinary babies were able to adjust their body thermostats to frigid air for very short periods, and Jack was particularly adept at the trick.

"And I'm sure he has all kinds of other talents that we haven't even begun to discover yet," she said proudly. "Just wait until Papa meets you, Jack!" She looked brightly at Denis. "I suppose Paul plans to come to see us in Kauai as soon as he gets back to Earth."

"He doesn't think it would be wise to have any contact with you," Denis said regretfully, "until the family lawyers have assessed the situation."

"Foutre!" exclaimed Rogi indignantly.

Teresa's face froze. But an instant later, she was smiling as she began to undress the baby. "It's quite all right. I understand perfectly. We'll do whatever Paul thinks is best. Won't we, Jack?"

The baby stared at her with enormous eyes, his mind remote and silent.

28

HANOVER, NEW HAMPSHIRE, EARTH
25 MARCH 2052

By the calendar, spring had come to North America. But the calendar lied where New Hampshire was concerned, and it was almost enough to make Marc wish he were back in the climate-controlled perfection of Concilium Orb.

Freezing rain mixed with sleet beat against his leathers as he drove back to the frat house on his turbocycle after finishing his first full day at Dartmouth College. Grassy parts of the campus, rooftops, fences, and other unwarmed surfaces were beginning to glaze now that the sun had gone down. The bare branches of the big elm trees and the shrubs glittered in the streetlights. Pedestrian students slogged along, emanating misery and dodging sprays of slush from passing ground-cars. Driving north on College Street, Marc got sprayed even more than those who were afoot. And his bike was balking worse than ever, fighting back every time he tried to change its vector. It had to be the guidance helmet. His tinkering with it after he discovered the weird brainboard interference must have screwed something up. The poor old turbocycle was probably receiving conflicting orders from his mind and the phantom glitch, and it didn't know whether to shit or go blind.

Marc finally killed the cerebroguidance. He came onto slippery Clement Road, where the melting grids seemed to be on the fritz, then entered the driveway of the Mu Psi Omega house. He'd moved in the day before, less than a week after finally returning to Earth. The driveway was a sheet of glass. He could have deployed the ice spikes, but in his present mood he chose instead to kill the engine and simply horse the heavy BMW along with his PK. No sense pissing off his new meta frat brothers with something so mundane as tearing up their driveway. The garage door opened in response to his mental nudge of the old-fashioned electronic opener. He rolled inside and put the machine in its allotted space in the cramped freshman section, between Alex Manion's 10-speed bicycle and Boom-Boom Laroche's Kawasaki Jet-Scoot.

He took the guidance helmet off and frowned at its complex interior. The needle electrodes gleamed faintly red with his blood before retracting into the cage, automatically heating up and sterilizing themselves with tiny puffs of smoke. Even as Marc summoned an ultrasensory view of the suspect microsystem, he knew that simply looking at the damn thing wouldn't tell him diddly-squat. He would either have to take it apart and test it himself—and with all the makeup work from his two missed terms, it wouldn't be easy to spare the time—or else give it to Alex and see if *he* had any bright ideas.

Marc took his IBM notebook and a large sack of buttermilk donuts from the turbocycle's carrier and trudged up the slushy back walk. In the mud room, he stripped off his environmental leathers and boots and put them in his locker to dry, then tramped into the back parlor stocking-footed. Alex was there, and so were Boom-Boom and Pete Dalembert and Shig Morita and a couple of sophomores he didn't know, watching a Soviet football game on the Tri-D.

"Hey, Marc," Alex said. The other three freshmen also murmured greetings.

"Small contribution to the general jollification," said Marc, dumping the donut sack. Everybody but Shig, who was already munching dried seaweed from a plass packet, pounced. The sophomores took extras.

"Shitty weather," Boom-Boom said, with his mouth full, "but very commendable quasi toruses."

"Tori," Alex corrected.

"But never torii," Shig Morita said, his eyes never leaving the game, "because *that's* not a bag of donuts at all but a Japanese gate! . . . Aaagh! Would you believe the way that Ostrovsky can boot the ball back over his head? The clot's gotta be a closet PK meta!"

"No way," said Pete Dalembert. "The refs would spot his noodling."

"Not if the guy's a gonzo screener," said one of the sophs.

"A psychokinetic topspin on the ball is detectable if an operant referee is looking for it," Alex said. "And if the player tried to screen it, the *screen* would be detectable. Right, Marc?"

"Most of the time it would," Marc said gravely. "I could probably fudge it, but I doubt if many other heads could."

"Oh, hey! *What* have we here?" The bulkiest of the sophomores, a patronizing grin on his face, tossed an inexpert mental probe at Marc. It did not even bounce; it was absorbed without a trace. "Ooo! Captain Marvel comes to Animal House! Lucky, lucky us. What did you say your name was, young donut peddler?"

"Lay off him, Eric," said Boom-Boom in a warning tone. Although the sophomore was three years older, the hulking fourteen-year-old freshman outweighed him by ten kilos. "He's one of our buddies from Brebeuf."

"I'm Marc Remillard." Marc spoke absently. He was having a swift telepathic conversation with Alex Manion about the malfunctioning helmet.

The second sophomore groaned. "Another Jebbie ass-wipe! The house is crawling with you precocious little pricks."

"Remillard . . . ?" The boy named Eric was frowning. "Don't tell me you're the one who—"

A donut levitated from Boom-Boom's paw and neatly stoppered Eric's open mouth.

"Marc's okay," said Pete Dalembert quietly. "Sometimes he comes on a little weird, but in time you get used to it. He's not really shy, only arrogant."

"Our glorious leader," Shig said. "You sophs are going to love him even more than the rest of us."

Eric slowly chewed his donut. His eyes had gone narrow and thoughtful.

Marc tossed the black helmet to Alex, who caught it one-handed. "There's the wonky brain-bucket. I'm fresh out of easy fixes myself. Want to check it out?"

"Sure." Alex Manion licked sugary leftovers off his unencumbered hand and got up slowly from his chair.

"That a CE hat you got there?" Eric brightened. "I've heard of them but never seen one. What model?"

"Homemade," Marc said. "Built it myself. It drives my BMW bike."

"Jeez Louise!" exclaimed the second sophomore. "You really made it, kid? Lemme check 'er out. I'm majoring in cerebroenergetics."

"It's broken," Marc said shortly. "Maybe some other time."

"Let's take it up to my room and run a quickie test," said Alex. "There's time before dinner."

The two of them climbed the back stairs of the frat house together, hearing Boom-Boom and Shig filling in the suddenly attentive sophomores on Marc's family antecedents and metapsychic armamentarium. A rich scent of clam chowder wafted up from the kitchen. Somebody was playing "Lush Life" very badly on a saxophone. From the sun room and the front parlor came sounds of laughter and a mélange of declamatory mental speech, mostly jocose and semi-obscene and concerned with coy women and hoped-for Friday-night dates. Alex addressed Marc on his intimate mode:

Sorry I missed you this morning. How they hanging?

Goodenough. These first days back are bound to be glarfy the worst will be wangling the lost labtime but fear not I'll catchup I did a lot of the swotwork while I was in Orb.

Hey burdens of being wellconnected! Tough you missed Winter-Carnival icecycle racing this year was *noteworthy* but it musta been somekinda zorch seeing ConciliumOrb and mingling with the MagnatizedMob + **LYLMIK OVERLORDS IN HUMAN FORM**!!

"Ha," Marc said without humor. "You don't know the halvesies."

They went into Alex's room, a tiny cubicle where the floor, desk, and two chairs were nearly buried in a junkshop tangle of microelectronic gear, homemade boxes of mysterious function, and miscellaneous equipment ranging from miglom analyzers to miniature dy-field generators. The place stank of fried insulation and Forte cement. On the wall was a holo poster advertising the New D'Oyly Carte Opera Company production of *The Mikado*.

"Didn't take you long to make yourself at home," Marc observed, taking in the chaos of the room. He sat down on the bed, the only reasonably clear surface available. "Your mom must be singing hallelujah, getting all this crapdoodle out of your house at long last. Her fire insurance probably dropped a few kilobux, too."

Alex was Marc's best friend and his former prep school roommate, a sturdy, bulldog-jawed youth whose eyes were dark and wide-set, with heavy lids that gave him a sleepy expression. He was the only person who had ever beat Marc at three-dimensional chess, and the only other undergraduate at Dartmouth with an intelligence quotient classed "unmeasurable." He was an amateur computer engineer of considerable talent and intended to specialize in theoretical physics. His creativity was grandmasterclass and his other powers mediocre.

Alex pulled a clamp vise from behind an overflowing trash basket, fastened it to the worktable after making room, and immobilized the CE helmet. Deftly as a surgical nurse prepping a patient, he removed the visor, the ear padding and phones, the needle-electrode cage, and the environmental unit. "Mom's got her hands full with your Uncle Rogi's bookshop, and no time left to fret about anything so piddling as my little hobbies." He positioned a microscanner and a slave manipulator, then laid out the slave's tool kit, the virtual glove, and the goggles. Poking around among the junk on a nearby shelf, he found what looked like a jeweler's ring box, made of crystal and silvery metal. He plugged a little cable into it and mated it to the scanner. "Will your family close the bookshop, now that the old man's passed away?"

"No," said Marc tersely.

Alex fiddled with his IBM Main Shoebox, coupling the powerful little computer to the scanner as well. The Tri-D monitor lit up. Alex began configuring for the job, whispering parameters into the hand mike. His mind said: I'm really sorry Marc. About Uncle Rogi and your mother.

Don't be.

. . . ?

It'll be made public eventually but keep it under your hair until the poop hits: Uncle Rogi and Mama aren't dead.

Alex's jaw dropped open. He stared at his friend in shock.

Marc said: It was all a hoax. I engineered most of it with Uncle Rogi's help. Mama was preggers in violation of the Repro Statutes and determined to have the baby. His fetal genetic assay said he was chock-full of lethals but Mama proved to me that his mind was superior to anybody's in our family. Including mine. I decided the kid deserved to live and so I hid Mama in the Canadian bush with Uncle Rogi to take care of her. My father and the rest of the family found out but they didn't know where I'd stashed them and knew they couldn't pry it out of me and they were wild to suppress the scandal so they let it be. They sent me to Orb to keep me out of shitway and kept me there after most of the human magnates had already gone home. My grandfather finally found out where I'd hidden Mama and Rogi and took them out of the hiding place up in Canada and put them somewhere else. Our lawyers have been working to find a way to deal with Mama's legal problems. Rogi's too of course. And the baby's. His name is Jack. I haven't seen him or Mama or Rogi or even farspoken them since last August.

God . . . Can your mother really beat the rap? An operant's violation of the Repro Statutes carries the death penalty!

Under the Simbiari Proctorship it did. Papa&Dynasty have been humping away down in Concord trying to change the law get Mama a pardon or retroactive exoneration or some damned thing. That may take months. But the resolution to modify the Repro Statutes finally passed in the Intendant Assembly three weeks ago and went to committee. That's when I was finally allowed to leave Orb.

Can they nail *you* for anything?

Probably not. Uncle Rogi will most likely claim that the whole thing was his doing. There's no percentage in my contradicting him.

Holy shit . . . and you say this little brother of yours is a real longbrain?

"He'd better be," said Marc out loud.

Alex blinked, then ventured to ask, "What about the snuff genes?"

"I don't know," Marc said in a low voice. "I just don't know."

Alex didn't say anything else. He turned on the microscanner, aimed it at the relevant circuitry of the helmet, then slipped on the virtual glove and goggles. The slave manipulator delicately picked up an instrument in obedience to the analogous movements of the gloved hand. Alex seemed to be prying up an invisible thing as the glove moved in empty air. On the microscan monitor, Marc could see an enlargement of the actual tiny tool removing an infinitesimal electronic chip from its seating in the brainboard.

"You say you replaced this chip when the hat first began to act up," Alex said. In the virtual world depicted in his goggles, he saw the chip as a thing larger than a book-plaque. The microscopic tool seemed the size of a small crowbar, gripped firmly in his gloved hand.

"Right. I was getting oddball feedback from the executive miglom. Mental imagery that wasn't mine and didn't make any sense. Weird pictures. I thought I had traced it to that chip of the brainboard and put in a new one. Then today the exec mode balked out completely and the bike fought back every time I thought it an order."

Alex mimed moving something. The slave swooped away from the helmet and extended an arm toward the ring box. An opening appeared in the box's top, and the slave, directed by Alex's glove, inserted the microscopic electronic device into the function-tester. "This little hummer is certainly the obvious point of origin for spurious commands. Putting it through its paces in the glom analyzer ought to flush out any exec glitch."

"It tested okay on miglom. I didn't try ceep."

"Let's do that." Alex took the glove off and picked up the mike again. In a few minutes the computer's monitor began to display the chip's secrets. The two boys studied the flickering complexities, now and then making remarks. After about ten minutes, Alex said, "The chip is functioning perfectly in cpglom *and* miglom."

"Shit," said Marc.

Alex shrugged. "You want me to trace the board's executive circuitry? It'll take a while."

"It's impervious, and I never touched it. Only the one chip. There must be some other explanation."

"Wear and tear," Alex suggested. "Sweat in the board. Electric dandruff."

"Come on! You saw how well sealed the brainboard is, and the helmet was working perfectly before I got shipped off to Orb. Now it starts gibbering and flashing goofy images and countermanding my orders! A tired chip in the BI exec was the obvious fix. Eliminate that, and what's left?"

Alex considered for a minute. "Is there any way that somebody could have tampered with the helmet while you were away?"

"It was locked in the boot of the bike, in our garage at home. Who the hell would bother?"

"Beats the hell out of me," said Alex. He hesitated. "You know, my man, the most obvious explanation for malfunction is that the glitch is in your own neuronic software. You've had a hard time of it during the past months. The spurious commands could result from some mental conflict that has nothing at all to do with turbocycle steering."

"Horse puckey," Marc scoffed.

"You know CE devices have always had a bad rep for screwing up the operator's mind . . . You want my advice?"

"Not if it's what I think it is."

His friend persisted. "Give this brain bucket a rest. Drive your bike like a normal. At least until your family problems are resolved and you're positive you're thinking straight—"

"I always think straight, dammit! There has to be some other explanation."

"Is it possible that another mind could inadvertently interfere with this CE system of yours? Say, through some gross slopover of the creative metafunction into the brain interface?"

"I don't think so. But cerebroenergetics is one of those damned sciences where things are being discovered so fast that the new data are obsolete before they're published. I suppose it's theoretically possible to diddle the BI voluntary nodes, given a humongously talented grandmasterly creativity maven."

"Now if you only had a twin," Alex postulated idly, "and he was shadowing you on a second turbocycle wearing an identical guidance helmet . . ."

Marc did a double take. "I *did* have a twin brother . . . but he died when we were born. His name was Matthieu."

"I'll be a horse's patoot!"

"Uncle Rogi told the story to me in the bookshop one day when I caught him maudlin drunk and he didn't know what he was doing. He said that the two of us babies were mental antagonists almost from the first time we attained consciousness. Matt was born first, dead, and when I was born they found my umbilical cord wrapped around my neck and my little hands locked in a vise grip on Matt's cord. Evidently I cut off my twin's blood supply before he could finish throttling me."

"Christ! You really tried to kill each other? Two unborn fetuses?"

"I asked Papa about it after hearing Uncle Rogi's story. It was never really clear what happened. We twins learned to mind-screen in the womb at eight months. Matt was supposed to have been larger and mentally more powerful than me. Maybe he didn't like competition."

"Craziest damn thing I ever heard of." Alex slipped the virtual glove and goggles back on and in a few minutes replaced the chip. The complete reassembly of the helmet took a little longer, after which Alex handed the gleaming black thing back to Marc. "Don't blame me if it drives you batshit."

"Wouldn't dream of it." Marc headed for the door. "Thanks for the test. See you at dinner." The door slammed.

"Craziest thing," Alex repeated to himself.

He pulled the Shoebox closer, called up the ABNORMAL PSYCHOLOGY database, and began to search through the more bizarre permutations of sibling rivalry.

Marc went to his own room, a chamber no larger than Alex's that managed to look twice as spacious because everything was meticulously in order. The teleview had its red light on, and he hit it for the recorded message.

An anonymous male face appeared on the screen. "Mr. Remillard, I'm Elihu Peters from the Office of the Dean of Freshmen. We're having a good deal of difficulty reconciling your application for a two-year dual-major accelerated honors program with the basic requirements for the bachelor's degree. Please arrange to see me *in person* no later than Tuesday about this. I want to emphasize that it's necessary that I confer with you yourself, not with some employee of your family." The screen went blank.

"Beautiful," Marc groaned. Aunt Anne had promised to cope with the college bureaucracy, and she'd evidently shoved the job off onto some minion, who had even more evidently blown it—and maybe antagonized the Dean's Office in the bargain. What the hell was he going to do if the college dug its hoofs in and insisted that he waste his time studying undergraduate fiddle-faddle instead of the courses he was really interested in? He couldn't go whining to Anne, and he'd die rather than ask Paul for help, like a spoiled brat expecting his powerful daddy to put in the fix. Grandpère? Maybe. Denis certainly knew the academic jungle inside out. He might have suggestions on which buttons to push. But it might be best to phone rather than farspeak him—

Marc.

He stood as if paralyzed, one hand poised above the teleview's keypad.

Marcdear it's ME!

Mama . . . ? Where—

Jack&Iareback!!we'reatthefarm!!withGrandpère&Grandmère!!canyoucome?

Mama is it . . . *safe* for you to be here?

Yes!! Please come assoonas you can I realize it's a dreadful night so you'd better call an eggtaxi the roads are getting very slippery out in the country.

"I'm on my way!"

He snatched up the helmet and raced down the stairs for the back door. Somebody called after him that dinner was almost ready, but he struggled into his things and dashed out into the sleetstorm.

The bike met him on the driveway, turbs hot and headlight blazing. He leapt aboard, coasted down to the street, and was off and roaring. South on steaming Main Street to Wheelock, coercing the walkers and the groundcars out of his way when he couldn't skid around them, fuzzing his identity creatively so the cops wouldn't know who to pinch. The street-melting grids stopped at the urban boundary, and Trescott Road was solid ice. The New Hampshire Department of Transportation probably figured no one but a lunatic would take a ground vehicle onto a secondary highway on such a night, so morning was soon enough to send out the sand trucks.

The bike began to skid perilously in spite of Marc's PK. It was illegal to deploy the wheel spikes, which were strictly for off-road use, but this time the boy had no qualms. The sharp steel fangs extruded from the tires and dug in. Then he really smoked the old Beemer, and only the spoilers kept him from going airborne. The bike guided like a dream. Whatever flaw had haunted the exec circuits earlier was gone with the wind.

For prudence's sake he upped spikes a few hundred meters before Grandpère's gate and kept his machine more or less straight and level with PK. There was no sign of any special activity about the place, only a single unfamiliar egg parked at the front of the farmhouse driveway. Sleet pelted him like a fusillade of ball bearings as he ran for the porch. Denis opened the door immediately, and Marc was aware of Uncle Rogi hovering in the background.

Denis exclaimed, "You drove your motorcycle out here in this storm? You young idiot!"

Rogi said, "She and the baby are in the big guest room."

Marc threw him a grateful glance and ignored Denis's indignant protests as he pounded up the staircase to the second floor, leaving globs of muddy slush and wet bootprints in his wake. He flung open the guest room door.

She was there in a chintz-covered rocking chair in front of the fire, with a shawl-wrapped bundle in her arms. Her dark hair was much longer than he remembered it, plaited into braids. She wore a gown and a night robe of blue, smocked and embroidered so elaborately that she looked like some medieval madonna.

Marc entered, keeping his mind opaque. His smile was tentative and quirkily one-sided, and his sodden black leathers gleamed in the firelight. He carried the helmet under his arm.

"Mama."

"Hello, Marc. You didn't take a taxi after all."

"No."

She nodded serenely. "It doesn't matter."

"Are—are you all right?"

"Quite all right. And so is Uncle Rogi . . . and so is your baby brother. We are technically under house arrest. The family lawyers have surrendered me to the jurisdiction of the Human Magistratum. I'm afraid I didn't pay too much attention to the legal details, but it seems that after Rogi and I are arraigned tomorrow, we will be granted bail and be free until—until the matter is resolved. We'll be able to go home."

"And you're going to be pardoned?"

"I really don't know what will happen. But the lawyers seem certain that everything will work out. Your Uncle Rogi told them that he conceived our escape plan serendipitously after the canoe upset, when we two found ourselves washed up on the riverbank." She smiled. "You knew nothing about it, of course, since you were carried further downstream."

Marc nodded and was silent for a time. Then: "The family shanghaied me and sent me to Concilium Orb. I *tried* to return to Earth so I could bring you more food, but—"

"We managed well enough. Uncle Rogi shot an enormous moose." She laughed softly and laid the baby flat on her lap. "Only Jack's diet was more monotonous than ours during those last weeks at Ape Lake. But we were never really hungry or ill-nourished. Denis came and took us away two months ago. We've stayed secretly at my family's old beach place on Kauai since then."

"I'm glad it worked out," Marc said stiffly. "And the baby . . . is he really okay?"

"Come closer and see," she invited him, indicating the small form.

"But I'm all wet."

"He won't mind."

Marc's black-gloved hands were trembling slightly. Disgusted with the evidence of his own physical weakness and the emotion that had provoked it, the boy steeled himself behind his mental barriers. The thing he had put completely out of his mind now had to be faced, the terrible potentiality in the baby that Marc had shunted aside and denied from the very beginning of the adventure: the lethal genes.

"Go ahead, dear," his mother urged. "Open the shawl."

The baby seemed to be asleep. He was very small, with dark hair. Marc reached out a gloved hand, took hold of the wool covering, and then twitched it aside.

The baby lay revealed, unclothed, perfect.

Mama he's all right! Papa was wrong the genetic assay was wrong—

Yes dear wrong wrong wrong little Jack's body is normal and his mind *his mind!* Oh Marc dear his mind just speak to him it's wonderful don't be afraid to wake him . . .

The baby's delicate eyelids opened. He looked at Marc and smiled, and the bonding of the infant to the older brother was instantaneous. Jack loved.

Marc held back.

Why? Whywhywhy are you shut tight? Open to me talk to me you helped to save me I love you I want to know you! Open! *Open!*

"Hello, baby. Jack." Don't be pushy it's not polite. You don't order people to open their minds to you. You wait for them to do it in their own sweet time.

Oh.

Are you [image] okay?

?? My body functions properly. My mind craves more challenging stimuli and I would like to discuss certain ideas with a mind more [*complex image*] than that of Mama. Or Uncle Rogi.

Well you've got Grandpère Denis to talk to now. He's more [*complex image*] than anybody short of a Lylmik.

Your mind is more congenial. I would prefer to talk to you. I demand it!

"Oh, you do, do you?" Hands on hips, Marc studied the infant with an expression of bemused consternation on his face. "Mama, this kid is overdue for a course in operant etiquette."

"Isn't he marvelous?" Teresa put the naked baby over her shoulder, got up, and took him to a changing table. "Now that you've seen that his body is perfectly normal, I'll dress him again. What did he say to you?"

"He was trying to boss me around."

Teresa laughed delightedly. "You'll have to help me civilize him. I know you two will be very close."

Jack said: *We will Mama.* [COERCION.]

Marc said to the baby, "Not if you keep pushing my face, peewee. Quit trying to probe me!"

"Oh, Jack," said Teresa reproachfully. "You know that's not friendly."

The infant spoke urgently to Marc on his intimate mode: Explain to me what a lethal gene is. Tell me why you worry about this concept and what it has to do with me. *Open your mind further!*

Marc said: No.

Jack began to scream.

Teresa picked the baby up to comfort him, but he howled on. "What's wrong? Whatever were you two talking about?"

"I only refused to let him root around in my mind. He wouldn't take no for an answer and tried to squirm under my screen, and I had to slam it down. He's incredibly strong in coercion, Mama."

"You were every bit as obnoxiously assertive when you were young. I distinctly remember how you used to bully—"

Tell me tell me Marc OR DO YOU WANT ME TO ASK HER?

It would frighten her and she knows almost nothing about it. My own knowledge is incomplete. If you insist on knowing I'll scrape up all the data I can find and give it to you in a few days. But you lack the emotional resources to deal with the impact this information will have upon your psyche. It'll scare the shit out of you Baby Brother.

Irrelevant. [Diapers.] *Tell me!*

!!Have it your own way!!

Yes.

"There," said Marc, "he's finally calmed down. I had a few words with him, man to man."

Teresa's smile was uncertain. "I know he's difficult, Marc. But be gentle with him, won't you? Be his friend. He needs close contact with another powerful operant if his mind is to develop properly. I won't be able to cope with his needs by myself, and for some reason he's suspicious of Lucille and Denis. He can't bring himself to trust them fully."

"There's Papa," Marc said.

Teresa looked away. "He came to see us before we left Kauai. With the lawyers and Colette Roy. Your father was very kind to me and Jack, but he made it quite clear that—that other, very important matters will take up most of his time for the immediate future."

"I see." Marc stood motionless, keeping the abrupt surge of anger and disappointment walled away from her perception. Poor Mama. Even pardoned, Teresa Kendall and the offspring of her crime would always be political liabilities to an ambitious First Magnate of the Concilium.

Teresa was saying, "Lucille has gone to fetch Marie and Maddy and Luc in her egg so that they can meet their baby brother, too. I know they're going to do their best to help with Jack. But he needs more than a group of loving brothers and sisters, Marc. He needs someone very strong. Like you. I wouldn't dream of asking you to move out of the fraternity house, but—will you make some time for Jack?"

"All right. I'm up to the eyeballs in college work, but I'll find a way to be with him. Farspeaking, too, if he can just learn to control himself."

I will! I will!

No more stupid brat tricks?

I promise.

"Thank you, Marc." Teresa put Jack into the beautiful old maple cradle that Lucille had used for her seven children. She went with Marc to the door and kissed him. "Try not to judge your father too harshly. He has so many demands on him—and in his way, he's trying to do the best he can for us."

Marc said only, "Goodbye, Mama." *Catch you later Jack.*

Then he hurried downstairs, where Uncle Rogi waylaid him before he could be out and away.

"How'd it go?" the old man inquired. His gaunt face was tanned from the tropical sun, and he wore a Hawaiian shirt under his old cord jacket with the leather elbow patches.

"She forgives Papa!" Marc was incredulous.

"You better, too, if you know what's good for you."

Marc stared coldly at Rogi. "Papa's not going to just wash his hands of Mama like she was some—some—"

"She won't thank you for confronting Paul, and she doesn't need you to be her knight in shining armor. There's nothing you can do to make your father change his mind about dealing with this matter any way he chooses to. But he won't subject Teresa to any humiliation. There'll be no divorce or open separation."

"That's considerate of him. And politically expedient as all hell!"

"Now you listen to me," Rogi said ferociously. "Teresa's accepted the situation, and you damn well better accept it, too! There's all kinds of fresh trouble facing your poor mother in the very near future, and you better not let me catch you acting like a vindictive young asshole and being a part of the problem!"

"I wouldn't dream of it. You may be interested to know that I've already received instructions from a higher authority regarding my filial responsibilities. Although it beats me why the Lylmik have condescended to meddle in our family affairs."

Rogi said, "Well, I'll be damned. So they decided to work you over, too, eh?"

Marc ignored the comment. "I'm going to be spending a lot of time with Jack and Mama. She thinks the baby needs me, and she's probably right. I'll keep up a cheerful front, and Papa will never know what I really think of him. Satisfied?"

The two of them glowered at each other. Then, abruptly, the tall old man's eyes filled, and he caught up his great-grandnephew in a bear hug.

"Oh, God, Uncle Rogi," Marc whispered, his face against the worn corduroy.

"Bon courage, mon petit gars."

"It's not only Mama . . . Jack pried inside my mind. I was off guard, and I had no idea he'd be able to do such a thing. He made me promise to explain the lethal genes."

"Merde alors." Rogi took a resolute breath. "Then you'll just have to do it."

Marc pulled free. "Mama said that Colette Roy came to the island along with Papa and the lawyers."

"Yes. She took tissue samples from the baby for a comprehensive assay at the Gilman Human Genetics Center. You remember that the original tests were done on the sly by your Uncle Severin, who's hardly an expert. Paul expects the results in about three days. If therapy is called for, it'll be done here, at Dartmouth, under Colette's supervision."

"Mama is convinced that Jack is perfectly normal."

"I know. He looks and acts normal, and has since he was born. I know that doesn't necessarily mean that he *is* normal. But your Mama seems to have put any idea of congenital disease in the baby clear out of her mind."

"As you said, Uncle Sevvy's no expert. Even though he was a pretty decent neurosurgeon, he wasn't trained in genetics. Still, it doesn't seem likely he could have mistakenly diagnosed three lethals . . ." Marc put on his helmet and gloves. As if reassuring himself, he said, "But the docs managed to fix Luc, and look what a mess he was."

"That's right. When you talk to Jack, tell him about the wonders of modern genetic therapy. Lethal genes aren't the death sentence they were in the old days. No way!" Rogi gave the boy an encouraging clap on the shoulder.

Then Marc was gone. For a few minutes, Rogi used his farsight to watch the turbocycle roar away into the storm. Then he shook his head and went off to burgle Denis's supply of fine cognac.

< The CE helmet ploy was a complete fiasco, just as I suspected it would be. >

I don't agree. I was actually able to deflect Marc's will. Stop him from doing something he wanted to do. My hunch paid off: the cerebroenergetic technology provides a genuine entry port into his mind—a bypass of all his mental screens. So what if nothing much came of it this first time? I'll think of other angles. *You* never managed to get that far!

< You're feeling very cocksure. And insolent. >

Well give me *some* credit!

< Very well. I withdraw my original assessment. Your maneuver was ingenious and may yet prove valuable—if you are ever able to refine your technique so that Marc is unaware of losing control. But that possibility is statistically remote. He's always on guard. It's part of his nature never to trust. >

I'm going to keep trying. I'm studying very hard.

<Good . . . Do you know that Marc has agreed to be Jack's mentor?>

No! Oh shit. I got absolutely nowhere in my first contact with the baby. *He's* an instinctive mind-guarder too. With Marc hanging around now things will be impossible! If you *really* want Jack you're going to have to let me kill Marc.

<No.>

I could get him through the helmet brainboard. I know it. Let me try. I could make him crash the cycle—

<No. The baby has the greater mental potential of the two but he may not live. And Marc . . . even if he is not under my control he instinctively furthers my great plan. You may NOT kill him.>

[Jealousy. Impatience.]

<You are going to ruin everything if you persist in defying me. My way is the only way. If you no longer love and cannot follow—>

I will follow! I do still love you! But—

<Dear one. I've given you free access to the nervebomb.>

That's not as good as it used to be. I need operant lifeforce! I need it to grow. I NEED IT TO METAMORPHOSE.

<Perhaps you do. Yes . . .>

You want me to be strong! Strong enough to take on the best of the Grand Masters. Strong enough to kill your Great Enemy!

<But we can't risk betraying you through reckless behavior. We have to energize you tracelessly. I must think.>

Don't take too long, Fury. I've grown already and I've GOT to continue to grow. In one way or another.

[29]

FROM THE MEMOIRS
OF ROGATIEN REMILLARD

When I was still moderately young, back in the last decade of the twentieth century, genetic engineering was in its infancy and all kinds of wild predictions were made about how, in the future, we would be able to have "designer" children, with bodies and minds tailor-made through manipulating the DNA codes that form the blueprint for the human species. It went without saying that all inherited abnormalities and diseases would be wiped out. No more sickle-cell anemia, no more hemophilia or cystic fibrosis, no more jerry-built eyeballs that made you myopic, no more saddle-bag flab or hay fever or dinky cocks or bald heads twinkling in the moonlight to put a damper on romance. Genetic engineering would fix it all.

The more flamboyant scientific soothsayers went even further and said that we'd routinely be able to order up desirable traits for our unborn babies, like long eyelashes and clear skin and handsome features and white teeth and an IQ of 300—just by selecting from a shopping list of "superior" genes that the heredity manipulators would offer to prospective parents. And this was only for eugenic starters! When population-pressured Earthlings set out to colonize other worlds and we decided we needed colonists with gills for watery planets, or lizard-skinned folks for hot planets, or even turtle-bodied humans for heavy-gravity planets—why, hey! It'd be easy as pie to engender a whole new population of modified bods and superminds to order.

Some of those science-fictional genetic predictions did come true. But not all of them—unfortunately for a whole lot of sick and unhappy human beings, including my little great-grandnephew Jon Remillard.

In the months following Jack's homecoming, I was to learn more about human genetics and genetic engineering's limitations than I ever wanted to know. Most of my education came from good old Colette Roy, who took charge of the baby's therapy from the hopeful beginnings in 2052 until the horrifying and transcendent culmination in 2054.

When she agreed to supervise Jack's treatment, Colette Roy was ninety-two years old. She was one of the original Dartmouth Coterie, that close-knit group of students with operant mindpowers who befriended young Denis when he first came to the college as a timid twelve-year-old prodigy in 1979. Like most members of the Coterie, Colette took a medical degree with graduate studies in psychiatry. She was an associate of Denis's later in the new Department of Metapsychology, doing clinical work with operants and suboperants.

In 1985 Colette married Glenn Dalembert, a colleague and another member of the original Coterie, who died in 2031. She and Glenn had one son, Martin Dalembert, who became a distinguished genetics researcher and the father of three children—Aurelie, Jeanne, and Peter Paul. Aurelie married Philip Remillard and Jeanne married his brother Maurice. Peter Paul and his wife Alice Waddell had a single child, Peter Paul Junior—called Pete—who became one of Marc's closest friends and a fellow Metapsychic Rebel.

After the Intervention, Colette herself turned to genetic research as a result of Martin's influence and made a second academic career for herself in what she thought would be her twilight years, studying the genetic aspects of the higher mindpowers and teaching graduate courses in the subject that became world famous. She continued to be a close friend of Denis and Lucille's and was Paul Remillard's godmother. As she grew older, she continued to participate in research even in semiretirement, and was one of the first to submit to experimental regeneration tank therapy in 2035. Her rejuvenation was an unqualified success, and at the age of seventy-five, Colette found herself once again possessed of the body and brain cells she had enjoyed as a thirty-year-old.

When she agreed to try to help baby Jack, Colette Roy knew that she faced the premier challenge of her long life. Even though the infant still looked perfectly normal at three months of age, the defective genetic blueprint within his body cells had already begun to program his inevitable death. Comprehensive tests showed that Jack had not three intractable lethal equivalent genes, as Severin's hasty and incompetent assay had showed, but *thirty-four*—some of them never before encountered in the human gene map. Any one of those defective bits of DNA would have been sufficient to kill the little boy before he reached the age of five years. All of them had heretofore proved resistant to genetic therapy; but Colette was going to treat them anyway, hoping that Jack's genetic makeup was as extraordinary as his mind.

The human species has more than 100,000 genes, the DNA "code words" that program every cell in our bodies to take this shape or that, and perform this function or that, in this organ or that. A detailed map of human genetic material has been made, but the map is not always a straightforward thing. One gene does not always control one trait. On the contrary, the *usual* thing is for one gene to affect several traits or body functions, something geneticists call pleiotropy. (The ramifications of pleiotropy were still being studied as the twenty-first century rolled to a close.) In a flip side to pleiotropy, a number of completely different genes are capable of producing the same effect or trait. And in a given environment—for example, adequate or inadequate nutrition in the womb or in early years, or in the presence of carcinogenic agents—genes can influence the bodies in widely varying ways. To complicate things even further, our human-species collection of DNA is fraught with mysterious "extras"—ornaments or doodles on the basic blueprint that seem to be totally unnecessary . . . perhaps.

The entry of the human race into the Galactic Age gave us access to high technology, but it did not instantly improve the techniques of genetic engineering. We still had the same human genes to cope with, and they were, by and large, more complex in their interaction than were the genes of the other Milieu races. It became possible to identify pleiotropic human genes more precisely using Milieu science; but modifying these genes to avoid undesired side effects during therapy was accomplished only very slowly, over a long period of time.

It was not until 2040 that the genetic engineering triumph known as the regeneration tank came into widespread use, enabling humans to regrow lost or defective organs and rejuvenate aging bodies to a reasonable equivalent of young adulthood. As a side benefit to truly necessary (and expensive) regeneration therapy in the tank, a person could also be reprogrammed genetically for modest types of enhancement genetic engineering, such as the modification of muscle mass and inherited fat deposition patterns, the resculpting of facial features, the elimination of male-pattern baldness, and the changing of various body pigments. During the Simbiari Proctorship and for some decades thereafter, until tank therapy became inexpensive, reliable, and routine, purely cosmetic or otherwise frivolous alteration of the genes was forbidden by law. Human nature being what it is, however, persons with enough money to spend were very often able to get what they wanted, law or no law.

Even the most carefully executed genetic engineering procedures still carried some risks all throughout the twenty-first century, since inserting extra genes into a person's blueprint might produce unexpectedly disastrous effects through some hitherto unknown action of pleiotropy. There was also the perplexing matter of self-redaction, in which a person's mind was known to influence the way that genes "expressed" themselves for better or worse.

Certain gene complexes causing serious defects proved to be completely intractable to engineering, and so did some "good" genes that might have been used eugenically. Traits such as intelligence and personality turned out to be controlled by a bewildering interaction among more than sixteen thousand different genes—effectively banishing any possibility of genetically engineering the brain. As the reader of these Memoirs has probably already suspected, the so-called immortality gene complex occurring in the Remillard family was never successfully transplanted either, except by the good old-fashioned technique called sexual intercourse.

Nevertheless, by the time of Jon Remillard's birth, the "bad" genes responsible for a host of congenital human diseases had been pinpointed, and a goodly number of the worst of them had succumbed to the type of genetic engineering called somatic cell gene therapy. In this, DNA containing a "correction" of the flawed gene is inserted into the patient's body, and if all goes well, the genetic blueprint will be successfully revised, and abnormality will give way to normality.

The flawed codons still existed within the cured patient's germ cells, however, and could be passed on to the offspring. In order to eradicate a genetic flaw permanently from an affected family, the much trickier expedient called germ line gene therapy is required. The delicate fertilized egg itself must have the genetic correction inserted into it, so that all cells of the developing embryo, including the embryo's own germ cells, will carry the revised blueprint.

Germ line gene therapy was very successful in plants and in some animals. But in the highly organized human body with its pleiotropy, the results were usually unsatisfactory, with the DNA often latching onto inappropriate parts of the embryo's chromosomes. Even before the Intervention, ethical genetic scientists had decided that the risks in the procedure outweighed potential benefits.

The Simbiari Proctorship confirmed this judgment and set up the infamous Reproductive Statutes in order to prevent the propagation of the genetic flaws deemed most injurious to human society as a whole. All humans were obliged to submit to genetic assay before they were issued a reproduction license. Those with the cleanest gene map—especially the operants—were encouraged to have the most children, while somewhat less fortunate types were apt to be restricted to a single offspring. Persons having genetic flaws were counseled as to the risks they faced and the possibility of successful genetic therapy. Those who carried the worst category of deleterious genes were prohibited by law from having any children at all, with the penalty varying with the seriousness of the genetic defect and the metapsychic status of the individuals involved. All fetuses had to be tested for flaws within two months of conception, and those with intractable genetic disease were aborted. If nonoperant parents evaded the restrictions and persisted in having a seriously flawed baby, they were subject to fines, their health insurance was canceled, and they were obliged to assume all expenses involved in treating and rearing the diseased child. Operant parents, being in the eyes of the Simbiari Proctorship the standard-bearers for humanity's future, were subject to the death penalty for committing the same reproductive crime. And so was the flawed fetus, if it still resided within the womb of the criminal mother.

As a result of Teresa Kendall's case, the deliberate contravention of the Reproductive Statutes by an operant was eventually reduced from a Class One to a Class Two felony, no longer carrying the death penalty, and the child involved in such a crime was deemed totally innocent and given the right to the best medical treatment that society could provide. The operant parent or parents found guilty under the new law were deprived of custody of the illicit child, heavily fined, and obliged to perform ten years of public service.

Paul and his powerful siblings did not oppose the proposed new law as it was debated in the Intendant Assembly but rather gave it their enthusiastic support. The measure was passed by a simple majority, ratified by the Human Magnates of the Concilium, and became law with the affirming signature of the Dirigent for Earth, David Somerled MacGregor, on 10 May 2052.

A rider that would have pardoned Teresa Kendall and Rogatien Remillard was stricken from the measure during the final floor debates. The members of the Dynasty, with a single exception, had voted to keep the rider.

But Paul had voted against it.

I was fit to be tied when the news reached me that day in the bookshop, and it was Anne, not Paul, who transmitted the details to me from Concord in brisk, emotionless farspeech. I immediately went galloping out of the shop and around the corner and down to Teresa's house. It was a nice sunny day, and the new roses in the bed that she had planted on the side of the house facing the library were blooming their heads off. Marc's turbocycle stood in the driveway, signaling that he'd got the news from the capital even faster than I had.

I went slam-banging into the house and found Teresa and all five of her children in the cool, dim living room. Jack was suspended in his papoose-frame, which stood at his mother's side. Marie, cuddling Luc, and Madeleine sat at Teresa's feet. Marc was standing at one of the windows, staring morosely outside.

"You don't have to worry!" I blustered. "They won't take Jack away from you. There still has to be a trial—due process!"

She looked at me with that calm, madonna expression. "I've been telling the children what their Aunt Anne explained to me about that. You and I are not scheduled to go to trial until November, but there are two other legal avenues open for pardoning us before that. The first—and the one Anne thinks most likely, because she's a member— is through the ten-person Directorate of the Human Polity of the Concilium. Anne thinks Paul felt obliged to make a public gesture deploring my deliberate defiance of the law, and that's why he voted to defeat the pardon rider. It didn't have enough support to pass the Assembly anyhow. But when the application for pardon comes before him and Anne and the other eight Concilium Directors, they'll prevail on the others to let us go free."

"H'mph!" snorted I. "They damn well better! If we go to trial, we'll be convicted. *You* can afford to pay almost any fine, and your ten years of public service would probably consist of giving music lessons on that damned Siberian planet. But my poor old bookstore has always tippy-toed along the brink of insolvency, and any sort of fine would bankrupt me. I'll be damned if I want to spend my next immortal decade planting baby evergreens in a Maine tree farm while mosquitoes drill my ass!"

Maddy giggled.

Luc wailed, "I don't want Mama to go to jail! Not when we just got her back."

Baby Jack asked: What is jail?

Maddy said, "It's really awful!" And she simultaneously transmitted a horrific mental image of a dungeon cum torture chamber, whereupon the infant began to cry.

"Mama won't go to jail, silly," Marie declared. She gave Madeleine a PK poke. "And neither will Uncle Rogi. Nobody goes to jail except *really* wicked people."

Still mewling and hiccuping, Jack said: Was bringing about my birth only moderately wicked?

Teresa burst out laughing, lifted the baby from his swing, and kissed him. "Certainly not! It wasn't wicked at all, only illegal. There's a big difference, and Marie is going to take you upstairs and explain it to you, and then it's time for your nap. Nana Colette is coming later with more good genes for you, and you must be well rested and full of the best possible redactive thoughts in order for them to work."

The baby said: Very well Mama.

Teresa gave the baby to Marie and told Maddy and Luc to go out and play. When the youngsters were gone, Marc turned away from the window.

"What happens if Papa and Aunt Anne *don't* convince the Directorate to pardon you and Uncle Rogi?"

"Then we can appeal to Davy MacGregor," she replied calmly. "The Planetary Dirigent can issue an order of executive clemency all by himself, and not even the Lylmik can countermand it."

"If MacGregor is charitably inclined," I muttered.

"You probably have a better chance with him than with Papa," Marc said.

"I won't have you talking that way," Teresa reproved him.

"How much vindication for Jack's birth does Papa need?" Marc demanded hotly. "Even the preliminary assessment of the baby's armamentarium shows that he has the most powerful mind the human race has ever produced! You were right to save him from being aborted! Someday he could be a super-Einstein! But all Papa can think of are his precious principles and what the goddam Simbiari and Krondaku think. He won't even come and see Jack!"

Teresa's resolution wavered. Her eyes began to fill, and she shrank back into the corner of the couch. She appealed to me mutely on my intimate mode.

"Okay," I said to Marc shortly. "You've expressed your righteous indignation. Now scram."

The boy finally had sense enough to be ashamed of himself. He made a gruff apology to his mother, promised to visit Jack tomorrow, and slouched away. I waited until the roar of his turbocycle had dwindled into the distance before speaking to Teresa again.

"He's only fourteen. The intellect of a grown man, the tact and forbearance of a teenage twit."

"I know . . . and he's been marvelous with Jack, coming almost every day in spite of his heavy course load at college."

"Is it true—what he said about Jack's mind? I've always felt in my guts that the kid was hot stuff, but have the psychologists actually proved it?"

She shrugged. "Apparently yes. Colette told me last week. I'm sorry that I forgot to tell you, Rogi. You see, I never doubted that Jack was extraordinary, and the mental-test results only seemed to confirm what I knew all along was true. My little son is going to do wonderful things for humanity. It . . . hurts that Paul still seems to think of him as an embarrassment rather than a source of pride. I can only keep praying that he'll change his mind after we're finally pardoned." Her eyes met mine. "And we will be. I know it. Please don't worry about it, dear."

I mumbled something reassuring, then said I'd better be getting back to the shop. Teresa walked me to the front door. Colette Roy's groundcar was just pulling up in front of the house.

"How's the therapy going?" I asked Teresa.

She smiled again. "Colette says everything is going very well. As you saw, Jack is perfectly healthy. It's entirely possible that his mind is fending off the harmful effects of the damaged genes."

"Good for him," I said heartily, and fled, giving Colette only a hasty wave.

Two weeks later, Colette Roy was able to tell the family that replacement genes to counteract all of Jack's defects had been successfully implanted within his body. Now we could only wait and see whether the therapy succeeded. From time to time the baby would be given full-body scans at the old Hitchcock Hospital, which was part of the Genetics Center; and he would also wear a tiny vital-signs monitor that would alert Colette to any problems.

Meanwhile, Jack was able to live the life of a normal infant, so Teresa and all the children joined the rest of the family at Adrien and Cheri's place in Rye, on the New Hampshire shore, for the Memorial Day holiday weekend, the traditional opening of the summer boating season. Teresa and Jack returned to Hanover on the following Tuesday, May 28, so that the baby could undergo some special tests of his self-redactive faculty at the Ferrand Mental Science Center, and Marc came with them to take his spring finals. The other three children and Herta, their nanny, stayed at Cheri's with a horde of younger cousins throughout the rest of the week.

On 29 May, in Wallis Sands Park, about two kilometers north of Rye, an operant woman named Frances Schroeder disappeared while swimming in the sea. A day later, an operant young man named Scott Lynch vanished from the Hampton Beach Park, a few kloms south of Rye. Neither body was ever recovered.

Madeleine Remillard, age twelve, who had been sailing along the shore in a small catamaran on both days, claimed to have seen a shark fin. The other four children in the boat, her cousins Celine, Quint, Gordo, and Parni, noticed nothing unusual. The Coast Guard issued a Shark Watch, which was to stay in effect throughout most of the summer.

From July through August, Marie, Madeleine, and Luc stayed at the shore, either with Cheri or with Lucille and Denis at their summer cottage. Many of the other young Remillard and McAllister cousins were also there off and on. Two more apparent shark deaths took place—one victim an operant man whose overturned sailing dinghy was found drifting off the Isles of Shoals, the other an operant woman who disappeared while on a dawn swim off Salisbury beach, just south of the New Hampshire border in Massachusetts.

The parents of the Remillard clan took a sensible view of the tragedies and did not prohibit their offspring from entering the water. Provided that the children always swam prudently in groups and kept their farsenses alert for marine predators, they would almost certainly be perfectly safe.

[30]

RYE, NEW HAMPSHIRE, EARTH
2 SEPTEMBER 2052

The bonfire had burned in the beach cooking pit all afternoon until the stone lining was red hot, and now Adrien Remillard carefully raked out the last glowing coals. The four youngsters who were designated cooks-of-the-day, togged out in gaudy aprons over their bathing suits, had baskets and boxes of food ready. Those of the other children who weren't sailboarding or playing with Frisbees or swimming stood around making smart remarks.

"Looking good," Adrien sang out, tossing aside the last smoking brand. "Carry on, you cooks!"

His eldest daughter Adrienne, wearing a tall white chef's toque in addition to her apron, gave a telepathic command to Marc and Duggie McAllister, who began to fork up damp seaweed from a big pile on a plass tarp and heave it into the cooking pit. A great hiss and a tremendous cloud of iodine-smelling steam rose up, and the little kids screamed. When there was a good layer of weed in the pit bottom, Adrienne commanded: "In with the potatoes!"

She and her cousin Caroline began tossing in foil-wrapped tubers, using their farsight and PK to do the job properly amid the smoke and steam. When the potatoes were all in, Marc and Duggie forked a thinner layer of seaweed on top of them. Then it was time to put in the lobsters and the crabs, a task that required the efforts of all four cooks. Tenderhearted Adrienne insisted that Marc mind-zap each living crustacean just before it was consigned to the pit, which drew hoots of laughter from Duggie and most of the audience. Another layer of weed covered the sacrificed creatures, and then Adrienne cried, "In with the corn!" She and Caroline flung in armloads of unshucked sweet corn, the boys heaped the rest of the weed over it, and then all four of the cooks raked a big pile of sand on top of everything to seal in the heat and steam. The spectators cheered and began to drift away.

It would be several hours before the feast would be ready. Then the entire family would gather at the rustic picnic tables on the beach to stuff themselves with the bounty from the pit and with salad and peach shortcake that the cooks would have to prepare later and bring down from the house.

Luc came up, big-eyed and solemn, as Marc was rinsing off the messy seaweed tarp in the booming waves. "I'm glad you killed the animals before they went into the pit," he said softly to his brother. "Some of the other guys . . . were waiting to hear 'em mind-shriek. You know. As they roasted."

"Sadistic little shits," Marc muttered. "Grab a corner of the tarp and help me slosh."

Luc obeyed. "Maddy killed a moth for Jack once. She said she wanted him to emp—empathize. She wanted to kill a sparrow for him, too, but he wouldn't let her. He said he'd already grasped the concept. She was disappointed, just like she was today when you zapped the lobsters and crabs."

"Christ—the little creep! No wonder Jack told me he doesn't like her. I'm going to have to have a long talk with Maddy one of these days." He saw his younger sister down the shore a few hundred meters, shoving the Hobie Cat into the water together with Quint, Gordo, Parni, and Celine. He farspoke the lot of them: *You guys watch out for sharks!*

They said: *Yes SIR Officer Friendly SIR!*

Luc's face was troubled. "Is it hard to kill things, Marco?"

"Not critters like lobsters and crabs. Or worms or bugs or other small things."

"Have you ever killed anything *big?*"

"No," said Marc brusquely. "Quit being morbid." He shook out the tarp and folded it. "You want to help? Take this up to the house and put it on the back porch."

"I could never kill anything. Not even mosquitoes. I just push 'em away."

"Great, if it makes you happy. Just don't go pushing 'em at *me.*"

Marc started back to the pit, and Luc trailed after. Adrienne was ordering Duggie and Caroline to help her gather up the shellfish baskets and pitchforks and things.

"If a shark came after you, could you kill it, Marco?" Luc asked.

"I don't know. Sharks are weird. Joe Canaletto told me that if you cut the head off one, the head can still bite."

Luc shuddered. "There are sharks out there. Everybody says so. I'm never going swimming in the ocean ever again."

"You don't have to be afraid. Just keep your farsight alert, and if you see a shark, you just tell it: 'I'm not good to eat. Go away.' "

"That didn't help those four operants who disappeared," Luc said dubiously.

"They were swimming or sailing alone and probably not paying attention to what they were doing. Now get along up to the house with that tarp."

He watched the little boy, pathetically skinny in his bathing trunks, trudge away. Luc would never be physically strong until his body was finally completely restored in the regen-tank, after he reached puberty. And although his mindpowers assayed at the grandmaster level, he was still almost completely unable to utilize them. His early ordeals had turned him into a metapsychic invalid, and it was questionable whether he would ever be raised from latency. Marc wondered whether the same thing would happen to Jack if his genetic flaws resisted therapy.

"Help me take away these gunnysacks the seaweed came in," Adrienne called.

"Yo," said Marc. The other two cooks had already gone off with the pitchforks and the empty baskets. The mound above the fire pit now steamed gently, and a young gull poked through scattered bits of leftover seaweed. Adrienne was using a sack to brush sand and bird droppings off the picnic tables. "All we have to do now is take these sacks up and wash them at the pump, and then we're off duty until the food is cooked."

"Cosmic," said Marc. He collected his share of the slimy jute bags, and the two of them headed back through low sand dunes to the huge old gray-and-white shore house. Some of the adults were sitting on the long front veranda, and as Marc and Adrienne went around to the rear, where the old pump stood on a concrete slab, Teresa waved at them and baby Jack said: *Hi!*

In the backyard, which was already deeply shaded from the westering sun, they heard laughter and caught a glimpse of Duggie and Caroline running off into the trees. Caroline was carrying a blanket.

Marc scowled. "Well, now we know how *they* plan to spend the next few hours." He took hold of the red-painted iron handle and began to pump.

"They're in love." Adrienne pulled a sack inside out and held it under the gushing water. "They've had a thing going all summer. Most of the older kids know. I'm surprised you don't."

"Poor shmucks."

"I think it's beautiful! And they're both sixteen, so they have a perfect right to love each other—"

Marc cut her off with a scornful laugh. "To use each other, you mean. Love! It's just biology. One set of overactive adolescent gonads calling to another, causing all kinds of complicated emotional shit and grief en route to the propagation of the species."

"Human love," Adrienne declared, wringing out a sack, "is noble and sacred. All the philosophers say so."

"About as sacred as taking a leak! If you want my opinion, Addie, the whole sex thing is a bloody bore and a time-waster. Just think of the famous people—smart people!—throughout history who acted like complete idiots because of sex: Saint Augustine, Mary Queen of Scots, Henry the Eighth, Oscar Wilde, John F. Kennedy, Dr. Louise Randazzo! To say nothing of the millions and millions of men and women who ruined themselves or accomplished nothing in their lives because they were too busy chasing members of the opposite sex, or taking care of one damn baby after another, or working like dogs to support all the children they fathered because they couldn't keep their paws off their wives . . . The human race would be better off if we were all cooked up in jars, like the nonborns they're growing to help populate the colonial planets."

Adrienne straightened up and glared at him. She was wearing the ridiculous chef's hat, and her dark hair was sweaty and straggling, and she was sunburned and peeling slightly on the bridge of her nose. "Is *that* what they taught you at Dartmouth?"

"No," Marc said archly. "I figured it out for myself, through keen observation and deduction. And what are they teaching you math majors down there at MIT this summer? How to be noble, sacred sexpots?"

"Surely you jest." Adrienne struck a pose and sang:

"Root-ti-toot! Root-ti-toot!
We are the girls from the Institute.
We don't neck.
We don't screw.
We don't go with boys who do."

Marc howled with laughter, and then he gave the pump handle a mighty thrust, and stuck his hand into the spigot so that she was sprayed with water, and she shrieked and walloped him with a sopping-wet gunnysack, and then they stood there grinning at each other.

"God," she drawled, "what a pair of superior metapsychic lifeforms we truly are." She dropped the wet sack and stepped close to him. Her chef's hat had fallen off. "I'm homely and brilliant, and you're gorgeous and brilliant, and we're sweet fourteen and never been kissed . . . Marco, let's do it."

"Good God, no!"

She was laughing, but there was something else lurking behind her eyes. "Think of it," she said lightly, "as an exercise in empiricism. Or are you afraid to verify your antisexual hypothesis experimentally?"

He stopped smiling. His emotions were barricaded, and his gray eyes were like polished granite. He suddenly took hold of her head in both wet hands and bent over her upturned face. Their lips met and hers were chilled from fear and audacity and his were warm and slightly parted. Both of them still had their eyes wide open, and she felt herself melt as his tongue stole gently through her teeth and then thrust strongly. It seemed that she tasted perfumed honey, and then smoldering musk, and finally the acidic tingle of a Winesap apple, strong enough to make her dizzy, to dissolve all the carefully woven mental screens she had always locked tightly into place whenever she came near him. Her own eyes closed as the sweet aching wonder began to flood through her; but she still saw Marc and knew that he saw her—body and brain and everything. And knew.

Then they stood awkward and apart, still in their silly aprons, barefooted, their legs and arms all sticky with sand and seaweed slime and bits of cornsilk. He had that maddening little lopsided smile on his face, and his inner self was as impenetrable as ever.

"Addie, you silly broad. You can't possibly love me. It's only sex."

"I never wanted you to know," she whispered, contrite now for having tricked him. She hesitated. "Didn't you feel *anything?*"

He was silent.

She flung her hands wide in helpless, comical exasperation. "There's nothing at all I can do about it, Marco. It's there. Those damned adolescent gonads! But you needn't worry that I'll make a dreary mooning pest of myself. No brokenhearted complicated emotional shit. We'll go on as before. Platonic cousin-pals. Okay?"

"Okay," he said, grinning at last.

"What about a swim?" she suggested briskly. "We're both filthy, and at least *one* of us needs cooling off."

Marc made an almost imperceptible gesture toward the blazing sky. Adrienne looked up and saw a silver rhocraft wafting toward them from the west. "It's my father," he said. "I have to see him. I'll wash off here at the pump."

"Right. But remember— I want you in the kitchen no later than nineteen hundred hours to help with the salad and peaches. God only knows if those idiots Caroline and Duggie will show up."

She went running away to the beach then, her unrequited love for Marc once again locked safely away. Flinging the apron onto one of the tables, she sprinted across the hot sand, dived into the breakers, and swam strongly toward deep water.

Much farther out, the catamaran danced on the sparkling waves.

Fury watched from above, watched the swimmer suddenly change direction and head directly for the Hobie Cat in response to the irresistible coercion. The little boat was far enough offshore that none of the beach loungers was paying any particular attention to it.

< All the same, > Fury told Hydra, < take her well out to sea before you do it. >

YesyesyesyesYES! I'm so glad the last one will be her. I *hate* her!

< You've fed well this summer darling Hydra. Now you must rest and ripen in preparation for your metamorphosis. A period of danger is coming for us and we must be very discreet. >

It's allright I can wait I'll be good I'm getting stronger&stronger ah Fury it's *so* good I love you so much and I WILL mature and then it will be Marc's turn won't it please won't it and then I'll be strong enough strong enough for Jack and all the others . . .

< We'll see. Enjoy your last mindmeal my darling little one and then rest. Rest quietly and wait for me to awaken you. >

The traditional American Labor Day holiday was not celebrated in the Galactic Milieu, and the Directorate of the Human Polity of the Concilium had put in a full Monday's work in Concord. Most of the time had been spent on the final arguments and the voting on the pardon applications of Teresa Kendall and Rogatien Remillard.

Paul was exhausted and dispirited, and if there had been any honorable way that he could have avoided going to the last beach party of the season, he would have stayed in his apartment in the capital. But the final ruling of the Directorate would be reported on the evening news, and he would have to face Teresa and the family eventually anyhow, and so he bit the bullet.

As he guided the silver egg in for a landing behind the big house he perceived Marc waiting for him. That provoked a suppressed subliminal obscenity from the First Magnate, followed by a sense of relief. At least the damned kid was off the hook. The Human Magistratum had accepted without demur Uncle Rogi's simple statement that he was solely responsible for Teresa's flight and concealment. It had helped that the media made a hero out of the old man—to say nothing of idolizing Teresa herself. The pair of them were universally regarded as martyrs to human freedom, and there had been clamorous dismay among the citizenry, both operant and non, when the first attempt at pardoning them fell through.

The PR repercussions of today's Directorate ruling would cause an even bigger hullabaloo.

Marc, wearing only swim trunks, greeted his father without emotion as he stepped out of the egg. It did Paul no good to erect a thought-screen when that young devil was around—not that the lowliest normal could have failed to read on Paul's face what the decision had been.

"I'm sorry, son. The Directors voted against pardoning, five to four. I abstained. It would have accomplished nothing to tie the vote and throw the decision onto a vote of the full Concilium."

"I suppose not." They walked side by side up the garden path toward the house. Cheri had planted haphazard masses of colorful annuals—zinnias and marigolds and petunias and cosmos—and the flowers were alive with butterflies. "Who were the nay-sayers?" Marc asked.

"Vijaya Mukherjee, the Director for Arts—and I admit that was a nasty surprise. Kwok Zhen-yu, the economics boffin. Rikky Cisneros, who's a Director at Large. The Colonial Affairs Director, Larry Atlin . . . and your Aunt Anne."

"Anne!" Marc stopped in his tracks. "In the Intendant Assembly, she voted to include the pardon rider—and she *said* she'd vote in favor when the petition came before the Directorate."

"She reviewed her decision when it became very obvious that most of the Directors favoring the pardons were the ones who are—shall we say—the least committed to Human Milieu solidarity."

Marc pricked up his ears. "Oh? That Russian woman who's the Science Director? The one who made the speech demanding that more colonial planets be opened for nonoperants?"

Paul nodded. "Anna Gawrys-Sakhvadze. And two other at-large members who are cronies of hers—Hiroshi Kodama and Esi Damatura. Esi always was an anti-Milieu troublemaker in the African Intendancy, and the Asians have a lingering resentment of the fact that such a large percentage of Human Magnates come from the Caucasian and Amerind racial groups. The fourth yes vote came from Nyssa Holualoa, understandable given her Polynesian descent. In her heart, Nyssa thinks of Teresa as a Hawaiian, not a citizen of the Milieu."

They went up the side stairs and walked around to the front veranda, where Cheri, Teresa and the baby, Denis, Lucille, and Aurelie Dalembert were sitting.

Jack bounced in his papoose swing. He gurgled and exclaimed: Marc! Take me for a walk along the beach!

"Is it okay?" Marc asked his mother.

"Yes, dear. Just keep his head covered from the sun."

"Okay, brat! Let's hike." The boy detached his swaddled infant brother from Uncle Rogi's invention, adjusted the shoulder straps of the carrier, and hiked off through the beach plums with Jack on his back, squeaking happily.

Paul sighed and helped himself to iced lemonade. He had conveyed the Directorate ruling to the others almost instantaneously in baldly stated telepathy, in the manner that operants often used to deliver the worst of news.

Lucille said, "What a shame." Paul sat down beside her, at some distance from Teresa.

"Have you told Uncle Rogi?" Aurelie asked.

"I farspoke him right after the vote. But I felt I owed it to Teresa to come here."

"Thank you," Teresa said in a neutral tone.

"I agree that forcing the decision onto the entire Concilium would have been a bad move," Denis said. "Davy MacGregor is bound to come through for us with executive clemency."

"Do you really think so?" Cheri asked anxiously.

"He and I are very old friends." Denis's face was serene. He was staring out to sea. "All the political shenanigans are over and done with now. Paul's made his grand high-principled gesture—"

"Dammit, Papa!" Paul cried.

But Denis sailed on. "—and Anne's made hers, and the Milieu loyalists have had their day in the media limelight and so have the advocates of human reproductive freedom. Now it all comes down to the simple matter of whether two harmless, well-meaning people should be severely punished for giving life to a supremely intelligent baby."

"Paul—do *you* think it's a foregone conclusion that the Dirigent will let them off?" Cheri asked.

"Yes." The First Magnate kept his eyes lowered. There was a silence.

Then Teresa said abruptly, "I've been asked to sing Turandot at the Met opening. Kumiko Minotani canceled out. I'm going to accept."

"Super!" Cheri exclaimed.

"My God," Paul groaned. "Is that all you can think of?"

Lucille was solicitous of her daughter-in-law. "Do you think you're really up to it, dear?"

"It's more of a lyric-dramatic than a coloratura role, and not exceptionally strenuous—except for having to up the decibels in the finale. Of course, I've been away for a long time. But there's nothing whatsoever the matter with me physically anymore. If anything, being exiled at Ape Lake did me good. I've been practicing like mad, and my voice is coming along nicely, and by the end of the month I ought to be ready."

"How marvelous!" Aurelie said. "We'll all come down to New York to cheer you on opening night."

"I hope so." Teresa's eyes were on Paul, but he continued to stare at the porch floor. Cheri tactfully changed the subject, and they chatted in a desultory fashion for another half hour or so. Then Paul left them, saying he wanted to go swimming while the sun was still up.

When he was gone, Teresa said, "He never asked about Jack."

"He has too many other things on his mind," Denis said. "The Directorate turning down your application for pardon will mean another media circus."

"I'm sure Paul's been keeping a close eye on the baby's progress," Aurelie said comfortingly, "just as we all have. Little Jack's always in our prayers."

"And he looks just wonderful," Cheri added. "I didn't want to say anything while the baby was here—but how's the therapy going?"

Lucille said, "Colette is very encouraged. The three lethals on Chromosome 11 are expunged, and it looks as though seven or eight of the other defective enzyme genes are surrendering to the inserts."

"And his body still shows no bad effects from the active lethals he still carries," said Teresa. "It's his mind fending them off. I know it."

Denis nodded. "It could very well be. Jack is one very extraordinary human being. Marty Dalembert told me that if his brain continues to mature at its present rate, it'll be fully developed by the time Jack is four or five. Of course, that's consonant with the rapid prenatal development."

"He doesn't have the immortality complex," Lucille said, her voice low. "Colette is at a loss to explain it, since it seems to be a genetic dominant."

"Mutation," Denis suggested. "A pity—but the baby has other anomalously programmed DNA as well."

Teresa only laughed. She got to her feet and headed for the interior door. "It doesn't make one bit of difference! The regen-tank has made the whole human race as immortal as we want to be." She flipped her unbound dark hair gaily. "I think I'll go swimming, too!" And she was gone.

"That dear, brave woman," Cheri marveled. "I don't know how she does it. If only . . ."

She left the thought unsaid, but all their eyes strayed to the beach path, where Paul Remillard was striding along toward the sea with a towel flung over one shoulder, not looking back.

Marc and Jack spent some time discussing a thrown Frisbee, comparing its peculiar flight path to the more easily analyzed trajectory of a volleyball that some of the cousins were tossing around. Then, when the joys of simple physics palled, Jack wanted to know the life cycles of the American lobster and blue crab, which he had studied with his deepsight as they steamed inside the cooking pit. Marc said he didn't have the faintest idea how the crustaceans lived, and he was equally ignorant of the natural history of the potato and the much-hybridized maize cooking along with them.

"All I know," the older boy said, "is that they all taste fantastic, especially if you slather them with butter and a little bit of salt."

Jack said: I would like to try them.

"Tough titties for you, sprout. You need a full set of teeth for that, and you've only got four."

The baby said: In my judgment the mealy substance of the potato would be perfectly compatible with my limited dentition. Especially with butter.

Marc laughed. "We'll give it a try if Mama okays it."

Jack's mind fell silent. He was ruminating over something, but Marc hadn't a hope of eavesdropping. The baby was a better screener than he ever hoped to be, zipped up tighter than a Lylmik. The two of them were about half a klom down the beach from the house, resting at the foot of a miniature sand cliff topped with marram grass and sandbur and scrawny shrubs. The infant was propped upright on his papoose board so he could watch the marine scene, and Marc lay flat on his back, idly studying the small cumulus clouds overhead and seeing if he could influence their changing shapes with his creativity.

Then: Marco?

"H'mm?"

Please explain why Cousin Adrienne's physiological response to your kiss differs so drastically from my response to Mama's kiss.

Marc floundered up in a cloud of sand. *"What?!* Oh, you damned little Peeping Tom! You were spying on us!"

Jack uttered a surprised whimper. Marc was on his knees, shaking his index finger in the infant's face. "Don't you ever do that again, you hear me? It's rotten. It's an invasion of privacy. It's something operants don't do unless they're perverted voyeuristic dipshits!"

Oh . . . Like not watching Grandpère and Grandmère in bed when we stay at their cottage?

"Yes."

I had not realized that kissing could sometimes be classified as a sexual activity.

"Well, it can, sometimes. So watch it."

I will. I'm sorry I made you angry. I want to be a civilized person.

"Yeah, yeah," Marc muttered. He stood up and stared stonily out to sea. There were a handful of powerboats puttering around, and a beautiful schooner he'd never seen before was entering Rye Harbor.

The baby said: I was puzzled you see at the explosive discharge of neural energies that occurred in the body of Cousin Adrienne when—

"Will you belt up? I don't want to discuss it!"

She died you know.

Marc turned slowly, then knelt beside his tiny brother. "She *what?*"

Died. Cousin Adrienne. I wondered if the seven subsequent discharges of energy from her body just prior to her life's end might have had a connection with the lesser paroxysm following your kiss.

"Oh, Jesus. Oh, Jesus . . ." Marc had leapt to his feet again and began desperately scanning the ocean for Addie's aura. "I can't find her! She's gone! . . . What do you mean, she's dead? Are you sure? When did it happen? Did she drown? It wasn't the damned shark—"

No. People have been talking about sharks [image] that eat people all summer long but there are no sharks doing that. I would have been glad to clarify the situation if anyone had asked me. It was not a shark doing the killing but a Hydra [peculiar fuzzy image]. It absorbed the vital energies drained from Cousin Adrienne about eight minutes ago. While you watched the clouds.

"What the hell do you mean?" Marc whirled back to the baby. A terrible hollow nausea clawed at his guts. "Jack, did you really see Adrienne with your ultrasenses when—when she died?"

Not exactly.

"Can you farsee her body now?" he cried, frantic with dread.

It is macerated except for the bones and teeth. *They are sinking toward the sea bottom and the bits of flesh will soon all be consumed by fishes and other marine animals.*

"Oh, God, no. No! Not Addie. Not poor old Addie—"

I'm sorry too Marco. She was a domineering individual but she was kind to me. She put grape jelly on my pacifier this morning. But there was really nothing I could do to stop the Hydra from eating her—

Whattheflaminghell is a *Hydra?*

I don't know how to classify it nor can I obtain a clear image. It's ʃinı *and another very strange mind called Fury sustains it and controls it and loves it. I'm not sure but I think you would call Hydra and Fury evil. Hydra ate the energies of six other operants besides Adrienne. As it feeds it produces sequential lesions of radially symmetrical form on the body of the victim* [images].

Marc snatched up the cradleboard. He began to run. He ran faster than he had ever run in his life, mind-screaming on his father's intimate mode:

Papa! PapacomeoutofthewaterCOMEOUTOFTHEWATERCOMEOUT-**COMEOUT** . . .

Paul Remillard surfaced, shook his wet hair out of his eyes, and envisioned his two sons back on the shore. The infant was calm and the adolescent wildly agitated. Both had impervious mind-shields in place.

Torn between annoyance and concern, Paul headed back to shore with powerful, steady strokes.

[**31**]

FROM THE MEMOIRS
OF ROGATIEN REMILLARD

The tragic disappearance of Adrienne Remillard was officially attributed to a fifth fatal shark attack, the last of the summer. Not even her mother, Cheri, knew the truth until years later, nor did Teresa, nor any of the other dynastic wives, nor the gaggle of young cousins. Saying nothing of his suspicions to the Human Magistratum, Paul resolved that he would conduct his own investigation into the crimes of the monster called Hydra. He felt with sick certainty that it was somehow intimately connected to the Remillard family and that it posed a mortal threat not only to them but to the entire Human Polity under the conditions of the probation.

Marc and baby Jack were willy-nilly part of the new conspiracy. Only Marc had been able to get young Jack to agree to a voluntary scan of his memories. The child flatly refused to open to his father. He trusted only Marc to rummage around in his brain, and it was Marc who transmitted to the shocked Paul the damning mental depiction of the monster called Hydra, and showed the seven lifeforce-draining chakras inflicted by it that Jack had perceived for the merest instant before Adrienne's body was quietly disintegrated and consigned to the depths.

At this point Paul took Denis into his confidence, because of his father's special knowledge of Victor. The two of them then asked Marc to determine if the baby had any other concrete data pertaining to the entity called Hydra. Marc showed them the puzzling fivefold image that was Jack's representation of the murderous thing—an image that seemed to correspond to no sapient lifeform in the known Galaxy. No creature had a fivefold mind. But Paul was only too aware of the enigmatic thought that Margaret Strayhorn had projected to Davy MacGregor as she died. She had said: *Five.* And now it seemed undeniable that Margaret, like Brett McAllister and poor Adrienne, and doubtless the four alleged victims of nonexistent sharks, had all been victims of Hydra.

Hydra, the thing that killed as Victor had killed but was not Victor.

Hydra, that was somehow quintuple—perhaps a metaconcert of five minds, perhaps a single perverted mind that had somehow split into five distinct personalities.

Paul and Denis managed to impress upon Jack the necessity of keeping his dangerous knowledge to himself. They also warned him as discreetly as they could to be on guard himself and to immediately notify them or Marc if he should ever perceive the least trace of Hydra again. The two adults enjoined Marc to secrecy, too, citing the potential danger to himself, to Jack, to the other members of the family, and even to the human race, should the exotics of the Concilium get wind of the new Hydra killings. Marc promised to keep mum.

But as soon as he returned to Hanover, he came rushing to my bookshop to tell me everything.

It was my first inkling of the activities of the Hydra, for the exact nature of Brett McAllister's killing had never been made public, nor had the grave suspicions of the Magistratum and the family about the "suicide" of Margaret Strayhorn. I sat appalled as Marc gave me a recap of everything Paul had told him about the two earlier deaths, plus his own account of the Labor Day tragedy and its probable relation to the four operant deaths that had been attributed to sharks.

"What a crock of shit," I groaned, when the boy finally seemed to have finished. "And the only genuine witness to poor Adrienne's death is a precocious eight-month-old baby! No wonder Paul and Denis want to keep the thing under wraps. Can you imagine Ti-Jean being examined by forensic redactors?"

"They wouldn't have a chance of probing him," Marc averred. "The kid's mind is invulnerable. He wouldn't even let *me* really get into him. All he did was rerun the memory, and I transmitted it on to Papa and Grandpère—slightly edited."

"Oh?" My suspicions were immediately aroused.

The boy was sitting on a stool in the messy little back room of the shop, scratching my cat Marcel behind the ears. His face was a mask of unremitting gloom. "There was something Jack said out there on the beach that really bothered me. I—I couldn't bring myself to tell Papa about it, or Grandpère either . . . just in case."

"Just in case of what, for God's sake? What are you talking about? If you won't open your mind far enough to clarify your damned thoughts, then *explain!*"

"It was bad enough finding out about this Hydra. But it's not the only monster out there. Jack said Hydra was 'sustained and controlled and loved'—his exact thoughts!—by still *another* mind. I looked at the faint image of this second thing, which was all Jack could perceive, and it wasn't the same kind of entity as Hydra. Hydra wasn't human. But the other thing was—and what's more, it was vaguely familiar to me."

"Nom de dieu! Was the second thing Victor?"

"I wondered about that, too. And so I replayed my own childhood memories from that last Good Friday vigil twelve years ago to see whether I'd stored any data at all on Uncle Vic. I found no trace of any mentality that I could positively identify as his . . . but there *was* a faint recollection of someone very frightening. My infantile self-redaction had done its best to erase the memory because it had really traumatized my little mind. But I was able to catch this mnemonic glimmer. I'd been scared by a human person way back then, and it was nobody that I knew *at the time*. But I'd stake my life that the scary person who tried to make mental contact with me when Uncle Vic died and the entity who sustains the Hydra are the same."

"And you have no notion of this—this controller's identity?"

"None at all. But Jack called it Fury."

I whispered, "Oh, Christ!"

I tottered up out of my chair, ripped open the filing cabinet drawer, grabbed the bottle of Wild Turkey I had stashed inside, and downed three great gulps of the whiskey right before the eyes of the scandalized boy. And then I flopped back into my seat with a crash that sent Marcel leaping a meter straight up into the air. I sat there with my eyes bugging out from terror and clammy sweat breaking out all over me as my *own* twelve-year-old memories suddenly came rushing to the fore, escaping from the limbo I'd banished them to.

Fury.

. . . I'd refused to go into Denis's metaconcert with the others. I'd lurked somewhere in the mental lattices outside. And I'd seen it.

Who are you? I asked.

And it said: I am Fury.

Where did you come from? I asked.

I am newborn. Inevitably.

What do you want? I asked.

And it said: All of you.

Marc said, very calmly, "It's one of them. One of the family members who were there at Uncle Vic's deathbed. As he died, he somehow . . . I don't know what he did. Infected? Merged? Coerced? Transferred his perverted ambition—"

"Such a thing isn't possible!" I cried.

But Marc was lost in his own thoughts, speaking aloud. "And that's why my own unconscious made me hold back from telling Papa about Fury. Fury could be any of them! . . . No, wait, not the wives, and certainly not poor Uncle Brett. Fury has to be a Remillard. He could even be Papa himself—maybe a disjunctive part of his personality that he's not aware of."

"Then who the fuck is *Hydra?*" I croaked. "Some other member of the family? *Five of them?*"

Marc frowned but only shook his head.

I took another slug of whiskey to quell the shudders. It didn't work. But the old eau-de-vie must have given a momentary boost to my frazzled cerebral synapses, because a brilliant thought popped into my head.

"Adrien's out of it!"

Marc stared at me in perplexity.

"Your Uncle Adrien. He was here on Earth when Margaret Strayhorn died on Orb, ergo he's not Fury or Hydra! He's the one member of the Dynasty who stayed behind. All the others were in Concilium Orb at the same time Margaret was . . . And your Aunt Anne is safe, too! When Margaret was attacked on Halloween, Anne had already gone with you to Orb, in advance of the rest of the family."

The young face was doubtful. "You infer that Fury and Hydra are inseparable. I don't think the assumption is warranted."

I was crestfallen. "Maybe not. But it seems logical. Adrien was crazy about his daughter and he's been a wreck since she died. And Anne . . . Oh, shit. Any of 'em could be Fury! Even you." I lifted the bottle to my lips again.

But this time Marc's coercion stopped me. I was compelled to put the liquor down on the desk. The boy came up close to me and took my sweating head in both his hands, and our eyes locked.

Coercion. He had me cold. My mental screen hadn't a hope in hell of keeping him out, and for the merest instant he showed me what lay behind his own mental barrier. He showed me who he was. He said: I AM NOT FURY.

My mind uttered a silent yelp of amazement. I'd seen a veiled version of Jack's incredible infant mind, and I'd known Paul's awesome inner resources and those of Denis. Marc's mentality was different—deeper and darker than the mind of his father or grandfather, of a completely different order from Jack's—more frightening to me than any of the other three. But he'd spoken the truth to me: he wasn't Fury. I remembered Fury from Good Friday and I remembered him from a later time as well. A time I had forgotten until this very moment.

Fury had also been present when Jack was coming down the birth canal. He had tried to take control of the baby even before he drew his first breath.

This time I howled out loud.

Marc's coercion tightened like an iron vise.

UncleRogiI'vegottodothispleaseunderstand! I *need* you and I can't have you getting drunk and going all to pieces you and Jack are the only ones I can really trust FURY COULD BE ANY OF THEM and we know what *he* wants even if we don't know about Hydra FURY WANTS ALL OF US. He told you so. Whoever he is whatever he is however he's managed to concoct this Hydra HE IS THE REAL MONSTER and we're the only ones who can stop him! . . . So I'm going to fix you. I'm going to delete your alcoholism.

Marc was an uncertified Grand Master in coercion, but not even he could sustain control of me indefinitely. To really bend my mind, he would have to exert another mindpower, one he was equally expert in: redaction, the faculty that could be used to heal minds, or to destroy them.

I had always refused to let metapsychiatrists mess with my head. Again and again Denis and Lucille had pleaded with me to let clinical metapsychic practitioners root out the most perverse of the geraniums in my cranium, especially my propensity to abuse alcohol, but I had always balked. I refused to let mental healers "edit" the parts of my personality that others found reprehensible. I admit that I am neurotic and bibulous. It's the self I'm familiar with, the one that somehow manages to survive. I have no desire to change. But now here was my awful great-grandnephew prepared to drag me kicking and screaming into the pitiless glare of permanent sobriety, merely to serve his own selfish needs—and perhaps the well-being of the family and the Human Polity of the Galactic Milieu. I screamed:

NO! FortheloveofGod *not the booze!* You plant that damned inhibition in me and I'll go stark staring MAD I'm not a true alcoholic Lucille found that out years ago don't you know the liquor's a safety-valve for a supersensitiveegocentriccowardly personality? *GHOST! DON'T LET HIM!!*

Marc hesitated.

"If you zap me," I whispered, "you're no better than a monster yourself."

The gray eyes were unblinking. He could do it. Oh, yes he could. Even though he was still only a boy and not the metapsychic titan he was to become as an adult, he could have exerted his redaction and fixed me so that I could never take another sip of alcohol again without puking my guts out. Fixed me so that I'd never find sweet oblivion again.

But he didn't.

He let go of my skull and whirled away in a rage of frustration and stood with his back to me and both fists clenched. "Damn you, Uncle Rogi! I don't want to hurt you or make you miserable; I want to help you! So you can help *me.* Please . . ."

Shakily, I got up and put a hand on his shoulder. "I'll do the best I can. That's all any man can do. You can't force a person to be better than he is."

The clenched hands slowly relaxed. Marcel the Maine Coon cat came out from wherever he'd been hiding during the rumpus and rubbed against Marc's calves. The boy turned around. The words seemed forced through his teeth. "I'm—sorry."

I sighed. "De rien, mon enfant."

"It's just that I don't know what to do! Five or six members of the Dynasty—my own aunts and uncles, maybe even my own father—might be mental monsters! But there's no proof. I can't go to the Magistratum. Even if humans are running it now, they're still so new at the game that they'd call in the exotics like a shot over something as big as this."

"Probably."

"I couldn't do it!"

"No."

"But I don't know what else I can do."

"Neither do I. Tell you what: we'll both do nothing at all for the time being. Just get on with our regular work and try to think about this affair as calmly and rationally as we can. We may get a brainstorm, or we may find some kind of useful clue that will prove things one way or another. There's even a chance that *Paul* will discover something, if he's not Fury himself."

Marc slumped down onto the stool, drained. The cat continued his furry consolation. It was pushing suppertime, and Marcel was really asking for food on the feline telepathic mode, but both of us had heartlessly tuned him out.

"I thought I hated Papa," Marc said. "But when there was deadly danger, I called *him.*"

I didn't say anything.

"When you were in a panic, you called on a ghost, Uncle Rogi."

"Bullshit," said I, stoutly.

But he wouldn't be deflected. "I heard you do it. A ghost—and not a Holy Ghost, either! The mental image attached to the concept was ... strange." For just an instant, he seemed poised to coerce it out of me. And then he caught himself and made a hasty gesture of self-deprecation, pretending to slice his throat. "Never mind. I'm sorry. I'm poking where I shouldn't again."

Are you? . . . The only two persons who might possibly be able to save me and the rest of the Remillards from Fury and Hydra and other things that go bump in the night were my old Lylmik friend who called himself the Family Ghost and this boy. Maybe it was about time Marc knew he had some sort of an ally!

I lurched up out of my chair and clapped Marc on the shoulder. "Hell, I don't see why I shouldn't share my ghost story with you. But not here. It's getting late. Why don't I take you over to the Peter Christian Tavern and buy you supper, and along with it I'll tell you a few tales about my misspent youth."

[32]

CONCORD, HUMAN POLITY CAPITAL, EARTH, 20 SEPTEMBER 2052

The lawyers had their driver land in the rhocraft lot of Europa Tower, and from there they took Rogi and Teresa in on the subway to Dirigent House, a good two kilometers away. But someone who was either operant or wired must have spotted them somewhere along the line, because a baying pack of media people awaited them when they stepped out of the subway car, brandishing camcorders and microphones and shouting questions in dozens of different accents of Standard English. There were even two Gi and a Poltroyan among the reporters. Teresa seemed more pleased than annoyed as the shouting echoed through the little subway station.

"Miz Kendall! Tell us how you feel as you make your final plea to be pardoned!"

"Miz Kendall! Do you believe the third time is going to be the charm?"

"Miz Kendall! Do you think you've been treated fairly?"

"Will you still be singing on opening night at the Met next week if you have to stand trial?"

"How's little Jack bearing up?"

"Look this way just for a second, Miz Kendall!"

"Is it true that you and the First Magnate are estranged?"

"Miz Kendall, will you be making a personal appeal to the Dirigent, or will your attorneys speak for you?"

"Miz Kendall—"

Rogi grabbed one of her arms and Chester Kopinski took the other, and they attempted to haul her toward the elevator while Sam Goldsmith and Woody Bates ran interference. Woody kept shouting, "No comment! No comment!" Teresa, a bright smile on her face, insisted on trying to answer the questions. The senior attorney, Spencer Delevan, stood just outside the mob fringe, clutching his briefcase to his tailored bosom and talking frantically into a portaphone.

Finally the police came and order was restored. Teresa and Rogi and the lawyers got into the elevator and ascended to the offices of the Dirigent for Earth, David Somerled MacGregor.

"The media hawks will still be waiting when we come out," Chester predicted darkly.

"We'd better ask the ODE for permission to take Teresa and Rogi off from the roof," said Sam, sotto voce. "Especially if we get a turndown."

"I really don't mind answering their questions," Teresa said. "And we won't be turned down."

"Now, Teresa," Woody chided. "You know what you promised. Leave it all to us."

Nobody paid a bit of attention to Rogi.

Ommm, said the elevator, and they all exited into the reception area, an atrium of no particular distinction, done in the popular neo-Romanesque style. There was a mosaic floor, a white marble pool at the center with small fountains and large fishes, a glass roof, and an abundance of potted greenery. To Rogi's surprise, there were nearly two dozen people sitting about, apparently waiting to see the Dirigent. They didn't look like lawyers or other bureaucratic types, either: only ordinary citizens. One young woman had two little children with her, who were leaning over the edge of the atrium pool teasing the koi.

"I'd heard rumors that the Dirigent had decided to treat his office as a kind of glorified ombudsmanship," Rogi murmured to Chester, "but this is a bit much. Do you suppose we'll have to take a number?"

"We have an appointment for ten hundred hours," Kopinski said, glancing at his old-fashioned gold pocket watch, "and we're right on time."

Teresa was astonished, studying the people who were waiting. "You mean that *anybody* can see the Planetary Dirigent?"

"Anyone may apply for an appointment," Spencer Delevan said austerely. "Frivolous requests are denied, and matters that can best be handled by other authorities are appropriately shunted. Dirigent House has a very large staff as well, and only specially selected matters are referred to MacGregor himself."

"Well, I'll be damned," Rogi said. "I thought a dirigent was kind of like top dog of the Intendant Assembly—the king of the world."

"Certainly not," sniffed Delevan. "The Dirigent is independent of the ordinary planetary legislature. He is accountable to the entire Galactic Concilium, not merely to the Human Polity."

Sam Goldsmith remarked, "You're not alone in being confused, Rogi. The legal profession is still trying to sort out the way the Dirigency operates, and some of us suspect that Davy MacGregor is making up the rules as he goes along! By definition, the Dirigent is the primary *metapsychic* official of a planet, providing a direct link between the ordinary citizenry and the Concilium. Each Milieu Polity views the office a bit differently, but generally speaking, the Dirigent is more of an overseer or a public advocate than an administrator. When this probationary period is over, every one of our colonial worlds will have its own dirigent, and he or she will be solemnly charged with the nurturing and guidance of the planetary Mind."

"Sounds to me," Rogi said, "like MacGregor is more of a glorified nanny than anything else."

Goldsmith laughed, but the other lawyers looked pained.

"It must be a very difficult job," said Teresa.

Goldsmith said, "A Poltroyan friend of mine told me that most of their dirigents burn out after only a few years in office."

"Goodness!"

"Here comes one of the staff," Woody Bates said. "It's about time."

A slender young man with sandy hair, wearing a blazer with the ODE insignia, picked out the two petitioners immediately. "Hi, there! Teresa Kendall and Rogatien Remillard, I presume? I'm Bart Ziegfield, one of the Dirigent's assistants. Would you two like to follow me? He's ready to see you right now—"

Spencer Delevan interrupted smoothly. "We are the legal counselors for Citizens Kendall and Remillard, and we respectfully request that we be allowed to accompany our clients and present their petition to Dirigent MacGregor."

"Sorry," said Ziegfield with good-humored firmness. "You were told when the application was accepted that the Dirigent would see the principals only. This isn't a law court."

Delevan flushed. "But—"

Rogi pushed forward. "We get the picture. Come on, Teresa."

Ziegfield winked at the disconcerted attorneys, then led Rogi and Teresa out of the atrium into a long corridor. It was very quiet, with handsome Chinese carpets on a parquet floor and many tall, anonymous doors. The paneled walls were hung with impressive paintings.

"Can that possibly be a real Van Gogh?" Teresa asked.

"Oh, yes," their guide replied. "Dirigent MacGregor has always been a keen art buff, and he was very quick to take up the perquisites of the office, along with the duties and responsibilities. The paintings are on loan, of course. Lovely little Fra Angelico there . . . and don't you just adore Hieronymus Bosch's *Ship of Fools?* It's the Dirigent's favorite."

The assistant knocked on a door that looked no different from the others they had passed. "There you go," Ziegfield said cheerfully. He gestured for them to enter and then hurried away, leaving them standing there.

Rogi and Teresa. Please come in.

The old man gave a violent start. He took hold of the doorknob, opened the door, and stood aside to let Teresa precede him.

The room was small, even cozy. There was a fireplace where a few birch logs lay on a grate, ready to light. A pine credenza against one wall had an elaborate data-retrieval station built into it, but there was no other evidence of modern technology to be seen. Behind the pine table-desk with its nut-brown leather morris chair was a single window with homespun drapes, which looked out over the Merrimack Valley.

Davy MacGregor came out from behind his desk to meet them. Rogi had not seen the former Intendant Associate for Europe in person since his rejuvenation, and he was reminded anew of Davy's strong resemblance to his late father. The hair was a different color, but the dundreary side-whiskers were the same, and Davy even wore a tweed jacket and a vest of the MacGregor tartan with staghorn buttons, that were virtual duplicates of Jamie's favorites. He shook hands as though Rogi and Teresa were welcome guests, drew up two ladder-back chairs with crewel seats, complimented Teresa on her dress, and inquired after baby Jack. Returning to his seat behind the desk, he asked Rogi to keep an eye out for a fine copy of L. Sprague de Camp's *Wheels of If,* with the Hannes Bok dust jacket, which he said he was eager to add to his personal fantasy collection.

"I've got one in stock," the bookseller managed to say. "All deacidified and permeditioned. I'll have it shipped. My compliments."

MacGregor's dark eyes twinkled. "Have it shipped with an invoice, Rogi," he insisted.

"Uh—of course."

There was a silence.

Davy MacGregor said, "I've already done my own investigation of your case. There is only one thing I want to ask you, Teresa: Knowing what you do about young Jack, would you conceive another child?"

She answered with her head high. "No. But I still feel certain it was right to have *him.*"

MacGregor turned to Rogi. "Why didn't you tell the Human Magistratum the truth about Marc's role in the flight and concealment of Teresa?"

The old man felt his throat constrict. He'd been living in a fool's paradise, thinking he'd successfully diddled the cops by taking the full blame. Rogi took a slow, deep breath. He said: "I'm an old man who earns his living in an unimportant trade. If I get sent down for ten years, it's no big deal. The other accessory to the crime is a juvenile. He's at a critical point in his education, and he'll doubtless mature into an important person. I thought it was the better part of prudence to shield him. To let him enter adult life free of stigma."

MacGregor's gaze lowered to his own hands, lightly clasped on the polished dark wood of the desk. He still wore a wide golden wedding band.

"Both of you deliberately broke the laws of the Proctorship. You, Teresa, were driven by a subrational compulsion—a species of metacoercion recognized but not understood by the exotic races of the Milieu. Ancient humans would have said you were God-driven. Perhaps they would have been right."

He lifted his eyes to Rogi. "You didn't really want to break the law by helping her. You were also compelled—by two persons. One of them was Marc Remillard, and the other . . . you know who the other was."

Teresa turned to the old man in surprise. "But you never told me—"

Davy MacGregor silenced her with his coercion. "I believe that the circumstances justify pardoning you both without condition."

Teresa was instantly on her feet, bursting into tears of joy, stammering out her thanks. The door opened and Bart Ziegfield came in, took her gently by the arm, and led her away. The door closed behind him.

"I'd like to thank you, too," Rogi began, rising and holding out his hand.

But MacGregor ignored it and motioned for him to sit down again. His face was grave. "You and I aren't finished, Rogi."

Rogi heaved a sigh. Only one person could have told Davy MacGregor his own motivation, to say nothing of Teresa's. Rogi found himself wondering just what kind of training had been given to the Dirigent by the Lylmik.

Davy MacGregor smiled. "It was rough, my lad. Damned rough. But the details are none of your business, for all that you've had a bit of the treatment yourself."

"Hah!" Rogi said, his eyes lighting up.

"It's not camaraderie I want from you," MacGregor said curtly. He was no longer smiling. "It's something quite different, and you'll cooperate or suffer some serious consequences."

Rogi stared at him, openmouthed.

"Now, you might not be aware," MacGregor said matter-of-factly, "of the trick certain Remillards have of shutting others out of their minds while appearing to submit to coercive-redactive probes. We're going to be able to do something about that, as you lot will find out. It will take precious time to implement, however, the Magistratum being subject to the constraints of due process and the laws governing evidence-gathering, and such tedious things. But the Dirigent has the option to cut a few corners in a good cause. Having you here in my web, so to speak, I'm opting for a simpler and more direct method of information-gathering."

"About what?" Rogi bleated.

MacGregor seemed not to have heard him. "The simplest and least painful option open to you is to tell me the truth freely, and then just open wide and let me see into your mind to confirm it."

"But you've just pardoned Teresa and me—"

"I'm no longer interested in Teresa's crime. It's something infinitely more important you're going to tell me about. You can do it voluntarily, or you can refuse. In which case I'll be forced to apply my very own brand of mind-ream, which is still a very rough-and-ready instrument, even after the Lylmik training regimen. Now I concede that my ream wouldn't get me much if I tried it on Paul Remillard or on his eldest son. But I guarantee it'll turn *your* brain permanently to clotted porridge if you try to fight back."

"For God's sake!" Rogi cried. "Just tell me what the hell you want to know!"

"Everything you know about the person or persons who murdered Brett McAllister and my wife, Margaret Strayhorn. Or by God, you won't leave this place a sane man."

Davy MacGregor had lied.

He admitted it after Rogi had spilled his guts in a pool of muck sweat and confessed everything he knew about Fury, Hydra, Vic, baby Jack, and the seven deaths. After Rogi had recovered from the ordeal (with the help of four fingers of Lagavulin Limited Edition), Davy admitted that he would not really have mind-probed the old bookseller to the point of madness.

"Not that I'm incapable of it, old son," the Dirigent said amiably, "because my coercive-redactive faculties have assayed out at some really filthy potential, and the Lylmik did teach me a thing or two. But I'm actually a kindly sort of chap who wouldn't hurt a fly—and besides, my authority doesn't quite extend to the infliction of mental mayhem, even though I do have more leeway than the Magistratum in questioning Earth citizens."

Rogi snarled and whined about the unfairness of it all, but Davy only said he intended to get to the heart of the killings by what he suspected would be the most direct route available—to wit, Rogi himself. And while Milieu law protected Magnates of the Concilium such as the Remillard Dynasty from being mind-probed without firm grounds, a mere private citizen was dead meat if the Dirigent decided to dig.

"Now I have some information to give you," Davy said, still smiling, "and I want you to be sure to pass it on to the members of your family. Within a month, the Human Magistratum will have a new mechanical interrogation device at its disposal that will be able to get an accurate true-or-false reading out of even the most stalwart mental screeners. Thanks to you, there are now legal grounds for questioning the seven Remillard magnates with the machine—based upon information received. If they agree to submit voluntarily to the machine here in my offices, without me having to turn the matter over to the Magistratum for the lengthy legal rigamarole, then the testing will be done under strict confidentiality. No one's reputation will be even slightly besmirched, provided they're innocent. Again thanks to your cooperation, we now know just what questions to ask."

"Beautiful," Rogi said bitterly. "I can add stool pigeon to my personal roster of guilt trips."

The kindly façade melted from Davy MacGregor's face, leaving Caledonian rock. "The devil take your wounded sensibilities! The only thing that matters is finding the fiends who killed my poor Maggie and the others, and sending them straight to hell. Tell *that* to your precious Remillard Dynasty."

[33]

FROM THE MEMOIRS
OF ROGATIEN REMILLARD

Teresa's opening-night portrayal of the icy Chinese princess Turandot, whose heart is finally softened by love, was one of the great triumphs of her career. She had wisely chosen a role that showcased her brilliance as a singing actress and a vocalist of rich and apparently effortless power. No one noticed that her voice was no longer as agile as it had been in her youth or that the exceptional high notes that had been her trademark were now few and far between. Her Turandot was a stunning comeback, and if the critics noticed that she was not the paragon of yore, they were not about to mention it and risk being lynched.

The entire family was there in New York on opening night, including Paul, and after the standing ovation given the performance, he dashed to her dressing room with tears running down his cheeks. The two of them frustrated her adoring fans and irritated the media by staying sequestered for nearly an hour. When they emerged, they came arm in arm, with dazed grins on their faces, to ironic applause and whistles. Baby Jack, who was being toted in a backpack by Marc, apparently made some telepathic remark that caused his older brother to blush to the ears.

The next day, Paul moved back into the family home in Hanover.

Teresa had signed to do seven more performances of the opera, scattered throughout October and early November, and during this time she commuted between New Hampshire and New York City, with Paul attending every performance but one. He missed the matinee on October 19, because that was the day the family submitted en masse to the Cambridge mechanical mind-ream, which was moved from Magistratum Headquarters to the Office of the Dirigent for Earth by special order of Davy MacGregor.

Not only the Dynasty but also their wives, Denis, Lucille, and Marc were questioned. (Teresa was tested the next day.) The machine was operated by Drs. Van Wyk and Kramer, and since both men were respected scientists and also magnates, the confidentiality of the procedure was erroneously presumed to be assured.

Because of the traumatic nature of the examination, only ten yes-or-no questions were asked of the examinees:

1. Are you the entity called Fury?

2. Do you know who or what Fury is?

3. Are you the entity called Hydra, or a part of that entity?

4. Do you know who Hydra is?

5. Do you know who or what killed Brett McAllister?

6. Do you know who or what killed Margaret Strayhorn?

7. Do you know who or what killed Adrienne Remillard?

8. Do you know who or what killed the four operants who disappeared in the vicinity of the New Hampshire seacoast last summer?

9. Do you know for a fact that Victor Remillard is alive?

10. Do you suspect that the Fury-Hydra murders of McAllister, Strayhorn, Adrienne Remillard, and the others have some connection to the Remillard family?

All of the persons examined answered "No" to the first nine questions and were ascertained to have told the truth.

Aurelie Dalembert the wife of Philip Remillard; Cecilia Ashe the wife of Maurice Remillard; Cheri Losier-Drake the wife of Adrien Remillard; and Teresa Kaulana Kendall the wife of Paul Remillard, answered "No" to the tenth question and were ascertained to have told the truth.

Lucille Cartier answered "No" to the tenth question and lied.

Philip, Maurice, Severin, Anne, Catherine, Adrien, Paul, Denis, and Marc answered "Yes" to the tenth question and told the truth.

Because of the overly broad nature of the tenth question, Dirigent David Somerled MacGregor appealed directly to the Lylmik Supervisors for a ruling on whether he had grounds to continue his investigation of the family. The Supervisors ruled that, at the present time, he did not. They also reminded him that he was not the one who would ferret out the murderer of his wife.

The results of the interrogation were sealed by the Dirigent and not turned over to the Human Magistratum.

[34]

SWAFFHAM ABBAS,
CAMBRIDGESHIRE, ENGLAND, EARTH,
2 NOVEMBER 2052

The moon shone down on the Devil's Ditch, and the inevitable wind of East Anglia rattled the windowpanes of the cottage that was quaintly English on the outside and peculiarly Russian inside. Flames crackled in the stone hearth, Mozart played softly on the stereo, and eight of the persons who had informally dubbed themselves the Metapsychic Rebels settled down with great relief and prepared to drink to the health of the newest of their number.

Anna Gawrys-Sakhvadze filled silver-mounted glasses with steaming tea from a brass samovar and had her nephew Alan Sakhvadze serve them. She herself offered a lacing of Georgian brandy to those who wished it. Gerrit Van Wyk accepted with his usual enthusiasm, and so did Will MacGregor and Alan. Hiroshi Kodama took a few drops. Oljanna Gathen, Jordan Kramer, and Adrien Remillard declined.

"And you, Esi, my dear?" Anna poised the bottle above the glass of the newcomer. "Perhaps after your experience with our nasty little lie detector machine over at the IDFS, you would like something to calm your nerves."

"No, thank you. My nerves are recovering nicely," declared Esi Damatura. "But I don't mind telling you that I'm glad Gerry and Jordy had only a single question to ask me."

"Poor Adrien recently had to endure ten in a row from those two," Anna said, topping off her own glass and then taking a seat. "But we will discuss that after our little toast . . . Hiroshi, will you do the honors?"

"It will be my great pleasure." Hiroshi Kodama rose to his feet. They were all sitting around the fire, and the rest of the room, filled with relics of Anna's former homes in Moscow and Central Asia, was in deep shadow except for flickering flamelight. "I have known Esi Damatura for over nine years. Even though she served on the African Intendancy and I on the Asian, we learned very early on that both of us had an abiding love for this planet and its people, and an uneasy feeling toward those who, not being human themselves, nevertheless felt convinced that they knew what was best for our human race. I was overjoyed when Esi, like Anna and myself, was appointed to the Human Directorate of the Galactic Concilium. I was even more gratified when she joined me in urging that Teresa Kendall and Rogatien Remillard be pardoned for conspiring to violate the Reproductive Statutes. Even though we did not carry the day in that infamous vote, Esi's heartfelt defense of human reproductive freedom led me to approach her at last about the possibility of her joining our little group, and ultimately to my bringing her here tonight for the final affirmation of her acceptance. Jordy and Gerry did their duty as inquisitors, and the result is one we all witnessed . . . And so, my friends, I give you Director Esi Damatura, Magnate of the Concilium, Grand Master Farspeaker and Creator—and now also, of her own choice, a Metapsychic Rebel together with us."

He lifted his glass. The others rose to their feet and drank. Then Esi proposed a toast of her own.

"To that great countryman of Adrien's, Thomas Jefferson! For years he has been highly esteemed in Namibia, the land of my birth. Among other things, Jefferson said: 'A little rebellion now and then is a good thing.' "

The others all laughed and drank. Then Hiroshi asked Adrien, "What's this about your having to endure ten questions on the interrogation machine?"

"It was in connection with the Hydra killings. Which are by now the worst-kept secret in the Human Polity—among operants, at any rate."

"Well, I never heard of them," Esi declared. Oljanna Gathen, her husband Alan Sakhvadze, and Hiroshi Kodama echoed her.

"Then lean a little closer, fellow conspirators," Adrien Remillard urged, his mental tone grim in spite of the fact that he spoke lightly, "and I'll tell you a murder mystery to freeze your gizzards and confound your deductive faculties."

For the next quarter hour he regaled them with details of the affair, winding up with the disappearance of his eldest daughter and the interrogation of the Remillard family by the Dirigent. Jordan Kramer and Gerrit Van Wyk already knew a good deal of the background, since they had conducted the questioning; but the others, with the exception of Anna, who already knew almost everything, and Will MacGregor, who was aware of the suspicions about his stepmother's death, were fascinated and appalled by Adrien's story of a metapsychic vampire named Hydra that apparently killed by inflicting seven chakra-like wounds on its victims and was controlled by an unknown human named Fury.

When Adrien finished, the young starship captain, Oljanna Gathen, said flatly: "I don't believe it. Granted, Brett McAllister was murdered in this peculiar way. There's no real proof Margaret Strayhorn was killed by the same person; but I'll give that the benefit of the doubt. But the other deaths—? By your account, there is no hard evidence at all that your daughter and the others who died last summer were killed by this alleged monster. The entire story of Hydra and its fiendish puppeteer comes from the unsupported testimony—and *thirdhand* testimony, at that—of an infant! Has the child himself been questioned with the machine?"

"Can't be done," Jordan Kramer said. "The procedure is traumatic enough for adults. It could inflict irreparable mental damage on a baby, and this one isn't even in good health. As I understand it, he's undergoing therapy for nearly three dozen genetic defects."

"The poor thing," murmured Oljanna. "What's the prognosis?"

"Favorable, so far," Adrien said. "Little Jack is some kind of metapsychic wunderkind. No one can get past his mental screens, and he'll only let his older brother Marc examine his memories. But Davy MacGregor was willing enough to accept Uncle Rogi's account of Marc's examination of Jack."

"My father," Will MacGregor put in, grimacing, "is hardly unbiased. He nearly went out of his mind when Margaret died. He'd seize on any clue that might lead to her killer. Even something as fantastic as this."

"The burns on Brett McAllister," Hiroshi said thoughtfully. "They actually occurred at the seven chakra points and had a lotus form?"

Adrien said, "I saw them myself. Each brandlike pattern was slightly different from the others. They were white, ashen. The rest of the body looked as though it had been seared with a blowtorch. It was some kind of psychocreative flaming, evidently a side effect of the drain."

"Fascinating," said Hiroshi. "You are aware, of course, of the significance of the chakra points in Kundalini Yoga?" He projected a mental image. "But the yogi uses the seven body points in esoteric healing, or in endeavors to attain a higher level of consciousness. The vampiric Hydra has apparently perverted the yogic technique to cause a redactive outflow of the victim's vital energies. Amazing!"

"There was a clear connection between Brett McAllister's murder and the attack on Margaret at the Dartmouth president's house," Adrien said. "The strange burn on her scalp was identical to the one on Brett's head—and if we can believe my father, Brett's burns were identical to ones caused by Denis's late brother Victor, a family black sheep of the deepest dye, when he murdered two people many years ago."

"But there's no firm evidence that Margaret was actually killed that way," Alan said.

"No," Will admitted. "A suicide note was found. But my father is convinced that she *was* murdered, and he did claim to hear her far-spoken death shout saying, 'Five.' In his mind, this corroborates what the baby said about Hydra being a fivefold entity."

Oljanna shook her head. "Thin. Very thin."

"You might not think so," Adrien growled, "if you were better acquainted with the crimes of my late unlamented Granduncle Victor."

"Tell them, Adryushka," Anna commanded.

"I was only two years old at the time," Adrien said, "and I never knew Vic. But my older sibs, who did know him, rated him as an amoral opportunist with superior metafaculties who intended to conquer the world—and came damned close to managing it. He'd gained control of the Zap-Star laser-satellite net and one of the biggest corporate empires on Earth just before he was turned into a vegetable."

Gerrit Van Wyk had been listening wide-eyed. "When did that happen?"

Adrien gazed into the fire, cradling the tea glass in his hands. "It was the night of the Great Intervention."

"I was there," Anna said softly. "It was to be the last Metapsychic Congress, the farewell gathering of the beleaguered operant leaders of the world, held at this huge old hotel in New Hampshire in the U.S.A. I attended along with my mother Tamara and my dear grandfather, and my brothers Valery and Ilya and their wives. Our final banquet was held in a chalet on top of a mountain above the hotel, and this madman Victor Remillard conspired to kill us all by manipulating a group of anti-operant fanatics called the Sons of Earth. Surely you have read about it in your history books."

Hiroshi Kodama frowned. "There was nothing in the books about Victor Remillard engaging in psychic vampirism."

"No," Anna conceded. "But the entire world knows that he and a dissolute capitalist named Kieran O'Connor were behind the attack on the chalet. O'Connor's body was found on the mountain after the Intervention, marked with the seven chakra burns. His daughter was killed in the same way, and it is certain she was murdered by Victor. We learned this only afterward, of course. Victor himself attempted to blow up the chalet, with all the delegates of the Metapsychic Congress inside. Is this not so, Adrien?"

"It's true. But he failed. He was found later among the building piers, in a coma. My Great-granduncle Rogi seemed to have stopped him somehow—perhaps by inadvertent use of some powerful psycho-creative impulse. Ordinarily, Rogi's mindpowers are very weak. But Victor had tried to kill him there on the mountain, and we know that extreme stress can sometimes greatly augment a person's metafaculties. Rogi himself is hazy about what happened. What we're certain of is that somehow Victor was paralyzed and sense-deprived and rendered metapsychically latent, just as he was about to murder the cream of operant humanity. And Vic remained that way, completely helpless, until he died in 2040."

"But McAllister was killed eleven years after Victor died," Oljanna objected. "Surely you don't think that this—this Hydra is Victor's ghost!"

"We don't know what it is," Adrien said wearily. "Except it's not a member of my family. Neither is its controller, Fury. Gerry and Jordy proved that with their mind-reaming machine."

"We really didn't, you know," Jordan Kramer said in a low voice.

"What?" Adrien started in his chair as if he had been electroshocked.

"We didn't prove you lot were innocent. The machine ascertains truth or falsity only as it's perceived by the conscious mind of the examinee. If either Hydra or Fury is an artifact of the unconscious—if they're aspects of a multiple-personality disorder—then the guilty party wouldn't *know* that he or she was guilty unless the Hydra or Fury persona was on deck at the time of the testing."

Gerrit Van Wyk added: "With the guilty persona suppressed, your unknown fiend can deny that he's Hydra or Fury, or that he knows anything about them—and the machine will register that he's telling the truth."

Adrien cried out, horror-stricken: "Then it could even be me! I could be a part of Hydra, or even the controller. I could have ordered the murder of my own daughter!"

"Well," Gerry temporized, "we're psychophysicists, not clinical psychologists. But multiple-personality disorders are well documented in psychiatric literature. The—er—secondary mental aspect doesn't usually communicate with the original personality at all."

"There's no proof that Hydra or Fury exists," Oljanna reiterated. "All you know is what *Marc* maintains that the baby said."

"What will happen now in the investigation?" Hiroshi asked.

Adrien shook his head. "The Dirigent decided to do nothing. The investigation into Brett's murder is still open. Margaret's been declared dead, but the murder/suicide question is unresolved. All of the other disappearances, including my daughter's, are officially attributed to shark attacks."

"Is there any way," Esi Damatura asked slowly, "that *we* can make use of this affair?"

"Tame the Hydra and enlist it into our little conspiracy?" Van Wyk gave a shaky giggle. "There's a thought!"

"I was thinking of using it to discredit Paul." Esi regarded Van Wyk with poorly disguised distaste. "Get him out of the First Magnate chair. All we would have to do is spread details of the Dirigent's test—plus Jordy's second opinion on the exoneration."

"It would discredit not only Paul but all the rest of us as well," Adrien said in a neutral tone. "There'd be a public uproar, even though nothing's been proved. The Remillards would be castigated as operant Draculas—especially by the normal-minded Intendant Associates of North America and the American colonies. The non-ops never have been able to decide whether we're operant role models or a gang of unholy elitist schemers."

Anna tilted her head and regarded Esi with a shrewd glint in her eye. "Do you think that discrediting the Remillard Dynasty deserves a place in our strategy?"

"I don't know," the African woman replied doggedly. "But it would get both Paul and Anne out of the Human Polity Directorate and give us a chance to introduce more prohuman legislation in the Concilium. Even here on Earth, in the Assembly, Paul hews to the Milieu party line and throws his weight around every chance he gets. He tried to stomp all over me with hobnailed boots when I demanded more colonial planets for humans of color, and to hell with this operant quota thing the exotics forced on us. Why should the Europeans and the Americans and the Anzacs have thirteen ethnic planets out of the twenty? All Paul could do was cite metapsychic demographics! More operants among those groups! And so we Africans end up with only two worlds to colonize, and the Asians have only five."

"There are disproportionate numbers of Japanese and Chinese living happily on the cosmopolitan planets," Hiroshi pointed out mildly.

But Esi was not to be mollified. "Look at that bastard ethnic world Paul lobbied the Assembly to approve just before the clampdown: Denali—an *Alaskan* planet, if you please! In my book, it's just another colony of the U.S.A."

Anna hastily offered her guests more tea and brandy, and a few minutes later Esi was laughing at her own outburst and saying, "Well, hey. If we're rebels, we ought to act rebellious! Everybody knows what a professional gadfly I am . . . but what are the rest of you doing to further the glorious revolution?"

Oljanna Gathen said, "I have something very interesting to report. It will be announced officially next week, but I'm happy to let you all know now that Owen Blanchard has been put in command of the first of the three new human space armadas, the Twelfth Fleet. And my brother Ragnar has been appointed the Chief Operations Officer. The fleet will be based on Okanagon."

"Crikey!" exclaimed Will MacGregor. He turned an accusing glare on his colleague Alan Sakhvadze. "You must have known, and you didn't tell me!"

Alan only grinned. "I didn't spill the beans to Auntie Annushka, either. Oljanna would have had my guts for garters."

"Bozhe moi!" Anna cried. "This means that someday, if all goes well, we may have control of a fleet of armed starships . . ."

Gerry Van Wyk was blinking like a frenzied electronic calculator, his wide mouth agape. "You don't mean that we'd— No, of course not! We established at the very beginning of our—er—relationship that we'd seek to extricate humanity from the toils of the Milieu by peaceful means!"

"They won't let us go peacefully," Adrien said.

Gerry stopped blinking. "They won't?"

"If we try to withdraw from the confederation, the Milieu is prepared to ostracize us. Put us into perpetual quarantine. They'll toss us off the colonial worlds and sling our folks back into the solar system and take away our superluminal starships and slam the cell door on us. No more interstellar travel."

"But"—Gerry flailed his small hands furiously—"we'd *suffocate!*"

"Yes," Adrien said.

"All throughout the Simbiari Proctorship we were denied armed spacecraft," Oljanna pointed out. "Even our commercial fleet was restricted in its operations. Now that the Proctorship is over, we're permitted to travel anywhere we want in the Galaxy, and that means that we also must help enforce the law. It's just another privilege and duty of Milieu citizenship. Officially, the three human space fleets will be only an arm of the Magistratum. A glorified coast guard service and space patrol. But Owen and Ragnar know that the Twelfth Fleet could be much more."

"Good God, yes!" Jordan Kramer said. "Those of us with the appropriate scientific expertise could do clandestine weapons research! I can already think of several projects—"

"What about the other two fleets?" Hiroshi inquired.

"When there are enough trained personnel, a Thirteenth Fleet will be headquartered on Elysium and a Fourteenth on Assawompsett," Oljanna said. "But the Twelfth, being the mother fleet, as it were, will no doubt have a tactical advantage for a long time to come."

"It will take years to prepare ourselves," Anna warned. "We are still only a pitiful handful of people."

"Quite a handful," snapped Esi Damatura. In an instant, her expression changed and she smiled at Anna. "May I have just a bit more of that delicious tea? And then Hiroshi and I will have to think about egging back to Concord. The Directorate is considering setting up a blue-ribbon commission of philosophers and religious leaders to study the concept of Unity. Paul and Anne will push the resolution through, but I'm going to make damn sure that they don't pack the commission with Jesuits!"

The younger rebels exchanged blank looks.

"The most famous human apologist for Unity," Esi said darkly, "was a Froggie Jesuit who died in 1955, a paleontologist. They say he was also in on the Piltdown Man scam."

Anna handed Esi a refilled glass, then turned to a nearby bank of shelves and drew out a book-plaque. The title on the spine was *The Phenomenon of Man,* and the author was Pierre Teilhard de Chardin, S.J. Anna stepped to a duplicator and in a moment had a copy for each person in the room.

"Teilhard was not a perpetrator of paleontological hoaxes. That was proved long ago. What he was, was something much more dangerous. Take the plaques with you," she invited her fellow rebels. "Read the book, and then you may begin to understand what we are up against."

[35]

FROM THE MEMOIRS
OF ROGATIEN REMILLARD

After the earlier tragedies, that year of 2052 was blessed with a golden autumn and a sparkling early winter—at least so far as our family was concerned. Paul and Teresa were together again, Marc and his father were reconciled, and baby Jack still appeared to be responding favorably to the genetic therapy. There were no more mysterious deaths in the family or among its associates, and no sign whatsoever that the malevolent entities called Hydra and Fury were anything other than nightmarish figments of a supersensitive infant imagination.

Jack had begged for mental stimulation and sensory input: Marc gave it to him, and then some. He was unfailingly generous in his fostering of his little brother, even to the point of designing and constructing a special small environmental pod that could be perched at the back of his turbocycle, in which Jack happily rode on excursions throughout upper New England. The baby accompanied Marc two or three times a week to his classes at college and to the frat house. After Jack beat Alex Manion at three-dimensional chess, the other Mu Psi Omega men decided that he wasn't a human baby at all but a midget exotic savant in disguise. They made him their mascot and dressed him in tiny Dartmouth sweaters and warmups, and when Marc was otherwise occupied they toted him around the campus, letting him sop up the Ivy League ambiance and audit every kind of class from algorithm analysis to French Symbolist poetry. Jack went to football games with Boom-Boom Laroche, to plays and lectures with Shig Morita, and to the Shattuck Observatory with Pete Dalembert—where he made a pest of himself at the downlink station of the Hawking Orbital Telescope. He attended the performances of touring symphonies and chamber music ensembles and jazz groups and musical soloists and dance companies at Dartmouth's Hopkins Center. Together with other members of the Outing Club, Marc took Jack hiking along the

Appalachian Trail in the White Mountains. Riding in a modified back-pack, the baby visited the scene of the Great Intervention atop Mount Washington, where the restored chalet and cog railway attracted millions of visitors each year. When snow closed the mountains to hikers, Marc took his little brother trekking along Dartmouth's Skiway and on snowmobile rides in the deep woods north of Berlin—and nearly frightened him to death with a wild run up the frozen Connecticut River on the BMW turbocycle, with the ice spikes deployed.

I returned to the peaceful business of bookselling and very often entertained Marc and his fraternity brothers and Jack in the shop. Jack even learned how to walk there among the shelves of The Eloquent Page, rather to the dismay of Teresa, who had become just the least bit jealous of the closeness between her eldest and youngest sons. But she had other matters to keep her busy now. Because of the excessively long advance commitments customary in the opera business, she could not simply plunge back into a full-time musical career. But all the impresarios were wild to have her sing, and so she did pick up a fair number of other substitute engagements, similar to the one at the Met, and La Scala scheduled four special performances of Prokofiev's rarely heard psychoanalytical opera *The Fiery Angel* especially for her, just before the Christmas season. Its sexually obsessed heroine Renata was another role, like Turandot, where Teresa's acting ability and vocal power enabled her to score a triumph. She was home for the holiday itself, a tumultuous family gathering at Denis and Lucille's farm, and immediately afterward she and Paul went together to Kauai for ten days alone together, just prior to his leaving for Orb and the Concilium session.

Jack spent his first birthday quietly at home. Paul and Teresa gave him a beautiful Celestron telescope, Marc gave him an air guitar (which he had especially wanted), Marie gave him a teddy bear, Madeleine gave him a weighty treatise on theoretical cerebroenergetics, and Luc gave him a small tank with saltwater tropical fish. I gave him a new papoose carrier, since he had outgrown the old one.

For some time before and after Teresa and I were pardoned, my bookshop was overrun with curiosity-seekers and opera buffs wanting to felicitate and shake the hand of the hero who had rescued Teresa Kendall and stood by her during her ordeal in the Great White North. One idiot Tri-D producer even wanted to do a movie-of-the-week about our adventure and was dissuaded from pestering me only when I threatened to sic the Remco lawyers on him.

My notoriety (a gushing female commentator compared my daring rescue of Teresa to an escapade of the fictional Scarlet Pimpernel—leading Marc and his pals to dub me the Scarlet Pumpernickel) somehow also managed to get my hormones all a-burbling. I noticed belatedly that I was Man and Perdita Manion, my widowed assistant, was Woman, and a discreet literary affaire ensued. We were not really in love with each other. But she was a congenial person, and when one feels on top of the world, sex often demands to share the limelight. (It also tends to intrude when the world is falling to pieces around one's ears, but that's another story.)

Perdita and I fooled around a fair bit when business was slow in the dead of winter, 2053, and we made dinner for each other now and then in my flat or in her neat brick house over on Brockway Street. We went to Dartmouth's Winter Carnival together and canoodled afterward in the icy moonlight under a bearskin rug in Denis's antique sleigh over by Occam Pond, nearly freezing our silly pétards off. Family members began to grin at us with a knowing air, while Marc and Perdita's son Alex were first incredulous and then appalled at the evidence of superannuated lust. Perdita was then 51 years old, and I was a full-blooded 108. I don't know what might have happened had things continued to go smoothly.

But they didn't. Not long after the Winter Carnival, near the end of February, the first evidence appeared that Jack's body was rejecting the gene-transplantation therapy.

He was then thirteen months old. He had black hair and bright blue eyes and was a little below normal for his age in height and weight. He could creep faster than a fence lizard and toddle along fairly well on his chubby legs. He spoke in erudite sentences using an excruciatingly cute infantile accent. His metafaculties were coming along like gangbusters. By that time, Marc's accelerated honors course had brought him well into junior-class work, and he was charging ahead toward the attainment of his Bachelor of Science degree, with dual majors in metapsychology and theoretical physics.

Marc told me all the details of that snowy afternoon when Jack's life changed forever, replaying his searing memories so that now it seems that I was there myself. He and his pals Pete and Alex had the baby with them in the basement game room of the frat house. Marc was studying for an astrophysics credit and Jack was watching the other two boys play Ping-Pong, idly exercising his PK on a spare plass ball by making it creep up and down his arms and around his neck and head. When he tired of this game, he cupped the ball in both of his tiny hands for some time, sitting motionless with his eyes closed, and then called out:

"Pete, Alex—use my ball to play with for a while!" And he held out the white sphere.

Alex took it with a good-natured insult, tossed it up, and hit it with his paddle.

The ball was a blur as it flew to Pete's side of the table, eluded his paddle in a lightning bounce, and went sailing ten meters farther on. It impacted the wall at the far end of the room, then continued to bounce crazily among the furniture and video games as if it had a life of its own.

"Okay, shrimpo," Alex cried in disgust. "What's the big idea? You know you're not supposed to interrupt our game with juvenile PK shit!"

Jack grinned. "I didn't. I fixed the ball instead." And he burst into squeals of laughter.

Marc looked up from his book-plaque, and his shocked gaze met that of the other two boys. Without a word, he reached out with his own psychokinesis and snared the still wildly bouncing ball. He hefted it, smelled it, stared fixedly at it, and then carefully handed it to Alex. "It's not plass." His face had turned expressionless. Jack was still gurgling with self-congratulation.

Alex did his own quick examination, then dropped the ball onto the table from a height of about ten centimeters.

It bounced nearly to the ceiling.

Alex snatched it out of the air and handed it to the openmouthed Pete. He said to Jack: "All right. It was a regular Ping-Pong ball when I gave it to you. It's still even got the trademark on it. What'd you do to it?"

"Messed up its polymers," said the baby, grinning. A drop of drool hung from his pink lower lip. He had on his little green Dartmouth sweats and miniature Nikes.

"Just like that?" Pete cried. He shook the ball. "There's some kind of damned fluid in there!"

"It improves the coefficient of elasticity," Jack lisped. His mind broadcast the formulas of both the ball shell and its contents. "I've been practicing my creative metafaculty in secret for some time now. It was very difficult to learn how to revise small molecules. Very large ones are easier."

"Oh, God," said Marc. "What *else* have you been messing with?"

"Nothing important," Jack said. "Mostly I used air and accreted water vapor, and I have modified some things I took from wastebaskets. But my most versatile raw materials have been my own solid and gaseous body wastes. It's possible to convert them into ever so many interesting organic compounds. I formed various things as I practiced—mostly spheroids and cubes and prisms and other symmetrical objects, once I had discovered how to manipulate the different compounds with fair precision. When I had finished experimenting, I reconverted my samples into an amorphous shitlike substance and replaced them in my diaper so that Mama or Nanny Herta wouldn't find out . . . Do you know that it's *really* possible to fart flames? I thought it was only a metaphor for anger, but I discovered that the phenomenon is genuine! It's harmless to the body if you perform the experiment with extreme care. All you have to do is ignite the inflammable gases naturally produced by—"

The three older boys collapsed into near-hysterical laughter and whoops. A couple of other fraternity brothers ventured downstairs and asked if they could get in on the fun.

Marc scooped up his baby brother under his arm. "Just horsing around with the pygmy Einstein here."

"He's more laughs than a barrel of monkeys," Alex added hastily.

Marc said: *Upstairs. To my room. Pete hang on to that friggin' ball.*

They galloped up two flights of stairs, and when they were safe in Marc's cubicle sat Jack on the bed and began to throw questions at him:

Did he realize what he was doing when he altered the Ping-Pong ball? . . . Yes. He was exerting the metafaculty of creativity.

Did he have to exert creativity on each individual molecule to cause change? . . . Certainly not. The process, once initiated, "infected" adjacent molecules and spread under the mental direction of the creator's coercion.

Could he create matter out of nothing? . . . Of course not. On the other hand, there is indubitably a store of matter and energy trapped within certain of the dynamic-field lattices, and this, while not properly classed as "nothing," has negligible impact upon the Present Reality and is available to an ingenious creator.

Could he make matter out of energy? . . . Not yet. That would be a considerable challenge. It was rather easy to produce chemical energy from the disruption of molecules, however, and many interesting effects, such as the farting of flames, were—

Could he transmute elements? . . . No. He felt that theoretically this was possible; but the consequences to the creator were likely to be drastic. One even had to exert caution with chemical-type reactions because of the potentially hazardous energies involved. For example, the bed linen should optimally be soaking wet before one attempts to—

What was the most complicated thing he had ever made? . . . The wizzo Ping-Pong ball.

How long had he been able to exert his creativity in this fashion? . . . Almost from the time he was taken from Ape Lake to Kauai, and there taught how.

Who taught him? . . . An aged Hawaiian woman, Malama Johnson, who was the cook at the Kendall house on the island, had come creeping into his room when he was alone, soon after his arrival. She had greeted him with great dignity, treating him as an equal and not as a child, and told him that she was a kahuna, one of the magician-priests who had lived among the Polynesian people for thousands of years, long before they ever migrated to the Hawaiian Islands.

Malama had touched Jack and sung very softly, and then she told him that he was overflowing with mana loa—the strongest kind of metapsychic energy.

"She waved her hands, and there were hundreds of little sparks flying around, and then tiny little black things floated in the air," Jack said to the older boys. "They settled on my crib and made an awful mess, but later, when Mama saw them, she thought they had blown in the window from a fire in a canefield nearby. The black bits were carbon smuts. Malama had formed them psychocreatively from atmospheric carbon dioxide and ignited some of them."

Jack went on to tell his awed listeners how the kahuna had taught him this simple trick and then, in the weeks that followed, many others. She warned him that he should not let anyone know what he could do—not even his Mama or his Uncle Rogi—until all of his inner "selves" were more fully under his control.

This strange statement had a certain rightness about it that made a deep impression on Jack. Even when he was still in the womb he had felt that he had a Low Self and a High Self who contended within him, and he had asked my help keeping them in line as he was being born. Malama told him that the names of those two selves were unihipili and uhane. Haole wise men (who had only belatedly discovered what the kahuna had known from time immemorial and who still were very backward in their understanding of huna) sometimes called the two selves the unconscious and the conscious minds. But the uhane that Jack had mistaken for his High Self, she said, was actually his Middle Self. The true High Self, or amakua, was the superconscious, an integrating or unifying entity that was capable of binding together in perfect harmony the selves and the body they inhabited. The amakua had, she said, a special life of its own and was the font of mana loa. It was available to all thinking persons, but many did not make use of it. In time, she said, Jack would attain perfect access to the amakua, and then he would be able to accomplish a great work . . .

"Of course," Jack said to the college boys, "I have since recognized that what Malama called mana loa was what we would call the creative metafaculty, the higher mindpower that infuses and energizes all the others and the lower mindpowers as well. My very high metapsychic assay in creativity merely confirms what Malama observed when she first met me."

Marc asked: "And do you feel that your three selves *are* under control now?"

The small face clouded with perplexity. "I'm having problems. I *thought* that the Low Self and Middle Self were under my control, and I'm learning to communicate with the High Self. I barred both Hydra and Fury, who would have separated the three and then reintegrated them into a new person—"

Marc uttered an expletive, then said to Jack on the intimate mode: *Say no more about THIS to Alex&Pete we'll talk later!*

Jack said to Marc: Yes we must do that. You have been having troubling dreams, haven't you? About Fury.

How did you know that?!

For a time he troubled me. But I forced him to go away. You have listened to him even though what he says is—

Not now! Aloud, Marc said, "Tell me about the problems you've had trying to integrate your three selves."

"I've discovered that my body increasingly balks at accepting creative direction," Jack said. "Up until now, I've been able to make it operate in a normal human fashion, within the accepted parameters of good health. But lately there have been difficulties." He began to fumble ineffectively with the fastenings on one of his tiny athletic shoes. "Marco, *help* me."

"Imperfect motor coordination," Marc opined. "To be expected until your peripheral nervous system matures a bit more."

"No, that's not what I mean. Take off my sock and look at the toes."

Marc did so. The other two boys leaned closer.

"What's that on his little toe?" Pete pointed out. "Right at the base of the nail? Check it with your deepsight, guys."

"Looks like a sore," said Alex without certainty. "Maybe a little bitty blister rubbed raw. But my deepsight isn't worth shit."

Marc's, however, was extraordinary. He could magnify the tiny spot and see into it, and call up from his memories information stored from his biology studies.

"It's not . . . just a sore," Marc said. His two friends regarded him with astonishment. His usual shell of mental impermeability was faltering, as if attacked from the inside by some overwhelming emotion.

"I know it's not ordinary," Jack said calmly. "I could use self-redaction on a blister or scrape and make it disappear at once. But this small lesion is caused by a cellular anomaly, and it responds neither to autoredaction from my unconscious nor to the psychocreative and coercive impetus of voluntary self-redaction. It's very puzzling. I'm not yet very well educated in molecular biology, but it almost seems as though the lesion is a product of my body's own genetic apparatus."

Marc stared at his little brother for a long moment without speaking. His mind-screen was once again fully deployed. He smiled as he took both of Jack's little hands in his own and spoke quietly, coercively.

"The thing on your toe could be nothing at all. It also could be a sign that something isn't going quite right with your therapy. All those transplanted good genes have been racing around in your body trying to plug in, and your mind has evidently tried to help them. But now it may be that something's screwed up a little bit. So I'm going to bundle you up right now and také you down the street to Hitchcock Hospital, and we'll let Nana Colette take a look at this. Okay?"

"Okay," the infant agreed. Marc began to put on Jack's sock and shoe. "What do you call the thing on my toe, Marco?"

"It's a cancer," Marc said. "Upsy daisy, kiddo. Now we have to put on your snowsuit. Do you need to have your diaper changed first? No? Okay." Marc turned to his two stricken friends, who were hiding behind their own thought-screens. "Will one of you guys do me a favor and run down for the astrophysics plaque I left in the game room? I'll take it with me—in case I find myself with time on my hands while old Jacko here gets checked out."

[36]

FROM THE MEMOIRS
OF ROGATIEN REMILLARD

Now I come to a part of my Memoirs that I would rather skip over, for it covers the time during which Jack's body changed. It was a time when those of us who loved the child saw hope give way to horror and horror pass into numb despair and a desperate desire that the suffering baby would die and find peace, giving us peace as well. We could not know that Jack's body was as anomalous as his brilliant mind, that he was destined from his conception to be as he became. He was at once more than we humans are, and less. Prochronistic is the term the scientists eventually applied to him: a being born far ahead of its time, with a body that was not that of Homo sapiens at all. The beautiful, normal-appearing baby that Teresa had given birth to was only the larva, as it were, of the wondrous and terrible mature entity that Jack would become.

His transformation began in the spring of the year 2053.

I have to apologize again if the entity reading these Memoirs finds my explanation of the background of Jack's disincarnation to be overly facile and full of scientific half-truths and omissions. Human genetic science is a complex discipline, and Colette Roy's explanations to me were couched in the most elementary lay terminology, which I must inevitably fall back on in my writing. If I inadvertently slip from the path of scientific orthodoxy, remember that what was going on in Jack's body was subordinate to what was going on in his mind and the minds of those around him . . .

Beginning in the late twentieth century, genetic engineers had developed a number of different and reliable methods for inserting new genes into the human body. The most widely used, and the one that formed one of the principal mechanisms of the regeneration tank as well as the more specialized therapy used in the attempts to cure Jack, was the viral vector or transduction technique. In this, special viruses carrying the gene transplant were allowed to "infect" appropriate target cells in the patient. Over the years, hundreds of thousands of different viral vectors had been developed to carry and deliver genetic material safely and efficiently. The selection of the vector was done after a meticulous assay of the individual patient's gene map, in order to avoid a dangerous situation that cropped up all too often during the pioneer days of gene therapy—the activation of proto-oncogenes.

All of us have a mixed bag of proto-oncogenes in our heredity. They are two-faced bits of DNA that can lie doggo all throughout a person's life, acting just as though they were perfectly normal blueprints for body proteins or the switches turning processes on and off, doing the useful work they are supposed to do . . . unless some extraneous factor sets off a fatal trigger and transforms them into genuine oncogenes, the inducers of cancer. The trigger can be a virus, or radiation, or a carcinogenic chemical, or a mutant gene that is inherited, or even a failure of the body's autoredactive mechanism.

One of the commonest kinds of proto-oncogene used to cause lung cancer in people who smoked tobacco. Folks who had the P-O and smoked got the disease; folks who didn't have the P-O might smoke like chimneys for years and eventually die of something else. There were other ways of getting lung cancer—other chemical or psychological triggers, even different kinds of tobacco-cancer P-Os; but you get the idea.

Now, a cancer is not a simple thing, any more than a living human body is simple. A cancer is not an alien invader, as a germ is, but rather an uncontrolled growth that begins in a single cell that once was normal. We are marvelously made. So marvelous that, if you study molecular biology and get an inkling of just how many millions of little chemical and electrical and psychocreative reactions have to take place and coordinate perfectly from moment to moment in order for the body to function, you might wonder how we manage to live at all! But we do, because the genes present in our body cells give out instructional messages to keep things ticking. Most of the time, we tick properly. But when an oncogene is activated, the wrong messages are sent to the affected cell and it becomes transformed into a cancer cell.

Cancer cells multiply like mad and don't know when to stop. They have extraordinary vitality, a characteristic that has led some researchers to call them "immortal." They invade adjacent tissues, destroying normal cells as they go. They hog the blood supply. They seed themselves and spread throughout the body via the bloodstream or the lymphatic ducts, a process called metastasis. Cancers come in many different varieties, some slow-acting and some fast. The worst of them wreak havoc on normal tissues, interfere with vital body functions, and kill the victim unless they are stopped.

Another name for cancer is neoplasm, which means "new tissue." It's an appropriate name, because the DNA in cancer cells is different from the stuff in normal body cells, in that the harmless proto-oncogenes have been transformed into new, malignant oncogenes.

Now, none of baby Jack's original collection of lethal equivalent genes had been oncogenes, but some of his chromosomes did have the "fragility" factor that characterizes proto-oncogenes. When Colette Roy and her colleagues prepared his genetic map, they discovered not only the thirty-four potentially lethal DNA combinations but also a number of peculiar DNA novelties that occupied the "redundant" chromosomal regions, those that have no known effect upon normal bodily function. Colette went ahead with therapy to repair Jack's documented genetic defects, the ones that were guaranteed to be harmful, knowing that there was an off chance that the proto-oncogenes might be triggered. When the child passed his first birthday still showing no sign of genetic disease, she and her colleagues thought they had lucked out.

Until the first cancer appeared.

The thing on Ti-Jean's toe was a relatively sluggish little epidermoid carcinoma of the type that ordinarily is easily cured. After the scientists analyzed the cancer's DNA, they whipped up a correction and inserted it into the baby. Within a few weeks, all of the neoplasmic cells vanished, and Teresa and Paul and Marc and the rest of us breathed a sigh of relief.

Colette was not nearly so sanguine, although she did not then share her fears with the family. She thought at first that one or more of the viral vectors used to infect Jack with good genes might have set the P-Os off. But there was another, more ominous possibility: that the cancer had been triggered by messages sent from the mysterious redundant genes. If this was true, then Jack carried the blueprints for his own destruction in every single cell nucleus of his body. Less than a month later, in early May, another, completely different variety of cancer was detected during one of the weekly comprehensive body scans that Jack endured at Hitchcock Hospital. It was a much more malignant and fast-growing melanoma, and there were two of them, sited in Jack's testicles.

When I got the news I felt my own balls flinch in sympathy. I am sterile as the result of a painful complication of the mumps that I suffered in early adolescence, but aside from having no viable sperm, I function very well, thank you. Even though it eventually became possible to restore my ruined semeniferous tubules in the regen-tank, I have declined to be treated, for various reasons of my own.

Jack's case was far worse than mine, of course. His cancer would not only destroy his testicles; it would kill him very quickly unless drastic treatment put a stop to it. Once again, corrective genes were transplanted—but this time the cancer proved to be highly resistant. Even though the two lesions were still microscopic in size, they showed alarming signs of getting ready to metastasize—to seed replicas of themselves throughout the body. According to the medical state of the art in 2053, in the rare case when an adult or an older child suffered from metastatic cancer, the treatment of choice involved putting the patient into a regen-tank, where the "seeds" could be obliterated by rigorous treatment. But Jack was too young for the tank, which was contraindicated in individuals below the age of puberty. In order to prevent metastasis in Jack, they had to act very quickly and remove his testicles surgically.

The family was devastated, even though they knew that it would be possible to restore him when he was older. Jack suffered considerable pain following the operation, for he declined to take any analgesics, and Teresa fell into a mood of profound depression. She cornered Colette Roy and demanded to know what was setting off the oncogenes. Colette had to say that they didn't know for certain. Some unknown factor was "insulting" the baby's DNA, causing the proto-oncogenes to mutate. If the viral vectors used in the original gene transplants were responsible, then the doctors would continue making "repairs" until the situation stabilized. It was also possible, she admitted, that Jack's anomalous genome itself contained the cancer triggers . . . triggers with a built-in time-lapse function. A third and less likely possibility was that his autoredactive metafunction had gone awry, perhaps as a result of its working so hard in suppressing the expression of the lethals while the genetic transplant therapy was "taking." If this latter was the case, then voluntary redaction on Jack's part might restore his health—provided he was able to learn the appropriate metapsychic programs.

Teresa's apprehensions were far from calmed, even though Colette tried to put a good face on things by reminding her how Jack's older brother Luc had been restored. Luc's genetic anomalies had been completely different from Jack's, Teresa pointed out, and he had never had cancer. That formerly deadly condition had become readily treatable among humans at the midpoint of the twenty-first century, but the ancient fear of it lingered on. What would happen to Jack if more of the rapidly metastasizing cancers appeared? Colette calmly replied that they would be treated in whatever way was appropriate. She said nothing to Teresa of what the treatment might entail.

Just after Jack's operation, which Colette pronounced to be completely successful, Teresa gave a disastrous concert in Moscow, during which her voice broke several times. She immediately canceled the rest of her singing engagements for the year and moved into a room next to Jack's in the hospital, where he was still recovering and undergoing tests. She declared that she would not sing again until Jack was completely cured. Following this, Paul left the house on South Street and returned to his apartment down in Concord. There was no overt evidence of a fresh breach in the marriage, but neither Marc nor I needed a neon sign to indicate what was probably happening.

In mid-June little Jack was pronounced fit again, and he and Teresa returned to the family home, where he was pampered and carefully monitored. Henceforth the baby would be taken to the hospital every other day for scanning, so that any incipient problems could be nipped in the bud.

When the summer term at Dartmouth began and Marc started the last intensive push toward his goal of a bachelor's degree, he made a decision not to take Jack on long outings anymore until Colette was satisfied that the baby's health had stabilized. Feisty Ti-Jean deeply resented being confined to the house most of the time, and Marc did his best to be with him as often as possible and take him out for short trips. Jack's other three siblings, free from school for the summer, also seemed anxious to help the baby in his continuing thirst for intellectual input. His second sister Maddy, who was now thirteen and ready to begin her final year at the Granite Hill School in Vermont, was especially solicitous. She and Jack spent many long hours together studying cerebroenergetics, of all things. They made Marc show them the schematics of his homemade CE helmet and pestered him until he took the thing apart for them and explained it to the last detail.

Everything went well until early August, when the first act of the drama of Jack the Bodiless began to approach its climax. The scanner revealed several dozen ultramicroscopic cancerous lesions scattered in the child's long bones, pelvis, ribs, and scapulae. These were diagnosed as Ewing's sarcoma, a rare type of childhood-onset cancer with a propensity for rapid metastasis. Ordinarily, the Ewing oncogenes responded well to genetic engineering. In Jack's case, the attempt to insert replacement DNA failed. His variety of Ewing's was somehow different from the type already well known, having a different pleiotropic mechanism that undoubtedly accounted for its striking in so many places at once. Ferreting out that mechanism might take months. Given the multiple sites of the tiny cancers and their impending metastasis, amputation of the limbs and aggressive laser cautery and chemotherapy of the other diseased bones was the only course open to Colette and her colleagues.

When Teresa learned what would have to be done to Jack to save his life, no bright talk of future restoration in a regen-tank was able to distract her from the present catastrophe. She reacted so wildly that she had to be put under sedation. To his credit, Paul returned to her and attempted to use his own powerful redactive faculty to help her regain her mental equilibrium. He also spent long hours with Jack during the five weeks following the operations, transmitting to the precocious child every redactive healing program known to the human race at that time—plus numbers of them derived from the near-humanoid Poltroyans. In addition, he obtained from Denis and various other sources the most advanced metacoercive and creative programs, and force-fed the child the design principles for more complex multifaculty programs. Jack assimilated these recondite data gratefully, telling his father that he would make what use of it he could.

Now came those autumnal days, so crucial in the later lives of both Marc and Jack, when the older boy would come sneaking into the hospital, cloaked with invisibility, to steal his baby brother away. The original crude papoose-board backpack carrier that I had fashioned for Jack had gradually been transmogrified by Marc and his buddies into a high-tech wizard's cradle. Following Jack's quadruple amputations and entry into chemotherapy, the backpack became a virtual portable intensive-care unit, with only the baby's pale, bald little head visible within the transparent hooded top. The nurses at Hitchcock who were supposed to guard Jack were coerced and then convinced by posthypnotic suggestion that he never left his room. Marc craftily timed his excursions so that Colette Roy and the other operant doctors would be unlikely to discover what he and Jack were up to.

Most of the time, Marc carried his little brother away from the old hospital and walked north on Rope Ferry Road, along a path through the golf course and into a ravine carved ages ago by Girl Brook, where they entered a region of ancient pine trees and other evergreens called Pine Park. Until the Metapsychic Rebellion, the place was also one of my favorite walks, an undisturbed fragment of New England forest growing along the bank of the great Connecticut River. The place is full of ferns, and in its tiny glades there are wildflowers in season, and birdsong echoes beneath the 30-meter-tall pines as if in a hushed cathedral.

What did they talk about during those stolen hours? That they discussed the meaning of life goes without saying, for it seemed increasingly certain to Marc that little Jack was going to die. They discussed the science of death and the philosophy of it and the personal beliefs each one had on the subject, and how these contrasted with the tenets of the religion of their ancestors. Jack was often in considerable pain, although he never let it daunt him, and he steadfastly maintained that pain, like the paradoxical proto-oncogenes, would not have evolved in us and remained a part of the higher animal condition for so long unless it had more than a fleeting, avoidance-factor/signal-factor value. Jack recapitulated Teresa's naïve wisdom relating to the subject, which Marc tended to pooh-pooh. Jack also queried Marc's views on the notion, held by a fair number of thinkers, that pain was an educative tool and the ordeal a potential pathway to higher levels of consciousness. At first, Marc thought this was more sentimental poppycock, but later he came to share his brother's opinion.

Besides philosophizing, they argued. Among other things, about sex. At this point in his adolescence, the sexually repressed Marc was fighting what seemed to be a never-ending battle with his body's carnal urges. The usual avenues of relief open to a boy of his age seemed to him to be a craven cop-out, a surrender of the mind to the most primitive instincts of the body. He would learn to control himself in a dignified manner—in an operant manner!—or know the reason why.

Human sex, Marc argued, was a detriment to metapsychic advancement. The exotic races of the Milieu were a case in point: The most advanced were the ineffable Lylmik, who had no sex at all. Then came the Krondaku, with whom sex was so stately and well deliberated that it might be a formal dance ending in an exchange of gifts. The Simbiari, in spite of their racial immaturity and all the jokes cracked over their unesthetic physiology, ranked next on the ladder of metapsychic advancement. Their sex involved no intercourse or frenzied courtship ritual, the eggs being fertilized in their watery nest by sperm packets neatly supplied through a special orifice beneath the male's vestigial tail. The jolly but none-too-competent Poltroyans, as lusty a lot as ever copulated for the mere fun of it, were always letting sex make sentimental fools of them. And the Gi . . . ! They seemed to live for little else and were so scientifically backward that it was a wonder they had ever been accepted into the Milieu at all.

Humanity, in Marc's opinion, fell somewhere between the Poltroyans and the Gi.

They argued about many other things as well: About the validity of the Judeo-Christian tradition and the existence of God, and especially about the notion that a thinking, responsible person with well-defined goals was still somehow obligated to "trust" God. About whether continuing membership in the Galactic Milieu was apt to be a good or a bad thing for humanity in the long view. About eugenics, the deliberate attempts to "improve" the human organism, which had been forbidden under the Proctorship but was now coming to the fore again. About the desirability of mass-producing humans artificially to facilitate populating new planets with nonborns. About the underdog position of humans in the Galactic Concilium. And about the potential danger that Unity might pose to human individualism.

They also argued about Fury and Hydra, even though neither entity had manifested itself for over a year. Marc had had many troubling dreams of Fury, but his conscious mind by now had almost managed to convince itself that Jack had imagined the fearsome events attending Addie's death. Jack stubbornly maintained that there was a real Fury and a real Hydra, and that Marc should make a stronger effort to bar Fury from his dreams, or one of these days, when everyone least expected it, the monsters would be back.

The brother minds were very different. They were natural antagonists by nature, and one can see that the rivalry that eventually led to the Metapsychic Rebellion had its inception during these intimate, clandestine walks in the pine forest, when the warmth of Indian summer filled the air with the scent of resin and the two of them, weary at last of their colloquy, would simply stand watching the great river flow by, Jack fashioning tiny boats out of forest debris with his creativity and Marc influencing the wind and river currents with his to make the little things dance on the water.

In November, just as the last leaves had fallen and the frost began to settle in to stay, the scanner detected in Jack incipient adenocarcinoma of the pancreas, formerly one of the fastest-acting and most intractable cancers. Gene therapy was tried, and once again it failed. The child's pancreas had already been removed before the genetic procedures were attempted, and Colette hoped that no metastasis had taken place.

Unfortunately, it had. New deadly cancer seeds were detected soon afterward in vital organs adjacent to the pancreas—in the liver, the spleen, the stomach, the large and small intestines, the kidneys—and in the great blood vessels of the heart. Pinpoint chemotherapy and laser microsurgery were brought to bear, but no sooner had one crop of seeds been destroyed than another wave appeared to take its place. The baby was put on full cerebro-isolate life support while Colette, her colleagues, and consultants brought in from all over the world tried to find a way to get Jack into a regen-tank, wipe his genetic slate clean, and put him back together again.

None of the cancers or the therapies affected Jack's brain or his central nervous system. He remained alert, fully operant in all his metafaculties (except, apparently, self-redaction), and in considerable pain. He refused to accept any anodyne, chemical or electronic, saying that it would dull his mind and inhibit the "work" he was engaged in. What this work was he could not explain, and the mental images he projected were incomprehensible to Paul, Marc, and the professional attendants. Because of Jack's extraordinary precocity, both his father and the doctors acceded to his request, hoping that the "work" was some grand, all-encompassing mental program that would eventually initiate a spontaneous cure.

Paul still had a small hope that Jack would survive. Teresa was another matter. When the new and devastating pancreatic cancer was diagnosed, she insisted at first on visiting him daily, even though the sight of the awesome paraphernalia now enveloping him frightened her almost to the point of hysteria. When Jack truthfully admitted to her that the pain was intense, she begged him, day after day, to let the doctors install a blocking device. His continuing calm refusal and rapid physical deterioration as organ after organ shut down culminated in her having a nervous breakdown in Colette's hospital office, blaming herself for the baby's ordeal in an orgy of self-recrimination, saying Jack should never have been born, and demanding that he be removed from the machines and allowed to "die in peace."

Stress and guilt brought about Teresa's total collapse. Once it was determined that there was nothing wrong with her physically, she was given medication and put to bed in the house on South Street, with a full-time private duty nurse to keep an eye on her. Marie and Maddy were away in boarding school until the Christmas holidays, and Luc, who was tutored by the nanny, was shipped off with her to stay with Cheri and Adrien in their winter home in Loudon, just outside Concord. After several futile attempts to aid Teresa through his redaction (she shut him out, accusing him of damning their baby to a travesty of life), Paul left her once again.

For some weeks Teresa languished, eating very little and sunk in profound depression. She no longer had any desire to see Jack, and when I visited her from time to time, bringing from the bookshop rare musical tomes that I thought might interest her, she was sweetly apathetic. And then, just before Christmas, she suddenly began to speak of her youngest child in the past tense, and her condition greatly improved.

Imagining Jack dead, Marc told me without emotion, was apparently the only way his mother could retain her sanity. In Marc's opinion, she had made an eminently sensible adaptation, for unless the family was willing to keep the baby on total brain-isolate life support for over a decade, he was certainly doomed to die.

The bone cancers had returned, and they were attacking Jack's spine and skull in spite of everything the doctors could do.

[37]

HANOVER, NEW HAMPSHIRE, EARTH
24-25 DECEMBER 2053

Uncle Rogi was the one who organized the mob of cousins into carolers. With both Teresa and Jack unable to attend the family Christmas party at Denis and Lucille's, the old bookseller thought of this way to cheer the invalids a little, and the children of the Dynasty, both young adults and kids, agreed enthusiastically to participate. Two hours before they were all scheduled to attend midnight mass at the quaint fieldstone Catholic church on Sanborn Road, Rogi had all of the Remillard offspring assemble in his bookshop. He gave them songbook-plaques and then led them down South Street en masse to sing Christmas carols under Teresa's bedroom window.

It was snowing gently, with a crisp shallow layer already on the ground and sticking to the bare bushes and trees. Hanover looked impossibly lovely in the gleam of streetlights and house windows that framed illuminated Christmas trees. There were thirty-four children in the choir. The only ones missing were two toddlers belonging to Philip and Aurelie, who were too young to participate, Cheri and Adrien's little Cory, who had a cold . . . and Jack.

They sang "Adeste," and "Il est né, le divin enfant," and "The Holly and the Ivy," and "Gesù Bambino," and "Silent Night," and "Bring a Torch, Jeanette, Isabella" in both French and English. They sang the haunting "Coventry Carol" in its entirety, and some of the young voices broke when they reached the more unfamiliar verses on the book-plaques and realized that the carol was about the slaughter of the innocents by Herod, sung by the mothers of the dead babies:

Herod the King in his raging, chargèd he hath this day
His men of might, in his own sight, all young childrèn to slay.

Then woe is me, poor child, for thee! And ev'ry morn and day
For thy parting nay say nor sing: By, by, lully, lullay.

The somber mood was lifted when they swung into "Joy to the World" and then finished with the Remillard family's favorite carol, "Cantique de Noël."

The nurse, forewarned by Rogi, had helped Teresa to a chair by her window. She waved to the crowd when the concert ended, and immediately the front door opened and Jacqui Delarue, the matronly housekeeper, came out with paper cups of steaming cocoa. Rogi surreptitiously added to his a slug of rum from his pocket flask.

Then—voilà! The carolers heard a sound of bells jingling and horses puffing and clomping, and two large wagons filled with hay driven by Severin and Adrien came out of the little lane beyond the library and up to the front of the house. With happy shrieks, the younger children greeted Dobbin and Napoleon, who normally lived in Denis's neighbor's pasture as pensioners and were called upon only during Christmas and the Dartmouth Winter Carnival.

"Everybody into the wagons!" Rogi roared. "We'll roll over to the hospital now to carol for Jack. And as we go, everybody sing!"

So they wended their way through town to the strains of "Frosty the Snowman," and "Rudolph" in English and in bastard French, and "Chestnuts Roasting," and "Santa Claus Is Coming to Town," and "Have Yourself a Merry Little Christmas," and "Jingle Bell Rock." As the wagons rolled past the snow-covered expanse of the college green, Marc and several of the other older Remillards who were students sang Dartmouth's "Winter Song."

Then the bulk of the old hospital loomed up, its outline blurred by the snow, and the children fell silent. The happy holiday vibes that had engulfed the hayriders vanished as they all, except for the single uncomprehending five-year-old, withdrew behind their mental screens.

Jack.

Poor little ravaged Jack.

They were finally going to *see* him.

Rogi had carefully consulted with each family before having Marc ask Jack if he felt up to having a horde of visitors. The parents had tried to prepare their offspring by presenting a realistic mental image of Jack as he now was. His aspect was saddening but not ghastly, for the child's head was still normal in appearance, and his baldness would be hidden under a Santa cap, and the support unit that held him could be sheeted over to hide what was inside.

The parents told their youngest children not to look under the sheet, knowing that the admonition was futile even as they said it. They also reminded the children that Jack's mind was strong and well and there was still hope that his body could be restored.

The night supervisor of nursing met them at the front door and led them to where Jack waited. There was no need to tell the operant youngsters to keep quiet. When they reached Jack's room they filed in, one by one, to greet him and say a few words if they wished. Jack was tilted upright in the frame of his life-support apparatus. On one side of him was a bank of monitors and the controls of the machinery that kept him alive. On the other side was a top-of-the-line minimain computer with a brainboard box, no keypads or microphone, and a jumbo display monitor on a flexarm: a toy for the invalid child. Jack smiled a lot and spoke to his guests telepathically. There was no overt evidence that he was in pain.

Then came five-year-old Cousin Norman, one of Philip's large brood, who was the youngest caroler of the group. He asked Jack: "Why do you have to mindspeak us? Can't you talk?"

No, Jack said. I still have my voice box, but it's no good without lungs.

There were scattered sharp intakes of breath and gasps of dismay, but Norman plunged on. "Then you can't sing along with us. But that's okay. Your ears work, don't they?"

Yes. And my eyes are still fine, too.

"How about your heart?"

It's still there, but it doesn't beat. It's shut down.

"Oh," said Norman. He was squinting, and everyone knew he was using his deepsight to look under the sheet. His older sisters braced themselves to grab him and hustle him out of the room if he became frightened and made a scene, but all Norman said was: "You're really a mess in there, aren't you?"

Yes, said Jack. He was still smiling.

"Now it's time for the Christmas carols," the head nurse said briskly to the visitors, "and then Jack must rest."

Marc had already primed them on his little brother's favorites. They sang "Good King Wenceslaus," and "Angels We Have Heard on High," and "Jolly Old Saint Nicholas," and finally "Lo, How a Rose E'er Blooming."

When the last sweet harmony faded, Jack said: Thank you for a wonderful Christmas present. And now I have a little present for each of you! . . . Marc, open the top drawer of that computer stand for me. Sometimes it sticks.

Mystified, Marc complied. And discovered that the drawer was filled with miniature white roses.

Murmurs of interest came from the carolers, and these turned to exclamations and even squeals when the little flowers began flying out and affixing themselves to the children's coats like boutonnieres.

Jack said: Lo, how a rose e'er blooming! Merry Christmas!

"Merry Christmas, Jack!" they replied, the oldest of them with suspicious moisture in their eyes. And then they shuffled out.

The head nurse was looking into the now empty drawer and shaking her head, her lips pursed with disapproval. She glowered at Marc, who had lingered after the others left. "I suppose you were responsible for that, young man. Don't you know that live plants can carry viruses that might interfere with your little brother's genetic therapy?"

"I didn't bring the roses," Marc said. "If you want to know where those flowers came from, you'd better ask *him*. He did it with his creativity. It's one of the things he's good at, transforming one thing into another." He fingered the rose in the lapel of his mackinaw, inspecting it with a critical eye. "You goofed, Jacko. Forgot the sepals. Smells nice, though. Good job on the essential oils."

The nurse was incredulous. "Do you mean to tell me he *made* those roses? Out of *nothing?*"

Jack grinned.

Marc headed out the door. "No, he used an organic raw material. But if I were you, Nurse, I wouldn't ask what."

Even before the long midnight mass was completely over, Rogi slipped outside and trudged toward his apartment above the bookshop. He was dead beat after shepherding the kids, and the sip of consecrated wine he'd taken at communion had reminded him sacrilegiously that his flask had been emptied long before. When he passed the house he saw that the light in Teresa's bedroom was still on, as were many of the downstairs lights. Impulsively, he rang the doorbell. When Jacqui answered, he asked if Teresa was still up. Jacqui said that she had looked in about twenty minutes previously and found Teresa reading. The nurse was at midnight mass.

"I'll just go up and find out how Teresa liked the caroling," Rogi said, shedding his down jacket and stamping most of the snow off his boots. "Don't bother coming along to play chaperone. Teresa and I know all there is to know about each other."

Jacqui laughed dutifully at his old-fashioned notions of prudery and went off. Rogi climbed to the second floor and knocked on the door of the big master bedroom. There was no reply, and he hesitated. It never occurred to him to use his metafaculties.

Well, he thought, if she's gone off to sleep, I'll just tuck her in and turn out the lights.

He opened the door and nearly jumped out of his skin. For the merest instant, he imagined that he saw a tall man in evening clothes bending over Teresa as she lay sleeping, giving her a tender kiss on the forehead.

"Paul . . . ?"

But there was nobody there after all. Trembling, Rogi came into the room, thinking that the night's excitement really had been too much for him, and he'd have to think seriously about going on the wagon during the new year. Damned imagination! Next thing, he'd be seeing snakes or pink elephants instead of Paul.

. . . But it hadn't been Paul. The phantom had been beardless and of a more muscular build than Teresa's husband. But for all that, there had been a distinctly familiar air about him.

Espèce d'idiot, Rogi called himself.

He drew up the coverlet a bit, turned off the bedside lamp, and gave Teresa a gentle farewell pat on one hand.

The hand was cold.

Rogi stood stock-still. But Teresa was even more motionless, and when the truth finally penetrated and he frantically switched the lamp back on and snatched up the bedside phone, he saw the empty pill bottle.

[38]

FROM THE MEMOIRS
OF ROGATIEN REMILLARD

Not even Jack knew what Teresa had planned to do, so skilled was she in guarding her most secret thoughts. When she took the pills, her youngest son was asleep, exhausted from his visitors and from the psychocreative gifts he had fashioned for them. As his mother began to slip into death, Jack woke, for in her deranged state she sought to force him to accompany her, and the final transmutation of her vital energies lent her a terrible gentle strength that the child could barely countermand. When Teresa passed on at last, Jack was comatose for ten hours, and his medical attendants and his distraught father were certain that he would surely die, too. He did not, but his condition worsened, and a new crop of rapidly infiltrating malignancies appeared.

Teresa's suicide provoked a wave of prurient public interest in the Remillard family, its tragedies, and its personal affairs that reminded me uncomfortably of the media madness attending the family of the assassinated U.S. President John F. Kennedy. The actual condition of young Jack had been carefully hidden from reporters, who knew only that the First Magnate's youngest son was being treated for cancer; but with the vultures circling around more and more closely, it seemed only a matter of time before the child's bizarre condition would become known—and then there would be a fresh spate of adverse publicity.

In January 2054, Paul took a month-long leave of absence from his official duties and went into seclusion on the planet Denali, with Laura Tremblay accompanying him. The inhabitants of the frigid little world were so grateful for Paul's help in getting their colony established that they kept his place of refuge secret, frustrating any journalists who might have pursued him.

There had been a star-studded public memorial service for Teresa in Concord between Christmas and New Year's, overflowing the Catholic cathedral in the capital of Earth and covered by all the news services. Her interment was to be private, and since she had been cremated, the media and the general public assumed that her ashes would be scattered. However, in a handwritten codicil to her last will and testament, Teresa had requested that I return her ashes to Kauai, the island of her birth. Marc wanted to accompany me, but I held off until he assured me that he had successfully completed the work for his Bachelor of Science degree and was well along on his Master's thesis. Then, on 5 February, the day after Marc's sixteenth birthday, when he was finally able to pilot a rhocraft legally, he borrowed Paul's silver Maserati and flew us to Poipu. The two of us carried Teresa's remains in an elegantly carved little pine box.

We picked up Teresa's father at the beach house and flew almost immediately to a historic little old church out in the wild canefields, Saint Raphael's. The ninety-three-year-old astrophysicist Bernard Kané Kendall looked sallow and middle-aged when he greeted us, although he had undergone rejuvenation less than a decade earlier. His mind was in a perennial state of abstraction, rapt in cosmological mysteries; and although he mourned the loss of Teresa, Marc and I could see that he was anxious to get back to the great complex of observatories on the Big Island, where he lived and worked during most of the year.

Teresa's mother was not in attendance. Annarita Donovan Latimer, the only child of my onetime fiancée, Elaine Donovan, was seventy-eight years old at the time of her daughter's death and living as a recluse in New York City after a long and successful career as an actress. She had been separated from Kendall for over twenty years and was adamantly opposed to rejuvenation. (Annarita would succumb quietly to heart failure in 2056, the year that the new Teresa Kendall Opera House had its inaugural season on the cosmopolitan planet Avalon, thanks to the beneficence of the Remillard Foundation.)

Saint Raphael's Church was packed with islanders who had known and loved Teresa in her youth, many of them native Hawaiians. When the service was concluded, the people filed up to the altar, where the little box of ashes rested on a kind of wide wooden stand with handles at the corners, and draped it with gorgeous leis of island flowers. Four Hawaiian men wearing brightly patterned traditional shirts and horseshoe leis woven of ferns then took up the litter, and I thought there would be a procession to the local cemetery. To my surprise, the pallbearers and the file of mourners moved directly to our silver Maserati, where the priest said a last blessing and sprinkled the box of ashes with holy water. Then the people began to sing "Aloha Oe," and a plump brown hand fell upon my shoulder. I looked around, to discover Malama Johnson, the woman who had taken care of Teresa and Jack and me when we spent the last months of our exile at the Kendall beach house down in Poipu.

"Now you and I and Marc will take dear Kaulana's dust to Keaku," she whispered. "We will fly in your egg."

The box and most of the flowers fit in the backseat, and the three of us climbed into the front. Keaku, it seemed, was in the direction of cloud-cloaked Mount Waialeale, in the center of the island north of us. Our inertialess aircraft lofted us 1700 meters into the air in a few seconds under Marc's pilotage, and we flew noiselessly through thick clouds almost as featureless as the gray limbo of hyperspace.

The heights of Kauai are the wettest place on Earth, with an annual rainfall of over twelve meters. I knew only a little about the country up there. It is called the Alakai Swamp and is a windswept ancient volcanic plateau of almost perpetual rain and mist, where the bogs shelter rare plants and hundreds of waterfalls plunge over precipitate fern-clad cliffs into the fertile lowlands. Of all the Hawaiian Islands, Kauai is the greenest and, to me, the most inviting. It was also the island that had been the last refuge of the legendary Menehune—the dwarfish "magical" people whom the conquering Polynesians found and enslaved when they first migrated north from Tahiti.

The place Malama had indicated on the rhocraft's large-scale local navigation display was a lava cave on the southern edge of the swamp, near the head of Olokele Canyon. Marc had the egg on autopilot, and the terrain indicator warned us that we were about to touch down while the ship was still totally enveloped in cloud.

I stepped out into a cool drizzle that immediately soaked the white tropical suit I had chosen for the obsequies. All I could discern with my regular sight was swirling mist, gnarled little trees, and a lush growth of ferns and other rain-forest vegetation. There was a delicate fragrance like anise in the air.

Malama carried the box of ashes in her arms and started off among the bog pools. Marc and I followed, loaded with flower garlands, casting about with farsight and deepsight lest we sink into the muck. Almost immediately we came upon the cave, which was of a fair size, girt about with rampant, dripping greenery.

"You stay here," Malama told me sternly, "and keep your farsight under control." And then to Marc: "Boy, bring one lei strung with green berries and leaves—the mokihana and maile that belong to our island. And bring one other that you think your mother would have liked."

His face frozen, Marc took the modest green garland and another of white dendrobium orchids. The other flowers were left at the cave mouth. He followed the Hawaiian woman into the darkness, and dutifully, I did not spy. This remote spot wrapped in chill, sweet-smelling mist was not one I would have chosen as a last resting place, and somehow I found myself doubting that Teresa would approve of it, either. But neither Marc nor I had thought for a moment of going against the kahuna's command.

After less than ten minutes, the pair of them reappeared. We returned to the egg in silence and were back in sunny Poipu in short order. Dr. Kendall was already gone from the beach house, leaving only a curt note, and Malama disappeared almost as soon as we landed. Her husband Ola, an uncommunicative stocky fellow with grizzled, curly hair, showed us where we could dry out our clothes and then gave us a hearty lunch (which was actually supper for us New Englanders) of roast chicken, taro biscuits, a salad of corn, tomatoes, and watercress in spicy mayonnaise, and pineapple with sweet coconut sauce for dessert.

Marc said nothing during the meal. As we started back for the egg, he looked up with a grimace at the sky to the south, which was rapidly filling with black storm clouds.

"It's going to be pouring cats and dogs pretty soon," I said.

"Yeah." He talked to Air Traffic Control and got us a superexpress Vee all the way to Boston.

"You want to tell me what happened in the cave?" I asked.

But Marc had a question of his own. "Did Mama's will specify that Jack was to be cremated and interred with her?"

I had said nothing about that part of the will to Marc, and he'd shown no curiosity about the document up until now. But Teresa *had* left that instruction, as though she believed that the baby would soon join her in death, and I admitted it to Marc.

It was getting very dark outside, and a sudden blast of wind made the egg totter on its splayed landing pads. The environmental unit of the rhocraft was still working to counter the island heat and humidity that had filled its interior. Marc's face wore a sheen of perspiration and was illuminated eerily by the glow of the control-panel displays.

"Malama . . . In the cave, she said Mama tried to take Jack with her. As she died. She said Mama had used the anana, the kahuna death prayer."

"Mes couilles!" I scoffed. "That's complete bullshit."

"Malama said she was very disappointed in Teresa for doing that. She called Mama selfish and said she had committed a sin against huna that her Middle Self was now sorry for. She said—" He paused, gritting his teeth, then continued relentlessly. "She said Mama's soul was in purgatory, atoning for the sin, and her Low Self was still charged with mana and dangerous, and that's why her ashes would have to stay in Keaku Cave for the time being. So Jack wouldn't die now when he was especially vulnerable. Malama said Jack *wasn't* going to die. Do you think she could possibly be right, Uncle Rogi?"

I felt ice-cold ants creeping up my spine. We were getting into areas of metapsychology that science knew nothing about: the possible survival after death of malignant aspects of the personality, the "evil spirits" of legend . . . and maybe even things like Fury and Hydra. The egg rocked with another gust. Palm trees were flailing, and out to sea I could see a pitch-black wall getting closer and closer. I said, "What with your studies and the family hassles, you've been so busy during the past month that you haven't seen much of Ti-Jean. But I have, and I can tell you that Colette has just about lost hope for conquering his cancer through genetic engineering. On the other hand, the kid acts like he wants to live! He's always talking about integrating his three selves. And he still refuses painkillers, because he says they would interfere with some special 'work' he's doing. Would any of that matter worth a damn if he knew he was going to die in a few weeks?

Don't you think a mentality like Jack's would *know* if he was failing?"

"I think he'd know," Marc conceded. "And he would have surely said something during our daily farspeech skeds. I'm sorry I've been neglecting to visit him, but those media ghouls camped out around the hospital—"

"I'm sure he understands."

The rain came roaring up the rocky beach, obliterating everything behind it. In seconds we were in an imitation of the gray limbo again, only this time it wasn't hushed and mystical as it had been up above Mount Waialeale. A tumultuous din filled the egg's interior as the tropical downpour crashed down on us, hiding everything outside the egg from view.

"Malama knows about Fury, too," Marc said. "I'm supposed to be ... careful. And if Jack's ever in any *serious* trouble, we can call on her."

"Serious trouble?" I was incredulous. "How the hell much more trouble does the poor kid have to have? Trouble! Jesus! . . . She say anything about Hydra?"

"No. Malama is operant, of course. But in a funny way. Up in the cave, she seemed to think I'd been there before. Isn't that the stupidest damn thing?"

"No," said I abruptly. "The stupidest thing is us sitting here getting battered into the sand when we could be sailing home through the nice dry ionosphere. You want to get us out of here—or should *I* drive?"

He sighed and lit the rho-field, and for us, the rain stopped.

The very day after Marc and I returned from the islands, the media catastrophe that the family had long feared finally occurred. Jack's privacy was breached when an unfortunate nurse with financial problems sold the sensational details of his case, complete with videotapes taken while he was still comatose, to the highest bidder among the scandalmongering yellow networks of the Tri-D. There was a predictable furor among bleeding hearts and squeamish souls that even extended to the exotic races. The consensus of popular wisdom was that Teresa had been driven to take her life by the appalling and inhumane medical treatment that had prolonged the life of her doomed baby beyond any reasonable expectation of recovery. Paul, of course, was blamed. His political enemies could not use the scandal to attack him openly; but during the days immediately following the revelations, his authority was so seriously undermined that he actually offered to resign as First Magnate. This was vetoed by the Lylmik, who further astounded the Milieu by flatly prohibiting the university hospital authorities from discontinuing Jack's treatment or removing him from life support unless he himself requested it.

The sob sisters having been stymied and hospital security restored (the miscreant nurse was swiftly convicted of violating medical ethics and sentenced to a ten-year work tour on Valhall, the least attractive of the four cosmop planets), Paul took steps to refute charges that he had sentenced his helpless little son to cruel and unusual punishment. Colette Roy called in genetic specialists from the Krondaku, Poltroyan, and Simbiari races and had them study Jack's genome and compare their findings to those of the panel of human scientists who had already been consulted. The findings of both groups can be summarized as follows:

Jack suffered from certain unique genetic mutations. Among other things, these had triggered cancers that had largely destroyed his bones and many other vital body organs. His brain was untouched, however, thus far showing an ability to reject the cancer metastases. This could be attributed only to some redactive (i.e., mentally induced) activity on the part of the patient. In spite of the devouring cancers, the child's life could be sustained by using heroic medical techniques that might distress lay persons. Physicians and genetic specialists in charge of the case continued in their attempts to repair the faulty DNA triggering the malignancies. If this could be managed before the child's mental abilities were impaired, then he could look forward to having his body fully restored to health following the critical period when his brain's pituitary gland signaled the natural production of the important adult-body-growth and sex hormone testosterone—that is, at puberty. At that time Jack could safely endure the rigors of regeneration tank technology. The child himself, who had a personality with quasi-adult attributes, wanted to have the treatment continue in spite of its considerable "discomforts."

With the release of these findings on 12 February 2054, media interest in Jack's case simmered down, and the family was left in peace for the time being. It was not revealed to the public that Jack's physical condition had by then deteriorated to the point where he was reduced to little more than an artificially sustained brain. The new cancers had invaded his skull, the musculature and skin of his head, and the other remnants of his body, causing hideous deformity. The most hopelessly deteriorated organs were removed. He was blind and deaf now and deprived of all other sensations except pain. Nevertheless he communicated regularly with his visitors and operant attendants via telepathy and continued to insist that he was not yet ready to die.

[39]

HANOVER, NEW HAMPSHIRE, EARTH
13 FEBRUARY 2054

Marc had been afraid to visit Jack.

He admitted it to himself as he hesitated outside the door of his little brother's hospital room. He had faithfully farspoken the child every day since Jack had recovered from his coma, but he had carefully refrained from exerting farsight and had used the press of his studies and then the media donnybrook over Jack's condition as an excuse to stay away from Hitchcock.

But now Jack had asked him to come.

It was early Friday evening, and the Dartmouth Winter Carnival was in full swing. Marc was not planning to attend most of the festivities; but now that he was sixteen and legally an adult, he was finally eligible to enter the Junior Open Division of the ice-cycle races that would be held on the frozen Connecticut River the following night. He had a new bike, a Honda TXZ1700 that was a real chewer, and he intended to get in some practice after visiting Jack. He was already dressed in specially armored racing leathers, stitched up in a striking black-and-white pattern. He carried his CE helmet under his arm as he stood vacillating outside Jack's door.

Marco! Stop hanging around out there and come in.

Marc flinched. He opened the door and found a nurse on his way out. The man smiled wryly. "Your little brother just gave me the boot. He wants to talk to you in private. I'll be monitoring his vitals from my station."

There was more equipment in the room than there had been at the time of Marc's last visit, and the putrid smell of cancerous degeneration was stronger, in spite of the deodorizers. Standing just inside the door, Marc didn't see the little patient at all. A craven sense of relief flooded through him as he wondered whether the child might now be completely enclosed in the life-support unit. If so, it wouldn't be necessary to look at him.

But when Marc approached, he found that Jack's head was still visible. If it could be called a head.

At the sight of it, Marc began to weep for the first time in his life, overcome with pity and silent rage, his mind cursing God and his dead mother for having allowed such a thing to happen.

Stop being an asshole.

"Jack—"

God and Mama aren't responsible for the way I look. I am.

Marc dropped his helmet on the floor and fumbled with the velk fasteners of his gloves. He finally succeeded in tearing them off, and pulled paper tissues from a pocket above his knee and swabbed his face. "You don't know what the hell you're talking about!"

Of course I do. My body is doing what it was programmed to do. By the mutations. It would have done it even quicker if Colette hadn't tried to plug in new genes and if she and the others hadn't tried to fight the cancers. If I'd been left alone, my body would probably have dissolved a lot more tidily. Unfortunately, I didn't understand this until just recently.

"You're talking crazy!" Now Marc could not take his eyes from the monstrous thing that was his baby brother. The head was enclosed in a transparent container of liquid. A medusa tangle of tubes and wires sprouted from raw, formless flesh studded with ugly dark lesions. There were no eyes, no other features, nothing human remaining at all.

Jack said: I'm sane. I've spent quite a lot of time making sure of that. It was not always easy to ascertain . . . Please, Marc. Get a chair and sit beside me. If you like, I'll try to redact away your revulsion and sense of irrational guilt.

"Lea' me the hell alone," Marc muttered. But he obediently drew up a stool and perched on it, despising himself for having broken down and for blaming the poor dying baby for his own imbecility.

Jack said: I am doing my best not to die. There's a critical period coming up now. I must learn [indecipherable image] if I am to survive much longer, and I'm finding it very difficult. Things distract me. It was a terrible distraction when Mama died. I loved her very much. She should not have blamed herself for my special predicament. I tried to make that clear to her, but she refused to listen. In her own way, Mama was very strong, and this was both a good and a bad thing. I forgive her for what she tried to do to me, but it did make things much harder.

"You know about . . . what Malama Johnson did? With the ashes?"

Yes. Malama often comes to me in excorporeal excursion. Her actions and her words at Keaku Cave, you must understand, were symbolic and not to be taken literally. Her culture approaches metapsychology from a different point of view than ours and makes use of its own techniques. But her beliefs derive from an underlying truth. I *am* in considerable danger from malevolent entities that dwell in moral darkness, and so are you and Uncle Rogi.

"Mama's ghost?" Marc exclaimed, starting up from the stool with clenched fists. "That's—that's the most incredible *shit!*"

Marc. Be calm. You must help me, and I'll try to help you as much as I can. But please don't ignore what I'm about to tell you. Don't disassociate, or all of us may be lost! And then Fury will win.

"Fury . . ."

You've heard him in your dreams, haven't you.

"Yes." Marc dropped his head into his hands. His voice was muffled. "And sometimes, what he says makes a hell of a lot of sense. We don't belong in the goddam Milieu and—"

Marco, for God's sake shut up. Hydra's been doing it again. Killing.

Marc looked up, his face rigid with shock. "You're sure?"

Yes. I've been watching for it. Expecting it. Yesterday there were five suspicious disappearances of operants—all in different parts of New Hampshire and Vermont, all of them apparently taking place about the same time. Early in the evening. Two of the events were reported by PNN on the *2300 News*, and I pulled the other three out of the computer from police reports when I realized what might be happening.

"This is all the evidence you've got? Five disappearances?"

It's sufficient. It can't be coincidental. The odds are too great. Now listen to me. The fact that the five deaths were more or less simultaneous but separated in space confirms something I suspected about Hydra. Malama agrees with me, for what it's worth.

"What?"

Hydra has undergone a metamorphosis. That must have been why it was lying low for so many months. Before, it had to act in metaconcert to do its killing, because the five individual units were too weak to manage the draining of human lifeforce on their own. But now, if I've analyzed the situation correctly, they've matured. Each one of the five heads—the five individuals—can now kill an ordinary operant all by itself. Working in metaconcert, they can probably subdue someone who's masterclass. Or possibly even a Grand Master. This may be why Hydra has just killed. It might have fed to strengthen itself before attempting . . . something more difficult.

Marc's eyes were unfocused. He was shaking his head slowly, as if unable to assimilate what Jack was saying.

Jack said: I've combed the entire region with my seekersense, trying to search out anomalous auras, but I've found nothing. Papa and the other six members of the Remillard Dynasty were all in Concord last night at the time I made my search. There's no easy way to prove their guilt or innocence. I think we can safely assume that long-distance draining of operant lifeforce is impossible. The chakra killer must be in close proximity to the victim, probably even in physical contact, as Victor was. I've discovered that around the time the disappearances must have taken place, the seven Remillard magnates were all in their eggs or groundcars en route somewhere or other. With the speeds those vehicles are capable of, it's possible that any one of the siblings could be responsible for any or all of the disappearances. Of course, now Hydra will be careful to hide its victims' bodies. The truth behind these five new deaths may never come out.

"And you—you think it'll come after us? Hydra?"

If it knows we're on to it.

"If Fury's really been romping through my dreams and I haven't just been imagining things, then *he* knows."

If Fury knows, so must Hydra.

Marc swore briefly. He seemed to have recovered his normal mental equilibrium. "I can take care of myself, but what about you?"

I'll be all right. I'm well guarded here, and I'll have the security increased. From now on I'll forbid Papa and the others to visit me. They'll be glad to be spared the distressing experience . . . unless they're Hydra! But I'm still worried very much about you and Uncle Rogi.

"Shit! I forgot about him. Before I go out to practice with the bike, I'll go to the bookshop and warn him not to be alone with any of the

Dynasty. There isn't much else to be done. Dammit—if only there was a way we could guard our minds when we're asleep!"

It's ironic, Marco. You and Uncle Rogi are most vulnerable when you sleep, while I am weakest when I am awake! I have learned to withdraw into an impervious psychocreative shell when my Lower and Middle Selves disjoin and I am unconscious. Unfortunately, the program is not yet accessible to an operant of your stature. When you are somewhat more mature, I'll try to transmit it to you.

Marc only shook his head.

Jack said: No doubt someday an invincible mechanical mind-shield will be perfected, but this is no help to us now. You must sleep only in a securely locked room, and so must Uncle Rogi.

"Okay. Any other things you want me to do for you?"

Stop by the office of the nursing supervisor. Tell her there have been crank threats to kill me. To stop my so-called hopeless agony. Have the security of this room enhanced immediately. Tell her that the Remillard family will pay for special equipment and an operant guard and then arrange for it.

"Gotcha." Marc bent down to pick up his discarded gloves and helmet. His gray eyes beneath their dark winged brows now regarded the grotesque thing that was Jon Remillard with calm equanimity. All traces of his tears had vanished. "You watch me win the Junior Division in the ice-cycle races tomorrow. Hear me?"

I will, Marco. Good luck.

Marc stopped at Wally Van Zandt's station to top off the Honda with j-fuel, then drove across the street and parked in front of The Eloquent Page bookshop. Uncle Rogi was just getting ready to close. He had cut back on evening hours since his relationship with Perdita Manion had come to an end and she'd quit, and he looked up with a glum expression as the bell on the front door tinkled and Marc came in. "I thought the races were tomorrow," he remarked, assessing the boy's striking black-and-white apparel.

"They are. I just need to practice with the new bike. You remember, I gave the old one to Gordo McAllister. I've got to make sure the CE hat and this new Honda's on-board computer are communicating."

"I hate that damned helmet thing of yours. It's unnatural, plugging yourself into a machine. Becoming *part* of a machine!" The old man got up from his chair behind the register desk, stretched his lanky frame, and continued grumpily. "When I was young, driving a car or a motorcycle was supposed to give a guy a thrill of accomplishment. You were in control of the thing and all its horsepower, but it took a whole lot of skill and experience to be a really good driver."

"It's still true with the machine under cerebroenergetic control," Marc insisted.

Rogi only h'mphed. "Thinking like a bike? All that takes is a mechanical mind-set. How the hell can you get your adrenaline up when you just *operate?*"

"Trust me. It's possible."

"And how is it fair for you to race against drivers using manual control?"

"Well, for starters, I can't use my metafaculties or I'll be disqualified. So would other operant racers. We're being monitored. For seconds, a driver using CE isn't necessarily more competent than one controlling a machine in the usual way. That's why I can enter my bike in the Junior Open. Against a really experienced MX racer, I'm a babe in arms, and there'll be twenty-year-olds up against me who could eat me and the Honda for breakfast on a motocross track. But ice racing isn't dirt racing, so I figure I've got a good chance. You going to come out tomorrow and watch?"

"Damn tootin'. But God help you if you break your neck right before my eyes. I've had enough grief this week already, what with getting outbid on a Robinson-mint March 1952 *Planet Stories,* with Poul Anderson's "Captive of the Centaurianess" on the cover, and finding out that Perdita's going to marry some young twit in the college's Sociology Department."

"But you and Perdita were finished," Marc pointed out reasonably.

"Wouldn't expect *you* to understand," growled Rogi. He headed for the private door opening into the building's main interior stairway, which led to his third-floor apartment. The Maine Coon cat Marcel LaPlume, anticipating supper, emerged from some lurking spot among the bookshelves and trotted ahead of his master, nearly tripping Rogi up as the door opened. "See you tomorrow," the bookseller said to Marc. "Set the lock on your way out."

"Uncle Rogi, wait."

The old man turned around tiredly. "Well?"

"I was just visiting Jack. And he said—he *thinks* that Hydra's on the loose again."

Rogi uttered a Franco expletive, and when Marc explained the circumstances behind Jack's suspicions, Rogi's response was even more ingeniously obscene. "Go tell the Magistratum! Tell that superior prick Davy MacGregor! But don't tell me. I don't want to know."

Marc's voice was quiet. "Jack wants us to be careful. Not to be alone with Papa or any of the other members of the Dynasty, just in case. And to be especially careful when we're asleep. You should change the lock on your apartment door."

"What good would that do? Your Papa and your uncles and aunts are all PK wizards. They can pick any lock ever made. And if they're really part of Hydra—which I don't believe for a minute—they can zap me no matter what precautions I take. So I'm not going to do anything. I'm so sick of the whole business that I don't give a good goddam if Hydra and Fury both fly down the chimney and zorch me to Kundalini charcoal. I think poor Ti-Jean's imagining things, and if you had a whit of sense, you'd think so, too."

Marc stood glaring at the old man. "All right," he said at last. "Be a silly old coot! But will you at least stay sober until I can do some checking myself on these new operant disappearances? If Hydra really was responsible, Jack may need our help."

Rogi's martyred expression changed to one of apprehension. "Jack? You really think so?"

Completely exasperated, Marc headed for the outer door. "Just lay off the sauce for a few days, okay?"

Marcel meowed impatiently from the middle distance, and Rogi yelled, "Will you shut up? Is the whole goddam world out to bug me?"

"Take care, Uncle Rogi," Marc said, and went out to his waiting turbocycle.

The two-kilometer section of the river between the Wheelock Street Bridge and Girl Brook, where the race would be held, was flagged off-limits so that the surface wouldn't be too badly chopped up ahead of time, but the section just to the north was open to spike-bikers. It wasn't illuminated by portable lights as the racecourse was, and most of the other riders had put in their practice time during daylight. Day and night were immaterial to farseeing operants, though, and Marc found nearly a dozen other heads making the chips fly in the fairly straight part of the river between Girl Brook and the Rivercrest Bend. None of the other students in Junior Division steered with CE, but there were a few in Senior who used the technique. One of them, a graduate student who taught one of Marc's CE engineering courses, was working out when the boy arrived and farspoke a brief greeting.

An improvised slalom course had been marked with tall saplings hung with trail ribbon, and most of the riders were practicing on that, since jamming the in-and-outers would be the trickiest phase of the race. Marc gave the poles a few whirls, then worked on his fast turnarounds and jumps. The jumps weren't high, just a couple of meters. This amateur race had only one triple, but there were four doubles and ten bun-bouncers. Landing a spikester after taking to the air without nailing your bike to the ice or floundering in some other guy's slush crater took finesse, revving up both wheels just the right amount at the touch to prevent the big punch, then easing off so you wouldn't dig too deep a trench and go out of control. Marc knew that his jumps were his weakest maneuver so he worked on them for more than an hour, catching air above the iced-over heaps of snow bulldozed onto the ice until his shaken kidneys hollered for mercy.

Time for a single good long run flat-out, and then he'd pack it in. He rolled out of the practice area and cast upriver with his farsight, making sure he had a clean reach. There was only one other biker out there, and he was inbound at a moderate turn of speed. Marc tuned to the aura, and bedamned if it wasn't his fourteen-year-old cousin Gordo McAllister joyriding on the old BMW that Marc had made him a present of. He was in his final preppie semester at Brebeuf down in Old Concord and would be entering Dartmouth next fall. He must have come to Hanover for the Winter Carnival weekend. Most of the cousins tried not to miss it.

Hey Gordo!

. . . Yo Marc!

Been chewing up the river kiddo? How's the old Beemer handling?

Sweet&lovely but I sureashell wish I had a CE brainbucket like yours to goose her with.

Build your own mylad.

I'm trying . . . You wanna race?

No *way* I'm saving it for the real thing tomorrow just going out for a long run to make sure I didn't shake anything loose practicing hops.

[Disappointment.] Bet this goodole Beemer could take your Honda in the straightaway.

Probably. It's a road warrior. But this new bike of mine has the edge in agility and that's what wins ice-cycle races.

Gimme time Marco I'll be out there smokin' you.

Ha ha. Come out and watch tomorrow and find out how much you've got to learn babycakes! . . . And now watchit I'm coming right at you.

Eek. Be still myheart!

Marc flicked the Honda's headlight to high beam. No sense straining his farsight when he wanted to check out the bike's performance through the cerebroenergetic interface, which meant not only controlling the machine mentally but also simultaneously scrutinizing a mental projection of its system readouts. Full concentration was required.

He spooled up the turbos and then let the Honda charge into the white, shimmering night. In seconds he met Gordo and passed him in a cloud of flying ice crystals, and then he was completely alone on the frozen river. He flashed past two small islands, skirted the bigger one at the county line, tore around a bend, and roared beneath the two Thetford bridges. The Honda wound up to 195 kph on the unimpeded stretches and handled like a dream. The innards were go all the way, and the machine was as responsive as one of his own limbs, a perfect extension of his body.

Marc let himself relax. He cut the analysis and just let the bike howl. Above Orford there were almost no houses near the shore, and the surface of the ice was smooth. The moon came up, and he turned off his lights and sped up the broad white thoroughfare like a dark meteor trailing a silver glittering plume, throttling back just a tad when the great river began to meander in wide bends. He was the bike and the bike was him and the only thing that mattered was running in the moonlight, on and on and on . . .

He was dreaming.

No longer on the river, no longer on the machine. Elsewhere. In darkness shot with a billion colored stars above him and a black pit below. Paralyzing terror flooded his mind, and he tried to regain control of himself, to cancel the dreaming—tried tried tried—only to fail. Helpless! He was helpless. But it was only a dream, and soon he'd wake in his room in the fraternity house, and it would be morning—

Marc listen to me.

. . . Oh no! Oh Jesus! It was him it was him only THIS TIME IT WAS NOT A DREAM—

Marc.

GOD IT WAS REAL REAL *WHATDOYOUWANTWHO-AREYOULETGO—*

I want you Marc. You know perfectly well who I am. I'm Fury. The hope of the human race and the Remillard family. The only one who can save us all from eventual ruin abandonment enforced stagnation eternal imprisonment by the perfidious exotics who envy us and fear us because they know our potential is so much greater than theirs! Haven't you been listening when I spoke to you? Don't you agree that what I say makes sense?

No! . . . Yes. . . . I don't know. Go away! Let me alone!

I'm going to free us from exotic constraints that hold humanity back. Free us from the threat of so-called Unity! Do you know what Unity is Marc? It's a mind-homogenizing process that destroys in-dividuality among operants and makes them nothing more than cells in a single gigantic Overmind dominated by the Lylmik. Is that what you want for your race? for your family? for your *self?*

No.

Then help me destroy the Galactic Milieu and replace it with a confederation of worlds that is truly free. Work with me Marc. Open to me and let me show you—

Let you take control of me YOURSELF you fucker? *NO!* I know who you are you're Victor go to hell *go back to hell—*

I am not Victor.

Then who are you?!

[Hesitation.] I am Fury. I am born. Inevitably.

Who are you *really?* Are you my father? Are you part of a sick split personality? Tell me the truth if you really want me on your side!

I am Fury. I draw minds to me and enlighten and guide and reward the ones who are mine and the ones who oppose me perish in the most agonizing manner known in the present Reality. If you oppose me you will die this way.

Bullshit! You can't get at me unless I open to you and I never will. I know what kind of mind I have and so do you. I'm the best. The best ever born—

Jack is greater. But Jack is going to die. I don't want Jack I want *you*. Join me freely Marc trust me let me show you how to obtain everything your heart could possibly desire limitless power pleasure prestige I love you I can give it to you come with me come come come!

Fury . . . I almost think I *do* know you.

I burn for you! I've loved you so long needed you waited until the time you would be receptive you are so different from the others so free from venality from silly selfishness so noble in spirit so proud so clean so strong and still not yet mature oh Marc what you could be what I could help you to become . . . [Image.]

God—you really are insane.

No. This [image] can be you. You've dreamed of it! I've showed it to you! It's you Marc. More than human. An angelic being more powerful than the Lylmik unfettered by the tawdry limitations of flesh and blood [image] a being whose very essence is Mind. A Mental Man.

No! Get away from me! You're a liar a fucking conniving liar trying to trick me you don't even know who *you* really are and you think you can tell me who I can be? No dammit no!

If you will not join me I have only one choice. I will send my Hydra to kill you to suck your vital energies from one bodily font after another to drain you while inflicting the most excruciating torture as your body blackens and swells and bursts in the psychocreative flames—

"No!" Marc cried out loud. "No no no no—"

He seemed to see the dream image again, the luminous superhuman being that he himself had named Mental Man, the star-angel who shone immortal and transcendent over all humanity, paling the lesser stars, who would have one day lifted the human race to his own glorious level, making it perfect. Except . . . the angel was falling, plunging into the black pit, his glow dimming, until unending abyssal darkness engulfed him. And off among the little stars a black nebulous mass was glowing with birth-fire, in its heart five strangely colored lights coalescing, growing, becoming brighter, more powerful, sentient, sapient, imminent—

Marc awoke.

He was aboard the turbocycle, speeding through the night along a wide white frozen river. The velocity readout said he was traveling at 186.26 kph. The terrain display, blinking scarlet alarm in his mind, showed he was heading directly for one of the massive midriver concrete piers of the Route 302 bridge. His own eyes and his farsight confirmed it.

He screamed to the CE control to change vector.

The bike roared straight ahead. The pier was less than 100 meters away, and the Honda refused to respond to mental guidance. It was the same executive-circuit glitch he'd had earlier with the helmet, the malfunction he thought had been fixed—

Or was it? God! Had Alex been right after all about the helmet being tampered with?

He tried to cut off the CE input to the bike's onboard computer. Tried to revert to manual control. The Honda wouldn't respond.

The six-lane bridge loomed against the starry sky, golden strings of streetlamps along the roadway, ruby lights below marking the supporting legs. He was going to hit the right-hand pier in a few seconds unless—

As his mind kept trying in vain to override the CE system, he clawed at the quick-release helmet strap with both hands and tugged upward. He felt the needle electrodes tearing loose from his scalp, saw a blinding white flash, and knew the interface between his brain and the machine was finally broken. He grabbed hold of the handlebars again and used all his willpower and physical strength to wrench the bike to the left.

The helmet flew away, a black missile bounding over snow-covered ice. The turbocycle was in a flat skid, heading for the abutment on the western bank, the spiked wheels spewing chipped ice sky-high. He cut the throttle, englished the bike upright with his psychokinesis, got it straightened out, began noodging the brakes, slowed, slowed, and finally stopped.

He dismounted and immediately fell to his knees and vomited.

Redacting his guts into submission, he forced his body to stop shuddering, slowed his hammering heart and wheezing lungs. The cold air he'd gulped during his panic burned like fire for a few moments, and then he was all right. Apparently no one had seen the near disaster. His bike lights were still out, traffic on Route 302 was minimal, and the river towns flanking the bridge were sunk in late-evening winter torpor.

He got the Honda going again and drove slowly over toward the Vermont shore to retrieve his helmet. The wind froze his sweat-soaked scalp, and he hastened to envelop his head in a psychocreative bubble of warmth. No way was he going to put that frigging hard hat back on! He stowed it in the Honda's boot and followed his own track back to the bridge to see how close he'd come.

The life-saving skid began less than 20 centimeters from the rough concrete face of the pier.

Marc smiled his one-sided smile. He wouldn't be using the CE helmet again until he replaced the whole brainboard. Fury and Hydra would have to find a new way to get at him. But they weren't going to spoil his fun tomorrow. He'd drive the goddam race in manual, and he'd *still* win.

He revved the bike in neutral, settled into the saddle, then sped off down the river toward Hanover and the frat house.

[40]

HANOVER, NEW HAMPSHIRE, EARTH
14 FEBRUARY 2054

We *can* do it. I have a plan all worked out. [Image.]

> Hey
> not
> > bad!!
> > > IT STINKS. You know Fury was only trying to
> > > frighten Marc. He never intended to let us kill
> > > him.
> > > Probably not.
> > Worse luck.
> Fuck Marc. Fury's pet! He'd use Marc to supplant us
> faster than the speed of light if Marc ever turned.
> > Fat chance of that. The White Knight!
> > > Mr. Clean!

Will you LISTEN to me? We can put Marc down in spite
of what Fury thinks he wants.

> > > If we kill Marc against Fury's orders he'll kill *us*.

You are totally full of crap. Fury needs us! Without us he's
helpless! That's why we don't have to be afraid to carry out
this plan of mine. [Image.]

> I like it.
> > You know it really looks pretty good . . .
> > > Damn straight.
> > > > It would give us *away* you stupid shitheads!

Not if I fuzz my identity psychocreatively. Stay invisible
until I'm on the course. That way the witnesses would think
I was just one of the contestants in the big jam.

> > How about staying invisible while you nail Marc?
> > > Yeah! That way—

No go. I couldn't hack it. I need all my watts to do the job right under stress. Invisibility is too stressful . . . Look: I T-bone Marc. Perforate him with the spikes as the field swings around the big loop at the bottom of the course. Not too many spectators down there. A few referees maybe some media cameras. Marc's bound to be one of the leaders even without the CE hat so I just cut short across the U and POW! The Beemer outweighs his Honda by 50 kilos. I staple him to the ice.

> So you burgerize his flesh a little. They'll just put
> him in the regen-tank for a refit.

Not if his j-fuel burns. And melts the ice. And he goes into the hole. And dies down there underwater before the medics can reach him. No regen for deaders sweetheart!

> You are totally *batshit.*

It's our best chance to nail him. What do the rest of you think?

Looks good.

> I'm for it.

>> The rest of us could even help! Be on hand to make
>> sure the ice melts fast. Psychocreative blowtorching.

Hey ALL RIGHT!!

>> . . . How do you plan to get away?

See? I knew she'd come around.

> Ha

>> Ha

>>> Ha!

>>> . . . Well HOW damn you?

Fuzzing again. The ice surface down beyond the course is all torn up from the practice runs. They'll never think to follow my trail during the blowup but if the thought occurs to anybody later so what? Tracks all over the place. I go invisible after I take Marc out. Get some other bikes in a tangle and start the marshmallow roast. I coast away on PK and then come ashore at the old road by the gravel pit. Home free!

> I suppose it would work. If Fury wasn't
> eyeballing.

He'll be back near the finish line with the rest of the big
crowd if he's at the race at all. Just farseeing the lower end
of the track like all the top heads.
        You *think!* You *hope!*
    Picky
        picky
            picky!
                I'M ONLY THINKING OF US!
If Fury stops me he stops me. I eat a shit sandwich. Maybe
the rest of you do too. So what? He'll have to kiss and make
up sooner or later. Fury needs us I tell you! But a chance to
nail Marc in a perfectly *natural* manner like this comes along
once in a blue moon and we're fools not to take it.
            No. We can't do it.
        Oh yes we can!
            Yeah. You're outvoted.
                If you don't wanna play then belt up and stay out of
                the flak zone toodles.
Hold it! We all participate or I'm not putting my ass on the
line.
                . . . I suppose—oh all *right.*
        Truly
            excellent
        decision.
I'll be ready at 1400 hours in the woods down by Girl
Brook. See that the rest of you are there too.

    The amplified music of the Dartmouth Marching Band was playing
a jump-rock arrangement of the "Troika" from *Lieutenant Kijé.* The
crowd cheered as fifty-two ice-cycles rolled slowly around the 200-
meter-long oval that formed the beginning and the finish of the race.
The bikes were dangerous-looking things, with their glittering eight-
centimeter wheel spikes fully deployed and their colorfully attired
young drivers sitting as stiff in their saddles as knights promenading
before a tournament joust.
    Up in the bleachers, two young-old spectators settled into their
seats. Rogi grumbled to Denis that in the old days of the Winter
Carnival, an outré so-called sporting event like this one would never

have been allowed. And the only reason he was here today, Rogi added self-righteously, was to pray that that damn fool kid Marc wouldn't kill himself.

Denis only laughed. "The spike-bikes aren't quite as horrendous as they look, Uncle Rogi. The drivers have to be specially certified before they're allowed to race, and they're wearing what amounts to a suit of flexible armor. Ice-cycle racing has been going on in northern Europe for over seventy years. It's just taken a little longer to catch on over here. And it certainly has become one of the carnival's most popular events."

The temporary stands that had been erected along the eastern bank of the frozen Connecticut River were jammed with at least ten thousand people, and there were almost as many on the opposite side of the racecourse, camped out in informal mobs behind the bales of straw and the safety fence, wrapped in blankets and sleeping bags and electric comforters. The sky was a cloudless robin's-egg blue, the snowy landscape sparkled, the air was still, and the temperature was a brisk − 16 C. Vendors of hot food and drink were doing a roaring trade.

"A guy can still get torn to pieces if one of those damned machines rolls over him the wrong way," the old bookseller growled. "The last thing Marc needs is to float switch-off in a tank of goo for the next eight months growing a new arm and leg just for the sake of a few cheap thrills and a two-bit trophy."

The gargantuan viewscreen just south of the finish line, which would depict the remote action on the backstretch downriver, was flashing the names of the contestants and their racing accomplishments in alphabetical order. Raucous cheers and occasional catcalls greeted the stalwarts of the Senior Division, who occasionally responded with farspoken yells or epithets of their own. Most of the Juniors were given more decorous applause, but Rogi leapt to his feet and gave out an ear-splitting whistle when the screen announced:

[3 J] MARC REMILLARD—ROOKIE

He was rewarded with a wave from a black-and-white-clad figure near the procession's end.

Dropping back into his seat, Rogi was scowling. "Damn shame Paul couldn't find time to come. I don't notice the auras of any of the rest of the high-and-mighty Dynasty, either."

"There's a big vote coming up Monday in the Assembly," Denis said mildly. "Some of the magnates have pushed for the establishment of twenty new ethnic planets for the peoples of Africa and Asia just as soon as the probation period ends in the fall. The bill they want to put before the full Concilium would set aside the Milieu's usual requirement for twenty-percent operants among the founding population of human colonies. There's a lot of heat being generated and a lot of lobbying going on among the Assembly magnates, since each of them now carries a hundred-vote equivalency over the elected IAs."

"I say let the Chinks and the black folks have their planets," Rogi declared stoutly. "Anybody crazy enough to want to leave good old Earth and pioneer some godforsaken corner of the Galaxy deserves all the help they can get."

"That's just the problem, Uncle Rogi. Supporting colonies until they become self-sufficient and eventual economic assets to the Galactic confederation costs a lot of money. The Milieu's exotic races pay most of the tab, and they have a vested interest in promoting the increase of *operant* citizenry because of the way Unity works. Nonoperants aren't particularly desirable as planet colonists because they're less likely to be highly motivated to follow Milieu statutes and accept its operant-oriented policies. You might recall what a happy shock it was to us back in the early days of the Proctorship that the Human Polity was permitted to have *any* nonoperant colonists."

"Since I never considered shipping out, I never really paid much attention to it . . . Hey! The Juniors are heading for the starting line! And lookit there—Marc's got a position right in the front row. Hot damn!"

Denis's face wore a sly, boyish grin. "I thought you only came here to pray, tu vieux schnoque."

"Ferme ton clapet, ti-merdeux." Rogi surged up as the starting pistol fired and the brass section of the band brayed a discordant U.S. Cavalry "charge" call. "They're off!"

The eighteen riders of the Junior Division, whose post positions had already been determined by time trials held that morning, took off in a scream of turbines and a great smoky cloud of chipped ice. The portion of the outbound course in front of the bleachers featured a short slalom, a single jump, and then a longer slalom. All of the front-runners negotiated these obstacles successfully as the fans yelled and cheered. The rear guard was less lucky. On the second in-and-out, two of the riders collided and slid out of control into the straw bales. Unhurt, they remounted and continued on behind the others.

Once the bikes reached the part of the course beyond the bleachers, called the Long Stretch, the attention of most of the spectators shifted to the big screen and the announcer commenting on the distant action over the PA system. The operant fans having the ability to farsee were able to follow the racers with their mind's eye, but they tended to zero in on their favorites and ignore most of the rest of the field.

Rogi stayed with Marc. The boy was in a solid third-place position behind nonoperant Rusty Ragusa, an eighteen-year-old who was last season's Junior winner, and front-running Miko Kitei, a young female head who was also a rookie and had given the largely male Junior Division a nasty shock when she ranked first in the time trials. The three of them stayed neatly strung out as they took the next pair of single jumps and the first double. Then Marc began to overtake Rusty, and the two of them sailed side by side over the next pile. The fourth-place rider, Augie Schaumberg, then began to come up fast. The next jump was a tricky double humper made of a rather soft snow-ice mixture that Miko had already deeply scored with her spikes. Marc, Rusty, and Augie launched into it almost hip to hip—but Marc, on the outside right, had the misfortune of hitting Miko's trench. He slewed out, his skid throwing a tall rooster-tail of white, and when he regained control and started into the second slalom series he was a distant fourth, with the rest of the pack howling on his tail.

"Batège," moaned Rogi. "What a rotten piece of luck!"

"It's only the beginning of the race," Denis pointed out. He sipped his container of hot tea and watched the monitor screen, which was now focused on the very difficult triple jump marking the midway point of the Long Stretch. The triple was a frighteningly short distance from the last pole of the slalom, and Miko showed all her skill as she recovered swiftly from the final turn, gunned her bike until it shrieked—and took all three hills in a single soaring vault. The approving yells of the crowd changed to groans of dismay as she landed much too heavily and it seemed that her fishtailing machine would throw her as it veered wildly from side to side. The following drivers altered course to avoid colliding with her, and she managed to recover, but not before Rusty overtook her and seized the lead. Marc had to swerve far out of the way to avoid striking Augie, and this allowed another back-runner, Voli Kotewayo, to shoot past and join the leaders. Over the next sequence of single-single-double-single-single, Marc ran fifth, with Voli, Augie, Miko, and Rusty ahead of him. Two other up-comers were nipping at his heels, and if Marc faltered again he was likely to slip even farther behind.

In the last outbound slalom, Augie hit a pole. It was an automatic penalty, costing him his position, and he was forced to throttle back until both Voli and Marc passed him. Trapped in a cage of hard-chargers behind Marc, he was no longer a threat.

"Allons, allons-y!" Rogi yelled. "Go, Marc!"

Now only a double humper and two singles remained before the sharp turnaround loop at the bottom end of the course. Marc passed Voli on the double and overtook Miko coming off the second bouncer. Rusty, Marc, Miko, and Voli were tightly bunched as they began their controlled skids around the tight curve. Augie and five other racers rode in a close group less than four meters behind Voli. The entire gaggle of ten riders was sliding through different portions of the loop all at once, their spikes flinging up clouds of sparkling ice and their bike engines howling. The small crowd of spectators gathered around the loop was whooping and whistling and getting in the way of the squad of referees and the camera ops who were attempting to record the action for the big screen.

Rogi's imperfect farsight had lost track of Marc's snow-plastered form in the mêlée. He switched his attention to the monitor screen just in time to see that Marc had gained the lead at last, coming out of the big skid a full length ahead of Rusty.

Rogi was jumping up and down, cheering, when the disaster happened. An unidentifiable bike moved out of the pack and traveled at tremendous speed *across* the loop, apparently out of control, heading directly toward the pair of front-runners. The announcer shouted a futile warning. The spectators in the bleachers began to wail and scream. The bikers at the back of the pack who were just finishing the final jump and about to enter the loop either heard what was happening on their helmet intercoms or saw it with their ultrasenses and hastened to steer for the sidelines even as the referees began to wave the red torches.

The wild bike struck the front wheel of Marc's Honda, and both machines began to tumble. Rusty and Miko cut sharply left and snowplowed to a stop in the middle of the loop. There was a spurt of flame from the two machines in collision, and the shouting of the fans increased to a bedlam that even drowned out the amplified roaring of the engines. Other turbocycles were crashing, skidding, throwing their riders onto the ice. Referees with red torches darted about in the haze of smoke and icy powder. Rogi was on his feet, his eyes blind, his farsight fixed on the vision of what was taking place two kilometers up the river.

A tremendous blossom of orange and black blotted out the place where Marc and the other rider finally slid to a halt, entangled with their bikes. An instant later, the sound of the detonation reached the ears of the spectators in the stands. There was a beat of silent horror, and then the three aid cars and two fire engines that had been parked on the sidelines just beyond the bleachers went into action, tearing down the open shore corridor of the frozen river with their emergency lights flashing and sirens making a banshee din.

"No," Denis whispered, his farsenses disabled by emotion. "Oh, God, not that."

"I see him!" Rogi screamed. And he transmitted the vision to his stricken nephew—the wonderful, reassuring sight of a single tall young figure in scorched leather staggering and slipping away over half-melted ice from a flame-girt mass of twisted metal and plass and burning flesh and bone.

Marc! Rogi shouted, wept. *Marcareyouallright?*

Yes . . .

With tears streaming down his weathered face, Rogi caught up Denis in a crushing embrace of relief. "He's all right! Dieu merci, Marc's all right!"

A black column of smoke rose above the dark evergreens and leafless maples of Pine Park. People were running along the ice toward the accident scene. Denis stood motionless, his face white and his eyes gone hollow and lusterless. "We'd better get down there and see what we can do," he said. "But first let me farspeak Lucille and the others, so they won't worry. They may have been watching. The race was scheduled to be broadcast on ESN."

"And I'll tell Jack," Rogi added.

But when he farspoke the child in the hospital, Jack said that he already knew and that he had warned Marc to put on the brakes just in time to avoid being struck squarely in the body by the steel-spiked front wheel of the other turbocycle.

Rogi asked: Who was that other poor devil anyhow? There hasn't been any announcement.

Jack said: It was Gordon McAllister . . . Hydra.

Fury cursed. Fury howled like a demented thing. The imbeciles! The stupid fools! Because of their half-baked jealousy, one of their number was dead and the other four in mortal danger.

Oh, Hydra! You were Fivefold and Singular. You were approaching maturity. You were ready to begin the really important work, the elimination of opposing Magnates of the Concilium. Perhaps even ready to bring down Davy MacGregor, the Dirigent himself. And now the great scheme lies in ruins! There are only four of you, and those are shocked and diminished and moaning in fear behind mind-dikes of cowardice. Useless. Worse than that—liabilities! Liable to be found out, to be used as conduits.

Conduits to Fury.

Gordon McAllister's death would be adjudged a mysterious accident, a piece of adolescent insanity, perhaps envy-fueled. If he had simply attacked Marc and died, the danger would be remote. But Gordo had not died as himself. In the instant before he expired in fiery agony, he had shown his Hydra face—and one of the persons watching in horror had recognized him and would surely deduce the identity of the other four heads of the now whimpering, vitiated monster, knowing that Gordo had been the fifth.

This person, not Davy MacGregor, was now the Great Enemy. He would have to be killed as soon as possible, and the killing would not be easy.

The new enemy was not Marc, who had been too stunned to know who had hit him.

It was Jack.

The Great Enemy. The one Fury would have to kill himself.

[41]

HANOVER, NEW HAMPSHIRE, EARTH
15 FEBRUARY 2054

Marc slept, woke, and slept again. He knew he was not too seriously injured, knew that he was in the trauma unit of the big Dartmouth Medical Center at the southern edge of town, knew there was an urgent reason for him to stop sleeping, wake up, and take care of some important matter. He fell asleep again anyway.

And had the nightmare of the race again.

His dream bike was a fantastic futuristic machine with wheels as tall as his body and spikes a full 30 centimeters long. The other contestants were all adult humans or exotics, and the things they rode weren't ice-cycles at all but different kinds of clumsy armored vehicles bristling with weapons. At the starting gun of the race, Marc was off and away like a thunderbolt, leaving the freaks sucking smoked slush and blasting away at him futilely with their zappers while he laughed at them.

In the dream, Marc left the outdistanced hostile pack far behind. His two-wheeled juggernaut hissed and roared alone down a deserted, moonlit course with jumps as high as hills. Chomping up the ice as he approached each obstacle, he would rev the bike to the max and shoot into the dark sky at the crest like a rocket, trailing diamond crystals. When he landed he touched down feather-light and charging. The monster bike was under perfect mental control, for he wore his CE helmet. After taking an awesome triple-humper that was as high as Mount Washington, he reared back and pulled a triumphant wheelie and saw the whirling spikes flash above his head in the light of the moon, clean and sharp and deadly and ready for any opponent rash enough to threaten him for the lead.

The dream replayed itself each time he drifted back into sleep, and the frustrating climax of the race was always the same.

An old black BMW T99RT coming out of nowhere behind him, looking small and ridiculous, but still gaining on him steadily. The voice in the CE helmet circuitry warning him that the upcoming rider would beat him. Would win the race if he didn't—if he didn't—

At that point in the dream Marc's tall, invincible bike vanished. He was aboard his Honda again. The other rider, crouched low over the handlebars of the Beemer, drew closer, closer, until the Fury-voice was frantic and the spectators in the stands were going wild and the finish line was just ahead. The other bike came up beside him, its rider unarmored, wearing ordinary riding apparel, but enveloped in an impervious thought-screen. And now in the last seconds the rival was beginning to pull forward. Beginning to win. Would win, unless—

Fury shouted and Marc obeyed, wrenching his own bike viciously toward the enemy, smashing into him, riding over him, leaving him spinning, bleeding, torn hideously by the spikes, his face behind the helmet visor contorted in pain, incredulous, unable to believe what Marc had done.

The face. Somebody unfamiliar and familiar. Somebody Marc ought to know. Someone he couldn't recognize, *had to recognize* before he woke up and then slept again and the dream replayed forever . . .

"Marc. Can you hear me? Marc?"

He heard the voice, felt the gently coercive mental touch, opened his eyes. Saw the bronzed, high-cheekboned face of Tukwila Barnes, the longtime family friend who was now the Director of the Department of Metapsychology at the Ferrand Mental Science Center. It was Tucker who was prodding him awake, closing off the too tempting sleepway with its nightmare that still beckoned. Marc was aware of another operant, a woman in a white coat, who was doing something redactive to support Barnes. Marc knew her, too. It was Dr. Cecilia Ashe, Maurice's wife, his aunt. Marc gave up fighting against the pair of them. The dream faded, forgotten, and he remembered the other urgent matter and tried to struggle upright in the bed.

Tucker and Aunt Cele restrained him easily. "Whoa. Stay down. Give yourself a minute or two. Or three." Tucker was smiling, projecting vibes of relief. "We've got a few tubes and dinguses hooked onto you. Don't disturb them yet. If you're really coming out of it, we'll get you free in a little while."

Marc finally relaxed. Cecilia tossed an indecipherable telepathic query at Barnes and then hurried out of the room.

"Tucker?" Marc's voice was an anxious whisper. "What day is it?"

"The day after," said Barnes. "Sunday evening, 1840 hours, the fifteenth of February, Earth reckoning."

"Is Jack all right?"

The metapsychologist was thrown for a momentary loss by the question. "Jack . . . ? His condition is unchanged. Don't you care about yourself?"

Marc managed a small smile. "Okay, what kind of shape am I in?"

"You've got a few third-degree burns, a sprained left wrist, and a small subdural hematoma—a little blood clot on the brain caused by landing smack on the top of your head when you were thrown from your bike. Your hard hat absorbed most of the shock, and the clot will go away by itself. None of your injuries will keep you down for more than a week or so. You were in shock. Now you're out of it. You've got a tube up your nose giving you a little extra oxygen, and a couple of needles in your bad arm giving you sugar and water and stuff and monitoring your blood, and a catheter where you'd rather not have it collecting precious bodily fluids, and a batch of electrode bugs clinging to various other parts of your anatomy. Apart from that, you're in good condition."

Marc was levering himself upright again, and this time Barnes's coercion was impotent to stop him. "Tucker, I've got to get out of here. Got to go see Jack—"

The door to the hospital room opened. Paul came in, with Lucille and Denis and Cecilia Ashe. The woman doctor reacted swiftly to Marc's attempt to get out of bed. Her redaction did something unexpected to the motor area of his brain, and he dropped back onto his pillow as limp as a rag doll.

"Unless you want me to administer a sedative, young man, lie still!"

Marc glared at her. Then he quit fighting.

"That's better," Cecilia said. "Tucker and I will leave you to talk to your father and your grandparents for a few minutes if you promise to behave yourself."

Marc nodded.

Lucille opened her very large handbag and took out something that gleamed with a metallic luster. A trophy. "You won, Marc. The racing was halted for the day after the accident happened. Yours was the only trophy awarded." She set the thing on the convenience unit beside the bed.

Marc uttered a raspy little laugh and turned his head away.

"How are you feeling, son?" Paul asked. He and Denis and Lucille drew up chairs to the bedside.

"No pain I can't psych away," the boy said. The door closed behind Tucker and Cecilia. Marc's husky whisper fell nearly to the point of inaudibility. "He died, didn't he. Whoever he was . . ."

"Yes." Paul's face was expressionless. "It was your Cousin Gordon McAllister."

"Gordo!" Marc's mental screen thickened palpably. "Of course! I thought it was someone I knew. But it all happened so fast . . . God! Gordo! He must have been crazy. Poor Aunt Cat."

"Catherine's devastated," Paul said. "She said Gordon had been acting in a perfectly normal manner when she agreed to let him come up from Brebeuf for the Winter Carnival. He was staying at Phil and Aurelie's house with some of the other cousins, happy as a clam with your old bike, talking about entering the ice-cycle races himself someday. None of us can make any sense out of what happened. What Gordo thought he was doing. Whether it was some kind of idiotic prank, or whether—"

"He meant to kill me," Marc said.

Lucille gave a small cry.

"Are you certain?" Denis asked gravely.

"His intent was clear as glass, Grandpère. I didn't even know who he was when he came at me out of nowhere, but I sure as hell knew what he intended to do. Jack gave me a nanosecond's warning. I hit the brakes, and the Beemer's spikes rode over my front wheel instead of over me. The fire—I can't understand the fire. The fuel tanks of the bikes are safety-lined. They almost never burn in a crash. Poor old Gordo." Bespeaking Denis on his intimate mode, the boy added: *Was it quick?*

Denis said: *No. But Uncle Rogi and I lied to your Grandmother and Aunt Catherine about that, and you keep quiet.*

Okay.

Lucille rose from her chair. "We mustn't excite you any more, dear. Is there anything we can do for you now?"

"No, Grandmère. Thanks."

Paul said, "Now that I'm certain you're going to be all right, I'll have to get back to Concord. There's an important vote on Monday."

Marc lay quiet, his eyes fixed on the ceiling. "It's okay, Papa. I understand."

"I'll farspeak you from time to time," Paul continued. He touched Marc's unbandaged right hand. "Especially if there's any fresh news about the . . . accident. The police will want to question you about it tomorrow, when you're feeling better."

"What—what should I say?"

"Tell the truth," Denis said.

Paul nodded his agreement. "The truth, but no speculation. Your Uncle Sevvy is coercively redacting all the cousins who had any contact with Gordon over the past few days. If he finds out anything concrete about Gordon's motives, he'll pass it on to the authorities. It would be better if you stuck to the facts."

"All right."

Lucille bent down and kissed Marc on the forehead. She had on her favorite perfume, which Marc recalled had the incongruous name of Poison.

"Pray for poor Gordo, dear," she said softly. "And for Aunt Cat and the other McAllister children."

Marc only blinked. Denis lifted one hand in farewell, his compelling blue eyes downcast and his feelings veiled. Then the three of them were gone.

Cecilia came back with a nurse. They removed the intravenous equipment and the oxygen tube and the catheter, but left the bugs. Then the nurse left and Cecilia said that he would be served a small supper. After that, he could either listen to calming music or watch something fairly quiet on the private room's Tri-D for a little while. "But rest is what you really need now," she concluded. "Your self-redaction will probably heal the blood clot first, and then the burns, and the sprain and the bruises last. It works most efficiently when you're asleep. A nurse will be in to give you a sedative around 2030."

"No!" Marc protested. "I don't want to be knocked out."

"If you fall asleep normally, I'll forgo the downer," Cecilia conceded, "but it's important that you relax and don't get excited. You did suffer from severe shock in addition to your injuries. You'll find that your metafaculties are weakened and uncoordinated. Don't be concerned about that. Things will sort themselves out in a couple of days."

At last she left. Marc continued to stare at the ceiling for a while, thinking furiously. Then there was a soft chime from the bedside convenience unit, and a tray with hot food slid out on a jointed arm. It smelled like some kind of bland invalid's slop, but he decided he was starving to death. He maneuvered the bed up into a semisitting position and began investigating the covered dishes. Broth with a few bits of pasta. Some kind of custard, buttered toast, a small glass of milk. Yecch.

As he ate it, he farspoke Uncle Rogi:

You listening?

Tonnere! . . . You're back among the living, are you?

So they say. They also say it was Gordo.

Yes. Incredible. Totally—completely—horribly—incroyable. But true. It was GordorottenGordo never liked the little creep.

Uncle Rogi! Damn you, are you plastered?

No. Only a nice glow on.

Shit!

That's not nice. Not a nice thing to say. Especially when we were worried sick about you, ti-gars.

I'm all right. And I've figured something out about Hydra.

Gordo was Hydra. Jack said so. Damned Gordo. Never liked him.

It fits that Hydra should be one of the cousins. Gordo was in the right place at the right time to do the different killings, and he was also out on the river the night before last when I very nearly got creamed myself.

?! You *what—*

Fury got to me through the CE helmet. The cerebroenergetic interface is a perfect bypass of operant mind-screening. It never occurred to me that it could be dangerous. Fury, or possibly Hydra, tried to force me to crash the bike into the Woodsville Bridge while I was practicing for the race.

Jésus. And when that didn't work . . . he came after you *during* the race?

Uncle Rogi, that's not the worst of it. Hydra isn't one mind. Jack tried to tell us that when Addie died, and he tried to tell me again later on. But I didn't want to believe it. Now I think I've finally got the straights of it: Hydra is five minds. Five minds that were somehow touched by Victor when they were very vulnerable. When they were unborn. Five women were pregnant at Victor's death-bed in 2040—Cecilia, Severin's ex Maeve O'Neill, Cat, Cheri, and Mama. The children that were born later that year are Celine, Quint, Gordo, Parni—and my sister Maddy.

Non! Ça, c'n'est pas possible! Five innocent little chil-dren?! Le bon dieu, he doesn't allow such things to happen!

Uncle Rogi, Gordo wasn't innocent.

. . . Who's *Fury*, then?

I have no idea. If he really did invade my dreams, bespeak me there on the river before trying to have me killed, then I think he must be an adult. The mind-tone in my dream was mature. Very cold, very goal-oriented. Fury could be one of the Remillard Dynasty, someone who hates the Galactic Milieu, who's conceived some mad scheme to destroy it by killing off key human operants and subverting others to his cause. Fury wanted to recruit me—and, dammit, I was tempted!

No. It's obscene! Diabolical! What can we do? Who can we trust? OhGodohGod—

MacGregor is the only one who'd believe us without wasting a lot of time. Where are you?

I'm at the bookstore. Inventorying.

Drinking yourself blind, you mean! You're going to have to sober up and go down to Concord and see the Dirigent in person—and do it right now.

Can't . . . Chrissake it's supposed to storm like hell tonight, and I'm tight as a tick.

Dammit, I *warned* you! Never mind. Forget it. I'm not thinking too good myself. It's better if I farspeak Mac-Gregor and persuade him to have the four kids picked up, and *you* go and stay with Jack. You're not too far gone to

make it up to Hitchcock, are you? Or do I have to break out
of this hospital myself and—

No no no . . . I can do that. Merde alors, I can drive to
Hitchcock in my sleep.

No you don't! You stay awake! Make sure the security
around Jack's room isn't relaxed for a minute. I've got a
feeling he's in danger. Find a way to keep Papa and the rest
of the Dynasty away from him until the Hydras are in
custody and they tell us who Fury is.

Ti-Jean . . . ce pauvre petit. He knew Hydra was Gordo.
Told me so. But Jack's safe. I went to the hospital this
morning. They wouldn't let me in to see him. Armed operant security guard outside his door and a sigma-field and
alarm doohickeys all over the place.

Go to him anyhow. Make certain he's all right tonight.
Stay there with the guard. Please, Uncle Rogi!

All right all right. Just make sure you do *your* thing. Get
MacGregor to sic the Magistratum on those four damned
kids!

Yes. I'm going to do it right now.

Cecilia Ashe opened the door of Marc's room and entered, followed
by the nurse. The doctor's face was stiff with disapproval. "Marc,
didn't I emphasize how important it was for you to be quiet?
Your body bugs just set off nearly every alarm in the nurse's station
outside."

She was at his bedside in four rapid strides. Pushing aside the
robotic food tray, she took hold of Marc's good arm, whipped out a
transdermal infuser she had held concealed behind her back, and
applied it to Marc's neck. There was a hiss of compressed gas. A
microstream of powerful sedative entered Marc's left carotid artery.
The nurse helped to hold him down as he writhed.

"No!" Marc cried. "I've got to talk to Davy MacGregor! Please,
Aunt Cele . . . it's vital that . . . I farspeak . . ."

He sagged back, unconscious.

Dr. Ashe sighed. "Adolescents. And to think I believed this one was sensible! I might have known that any boy who raced those infernal ice machines was just a mite flakoid."

The nurse was sponging off Marc's brow and settling him in. "None of the body monitors was displaced, Doctor. Will you want the IVs and the catheter replaced?"

"I don't think so. We'll just let him sleep. He's a healthy young specimen and he's pretty well out of the woods. Let me know at once if there's any change, but unless I miss my guess, he'll probably sleep like a babe for ten hours."

A second nurse stuck her head in through the open door. "Dr. Ashe, your daughter Celine is on the teleview."

"Tell her I'll be right there," Cecilia said. She surveyed Marc one final time, shook her head, and said, "Pleasant dreams." The two women left the room and closed the door.

Marc groaned. With infinite slowness, his eyelids opened. The widely dilated pupils contracted even more slowly, and the eyes remained glazed and unblinking. Marc's breathing was slow and regular, and his heartbeat maintained a steady rhythm. After an interval, the boy's uninjured arm crept out from beneath the covers and moved toward his head. He touched a flattened lozenge-shaped thing clinging to his right temple. Awareness flickered in the gray eyes. His tongue stole out and moistened first his upper lip, then the lower. The questing hand moved with increasing confidence over his body, touching and counting the lozenges. There were seven all told, and their data-gathering mechanism was susceptible to looping. Slowly, one after another, Marc exerted his creative metafunction on the bugs so that they would continue to transmit repeated segments of unchanging data to the vital-signs monitor at the nursing station down the corridor. The nurses might notice the unnatural patterns if they paid close attention, but he was banking on their having set the machine's alarms to go off only at some gross abnormality.

When he was satisfied that he had executed the bug modifications correctly, Marc hauled himself into a sitting position, peeled off the small devices, and put them on his pillow. The drug was being rapidly metabolized by his redaction, but it still depressed his motor functions. He swung his legs to the floor with great effort, wincing a little from the pain of the burns on his left thigh. Gordo's spikes must have nailed him there after all, puncturing his armor.

He sat still for some time, cradling his sprained left wrist and burned hand, concentrating on husbanding his depleted mental energies. Then he exerted his farspeech, aiming the weakened thought-beam with as much precision as he could summon, attempting to bespeak Davy MacGregor in Earth's capital.

Concord was only 86 kilometers away. Nevertheless, there was no answering thought from the Dirigent.

Marc leaned across the bed to the convenience unit. A wave of nausea swept through his guts, and a sharp pain stabbed at the top of his head. He cursed silently and waited motionless until he was sure that he would not faint. Then he picked up the simple telephone handset, got the number of the Dirigent's office from information, and called it up.

The functionary who answered the 24-hour landline told him that MacGregor was en route to Concilium Orb. He could be reached by subspace communicator if the message was extremely urgent.

"How . . . long would that take?" Marc asked.

"You'll have to give me your message in its entirety. Then its relative importance and your own status will be evaluated by this office, and if a sufficiently high priority is confirmed, the message will be delivered within the hour. The Dirigent makes every effort to be accessible to all citizens, but you do understand that certain protocols must be observed."

"Yes . . ." Marc's head was spinning. If he gave his name, would they check back with Paul? No. He was legally an adult now. But this evaluation garbage— God! If he could only think straight . . .

"Citizen? Are you there? Do you wish to give me your name and message?"

"I—I'll get back to you," Marc said, and hung up the phone.

Jack, he called. *Jacko can you hear me?*

There was no response. Was his farspeech functioning at all? Again he paused, trying to muster up metapsychic strength. Redact the head pain, the nausea, the damned drug poisoning his nerves, the sweat breaking out on his forehead and chest. Bolster the motor function. Muscles—move!

He stood up. Exerted deepsight and farsight, breathed a brief prayer of thanks that they seemed to work.

There was a closet, and in it a robe and slippers. Outside in the corridor, two nurses were conversing at the station. Both were normals. There was no sign of Cecilia Ashe or Tukwila Barnes or any other operant.

Marc wondered if his coercion would function well enough to get him past the nurses and downstairs. If he would be able to overpower some poor devil and coerce his clothes and car away from him. If he would be able to drive back into Hanover to the old hospital where Jack was and make certain for himself that his little brother was safe. Uncle Rogi, that sozzled old fool, couldn't be trusted.

I have to do it, Marc told himself. I have to!

Very carefully, he began putting on the robe.

Rogi had started out working on inventory, it being Sunday night and the bookshop closed. He'd come down from his apartment in his moccasins after supper, leaving Marcel behind so he'd get a little peace. Then he had an attack of the horrors, seeing that damned ball of flame in his mind's eye again. There was a fresh bottle of Wild Turkey in the filing cabinet, and one thing had led to another.

Now, more groggy than panicked after Marc's mental communiqué, he had to go back upstairs to put on his boots and outdoor clothes before driving over to the hospital to Jack. He cursed Marc as he tied the boot laces with shaking fingers. Batège! Jack was safe as houses with the new security in place. MaxSec didn't have any masterclass heads on its payroll, but the operant rent-a-cop outside Jack's door would be able to hear if the child called for help telepathically. The hospital room was fenced with force-fields as well as mechanical and electronic alarms that would alert the Hancock police if anything should happen to the guard. What the hell good would it do for *him* to hang around the hospital all night?

But he'd promised Marc that he would go, and so he would.

Rogi made sure his heavy gloves were in the pocket of his parka. He saw through the bedroom window that it was beginning to snow again, and threw a bitter thought at Marcel, who was sound asleep in a warm nest in the middle of the down comforter on Rogi's king-sized bed. Checking to be sure he had his keys, the bookseller stumbled out the door and down the two flights of stairs.

Jack, he farspoke. *I'm coming to be with you boy! Marc thinks there's danger. Tell the guard at the door not to let anyone at all in not even nurses or doctors until I get there.* DO YOU HEAR ME TI-JEAN?

Nothing. The poor little guy was probably asleep.

His breath coming in harsh gasps, the old man emerged from the Main Street entrance to the old Gates Building. The garage was around the corner, attached to a little annex that housed an insurance agency. There were a few cars creeping along Main Street, but no pedestrians. Wally Van Zandt's energy station was closed and so was everything else in sight. The snow sifted down more thickly with every passing moment. The forecast had predicted an additional 15 cents by morning.

Rogi fumbled with the old-fashioned brass key to open the side door of the garage. He had a zapper in the groundcar to operate the overhead, but he'd balked at installing a modern electronic lock on the other door. The old Schlage was perfectly good for another century or two. Besides, crime was almost nonexistent in Hanover.

He got the door open at last and cast about gingerly within the dark garage with his farsight. The inside light had been broken for months. He was trembling a little and cursed himself for a cowardly old fool afraid of bogeymen. But in his semi-spifflicated and confused mental state Rogi half remembered looking into another dark space and seeing there the hideous sight of Shannon O'Connor Tremblay in the arms of Victor—the pair of them shimmering in a violet-blue aura as the monster drained her life from her. And Vic grinning as he raised his face from the last font of vital energy, at the base of her spine.

Victor had discarded Shannon's pitiable husk and taken control of *him.* Controlled him like a marionette until sheer chance had allowed him to escape. And then caught him again, down beneath the chalet with the storm winds shrieking and the mountain quaking—

Slowly he shuffled into the dark garage, and then gave a terrified squawk as he tripped over Marcel's old cat carrier, which he'd been meaning to clean out someday and donate to the next church rummage sale. Connard! Forgot to scan below his knees. If the monsters *had* been waiting, they could have cut him off at the ankles! . . . But enough of this foolishness. Into the car.

"Uncle Rogi? Are you in there?"

He gasped and gave a great start and spun around, and then almost gibbered in relief as he saw that it was only a girl silhouetted against the lamplit snowfall outside the garage. She had on a red skisuit.

"Uncle Rogi, it's Madeleine. I'm so glad I found you!" Her voice was tremulous. "Can you come down the street to the house? Something seems to have happened to Jacqui, and Herta's still at the movies with Marie!"

He stood with one hand on the groundcar's doorlatch, his mouth hanging open stupidly. Something happened to the housekeeper? Madeleine and young Luc home alone? If only he could think straight . . .

"Uncle Rogi, come on! Please!"

"Yes, of course. I'm coming."

"Hurry!" She was off, running ahead, and he groaned as he slogged along in her wake. It was a block and a half to Paul's house, across Currier Place, past the darkened library. Madeleine was almost there. Rogi was surprised to see an egg parked in the side driveway. Not Paul's silver Maserati, though. Who had a red rhocraft this year? Wasn't it Anne? And hadn't Maddy said she and Luc were home alone?

She was on the porch, and the front door was opening, and another teenage girl was there. Which cousin was it? Liane? Michelle? The half-screened auras of the adolescents made them scan all alike.

"Come quick, Uncle Rogi!" the second girl exclaimed.

Muttering under his breath, feeling very nearly sober again, he stumped up the snowy steps. Madeleine held the door open. He saw other youngsters inside, their minds emanating anxiety and fear. Saw a stocky adult form clad in slacks and a red sweater lying on the floor of the hallway behind the children.

Saw that the four young people waiting for him inside were Maddy, Celine, Quint, and Parni.

Remembered.

Rogi stopped. Eyes bulging, mouth open but incapable of utterance, he took hold of one of the porch trellis posts to steady himself.

"Quick!" one of the children said. "Jacqui doesn't seem to be breathing. Come in."

Rogi slowly shook his head.

"If you don't," Madeleine said, "we'll have to bring you in."

Her coercion reached for him, and so did that of the three others. But the Hydra metaconcert was a shaky one, for they were frightened, too. He slammed down his mental barrier and they lost their grip.

Closing his eyes against the horror of them, his mind screaming first for Marc, then for Jack, then finally for the Family Ghost, Rogi tore off one glove with his teeth and dug his bare hand beneath his parka into his pants pocket. The Hydra metaconcert was reorganizing itself, trying to make four as efficient as five had been.

"No, you don't, damn you!" he cried aloud.

He pulled a jingling little bundle free of the pocket fabric. With his eyes still tightly shut, he held high the key ring with the fob that looked like a red glass marble in a silvery cage. The fob that the kids had always jokingly referred to as the Great Carbuncle. The fob that the Family Ghost had given him, that had miraculously flashed and called down the Intervention—

Even behind his eyelids, Rogi saw the sudden blaze of light, heard the young voices and minds scream and then suddenly cut off.

He stood beside his groundcar, in the garage.

East South Street was quiet in the heavily falling snow.

"Sacré nom de nom, am I dreaming?"

There were keys in his hand. One glove was missing. He clawed open the car door, fell into the seat, started the vehicle, backed out onto the snow-covered pavement. For some reason, the melting grids had not yet been turned on. Probably the damned sensors were on the fritz again. It was always happening on the side streets—

There was a sound like a clap of thunder. Stunned, he stared in the direction of Paul's house. Not thunder, not an explosion—a sonic boom. A rhocraft taking off at illegal velocity, vanishing into the swirling whiteness in a split second.

Marc! Jack! They're getting away!

There was no farspoken reply.

Rogi called telepathically again, then gave it up with a curse of despair. Were both of them asleep? What should he do? There was no phone in the old Volvo, and his farsenses were too befuddled to follow the soaring egg more than a few hundred meters into the air. He couldn't make out the registration.

To hell with the little bastards! It was Jack who needed him. He gunned the car foolishly, making the wheels spin, nearly hitting a small tree. Then he regained control of the vehicle and himself and set off down Main Street as fast as he could go. He mind-called Jack's name every few minutes, growing more and more agitated when there was no reply, even though he knew very well that the child was locked in an impregnable mental refuge when he slept.

Rogi skirted the Green, went north on College Street past the Old Row and Rollins Chapel, past Steele Hall. He was almost there now. Just turn onto Maynard and into the old hospital parking lot. The streets were heated here and the pavement steaming. The snow and the steam intermingled and the streetlights gleamed fuzzy yellow and Rogi's car headlights made two white cones and the scattered lighted windows of the hospital were bluish-green and pale gold except for the one window that shone as red-orange as a setting sun.

Rogi stood beside his car, staring at that window dumfounded.

Another car swung around the corner onto Maynard, screeched up to him. The window hissed down, and he was amazed to hear Marc's voice shouting at him.

"Get in! No time to walk! We'll go to the emergency entrance!"

Then Rogi heard the approaching fire engines.

[42]

FROM THE MEMOIRS
OF ROGATIEN REMILLARD

The security guard had looked up from his book-plaque alertly as the elevator door opened, but then he relaxed, for he recognized the distinguished person who emerged and came up to him with an anxious expression, exuding vibes of authority and irresistible coercion.

"Dr. Colette Roy is on her way up. There's an abnormal readout showing on Jack's EEG monitor. He could be in serious trouble. Quickly, man! Open the door!"

It never occurred to the guard to refuse . . . even though he readily admitted afterward that he had been given specific orders to admit no one except the private-duty nurse and the night supervisor—most specifically no member of the Remillard family. The person must have coerced him, he declared.

Even when he was rigorously interrogated later by forensic redactors, the guard could not recall who that person was. His memories had been wiped blank. He did not even remember what happened after he deactivated the alarms and opened the door. Marc and I and the firefighters found him lying unconscious beside his chair in the hall, two bewildered nurses and a young physician attempting to revive him.

Jack's door was once again locked, and the medical personnel were unable to override the security system. They insisted to us that the young patient was perfectly all right, since the monitors at the nearby station showed no problem.

I grabbed the young doctor's hand and slammed it flat against the door. "Feel that, you blithering idiot!"

The man yelped. "Damn! That's hot!"

"Break the door down!" Marc cried. "The room's on fire, and the oxygen line is feeding it! My little brother's in there!"

The Fire Chief was examining the guard's elaborate control box, a thing the size of a small file cabinet. "According to this, there's a sigma-field laced through the walls and floor and ceiling and door. We'll have to cut it off before we can get in. And the door lock's time-set for two hours from now. Shit! It's probably cerametal, too. You guys bring in the heavy-duty laser blade and the rest of the gear. I'll get on the horn to MaxSec for the sigma override code."

Marc and I stared at each other in numb despair as the Chief began speaking urgently into the tiny boom mike of his helmet communicator. A room full of smoke and flame—and Jack's life being sustained by the most delicate kind of apparatus. He had probably perished almost as soon as the fire started.

The Chief began prodding the keypads of the control box, following the instructions being relayed from the security company headquarters. Something lit up green, and he said: "Field's off! Hit the lock!"

Clumsy in their protective garb, the firefighters shouldered us and the doctor and nurses aside and began trying to cut into the door with a dazzling yellow photon beam. I heard the hospital fire alarm go off belatedly, and the doctor and one nurse dashed off to do whatever they were supposed to do. The other nurse led the stupefied security man away.

"You called the fire department?" I asked Marc.

He nodded grimly. "I was finally able to scan Jack's room with my farsight when I was three blocks away, and I saw the flames. There was a phone in the car I stole."

Marc and I were forced to withdraw a short distance down the hall as the firefighters brought up still another piece of apparatus to attack the lock. The security company had done a very good job making Jack's hospital room unassailable. At that moment the ceiling sprinklers in the hall turned on, and I was vaguely aware of patients being efficiently evacuated. I remembered there were not too many housed in this wing, which was devoted to experimental forms of care. Somebody tried to force us to retreat, but Marc stonewalled him with his coercion and we huddled miserably together as the water sprayed down onto our heads and little gouts of molten metal popped here and there from the cutting torch like miniature meteors.

Progress was evidently being made. A technician wielding some kind of gargantuan drill had taken the place of the laser operator, attacking not the lock but the doorframe adjacent to it. Five firefighters hovered behind him, readying a hose and various kinds of nontoxic extinguishing chemicals. As the drill shrieked, the lights in the corridor suddenly went out. The firefighters switched on portable lanterns. The racket around us was numbing.

I had no idea what was going on behind that all-but-impervious door. I didn't want to know. My own farsight was worthless. Tears were pouring down my face along with the deluge from the sprinklers and I blubbered incoherently. Marc was silent at my side, his face pale as chalk and his eyes dark-circled. He had on a worn down coat and a pair of work boots without socks. He seemed to be wearing nothing but a bathrobe underneath.

The Fire Chief gave a triumphant shout, and the man with the drill stepped back. The Chief put something into the hole in the doorframe, stepped back, and punched a small hand-held keypad. There was a dull *whump!* followed by a little puff of smoke. The door now opened when the Chief kicked it with one booted foot.

A spurt of flame and a great cloud of dark smoke rolled out. The firefighters pressed forward, plying their hoses and chemical canisters. There were shouts. More firefighters hauled a smoke evacuator up, thrust its intake nozzle into the room, and switched it on. Marc and I crouched on the floor under the meager shelter of my sodden parka, coughing.

So this is the way it ends, I thought. The greatest mind the human race has ever known, kept alive against all odds by the best modern medical technology, perishing ignominiously in a fire, one of the most ancient of disasters. Had the four Hydras done it? At the time I thought so; but later, of course, the culprit was proved to be Fury. Unknown Fury, who had psychocreatively fuzzed his image so that even the room cameras had transmitted no identifiable picture to the security company, although the tapes showed how the fire had been started.

Fury had used the simplest kind of incendiary device: a glass bottle filled with flammable j-fuel, fitted with a wick. The oxygen line leading into Jack's life-support unit had been torn out, the blazing bottle smashed on the floor, and the door quickly slammed as the culprit fled. Meanwhile, the brilliant brain wrapped in rotting flesh had slept on oblivious, knowing himself to be safe from mental attack behind his own powerful mind-barriers, safe from physical attack inside an array of expensive security equipment.

Without the added oxygen, the fire might have burned itself out harmlessly in a few minutes. With oxygen to feed it, it had roared into an inferno, searing and melting the delicate and ingenious mechanisms that supported the last remnants of living tissue in which Jack's mind resided.

The Chief yelled something.

The ceiling sprinklers shut off, and so did the hoses held by the firefighters. No more smoke came from within the ruined sickroom. The Chief shone his lantern into the darkness. Suddenly Marc's lethargy fell away. He was on his feet, shoving the astonished man aside, stumbling into the sodden, charred mess.

I was behind him.

The window was broken, and snow blew in. Water dripped from the ceiling and pooled on the littered floor. Cooling metal ticked, and the wind moaned softly. The lantern light behind Marc and me dimly illuminated a scene of steaming chaos—twisted and blackened remnants of furniture, collapsed equipment cabinets, the ruined hulk of the life-support unit that had occupied the center of the room. There was a charcoal smell and a sharp chemical stench of melted plass. For the merest instant, as a fresh gust of icy wind blew in, I imagined that I smelled something else—something incongruously sweet, almost like Pernod or licorice or anise. I was weeping like a baby and could barely see, but memory told me that I had known that fragrance last on a misty plateau high above a tropical island, and in my dazed misery I had fleet recollections of Teresa: alive and embracing her newborn son in a snowbound cabin . . . lying still and cold in her bed . . . smiling at me from amid garlands of ferns and flowers.

Marc now stood just inside the door, with me and the firefighters pressing behind him. He grabbed one of the lanterns and swept the light about the large room.

We saw lingering wisps of steam laced with snowflakes. Contorted pieces of burned equipment like incinerated bones. Some fragments of pale, fragile ashy substance that reminded me for a second of the little white roses Jack had fashioned at Christmas with his creative metafaculty . . .

Psychocreativity.

He was so very good at that.

The lantern beam moved far to one side, to the dark corner at the left of the door. Both Marc and I saw him, and both of us cried out.

A man.

Crouched almost in a fetal position, with his arms curled protectively about his head, his body as perfect as that of Michelangelo's David, completely naked and clean except for his feet, ankle-deep in the filthy water. His arms moved. He raised his head to look at us, a bewildered expression on his face. He was perhaps in his twenties, dark-haired, quite good-looking, with the distinctive aquiline nose of the Remillards. He smiled hesitantly at Marc and me, and we goggled at him, bereft of speech and nearly frightened out of our wits. The Fire Chief was doing his best to push past us, cursing good-naturedly, trying to see what held us enthralled.

I've completed the first part of the work.

"Ti-Jean?" I whispered. "But it can't be you——"

The young man's face lost its bemused look. His perfect form seemed to dim and go translucent before my astounded eyes, becoming as insubstantial as the tendrils of steam that the storm wind plucked and tore. Instead of a beautiful mature male body I saw all at once a naked brain—not a raw or repugnant denuded organ but a thing supremely elegant and *correct*—suspended in air. It was attached to nothing and sustained by nothing except the atmosphere, photons of light, and its own conquering psychocreative mindpower.

And then the brain vanished in turn, and a little boy stood there in the corner, shivering slightly but still smiling. He seemed to be about three or four years old.

"This body is more appropriate for now," he said. "Don't you think so? At least until people get a little more used to me."

Marc handed me the lantern. I followed him as he walked into the room, and the Fire Chief and a couple of his cohorts pushed in behind me. They uttered awed exclamations.

Marc knelt in the muck, holding one of the little boy's hands in his own uninjured one. Jack was not a phantom or any other sort of illusion. Marc's hand was very dirty, and he soiled the child's clean flesh as they touched each other.

"Just like the Christmas roses?" Marc asked Jack.

"Not quite. But almost. I'm actually bodiless except for my brain, but clothed in a quasi-solid molecular envelope of optional form."

The Fire Chief said, "Merciful God, he's alive."

Marc turned to me. "I can't pick him up with this sprained wrist of mine, Uncle Rogi."

I bent down and took the small boy into my arms. Jack was warm, and the snowflakes melted as they struck him. "Can we all go to Uncle Rogi's place?" Jack said. "I think that would be the best for now. And it's been so long since I've seen Marcel."

Both Marc and I burst out laughing. Marc got to his feet. The firefighters drew aside, murmuring, as I came out into the hall carrying Jack the Bodiless. Then we all trooped into the undamaged part of the hospital and began to look around for something dry to wrap the little boy up in.

[43]

ISLAY, INNER HEBRIDES, SCOTLAND, EARTH, 16 FEBRUARY 2054

The gale winds of the North Atlantic lashed the great blunt headland of Ton Mhor, and the tall seas leapt and creamed about its foot and marched roaring into the bay of Sanaigmore around its eastern flank. In the gray first light, with a storm slowly abating, that northwest shore of the island seemed a grim place, broken cliffs and rocky reefs facing the sea and only a few patches of twisted conifers and winter-sere peat bogs and moorlands stretching between the small inland lochs. Un-metaled tracks and narrow roads led from the scattered small farms and homesteadings, many of them deserted and in ruins, toward the main highway that skirted the deep south-coast indentation of Loch Indaal. Along the gentler lee shores, lighted villages were dotted along the sands and tide flats like sparkling beads widely placed on a string. The bustling little distilleries of the south and west were lit like Christmas trees, for they operated day and night to fill the demand for those fine single-malt whiskies that were Islay's gift to the Galaxy. On the rest of the island there were sheep and berry farms, and some of Earth's most beautiful golf links, and holiday hotels that catered to bird-watchers and walkers and antiquarians.

But not in the northwest. There most of the old crofts and farms were long abandoned, as lifeless as the prehistoric standing stones and the tumbledown chapels and ornate crosses raised by the Celtic monks, and the castle the Macdonalds held when they were Lords of the Isles in the Middle Ages. The people who had once struggled to earn a hard living on Islay were almost all gone away now to the lovely "Scottish" planet of Caledonia. Islay's smaller modern population was prosperous and, thanks to the ubiquitous rhocraft, no longer isolated from the mainland. But there were parts of the island where locals and visitors seldom went, and one of them was isolated Sanaigmore Farm, once owned by relatives of the late metapsychic giant Jamie Mac-Gregor.

The red egg landed there at dawn.

Following Fury's instructions, the four surviving Hydra heads trundled the egg into the barn. It would have to stay there until the hue and cry died down, and it could be relicensed by fiddling the aircraft registration computer in Edinburgh.

The children found the house key where Fury said it would be and entered the dark farmhouse kitchen. It was clean and secure from the elements, and aside from a spider or two and a smell of mildew about the sink, reasonably inviting. Especially when one considered the alternatives.

Quint got the miniature fusion plant going to warm the place up and provide power for lights and cooking. Celine primed the well and flushed the antifreeze out of the plumbing. Parni checked out the food, found a more than adequate supply, as Fury had also said there would be, and solicited orders for breakfast. Maddy hunted out bed linen and ran it through the clothes dryer to freshen it. The pillows and mattresses were synthetic and not too musty. There were clothes and footgear in the closets.

Later, when they all sat around the kitchen table after eating, Celine dared to ask the burning question. "How long do you think we're going to be stuck here?"

"Till the flap cools down," Parni said gloomily. "And you can bet it'll be one helluva flap."

Maddy left the table and went to look out the kitchen window at the hills and bogs in the rain-soft dawn. "Why in the world do you suppose Fury sent us here?"

"He must have had a reason," Quint said. "And he said he'd come and explain as soon as it was safe."

"That could be a long time." Maddy sighed. "Damn that Gordo. It was all his fault, egging us on to go after Marc."

Celine huddled more deeply inside the big old sweater she'd found. "We're lucky Fury didn't just feed us to the wolves . . . Parni, turn up the thermostat. I'm still freezing."

"Fury needs us," Parni said. "At least old Gordo was right about that. Whatever the great scheme is, Fury can't do it by himself." After adjusting the environmental control on the kitchen wall, he went to the counter and got another mug of coffee from the brew machine. "I wonder who Fury really is?"

The other three Hydras shrugged.

"What are we going to *do* here?" Celine asked fretfully.

Quint leered. "At least now there's no odd man out."

"Oh, really?" Celine was arch. "On beyond nervebomb—is that your idea of few and simple pleasures on this tight little island? And is it going to be ladies' choice or love pile? Or were you thinking about stable monogamous relationships until we're all bored stiff?"

At the window, Maddy gave a low cry. She turned slowly to the others, a beatific smile spreading across her face. "We won't be bored here. It's a wonderful island. Fury knew what he was doing when he picked this place."

"How so?" Parni asked, still dubious.

"Natural suboperants," Maddy whispered. "Islay is chock-full of them. The best kind—untrained in the aggressive metafaculties and brimming over with lifeforce. I've been scanning with my seekersense, and the whole south coast of the island is alive with delicious bright auras."

Parni snapped his fingers delightedly. "Sure! Celtic genes! I forgot that this part of the world was one of the prime irruptive metapsychic foci."

"Fury didn't." Quint was grinning.

"This time," Maddy said firmly, "we're going to be extremely careful. No more flying off half cocked and giving the game away."

"No," the others agreed solemnly.

"Who knows how long we'll have to stay holed up here?" she added. "It might even be as long as a year. And we wouldn't want to deplete the natural resources."

FROM THE MEMOIRS
OF ROGATIEN REMILLARD

Marc and I took Jack to my apartment, as he had requested. The hospital personnel were aghast when we tried to carry the child out of there, and told us that Jack had to be kept for observation—at least until Colette Roy got there and pronounced him fit to be discharged. But Jack said very reasonably that *he* knew he was perfectly all right, and reminded everyone that the Lylmik had given him the right to pull the plug on himself if he chose. And he had chosen.

So we left, with the Fire Chief trailing after, declaring that it had been a goddam miracle the kid had survived, and this was a night he'd tell his grandchildren about. Like almost all of the general public, the Chief was familiar with Jack's case from the earlier media hooraw. But the bootleg tapes that the nurse had sold were made when Jack's head still had a normal appearance and his nearly decomposed lower body was hidden by the machines, and so the Chief had no notion of the real nature of the "miracle" that he and his fellow firefighters had witnessed. As far as the official reports of the fire went, Jack had saved himself by retiring inside a psychocreative bubble. It was a self-defensive ploy not unknown among powerful adult operants, and Jack was acknowledged to be an extraordinary child.

When the three of us got to my place, we put through the subspace call to Davy MacGregor. An all-points bulletin went out for the four children suspected of participation in the Hydra metaconcert. It was quickly determined that Anne Remillard's red rhocraft was missing. But she, like all the other members of the Dynasty, had been at Denis and Lucille's farmhouse, having supper and commiserating with Paul and Catherine, all throughout that evening. Anne's egg had apparently been stolen from its parking space in the farm's backyard. Colette Roy, Professor Tukwila Barnes, and Lucille's housekeeper, who were also at the supper, vouched for the fact that none of the seven Remillard magnates had been out of the house at the time arson experts determined that the fire had been set.

There was no record of the stolen egg having entered any Vee-route on the planet Earth. Wherever it had gone, it had traveled ex-vector and beneath the ubiquitous radar net of Air Traffic Control—almost certainly skimming along the surface of the Atlantic and coming ashore God knew where. Three satellites with equipment that might have recorded the path of the errant egg beneath widespread cloud cover suffered mysterious malfunctions that night. Fury had done a better job of covering the tracks of his protégés than Marc had done for Teresa and me. The red egg was never traced or recovered.

The Magistratum's investigation and the search for Madeleine, Celine, Quentin, and Parnell were kept strictly confidential, under orders from the Dirigent. The media and the public learned nothing about the existence of the vampiric little clique haunting the First Family of Metapsychology. The Remillards cooperated fully in the inquiry—most especially those parents whose children were under suspicion—and later the entire Fury-Hydra affair was discussed in a special week-long closed-door Special Session of the Human Magnates of the Concilium held in Concord. Marc's hypothesis of the origin of Hydra was debated and reluctantly given credence. Once again, the Dynasty was mind-reamed with the Cambridge machine and "proved" not to be Fury. No trace of the fugitive children was found.

Paul himself traveled to Orb and presented the findings of the Special Session to the full Concilium of exotic magnates. Among his recommendations were: that all the Remillards should resign their Concilium seats and be permanently incarcerated in a place of the Concilium's choice; and that the probation period postponing full acceptance of humanity into the Galactic Milieu be extended for an indefinite period, until Fury and Hydra were captured, or identified and proved dead.

The Simbiari, Poltroyan, Gi, and Krondak magnates voted to accept those two draconian proposals. The five members of the Lylmik Supervisory Body exercised their special privilege and summarily vetoed the decision.

The case was left open, and a special task force of human and exotic investigators assigned to it. Their efforts to find the Hydra monsters were to prove fruitless—as were the efforts of Jack himself. The four remained at large, doing what they were told to do, until nearly twenty-three Earth years had passed and the Dirigent Dorothea Macdonald, who came to be known as Diamond Mask, finally neutralized their threat—with a little help from a bumbling friend. That story will be told in the second book of this trilogy, *Diamond Mask*.

Fury was another matter entirely. His fate, like that of Marc and Jack the Bodiless and so many more of the characters who people these Memoirs, is inextricably entangled in the Metapsychic Rebellion.

The principal Rebels themselves, led by Adrien Remillard, Anna Gawrys-Sakhvadze, and Owen Blanchard, pursued their cause with discretion and determination until the culminating year of 2083. They drew more and more influential operants into their conspiracy as the wider implications of mental Unity and membership in the Galactic confederation were freely debated by the Human Polity. In time Marc would join them, just as Adrien had predicted, and assume their leadership. He would broaden the Rebel agenda with radical ideas of his own that went far beyond the original ideal of Human autonomy, and eventually threaten the life of the Galactic Milieu itself.

In these Memoirs I will reveal, as the Family Ghost permits, aspects of the Metapsychic Rebellion that Milieu historians haven't the least notion of, which I witnessed personally—and on more than one occasion even took an active part in. My own view of the cosmic conflict will be related in the third volume of the trilogy, entitled *Magnificat*.

I do not know whether the Ghost, in Its infinite wisdom, intends to release my chronicle to the Galaxy at large, or whether It intends simply to hide it away in some ineffable Lylmik archive. It refuses to reveal Its plans, just as It refuses to tell me whether I will long survive the telling of the tale.

Eh bien! Qu'est-ce que ça peut bien foutre? But it would be fun to watch the uproar.

Paul was back on Earth in time for Marc's college commencement on 14 June 2054, when the boy received both his B.S. and an M.S. in metapsychology. His thesis dealt with "The Cerebroenergetic Interface as a Potential Bypass of Grandmasterclass Mental Shielding." He had used himself as the guinea pig in his experiments.

Sitting between their father and me in the audience at the outdoor ceremony were Marc's sister Marie and his two younger brothers, Luc and Jack. Family friends congratulated Paul on Jack's wonderful recovery from cancer. Paul gave all the credit to Colette Roy and her medical colleagues. Unfortunately, Marc's second sister, Madeleine, missed the commencement. She was, Paul said, beginning her own higher education on the remote Poltroyan planet Toropon-su-Makon under a special student exchange program. The family did not expect to see too much of her for the next few years, but she was not expected to be too lonely. Three of her Remillard cousins were taking the same course of study.

On 3 October 2054, the probationary period of one Galactic year, a thousand Earth days, was declared complete. The Human Polity took its place beside the other races of the Milieu for better or worse, a full member of the confederation at last, with all the privileges and duties attending thereto.

A compromise was reached on the matter of the additional ethnic planets for humans of color: twelve new worlds were set aside that had no operant quota in their founding population. The colonies were rather remote from the home world, but they were attractive and richly endowed, and the people who settled them increased and multiplied and, in time, took a political position that would, ironically, place them in the forefront of the Metapsychic Rebellion fomented in the name of Mental Man.

Shortly after the Earth-wide festivities accompanying the human enfranchisement, Malama Johnson farspoke Marc with a special message. He and I and Jack egged to Kauai, removed Teresa's ashes from the kahuna's cave, and scattered them over the green island on a day when the sky was filled with sparkling showers and myriad rainbows.

Paul had been invited to come with us, but he declined. He was busier than ever now that the probation had ended, and lived most of the time in Concord or Concilium Orb. Laura Tremblay and a number of other attractive operant women were linked romantically with him from time to time.

Young Jack the Bodiless looked and behaved—almost always—like a normal preschool child, seeming to be a little in advance of his age physically, and decidedly precocious in his social development. He resumed his daytrips about the Dartmouth campus, sometimes in the company of Marc and his graduate-student associates, sometimes alone by special dispensation of the college president, Tom Spotted Owl, who became one of the child's dearest friends. Jack's extraordinary mindpowers were widely known in academic circles but given no publicity. The child's own grandmasterly coercivity ensured that he was never harassed by the media or by other busybodies, and the rest of his childhood seemed to pass peacefully without attracting the attention of the world outside Hanover, New Hampshire.

He wore his childish form when he lived at home or when he stayed with various friends or relatives in his extended family. There were also times when he chose to wear other bodies, both human and exotic, but he always did this with the utmost circumspection during his youth. Until he was nominated to the Concilium himself at the age of sixteen, only a handful of family members were aware of his true physical condition.

He visited me regularly in my bookshop and sought my opinion on some of the damnedest things, and it was easy for me to forget what Jack really was. Only on the coldest winter nights, when I sat by myself in the back of the shop, drinking and feeling lonely and sorry for myself, remembering Sunny and Elaine and Umi and even Teresa—women I had loved and lost—did I tell myself that there was one in the world even less lucky than I. At least I had known love's warmth. Three women had found me desirable and one had loved me like a father, and in Denis and Jack and even in Marc, the strange one, I had had foster sons.

But what woman would ever love poor Jack the Bodiless? And what kind of terrible, inhuman children could that laughing, brilliant little boy-brain ever hope to sire?

It was beyond imagining. Jack was happy now, growing in wisdom and grace, with his physical shells mimicking the human life processes in a manner that was nearly flawless. But his "bodies" were not the real thing, nor could they ever be. The fantastic biological complexity that houses the souls of each one of us is beyond the constructive abilities of even the most ingenious Grand Master of psychocreativity. Nor could Jack ever be reclothed in flesh through the technological miracle of the regeneration tank. His genes had programmed him to be as he was: a naked, self-sufficient brain. He was, if you like, a being midway on the ladder of evolution between Homo sapiens and the ethereal Lylmik.

He was unique. He was truly alone.

Sunk in my maudlin melancholy, I would drink a toast to poor Jack the Bodiless, who would never know human love, as the north wind moaned around the shopwindows, and the Great White Cold of the New Hampshire winter stalked abroad, and high in the sky the faraway star that was the sun of the planet Caledonia sparkled like the tiniest of diamonds.

How the Family Ghost must have laughed.

THE END

of

JACK THE BODILESS

Volume I of the Galactic Milieu Trilogy

Volume II, titled *Diamond Mask*,
gives the history of the early life of
Dorothea Macdonald, Dirigent of Caledonia,
together with the further adventures of
various members of the Family Remillard,
their friends, associates, and enemies.

REMILLARD FAMILY TREE

PHILIP   =   Aurelie Dalembert   [1] Jeanne Dalembert   =   MAURICE   =   [2] Cecilia Ashe
(1997–)   (2008–)   (2010–2037)   (1999–)   (2014–)

    m. 2030   m. 2033   m. 2040

    Joseph (2031–)   Robert (2034–)   Celine (2040–)
    Adele (2033–)   Caroline (2036–)   Roger (2042–)
    Louis (2034–)   Liane (2037–)   Roland (2044–)
    Gabrielle (2036–)
    Michelle (2036–)
    Charlaine (2038–)
    Richard (2041–)
    Emile (2044–)
    Denise (2044–)
    Samuel (2046–)
    Norman (2048–)
    Loren (2049–)
    Marianne (2050–)

      ANNE   CATHERINE   =   Brett McAllister
      (2005–)   (2009–2083)   (2012–2051)
      [no children]

                            m. 2035

                         Douglas (2036–)
                         Rene (2038–)
                         Ronald (2038–)
                         Gordon (2040–2054)

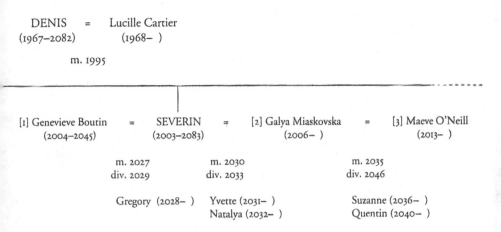

DENIS   =   Lucille Cartier
(1967–2082)   (1968–)

m. 1995

[1] Genevieve Boutin = SEVERIN = [2] Galya Miaskovska = [3] Maeve O'Neill
(2004–2045)   (2003–2083)   (2006–)   (2013–)

m. 2027   m. 2030   m. 2035
div. 2029   div. 2033   div. 2046

Gregory (2028–) Yvette (2031–)   Suzanne (2036–)
               Natalya (2032–)   Quentin (2040–)

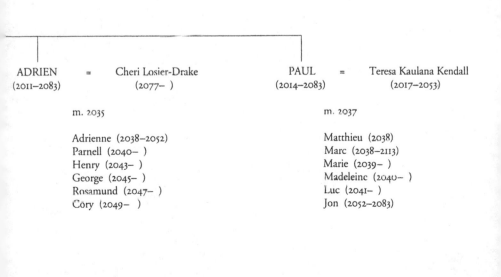

ADRIEN = Cheri Losier-Drake   PAUL = Teresa Kaulana Kendall
(2011–2083)   (2077–)   (2014–2083)   (2017–2053)

m. 2035   m. 2037

Adrienne (2038–2052)   Matthieu (2038)
Parnell (2040–)   Marc (2038–2113)
Henry (2043–)   Marie (2039–)
George (2045–)   Madeleine (2040–)
Rosamund (2047–)   Luc (2041–)
Cory (2049–)   Jon (2052–2083)

A NOTE ON THE TYPE

This book was set in a digitized version of Garamond. Jean Janson
has been identified as the designer of this face, which is based on
Garamond's original models but is much lighter and more open. The
italic is taken from a font of Granjon, which appeared in the repertory
of the Imprimerie Royale and was probably cut in the middle of the
sixteenth century.

Composed, printed, and bound by
The Haddon Craftsmen, Scranton, Pennsylvania
Designed by Virginia Tan